Praise for John Gilstrap and his thrillers

BLUE FIRE

"A John Gilstrap thriller, crammed with violence and testing of the soul, might be the perfect work of fiction to sink into in a tough time for the real world."
—*New York Journal of Books*

CRIMSON PHOENIX

"A nonstop roller coaster of suspense! *Crimson Phoenix* ticks every box for big-book thrillerdom."
—**Jeffery Deaver**

"Don't miss this powerful new series from a master thriller writer."
—**Jamie Freveletti**

"A single mother's smart, fierce determination to protect her sons turns this vivid day-after-tomorrow scenario into a gripping page-turner."
—**Taylor Stevens**

"*Crimson Phoenix* snaps with action from the very first page. It's certain to hit the 10-ring with old and new readers alike."
—**Marc Cameron**

STEALTH ATTACK

A BookBub Top Thriller of Summer
"Nobody does pacing and suspense better than Gilstrap. And in Grave he continues to grow with each entry. *Stealth Attack* is riveting and relentless reading entertainment."
—*The Providence Journal*

FRIENDLY FIRE

"If you only read one book this summer, make sure it's *Friendly Fire*, and be ready to be strapped in for the ride of your life."
—*Suspense Magazine*

"A blistering thriller that grabs your attention and doesn't let go for a second!"
—**The Real Book Spy**

NICK OF TIME

"A page-turning thriller with strong characters, exciting action, and a big heart."
—**Heather Graham**

AGAINST ALL ENEMIES
WINNER OF THE INTERNATIONAL THRILLER WRITERS AWARD FOR BEST PAPERBACK ORIGINAL
"Any John Gilstrap novel packs the punch of a rocket-propelled grenade—on steroids! Gilstrap grabs the reader's attention in a literary vise grip. A damn good read."
—**BookReporter.com**

"Tense, clever. . . . Series enthusiasts are bound to enjoy this new thriller."
—*Library Journal*

NO MERCY

"*No Mercy* grabs hold of you on page one and doesn't let go. Gilstrap's new series is terrific. It will leave you breathless. I can't wait to see what Jonathan Grave is up to next."
—**Harlan Coben**

"John Gilstrap is one of the finest thriller writers on the planet. *No Mercy* showcases his work at its finest—taut, action-packed, and impossible to put down!"
—**Tess Gerritsen**

"A great hero, a pulse-pounding story—and the launch of a really exciting series."
—**Joseph Finder**

"An entertaining, fast-paced tale of violence and revenge."
—*Publishers Weekly*

"No other writer is better able to combine in a single novel both rocket-paced suspense and heartfelt looks at family and the human spirit. And what a pleasure to meet Jonathan Grave, a hero for our time . . . and for all time."
—**Jeffery Deaver**

AT ALL COSTS

"Riveting . . . combines a great plot and realistic, likable characters with look-over-your-shoulder tension. A page-turner."
—*Kansas City Star*

Also by John Gilstrap

BLUE
FIRE

JOHN
GILSTRAP

PINNACLE BOOKS
Kensington Publishing Corp.
www.kensingtonbooks.com

PINNACLE BOOKS are published by

Kensington Publishing Corp.
119 West 40th Street
New York, NY 10018

All Kensington titles, imprints, and distributed lines are available at special quantity discounts for bulk purchases for sales promotion, premiums, fund-raising, educational, or institutional use.

Special book excerpts or customized printings can also be created to fit specific needs. For details, write or phone the office of the Kensington Sales Manager: Attn.: Sales Department. Kensington Publishing Corp., 119 West 40th Street, New York, NY 10018. Phone: 1-800-221-2647.

Pinnacle and the Pinnacle logo Reg US Pat. & TM Off.

First Hardcover Edition published: March 2022

First Paperback Printing: December 2022
ISBN: 978-0-7860-4666-9

ISBN: 978-1-4967-2858-6 (ebook)

10 9 8 7 6 5 4 3 2 1

Printed in the United States of America

To Joy

CHAPTER ONE

Hell Day + 34

VICTORIA EMERSON HEARD THE URGENCY IN THE TONE before she understood the words. She pivoted toward the back door as she rose from the table that she'd transformed into a makeshift desk in what used to be a diner called Maggie's Place. Since the days immediately following the war, Maggie's had served as an ersatz city hall. Victoria's knees scooted her chair across the wooden floor as she stood.

"What on earth is that?" asked Ellie Stewart. They'd been meeting about the status of the clothing bank, now that the air had begun to smell like winter.

"Whatever it is, it sounds important." Victoria opened the door.

A horse approached at a full gallop. Its rider—her fourteen-year-old son, Luke—hung tight to the saddle horn with his left hand, while he slapped the reins with his right. Never having sat a horse until a few weeks ago, he'd taken to it well, but he was pushing the beast way too hard on the asphalt roadway.

"Blue fire!" he yelled. "Coming down the river! Blue fire! Coming down the river!"

Victoria's heart doubled its rate.

"Is he shouting blue fire?" Ellie asked, standing. Everyone understood *blue fire* to be the code phrase for the highest level of alert. It meant imminent danger from deadly forces, whether man-made or from natural causes.

Victoria didn't answer. Instead, she reached back inside the door and grabbed the M4 rifle that was never more than a few feet away from her. It was a sad fact about feral, terrified humans that violence came more instinctively than kindness. That was a lesson hard learned in the first days after Hell Day—after the war.

Slinging the rifle over her shoulder, she adjusted the pistol that always rested on her hip to make room for the stock, and stepped the rest of the way outside. She waved, trying to get Luke's attention, but he was focused on spreading the word of imminent peril. She shivered against the chill of the autumn air and jogged around the side of the building toward the intersection of Mountain Road and Kanawha Road, the spot that had evolved, by silent consensus, to be the social and governmental center here in Ortho, West Virginia.

This unincorporated little burg had never had its own town government, instead taking leadership from a county whose real leaders had evaporated, either killed in the attacks and their aftermath, or just choosing to flee. Those who remained had survived the unspeakable destruction of Hell Day—the eight-hour conflict that left the world in ruins—but all the technology and conveniences of the twenty-first century were gone. Even the previous century was beyond reach. Electricity was a memory, and without it little else worked. Most of the homes that existed on Hell Day had propane in the tanks buried in their backyards, and as long as pressure remained, the gas could flow. But the clock was clicking down on that, too.

Equipment that utilized microcircuitry, or was even moderately computerized, had been transformed by electromagnetic pulse into paperweights and doorstops. A few ancient cars still worked, but without electricity to power pumps, it was a daunting challenge to raise gasoline from underground tanks, where it languished unused.

As she hurried toward the square, Victoria looked across the street and caught the eye of Army Major Joe McCrea, who returned a look of dread. He had not made the progress he'd been hoping for on the construction of barricades to provide some level of protection from miscreants and marauders. The town still reeled from the attack from the Grubbs gang, just a few weeks before.

Rifle in hand, McCrea jogged to intersect Victoria's path to the square. She slowed, but only slightly.

"This better not be a mistake," McCrea said, making a broad gesture to the dozens of people flooding the square. "That would be a bad way to start."

The emergency response protocol was new to everyone. Most agreed that swift action was key to mitigating any emergency, and they'd voted overwhelmingly to arm themselves while outside their homes. Those with access to long guns—in this part of the world, that meant just about everyone—agreed to keep them close at all times.

McCrea's biggest fear about the new protocol, which he'd voiced only to Victoria, was overreaction and alarm fatigue. People had different opinions of what emergencies looked like, and if miscalculations resulted in a series of false alarms, especially in the early days, the system would quickly fall apart.

The fact that Luke Emerson was the first Paul Revere to trigger the alert protocol made it even more important that the emergency be real. Victoria had risen to leadership in Ortho by default rather than by election, and while her support remained strong among the original residents of the town, the daily flood of newcomers placing demands on the community's already-limited resources were forcing her to make decisions that were increasingly unpopular.

"He's a smart boy," Victoria said, even though the past weeks had all but obliterated his prewar boyishness.

Luke continued his gallop in a wide loop down Kanawha Road, then left on Charleston Street, where he disappeared and reemerged from Fourth Street. As seconds passed, the shrill squeal of whistles billowed like a cloud of noise as residents reacted to Luke's warnings. Another critical element of the emergency plan included the distribution of a recently-discovered cache of coaches' whistles from the basement of Ortho Hardware, so that selected residents could spread the news of danger even farther. Whoever heard the whistle—the sound of which traveled many times farther than the sound of shouting—was instructed to blow their own whistle as they hurried toward either their designated rally stations or the town square.

Victoria felt embarrassed that her whistle remained dangling from its chain behind her flannel shirt. As she ran the last few yards to the square, she fished it out and gave it a sustained blow, adding her own noise to everyone else's.

By the time Luke pulled his horse to a halt at the square, nearly thirty people had assembled, and more were rushing in.

Victoria stepped forward and raised her hands. In the distance from behind, she heard a familiar voice shouting, "Wait! We're almost there!"

She turned to see her sixteen-year-old son, Caleb, sprinting toward them as best he could, his M4 carbine slapping against his unbuttoned coat. He'd taken a bullet through his butt cheek during the dustup with Jeffrey Grubbs and his gang and still moved with an awkward gait. Rory Stevenson, the town's only doctor and Caleb's nominal boss, kept up, step for step.

Victoria knew they'd be next to her by the time Luke got to the point. "What's going on?"

Luke struggled to catch his breath as he leaned over his saddle horn. "People in boats," he said. "Lots of them. All with guns. They're coming this way."

"What does *a lot* mean?" McCrea asked.

"I didn't count," Luke replied with an adolescent flash of *duh*. "Maybe fifty?"

"How many boats?" Victoria asked.

"I didn't count those, either. Ten, maybe?"

George Simmons, once the owner of Simmons Gas and Goodies, stepped forward. "Were the boats under power?"

"I don't think so. I didn't hear any motor noise. I think they were riding the current."

"Why is this an emergency?" Victoria asked. She thought she probably knew, but she wanted to hear it from her son.

"All the guns," he said. "And the way they looked at me."

"They *looked* at you?" Caleb asked. He was incapable of speaking to his little brother without a silent *you idiot* attached to the end. "How close were you?"

"I was on the shore," Luke replied. Victoria knew from his tone that he'd been doing something he shouldn't have, but she didn't want to press him on it now.

"I thought you were hunting," Caleb said.

"Do you want to hear or not?"

"Boys!" This from Joey Abbott, whose pawnshop had once been a major form of credit for locals, back when paper money had value. "For God's sake. Are we being invaded, or aren't we?"

"One of them pointed a rifle at me," Luke said.

McCrea seemed to inflate with anger. "Did he fire on you?"

"No, sir. But I think he wanted to scare me."

"Looks like it worked," Caleb said.

"Up yours."

"Stop!" Victoria was forever amazed by her sons' cluelessness about how interactions like that made them look small in the eyes of others. So much for the departure of boyishness.

"How far out are they?" McCrea asked.

Luke shook his head. "I don't know. A ten-minute gallop."

"One mile," Simmons said. "Maybe two."

"That's not much time," McCrea said. "We need to take this seriously. It could mean nothing, or it could mean everything." He raised his voice to address the crowd. "Most of you know where to go. If you don't, find some cover and get behind it. Snipers, don't be trigger-happy, but be sure and accurate." At those words, five of the assembled residents—the Emerson boys included—peeled off and trotted off to their sniper's nests. The others headed off to their assigned defensive stations.

As head of town security—by default rather than by choice—McCrea had trained every resident older than fourteen (older than twelve in the cases of some of the kids who wandered in from the country and were skilled shooters) always to fight from defended positions.

"Where is Paul?" Victoria asked, referring to First Sergeant Copley, the other half of Victoria's security team on the night the world ended.

"He was helping in Church Town, last I heard," McCrea said. It turned out that Paul Copley was damn near a master carpenter. With the constant influx of new people, and the approach of winter, the need for housing had become critical. Church Town was an eight-acre plot of land surrounding the Church of the Redeemer, about a mile down the road, on which Copley was overseeing the construction of at least twenty cabins.

As if on cue, the fast-approaching clatter of hooves drew their attention that direction in time to see First Sergeant Copley at a dead gallop ahead of a line of others on bicycles racing in to respond to the whistles.

Copley pulled his horse to a stop and dismounted a few yards away.

"Everybody to your assigned stations!" McCrea yelled. "Move quickly. We don't have much time!"

"What's going on?" Copley asked.

Victoria took ten seconds to fill him in on what they knew.

Copley turned to McCrea. "So, what's the plan?"

"That's up to them. If they sail by, they sail by. If they stop, here at the boat launch is pretty much their only option. In that case, we have a chat." Victoria imagined that in the before times, everything from bass boats to rowboats to houseboats lined up for their turn to launch from the concrete ramp that sloped from the street to the water's edge.

"Suppose they unload before getting to the launch?" Simmons asked. The way things shook out in this unelected management structure, George Simmons and Joey Abbott were both part of the unofficial government.

"There's really nowhere else for them to go," Joey said. "I guess they could pile out into the trees along the riverbank, but why would they?"

"Because they mean to do us harm," Simmons said.

"If that's what they do, then we'll know," McCrea said. He'd only recently abandoned his Army uniform in favor of a hybrid of camouflage uniform pants with a warm plaid flannel shirt.

"I don't like not having a plan," Copley said.

"We do have a plan," Victoria said. "People know where to go and to keep an eye on what's happening."

"That's more a standing procedure than a plan, Vick," McCrea said.

"Call it what you like," Victoria said. "We've got good people in this town. Smart people. And they will do what's necessary to defend it. If I didn't feel that way, I wouldn't be here. I certainly wouldn't put Luke and Caleb in harm's way."

"I worry about overreacting," McCrea said. "With everybody spun up since the last attack, I worry about somebody on our team picking a fight unnecessarily."

"We trained 'em," Copley said. "I thought they did pretty good." Victoria guessed him to be in his mid-thirties, and he looked like he'd been born to wear a uniform. Built like a weight lifter, he was a zero-bullshit straight shooter, and perhaps her boys' best friend in town.

"I see them!" someone yelled from one of the surrounding buildings.

Victoria admired the simplicity of McCrea's action plan. Not knowing what might come, he'd settled on a one-size-fits-all strategy. Whether the threat was coming from the road or from the water, Victoria and McCrea would serve as a greeting party. If all worked out peacefully, newcomers would never know that crosshairs had been settled on their brainpans. If things went other than peacefully, the attackers would be caught off guard by the number of hidden fighters facing them.

A flotilla of pleasure boats appeared one at a time from concealment behind the trees, first visible from about one hundred yards. Victoria didn't know one boat from another, but these were a mishmash of watercraft of the sort you'd pay for by the hour at a mid-level resort. At first glance, Victoria saw that Luke's estimates had been spot on. Fifty people, more or less, occupied exactly ten boats. While the watercraft were clearly civilian, the people on board appeared otherwise. The majority, if not all of them, wore green camouflage uniforms. Victoria had never seen so many firearms outside of a gun show.

"I don't have a great feeling about this," she mumbled. "I see a grenade launcher."

"This could get interesting in all the wrong ways," McCrea agreed. "Spread out a bit and be ready."

Per the plan, Simmons and Abbott spread out to the flanks, taking positions at the far edges of the boat launch ramp. Victoria and McCrea stayed in the middle, but separated by twenty feet. At times like this, you never wanted to bunch up. It was much harder to harm individuals than it was to harm a group.

The occupants of the boats used oars—some real, some makeshift—to turn toward shore. When they closed within fifty yards or so and showed no sign of stopping, Victoria shouted, "Stay away from the shore!"

"Stop or be fired upon!" McCrea yelled.

A man in the lead boat with captain's bars on the front tab of his uniform shirt called back, "I am Captain Roy Magill, of the Maryland National Guard. Put down your weapons or you will be arrested." Mid-thirties, with leathery skin that clearly had seen no sunscreen, his high-and-tight haircut had grown out over his ears. He projected menace in a way that Victoria had seen in many cops and military officers.

McCrea shouldered his M4. "Last chance!"

Captain Magill brought his weapon to bear and McCrea dropped to a knee. "We represent the United States Army!" the captain called. "Put down your weapons!"

"What is happening?" Victoria asked no one as she

darted to her right toward a tree that might provide cover.

"Do not advance!" McCrea yelled. "Don't turn this into—"

Victoria stepped forward and raised both hands into the air. She intended it as a gesture of mitigation, not surrender. "Stop this!" she yelled.

McCrea hissed, "Vicky, what are you doing?"

She didn't answer. She stepped closer to the water's edge. "Put your weapon down, Captain Magill. We've already had one war. We don't need another."

She sensed McCrea moving to her left, keeping his field of fire open. "You too, Major McCrea."

Magill clearly didn't know what to do. He broke his aim, but not by much.

"The next choice is yours, Captain," Victoria said. "Trust me when I tell you there are many more guns leveled at you than you think."

McCrea snapped his rifle back to his shoulder. "You in the second boat!" he yelled. "Put your weapon down!" At a whisper he added for Victoria's benefit, "You're giving them advantage."

"You can see how fragile this moment is, Captain," Victoria called. "If people die in the next few minutes, it will be because of you, not because of us." She wondered how far away people needed to be to hear the hammering of her heart.

"This is a mistake, Vicky," McCrea said.

"Hush, Major." Victoria watched as Magill worked through his options.

Magill never shifted his eyes from McCrea as he shouted to his troops, "Everyone stand down! Drop your muzzles. Let's not have a fight. Not now."

"Thank you," Victoria said, taking a step closer, until her boots were in the water. "I am Victoria Emerson. We need to start over again. First of all, you will arrest no one. And you will not help yourself to our stores. If that is your sole intent, then you need to move on."

Magill's eyes narrowed as he listened. "Victoria Emerson," he said, tasting the words. "Have we met?"

"Not that I remember," Victoria said, "but we may have."

"You look familiar."

"I get that a lot. Would you like to come ashore so we can talk?"

"What about my troops?"

"That depends on how our talk goes. You pointed rifles at my son. That's a crappy first step in a new relationship."

"How many people do you have in this town?"

Victoria said nothing.

"Are you the leader?" Magill asked. "The mayor or something?"

"Or something," Victoria said. "Captain Magill, we've arrived at the shit-or-get-off-the-pot moment. Either you come ashore and we talk, or you and yours press on. If you choose to fight, I guarantee you will lose."

"You've got a lot of swagger, I'll give you that."

"Call the ball, Captain."

"All right, Lieutenant MacIntosh, row us ashore." His eyes never moved from McCrea, his hand never left the grip of his M4.

An unhealthy-looking man behind Magill engaged his paddle and pulled them closer to shore. As the bow of their pleasure craft scraped onto the launching slip, Magill threw a line to Victoria.

She made no effort to catch it as it splashed into the water. She was the leader of Ortho, not his crewman.

"It's like that, is it?" Magill said as he hefted himself over the gunwale to land in shin-deep water. "Mack, come with me. Elliott?"

"Sir?" That came from a third man in Magill's boat.

"Keep everyone close. If this is a trap, we'll know it soon enough. Safeties on, but weapons at the ready."

That didn't sound good. "Major McCrea, come with me, please. George and Joey, you too."

McCrea called out, "First Sergeant Copley!"

From somewhere behind them: "Sir?"

"You know what to do."

"Yessir."

"Are you ganging up on me, Vicky?" Magill asked.

"It's Mrs. Emerson to you, Captain." She turned her back on Magill and headed back toward her office in Maggie's Place. Entering through the front door, she stopped at the second table she came to, turned and waited for them to join her.

When MacIntosh and Magill were in place, she pointed at the two seats that would put them with their backs to the door.

"Who's your second?" Victoria asked, indicating the wan lieutenant.

"Hunter MacIntosh," the man said. "People call me Mack."

"What are you in real life?" McCrea asked. "Outside the Reserves?"

Victoria bristled at the question. This was her meeting, not the major's. She was surrounded by military hotheads driven by testosterone, and she needed to exert civilian control.

"I worked in a warehouse. Shift supervisor."

"Forgive me for saying this," Victoria said, "but you don't look well." His eyes seemed to have sunken into his head, his color wasn't right, and he looked like he'd lost weight faster than his skin could accommodate.

"You don't have to say anything to her," Magill said.

"I think I might have been a little too close to the radiation," Mack said.

"How big is that problem with the rest of your people?" Victoria asked.

"Why is our health any concern to you?" Magill asked. "Radiation sickness, if that's what this is, is not contagious."

"No, it's not," Victoria agreed. "I don't believe I said it was. I was concerned about your friend's health, so I thought I'd ask him about it." That was not entirely true, of course. Sick people sucked up rare and valuable resources. Terminally sick patients could be a particularly difficult drain, and these folks were not from around here.

She decided to shift gears. "What are your intentions, Captain?"

He cocked his head to the side, but said nothing.

Victoria clarified her question. "We've had people wandering into town ever since Hell Day. You're the first group that came in threatening the other residents. Why would you come in hard and fast like that, threatening to arrest people?"

"I saw your weapons, and drew the wrong conclusion, I suppose."

McCrea shifted his stance as if preparing to speak, but backed off from Victoria's glare. "That's not true, Captain," she said. "You announced yourself as representing the United States government, and you ordered our townsfolk to put down their weapons or face arrest. You came in with a plan, and I want to know what that plan is."

"You're imagining things," Magill said with a dismissive flick of his hand. His eyes grew large as a thought occurred to him and he snapped his fingers. "Aren't you a congresswoman? I've seen you on television."

"I used to be," Victoria said. "We're not changing subjects. You say you think I'm imagining things. If that's the case, let me share those imaginings with you. I think you and your band of soldiers are on a foraging mission."

Magill made a puffing sound. "Don't be—"

"I'm speaking," Victoria said. "I'll tell you when it's your turn."

Magill's ears turned red.

"In my world, foraging is another word for stealing. You're not doing that. Not here in Ortho."

They glared at each other for a few seconds, and then Victoria said, "You may speak if you wish."

"I don't know who made you Queen Bitch—"

"Careful." George Simmons took a half step closer.

Magill stood. "If you really want to have a fight—"

Victoria slammed the table with her hand. "Stop it! Captain Magill, you can sit back down or you can leave. We can continue this chat or you can take your troops elsewhere, downriver."

Magill planted his fists on his hips and cocked his head again. The head thing clearly was a tell, but Victoria hadn't yet figured out for what.

"Look, *Mrs.* Emerson. Are you really so delusional that you can defy a lawful order from the United States Army and think that there will be no consequence?"

Victoria stood, taking her time doing it. "That sounded remarkably like a threat, Captain."

"My troops need stores," he said.

"So do the citizens of this town," Victoria said. "If you want your own meat, hunt it. If you want fresh vegetables, you're screwed till spring. If you want fresh water, pull it out of the river and purify it. What am I missing?"

Magill's shoulders sagged as some of the bravado bled away. Victoria didn't believe it. "You're talking about skills that we don't have."

"If you've got guns, you can shoot game," Victoria said. "Boiling water is not an advanced skill."

"But preparing meat that you've hunted is," Magill said.

"Then learn."

"Excuse me for interrupting, ma'am," McCrea said. "Do you have orders, Captain? Or are you just wandering?"

Magill seemed startled. "We're trying to help people."

"Bullshit," McCrea said. "First of all, you've just admitted that you have no help to bring. You're not the Army. There *is* no Army anymore, at least not in the way we used to think about it. Just as there's no longer a police force or a Department of Health and Human Services."

Magill's jaw set. He was losing his temper again.

"Pretty much everything that was, just isn't any-more, Captain. You may *think* you're on a noble mis-sion—though I don't believe you do—but what you really are is a roving gang. You're a team of former military people who are looking to survive, just like everybody else, but you're not willing to work for it."

"I did not come ashore for a lecture from you."

"And your words reinforce what Major McCrea is saying," Victoria observed. "That's an insubordinate tone."

"Fine," Magill said. "Think what you want. Say what you want. You say we need to learn, so teach us."

Victoria cast a glance to both George Simmons and Joey Abbott. They both shook their heads. They were subtle movements—twitches, really—but their mean-ing was clear.

"I'm sorry, Captain," she said. "I wish you well, but not here. There are other towns downstream, and maybe they'll help you—if people are still alive there. But once you pointed guns at my friends, you surren-dered trust." She pointed her forehead at McCrea. "See to it that they leave, please."

"You don't have the right—"

"We're done here," Victoria said. She turned to Mc-Crea. "See the gentlemen back to their boat, please."

George and Joey joined McCrea to form a loose cir-cle around Magill and Mack. "Time to go, gentlemen," McCrea said.

Mack rose with considerable effort. "Any sympathy for the sick guy?" he asked.

"I wish you a full recovery, Lieutenant," Victoria said. "Just not here."

Magill's demeanor changed as he left Maggie's Place. His back straightened and his swagger returned.

Victoria followed at a distance, her rifle still slung in front of her.

CHAPTER TWO

Hell Day + 34 (The Same Day)

*L*UKE EMERSON KEPT BOTH EYES OPEN, ONE BEHIND the scope of his M4 rifle and the other taking in the whole picture across the street. He'd thumbed his safety lever to single-fire when he saw the Army guy in the first boat start pulling hard for the shore, and he'd even moved his finger to the trigger. But then his mom had stepped out and started talking to the guy.

"Holy shit, Mom," Caleb grumbled. Luke's older brother had taken up position in the shadows behind the window of the same hardware store, almost directly across the street from the boat ramp. "Good way to get yourself shot."

Luke thumbed the lever back to SAFE and let out the breath he didn't know he'd been holding. If he'd pressed his trigger, there was a good chance that he'd have shot his mother in the head. If his scope were perfectly zeroed, the bullet would have gone over her by a couple of inches, but at this range—call it a hundred yards—even the smallest twitch would make a two-inch difference.

And no rifle stays perfectly zeroed for long.

"I almost did it," Luke confessed.

"But you didn't," Caleb said. "Take the win."

Caleb had changed since he'd gotten shot. It wasn't a life-threatening wound—just his ass cheek and the heel of his shoe—but that day had changed him. Maybe it had changed Luke, too, but changes were harder to see in yourself than they were in others. Caleb was still sixteen years old, but he acted as if he were thirty. He didn't laugh as much as he used to, and his teasing always had an edge to it. He seemed angry all the time.

It had never been their plan to settle in Ortho, West Virginia. They were supposed to be a hundred miles from here, at Top Hat Mountain, the bug-out reunion spot that they had planned on for as long as Luke could remember.

Back when they were a *real* family—back before Dad was killed in Iraq and Mom decided to run for Congress—Top Hat Mountain had been their refuge from the world. Luke wasn't exactly sure where it was located—such was life when you saw the world from the backseat of the SUV—but it was beautiful. It teemed with wildlife, from fish in the streams to game in the forest. Luke couldn't remember a single time that they had run into any other humans up there.

Mom and Dad had always been obsessive about planning for Armageddon. They had extra stores of food and the gun safe was filled with weapons and ammo. From an early age—barely past toddlerhood—

Luke had handled firearms. He and Caleb both were expert shots and experienced hunters. Their dad said that as an Army officer, he had seen what happens when supply chains break down and when governments get too much control. He wanted to protect his family against all of that.

Mom and Dad said it was all part of what they called the Concentric Circle Plan. It meant, essentially, that in times of emergency, you protect yourself and your family first. In good times, you helped extended family and close friends and acquaintances, but they all represented circles that were outside the inner ring. It was only that inner ring that you had to be willing to fight and die for.

The Emersons used to grow their own food at their little farm in the mountains, but after Mom got herself elected to the U.S. House of Representatives, they'd had to give up the farm to move to a tiny rental house in Arlington, Virginia, just outside of Washington, DC. That's where Major McCrea and First Sergeant Copley had snatched them on Hell Night.

Top Hat Mountain was the place they would all go if *the balloon went up*—one of Mom and Dad's favorite euphemisms for the shit hitting the fan. The plan had a long lead on it. If the balloon went up when family members were separated, and they were unable to get back together, they would make their way to Top Hat Mountain, where they would meet up at noon on the first Monday of the month. If you found yourself alone, or if someone was missing, you'd show up again on the first Monday of the next month, and like that until you lost hope or until the reunion happened.

Dad used to say that no battle plan survives the first

shot fired, and that turned out to be the case with the Emersons' bug-out plan. On the evening before Hell Day, Major McCrea and First Sergeant Copley arrived at their house and essentially kidnapped Mom to take her to some bunker in a big hotel. But once they got there, Mom found out that the bunker wouldn't let Luke and Caleb in. Mom quit on the spot and they left. They wanted to go back home—which really would have turned out to be stupid—but Major McCrea refused to take them. In fact, he insisted that he was ordered specifically *not* to take them back home.

Even though no one thought an actual war was coming—something about Israel and Iran, as Luke remembered—but it didn't matter.

By dawn the next morning, everything was gone. Fires burned everywhere and the only people they passed while they were walking were either dead or dangerously scared.

That was when they started walking toward Top Hat Mountain. Hopefully, their eighteen-year-old brother, Adam, would be doing the same thing.

But then they got to Ortho, and Mom fell right into queen-of-the-hill mode.

Luke had to admit that she was able to bring reason and calm to a situation where everyone else's hair was on fire.

And here they were. They'd already been shot at and they'd had to kill people. This was the new way, he supposed. It bothered Luke that shooting people wasn't harder to do. He was only fourteen, for crying out loud. He was at least supposed to lose sleep or something, but that hadn't been the case for him.

The only people he'd killed were people who'd have killed him first if they'd gotten the chance. Luke couldn't think of a single thing about society that hadn't changed since Hell Day. He didn't talk about these things with his mom because she had enough shit going on in her life without him adding to her burden.

He did mention it to First Sergeant Copley, though, who told him that there was nothing wrong with protecting yourself from predators.

From his perch in the window of the hardware store, Luke watched Mom and Major McCrea talk with a soldier from the boat. When they went into Maggie's Place, he felt tension drain from his shoulders.

"Do you think it's over?" he asked.

"Not as long as all those assholes with guns are floating out there," Caleb said. "Have you seen the grenade launchers?"

With no immediate threats to protect against, Luke used his scope to survey the rest of the people in the rickety little fleet. "Those are the big tubes under the rifle barrels?"

"Right."

"I only see one. The guy in the third boat out."

"That's all I see, too. But where there's one, there's got to be more."

Luke suppressed a chuckle. How the hell could he know how many *anythings* were out there?

Major McCrea had stressed during training that being a sniper was about more than being a good shot. It was also about not attracting return fire. That's why they stayed back in the shadows of the room there in the second floor of the hardware store. If they did have to shoot, the targets on the other team wouldn't know where the bullets were coming from. Major McCrea called that a "morale buster."

This sniper's nest checked all the boxes. It was elevated, it had a clear view of the enemy's position, and the windows allowed them to hang back in the shadows so their rifles would be invisible.

"What do you think they're talking about in there?" Luke asked his brother.

"Not a clue," Caleb replied. "But that Army guy's friends are getting nervous. Look at how they're fingering their rifles."

Through his four-power scope, Luke continued to scan the occupants of the boats. Everybody, it seemed, was standing, and there was something wrong with the way they were talking to each other. He couldn't make out the words, of course, and he'd never been any good at lip reading, but they tilted their heads close to each other when they talked. A few of them pointed toward the shore.

The ones closest to the shore looked especially nervous. It was the way they'd slung their rifles. It was natural to rest your hand on the pistol grip of an AR platform—it was the only comfortable place to put it, actually—but the guys in the front boat had their fingers extended along the trigger guards.

"One of them has his finger on his trigger," Luke observed aloud.

"Front boat? Guy on the right?"

"No," Luke said, and he shifted his scope to that soldier. "I was talking about the guy in the second boat. Right side."

"Got it," Caleb said. "You keep your reticle on your guy, and I'll keep mine on mine."

"How will we know when it's time to shoot?" Luke asked.

"Damn good question."

That was another point that the major had leaned on very hard when he delivered his training to the citizens of Ortho. Everybody was scared and hungry. *Everybody.* That meant that everyone was nervous as hell. Every potential enemy you encountered—and *everyone* was a potential enemy until proved otherwise—considered you, likewise, to be an enemy.

"These times require all of us to be polite and aware," the major liked to say. "If that doesn't work, the times require fast and decisive action. We just can't afford to be wrong."

"They're coming out of Maggie's," Caleb said.

Luke shifted his eyes to the right to see the short parade moving in a line back toward the boat ramp, but then returned his eyes to the guy in the boat. "How does your guy with the gun look?" he asked.

"Pissed off," Caleb replied.

"Mine too." Behind the one man with his finger on the trigger, a woman in uniform arose from her seat and stood next to him. Her finger was on her trigger, too. "I think they're getting ready to shoot."

Caleb didn't say anything.

"Should we shout out?"

"No." Caleb snapped the word out. "If they're going to hear from me, it's going to be a big bang."

The captain led the way as they walked back toward the boats, followed closely by a guy who didn't look like he belonged in a uniform.

As he neared the waterfront, the captain shouted to the other boats, "We're not welcome here!"

Luke was surprised how clear the words sounded, even at this distance.

"Says who?" someone shouted from one of the boats.

"We're moving on!" the captain said.

"We need supplies!" someone else called.

"This is not a discussion!" Magill yelled. "This is an order. Get moving!"

Luke fought the urge to look away from his scope. His guy with the gun leaned over to the girl next to him and whispered something. She nodded.

Then both of them brought their rifles to their shoulders.

The first shot came from behind Victoria. A soldier in the second boat dropped as if his plug had been pulled. When he rolled off into the river, he nearly swamped his own boat. A female soldier standing next to him went down next.

That's when the world came unglued. Gunfire erupted from everywhere. The soldiers in the boats fired toward the shore, but they were shooting from unstable platforms and their rounds went wide and wild.

The genie was out of the bottle.

Victoria brought her M4 to her shoulder, settled the reticle of her scope on the chest of a soldier in the boat closest to shore, then pressed her trigger. The soldier spun on his own axis and dropped. She shifted her aim to another soldier in the same boat and fired again. This shot missed, or if it hit, her target made no reaction other than fear. He ducked, presenting the crown of his head. She drilled it and the soldier died on his feet.

Instead of struggling to turn away in the face of gunfire, the three closest boats redoubled their efforts to get to shore. Within twenty seconds, those occupants were all dead, and one of the boats was so riddled with holes that it was listing.

Farther out in the river, the crews of the other boats pulled on their oars to turn back downstream and get out. A few of the soldiers continued to fire toward shore to cover their escape, but from what Victoria could tell, the snipers took them all out.

Luke wasn't aware of anything but the sounds of the gunfire and the view through his scope. There was nothing fair about this fight. He settled his reticle on a target, he pressed his trigger, and the target dropped.

"Don't worry about kill shots!" Caleb yelled over the hammering booms of God only knew how many guns that were in play. "Just get them to stop shooting. If they're down, you're done."

Locked in like this, with his rifle stable, it seemed impossible to miss. Even the soldiers way out in the river—the ones who continued to shoot—dropped when Luke touched them with his scope.

"Stop!" Caleb yelled. "Jesus, Luke, stop!" He was pointing out the window at Major McCrea, who was making a chopping motion in the air with a bladed hand.

* * *

"Cease-fire!" McCrea shouted. "Cease-fire! Cease-fire!"

Victoria lowered her rifle. The silence that followed felt overwhelming. Like a vacuum of sound. The opposite of sound.

"Keep sights on the boats!" McCrea hollered. "If they point at the shore, blow them away. Otherwise, let them go."

McCrea turned his back on the water to face back into town. "Is anybody hurt?" he called. "If you're wounded and can walk, get yourself to Doc Rory's. If you need help, blow your whistle."

No whistles blew. Not yet, anyway.

Victoria left her cover to join McCrea at the water's edge. "What the hell just happened? It was so . . . fast."

"I'm not sure," McCrea said. "All I know for sure is they lost a gunfight. George, Joey, help me get these bodies ashore." As he waded knee-deep into the river, he called out over his shoulder, "First Sergeant Copley! Front and center, please!"

Copley seemed to materialize out of nowhere, as he often did. Apparently, he'd taken cover behind a long-disabled Dodge Durango pickup truck. "Yes, sir?"

McCrea grabbed the remains of Captain Roy Magill by the back of his collar and dragged him up the concrete launch ramp, where he dumped the body faceup on a dry spot. Without looking, he gave his instructions to Copley. "Paul, this isn't over. They'll be back. I don't want to unzip our defenses, but we need to gather more ammo for everyone. Take care of that, will you?"

Copley looked like he stopped himself from saluting. "Yes, sir. I'll spread the word that people should leave their posts a few at a time to restock and come back. What do you want done with the weapons and ammo from the corpses?"

"Put it all in the armory." They'd established a central depository behind Maggie's for weapons and ammunition they acquired from abandoned homes and people who died.

"Got it," Copley said.

"Paul?" Victoria said.

The young man stopped, waited for it.

"When you send my boys, please have them bring some extra magazines for me." She trusted Copley to hear the subtext that she wanted him to check to be sure they were okay. They'd both proven themselves to be valiant fighters, and it wouldn't be helpful to either one if she was perceived as mommying them.

"Yes, ma'am." He left at a jog.

Within a minute or two, eight corpses were lined up on the concrete ramp, which now ran crimson with blood. Victoria assisted with the effort to turn their pockets out and search for identification, but they came up with nothing. No identification at all. No printed orders. Granted, there was little use for identification papers in the wake of Hell Day, but she found it strange. She still had her wallet and credit cards, though they were in her rucksack back in St. Thomas Catholic Church, next to her bunk.

"Joe, what do you think this is all about?"

McCrea stood and stretched. "I have no idea. But if you want my gut, I think we should take Captain Magill at his word. This is a group of soldiers that's tired of being refugees and saw an opportunity to take provisions that don't belong to them."

"Are they really soldiers?" George Simmons asked. "That's pretty aggressive behavior."

"You see what I see, George. The uniforms are a few years out of date, which adds credence to the idea that they're from the National Guard, and their weapons appear to be government issued."

"So, are you saying we just attacked U.S. forces?" Joey Abbott asked.

"Not exactly," McCrea said. "And remember, they attacked *us*."

"We fired the first shot," Joey said. "That's the way I heard it, anyway."

"Their intent was clear," McCrea said. "Makes no sense to let people take the first shot when you know what they're going to do."

Victoria wanted to move the conversation to a different track. "I think Major McCrea is saying that these are people in military uniforms that may or may not have been active duty when the war happened."

McCrea added, "I know for a fact that I'm a major in Uncle Sam's employ, and this is not how I would have conducted myself under similar circumstances."

Victoria added, "From everything we've heard from newcomers, all forms of communication are still trashed. I don't see a way that these soldiers could have received orders from National Command Authority."

"That assumes that NCA even exists anymore," McCrea said. Then for the benefit of the others, "National Command Authority is the president, vice president and secretary of defense. Without them at the top, official orders are hard to come by."

"So you're saying that these folks were marauders," Joey said.

"That's my guess, yes."

"And you think this is only the first wave?" Victoria asked.

McCrea rubbed the back of his neck and looked out toward the river, where no occupied boats were visible anymore. "Even if they're just marauders, we have to assume that they're marauders with military training. They just lost a gunfight in which some of their friends died. Where their commander died. If I were in their shoes, I'd be pretty pissed off."

"Especially since they'd been beaten by civilians," Simmons said. Back in the day, as a Marine, he'd done his share of capturing hearts and minds on behalf of Uncle Sam.

"That doesn't help at all," McCrea confirmed. "On the other hand, the fact that all our fighters are civilians will give them a sense of superiority."

"Even after this?" Victoria asked.

"This was just stupid," McCrea said, indicating the bodies that continued to bleed out onto the ramp. "Pure hubris. This never should have happened. They weren't prepared, and it'll be easy for them to shrug this debacle off as a freak accident. Unfortunately, they're less likely to underestimate us on their second try."

"How long do you think we have?"

"A while," McCrea said. "But not long enough."

Paul Copley walked toward the hardware store, where Caleb and Luke were still hanging back in the shadows, and launched a piercing finger-whistle. "Who's up there?" he called.

Luke stood from the table that had been his shooting platform and moved to the window. He waved. "Caleb and me."

Something changed behind Copley's eyes. A look of fear, maybe? "Stay right there," he said. "I'll be right up."

Luke felt his gut tighten. Paul Copley looked angry.

"Did he say he's coming up?" Caleb asked.

The sound of someone climbing the stairs answered him. A few seconds later, Copley appeared in the doorway. Luke liked Paul, and Paul liked him back. He didn't know how old he was—he guessed maybe thirty-five—but he acted much younger. At least when Major McCrea wasn't around. Paul liked to laugh, and he had a great eye for practical jokes. He was also strong as shit.

But now he looked worried. "Hi, guys," he said.

The boys grunted a hello in return. Caleb clearly felt the doom in Copley's tone, too.

They didn't have to wait long. "Did you fire the first shot at those soldiers?"

"Luke did," Caleb said. "But I was second or third."

"Why?" Copley asked. "What did you see?"

"The guys in the first two boats—"

"—They were fingering their triggers—"

"—A lady, too, on the second boat—"

"—They were getting ready to shoot—"

Copley held his hands out, a gesture for silence. "One at a time, guys. Luke, you said you fired first."

"Am I in trouble?"

"Just tell me what you saw."

Luke relayed the sense of menace they got from the people in the lead boats while Mom and Major McCrea were inside with the soldiers. "When the guy in my boat brought his gun up, I shot him."

"He didn't shoot first?"

"He was going to." Luke's sense of dread was blooming larger.

"He really was," Caleb confirmed. "The guys in my boat, too."

"You keep referring to *your* boats," Copley said. "What does that mean?"

"We assigned targets," Caleb said.

"Just like you and the major taught us to do," Luke added. "What's wrong?"

Paul went quiet as he thought about something. "Take a seat," he said, finally.

The boys sat. Copley shifted his weight to one leg while he pushed his rifle around to his back and crossed his arms. "Here's the thing. First of all, no, you didn't do anything wrong. In fact, it sounds like you did everything just about perfectly."

Luke blushed.

"But I won't lie to you and tell you that everyone is likely to feel the same way. I don't know if you've been dialed into the tension around town—"

"You mean the people who don't like Mom?" Caleb asked, cutting right to it.

Copley winced. "Well, I'm not sure I'd put it that harshly, but—"

"She's just trying to do the right thing by everybody," Luke said.

"You'll get no argument from me on that," Copley

said. "But doing the right thing almost always means that one half of any dispute leaves angry. All of that gets focused on your mom."

"Hey," Caleb said, "if someone wants to take over, that would be great. I don't want to be here, anyway."

Copley held out his hands again. "Come on, guys. Let's not get defensive. I'm just trying to present the facts as I see them. And the rumors as I hear them. There's dissent out there."

Luke was confused. "What does that have to do with what just happened?"

"We're Emersons," Caleb said. "People don't care about justice when they're pissed off. They just want to hurt the people who made them pissed."

Luke got it. "And we're the easiest way to get to her."

"Exactly," Copley said. "Now, don't take this to the extreme. I don't think people are out to get you, or that you shouldn't sleep soundly at night."

"I don't remember the last time I slept soundly," Caleb said.

Copley clapped his hands softly. "I think we're done here." He started to leave, but then turned around. "Oh, your mom wants you to bring her some more ammunition."

CHAPTER THREE

Hell Day + 34 (The Same Day)

VICTORIA SUMMONED MCCREA, JOEY ABBOTT, GEORGE
Simmons and Paul Copley to her office in Maggie's. It
wasn't a secret meeting, per se, but she was glad that
no hangers-on had decided to attend. In fact, Victoria
was opposed to secret meetings, given the current circumstances. Secrecy sowed mistrust during difficult
times. It bred unnecessary paranoia at a time when a
healthy dose of paranoia was probably a good idea.

In the before times, George Simmons had been the
proprietor of Simmons Gas and Goodies, an Exxon
distributor and snack store. Joey Abbott had run Joey's
Pawnshop. In the weeks since Hell Day, they had become important conduits between Victoria and the residents of Ortho, with whom the two men had grown up
and gone to school. She considered them both to be
friends and leaned on them for wise counsel.

"What's up?" McCrea asked as he pulled out a seat for himself.

In its previous life, Maggie's had been a combination general store, café and bar. Since Hell Day, it had evolved into the seat of the government that didn't officially exist. Because of its central location within the tiny town, it had become the primary meeting spot for all the various committees and work groups that had proven so helpful to Victoria's efforts to seed hope and limit chaos. From the clothing bank to the education committee to the construction committee, the citizens of Ortho had willingly and effectively stepped up to work on behalf of the common good.

Then came today's assault, which she feared would unsettle people to the point where fear would eclipse hope.

"Gentlemen," Victoria began, "you are the defense committee for Ortho. We cannot afford for what happened this afternoon to happen again."

"All due respect, Vicky," George said, "being out there taking care of business would be a lot more help than sitting in here talking about it."

"There's four of you," Victoria said. "Major, you're in charge and I don't want to step on your toes, but is there an overarching defense plan or are we just winging it?"

While her romantic relationship with Joe McCrea was a secret to no one, she preferred to call him by his rank in official interactions.

McCrea cleared his throat and recrossed his legs. "I wouldn't say we're *winging it*. As you know, we've organized the militia, such as it is, and I think they performed adequately today. More than adequately, in fact. They kicked ass."

"Why did we open fire?" Victoria asked.

McCrea scowled. "Did you not see what I saw? Captain Magill and his crew meant to do us harm."

"But he *hadn't* caused us harm," Victoria said. "In fact, by what I saw, he was on his way back to the boat when we opened fire."

Copley raised his hand. "Um, ma'am?"

"Yes, First Sergeant?"

"I have it on good authority that the first shots were fired on boat crews that were preparing to open fire on you."

"What good authority?"

"I'd rather not say."

"I don't care what you'd rather not do," Victoria snapped. "I want you to answer my question." If there was one principle to which she was 100 percent committed, it was that the military needed to report to civilian leadership—even if the military was a group of ragtag citizens and the leadership was never elected.

Copley cast a look to McCrea, a silent plea for help.

"Let's stay focused," McCrea said. "Nothing we say or don't say at this point can undo anything that's been done."

George Simmons said, "You want to talk about what's really broken? Talk about what happened and why we can't stop it from happening again?"

Victoria invited him to make his point with a dip of her forehead.

"Outsiders," George said, as if one word were a whole explanation. "Present company excepted, Vicky, we've got to stop this constant flow of refugees. They're a drain on every resource and most of them don't bring anything in exchange."

Victoria had heard this narrative in one form or another for weeks now. She held her tongue. Life was about more than work skills and resource preservation. The families that arrived in Ortho were often in desperate straits. Some had been walking for days or weeks. All were malnourished. Some died within days of arrival.

The worst among them were the ones whose jobs before Hell Day had focused on pushing paper and exchanging cash. The irony was not lost on Victoria— herself a lawyer before she went off to Congress—that people who paid hundreds of thousands of dollars for educations that would make them wealthy now were left with no useful skills.

"I don't see how the refugees are a security issue," McCrea said. "Security is what we're here to talk about."

"They have no loyalty," Joey Abbott said. "They don't see us as neighbors. They see us as a source of free stuff."

"That's not fair," Victoria said. "Even if it's mostly true, it's not fair. Hell Day was only a few weeks ago. These people are desperate because they've lost everything. We can't just turn our backs on them. There were close to two million residents in this state before the war, and God only knows how many of them were killed in the attacks. Our population has grown by only several hundred."

"We're seeing a lot more pilferage," George said. "Your innocent refugees are breaking into people's homes and helping themselves. If we don't get a lid on that, we'll have a whole new war zone to deal with."

"We've been through this already," Victoria said. "If someone is caught breaking the law, they will be tried and punished."

"You can flog only so many people," George said. "And carve so many foreheads." With incarceration not feasible, corporal punishment in the form of public floggings had become the standard for serious offenses, and it had only been employed once so far. People caught stealing had the letter T carved into their forehead with the blade of a knife.

"We haven't had any second offenses that I'm aware of," Victoria said. "So make me a recommendation. You bitch about this stuff. Tell me how we stop desperate people from seeking help. Build a big fence around the town? That would take forever and it still leaves us with a readily-available river. Go."

"At a minimum, we need checkpoints on the major roads," George said. "We should get a chance to figure out new people's intentions when they're coming in."

"Their intentions?" Victoria asked.

"Yeah. What they're looking for, what they have to offer. Are they armed? Do they have sickness in their party? That sort of thing."

"To what end?" Victoria asked.

"Jesus, Vicky. To *know.* There's nothing wrong with knowing who's gonna be the next burden, is there?"

"That's not helpful," McCrea scolded.

Joey offered, "Put a positive spin on it. When new people come in, shouldn't they have an idea of where to go first? I mean we have all of this *free stuff,* but they need to know where to go to get it. They need to know where the doc is, where the tent city is. Plus, we need to know what skills they have. We're sort of doing that, anyway, but why not organize it?"

Victoria liked the sound of that. The more people understood what was expected of them, the more likely they would be to become part of the town. "Should the people at these checkpoints be armed?"

"Yes" and "Absolutely" erupted as a chorus.

"They need to know that we take security seriously here," McCrea said. "We ask that everybody be armed all the time, anyway. I think it's safe to assume that most of the newcomers are going to have weapons, too. In fact, that will be a great time to tell them about the militia requirement."

All of this sounded perfectly reasonable. "Is that it? Will that give us the security that you're looking for?"

It was McCrea's turn to burst her bubble. "No. Roadblocks or checkpoints or whatever we're going to call them are fine for nice people arriving a few at a time. It's not enough to stop a coordinated attack."

"I don't know what that means," Victoria said. *"Coordinated attack."* Actually, she imagined that she did know what it meant, but she wanted to hear him describe it.

"Like what we saw at the waterfront today," McCrea said. "Or worse. People at checkpoints get complacent because they see the same thing over and over again. That makes them easy targets over time. By definition, they're going to be outnumbered. If the bad guys get the drop on them, it'll be a bloodbath."

"Put that in the form of a recommendation," Victoria said.

"We need some kind of early warning system."

"Watchtowers," George said, again offering up a phrase as if it were an explanation.

This time, Victoria just waited for the rest.

"I've been thinking about this a lot," George went on. "Spoke to Joey about it, too. If there's one thing we've got plenty of around here, it's trees. And if there's another, it's hunters. There's not ten guys within ten miles of here that don't have a tree stand or know how to build one. I say we position a bunch of them around the perimeter—as far out as you want to go—and assign people in shifts to keep watch. At the very least, they'll be able to alert the militia covering the checkpoints to be prepared for something."

Deer stands were elevated platforms where hunters could wait for prey to wander by. Most that Victoria had seen were site-built, with hunters hammering planks into tree trunks to serve as ladders, and then hammering more boards into the tree to serve as supports for the platform they would sit on. In the past twenty years, more and more companies were manufacturing portable tree stands that could be more easily transported, set up and removed. The manufactured ones lasted a lot longer.

Victoria looked to McCrea. "That sounds like a good idea. What do you think?"

McCrea pinched his lower lip as he thought it through. "Can we get an accurate map of this area? Preferably one that shows elevations and trails in addition to the roads?"

"I've got one on the wall in my house," Joey said. "I ordered it years ago from the Geological Survey. I thought it looked good over my fireplace."

"Is it still accurate?" Victoria asked.

George and Joey laughed in unison. "If Daniel Boone had made a map of this place, it still would be eighty percent accurate," George said.

"Have you thought through the communication system?" McCrea asked.

"Same whistles that we have now," Joey said.

George elaborated. "Each stand would have a whistle code. I don't know, one short and two long blasts for stand number one, and one short and three longs for stand two. We could code the messages, too, but that would get really complicated."

"Just to be clear," Victoria said, "when you say *blasts,* you mean tweets, right? Blasts of the whistle?"

"Exactly."

McCrea's face lit up with the idea. "We could establish a relay, then," he said. "To use your example, if stand one sounded an alert, stands two, three and four—or whatever—could relay stand one's code, so everyone would know where the problem is."

"That's a good idea," George said.

Victoria was seeing real potential for something good here. "The observers themselves would need to be rotated out pretty frequently. Otherwise, that's a burnout job."

"Well, you're a hunter, Vicky," Joey said with a laugh. "You know how freaking cold you can get when you're up in a tree stand."

"Exactly." She ran the system through her head. It was much better than building a fence that would never work, and a hell of a lot cheaper. Plus, it could be put in place almost immediately. "I'm going to need a procedure for this," she said.

"Oh, my God," George groaned. "You ain't in Washington anymore, Congresswoman. The last thing we need around here is bureaucracy."

"I'm not talking about bureaucracy, George. I'm talking about a plan. If this is what we're hanging our defenses on, then we've got to formalize it, so we know that everyone is thinking the same thing at the same time."

"Plus, we can hold people accountable," McCrea said. "If this is the basket for all our eggs, there have to be pretty severe penalties for not showing up or for falling asleep at your post."

"Come on, Major," Joey said. "We're asking people to climb into trees to freeze their nards off. Let's not make it a bigger burden than it needs to be."

"The major has a point," Victoria said. "Not about punishing people, per se, but we've got to make sure that the people we sign up for this duty are up to it."

"We didn't have any trouble forming the militia," McCrea said.

"This is different," Victoria argued. "It's one thing to ask people to keep their guns nearby and to rally when called. It's something else entirely to put the burden on them to be the first line of defense. With that commitment to blow a whistle comes the reality of being the first target if they're alerting to the approach of bad guys. That's a lot to ask."

"Oh, I don't know," Joey said. "They'll be defending their own families. That's a hell of an incentive, if you ask me."

Victoria turned back to George. "Have you given thought to how many of these watchtowers we would need?"

"More is better than less," he said. "The farther out

we go with the towers, the more warning we're going to get."

McCrea held up a hand. "Wait a second. Let's dial it back a little. How do we tell the difference between an attack and wandering refugees? We can't spin the militia up every time people go on a hike."

"Before Vicky proposes a committee to explore motivations"—George sold it with a wink—"we'll really shoot ourselves in the foot if we overregulate that stuff. We're going to have to trust people's judgment."

"Which brings us back to the need for solid personnel," Victoria said.

"Which, in turn, means solid incentives. Solid motivations."

"We can always pay them," Joey said. "I'll finance it through my credit card. I seem to have no limit anymore."

McCrea laughed. "Eight hundred dollars an hour," he said. "Nah, make it a thousand."

"We can sort of do that," Victoria said.

They all gaped in unison.

"We compensate them," she said. "We recruit the specific people we want to rotate through the towers and we train them. As a reward for their willingness to serve, we compensate them somehow."

"*Somehow* is a big word," Joey said. "What do you have in mind?"

Victoria winked. "Mostly, I want to hear what *your* ideas are."

They laughed. The irony of their current situation was that everyone needed so much, but no one had anything of value that was useful to others.

McCrea said, "Okay, I'll bite. Over the past few

weeks, a solid barter system has started to bloom. People still need stuff. If I really need a knife, and you really need a chair, maybe we can strike a deal."

"Oh, Lord," George scoffed. "We can't barter on behalf of other people. We don't know what they need."

"No, but we know what *everybody* needs," McCrea said. "Ammunition."

"Are you serious?" Joey said. "There must be tens of thousands of rounds of ammo just within a mile radius."

"I like it," Victoria said.

"We're going to ask these people to risk their lives and pay them with more of what they already have?"

Victoria pointed to the wall behind the bar. "We've got tens of thousands of rounds right back there in Maggie's safe, in the armory."

"Those are for the militia," McCrea said.

"They're for the common good," Victoria corrected. "And that's what we're talking about."

From the looks on their faces, she could see that she wasn't making her point clearly enough.

"Look," she said. "Think back to before Hell Day. We carried pieces of plastic for credit and pieces of paper for cash. Those things had no inherent value beyond a fraction of a penny for recycling. They worked as currency because we all agreed that the piece of paper with a five on it was five times more valuable than the exact same piece of paper with a one on it."

"Nice history lesson, Vicky," George said with a chuckle.

She pressed on. "It didn't matter that you were current on your bills, or that you had extra money in the bank. If you did a job, you expected to get more money, not because you needed it, but because you earned it."

They still weren't getting it.

"If we declare ammunition to be currency, people will treat it as such," Victoria said.

McCrea leaned in. "Because we *say* so?"

"Essentially, yes. We pay the watchtower militia, say, fifty rounds per week. That gives them two hundred rounds a month that they can use for additional hunting or just plinking. It's ammo they wouldn't otherwise have. That gives it value."

McCrea looked at the others. "I think this is a great point. Then, if they want goods or services from somebody else, they pay for it in ammo. That will get us out of the business of giving out stuff for free, just because people are in need."

"Or *claim* to be in need," George said. "Not everyone is as bad off as they pretend."

"We'll still be helping the people who need it," Victoria said.

"But we won't have to carry them forever anymore," Joey said. His tone sounded hopeful.

"Exactly," Victoria confirmed. "It will take a while for the details to shake out, but some people will save, and others will not."

"If ammo is the new money, we got some really wealthy folks here already," George quipped.

"There's another element that will shake out over time," Victoria said. "People will decide for themselves what the relative worth of things are."

"What about people who want to continue bartering?" Joey asked.

"Then that's what they do," Victoria said. "That's

the nature of economies, right? Is a venison backstrap worth five bullets or twenty? Is it worth a scarf or a quilt? It depends on the individuals' assignment of value."

McCrea thought aloud, "And if Joey charges more than I'm comfortable with, I'll buy it from George, instead."

Victoria held her arms out from her sides and grinned. "Capitalism, baby."

"Are you okay if I assign your boys to the tower teams?" McCrea asked.

"They aren't boys anymore," Victoria said. "After Hell Day, I'm not sure if there's such a thing as childhood anymore. There's only young and old. What they're capable of or what they're not."

Something about the way Copley shifted in his seat caught Victoria's attention. "Do you have something to say, Paul?"

"No, ma'am."

He clearly did, but she wasn't going to press him on it.

"I've got something," Joey said.

Victoria raised an eyebrow.

"It's about the most recent refugees," he said. "I forget their names, but they're the ones who came in from Atkins. Mom and dad with three kids."

Victoria knew who he was referring to, but there had been far too many arrivals for her to remember their names. Atkins was easily thirty miles away, and they'd been worked over hard by the long walk. "Yesterday?" she asked.

"Right. Late. Did you hear their stories about the gangs?"

Everyone sat up a little straighter at that. "Gangs?"

"Yeah. The husband—shit, I wish I could remember his name—talked about how they walked into a lot of different gangs as they were coming in from Atkins. That's what I thought those Army folks were going to be this morning. They're essentially raiding parties."

"You keep speaking of them in the plural," Victoria said.

"Right. So did they. Said there were a lot of them. A lot was their word, not mine. Said they were desperate and violent. They called it the Wild West."

"How did they get through all of that?" Copley asked.

"They gave them everything they wanted. That's why they had no stuff when they got here."

"So they just gave in," George said. The disdain in his voice was palpable.

"What can I say?" Joey said. "They're not fighters."

"Wolves and sheep," Copley said.

"So, in the very same meeting when we're talking about militias and watchtowers, we're welcoming in a family of sheep," George grumped.

"Hey," Victoria snapped. "Ease up, George. You don't know what they went through out there. Maybe it was ten to one. We don't know that, and we have no right to. What we do know is that parents are still alive to care for their children. Dying just to prove a point, or just to be tough, doesn't help anyone."

"I'm just saying—"

"*I'm* just saying that that attitude doesn't help anyone in this room, either. We all know that some are going to get through this experience and adjust better than others. Some will not make it at all. We've all heard about the suicides."

McCrea cleared his throat again. "Um, Vicky—"

"I'm not done, Major. As long as I'm in charge, Ortho is going to be a town that welcomes others. If Joey's description is right—if the world beyond this town is the Wild West, then this is Dodge City. Yes, people who can work will need to work. And, yes, those who need help will get it. We will have justice, and if we can make it work, we will have peace."

She turned her gaze to George, and only George. "You asked me a long time ago, shortly after we arrived, who died and appointed me queen. Do you remember that?"

George's jaw muscles were working hard, but he didn't say anything.

"I told you then, and I'm telling you now, that this job is open to anyone who wants to have it. But as long as it's mine, this will be a place where law and order are tempered with kindness. Can I possibly be any clearer on this point?"

He looked away.

"Okay, then this is done," Victoria said. "We need to keep moving forward without stopping every few steps to look back and reargue settled points."

She took a deep breath and placed her hands on the table. She forced her shoulders to relax.

"Thank you, gentlemen," she said. "Major McCrea and George, I'll look to you to figure out this whole pay structure thing. But let's get the watchtowers manned as soon as we can."

Everyone stood. As the men filed out of the room,

Victoria walked to a table that was stacked with books that had been collected from around town. With all other options for relaxation pretty much shut down, books had become important to people again. Mr. Jake— a Santa look-alike who, so far as she knew, had no last name—had been spearheading an effort to start a library, which, of course, would be headquartered here in Maggie's, along with everything else.

"Excuse me, ma'am?"

Victoria turned to see Copley standing inside the door he'd just exited.

"You were right," he said. "There is something I need to talk to you about."

CHAPTER FOUR

Hell Day + 20 (Fourteen Days Earlier)

THE UNITED STATES GOVERNMENT RELOCATION Center—not so affectionately known as the Annex—was a good idea when it first appeared on President Eisenhower's desk in the mid-1950s. Designed as the bunker to which members of the United States Senate and House of Representatives would be evacuated in the event of nuclear war, the predecessor of this relocation center rested under the Greenbrier Resort in White Sulphur Springs, West Virginia. That original facility had to be abandoned in 1992, however, after a Washington newspaper revealed its existence to the world in a sensational feature article.

For years, as a result of the disclosure, the continuation of government remained at risk while Uncle Sam thought of something else. The president and the executive branch had a separate evacuation site, as did the

Supreme Court, but if the balloon went up, the legislative branch would have been left homeless.

Almost immediately after the story broke, the USA started spending billions of dollars to create a replacement Annex, this one at the Hilltop Manor Resort, also in West Virginia. Equipped with the most sophisticated communications equipment, members of the House and Senate would continue the business of government, helping the president and the rest of the government apparatus to rebuild the country from whatever was left after the explosions stopped.

Of course, all of that was theater—an illusion of a plan that no one in the know ever believed. Perhaps in the 1950s, when the Red Threat would have been delivered by bomber crews after a long flight under harassment by U.S. antiaircraft batteries, there was enough time to make the hours-long trip by train out to the Greenbrier, but not in the twenty-first century. Not when submarines lay in wait barely outside territorial waters and the flight times of their missiles to their farthest targets clocked in at under ten minutes.

Through all his decades of service in the House of Representatives, Penn Glendale had never given much thought to the evacuation card he'd carried in his wallet. If the balloon went up, he assumed he'd fry in the million-degree fireball just like everyone else.

Now, as he sat safe and well fed in his spartan room in the new Annex, he contemplated all the actions and errors that had brought him here. He contemplated how wrong he'd been in his assumptions that the Annex could never work.

For all those years, as he rose from a junior congressman representing South Central Virginia to become

Speaker of the House—and now the president of the United States, thanks to some parliamentary sleight of hand, with which he was still not completely comfortable—there was one variable in play that he'd never considered, but which turned out to mean the difference between immolation and survival.

He'd never considered that America might launch the first strike. More accurately in this case, Israel was to be the one who launched the first strike, but the advance notice was the same.

The plan had been so simple on paper, and Penn had always believed that it was ill conceived. In fact, his last conversation with the now-late President Helen Blanton had been a bid to get her to withdraw her support for Israel's launch on Iran. Yes, Iran had gone live with nuclear weapons, and, yes, they had been threatening to destroy Israel, but they had been making those same threats since 1979, yet they'd never pulled the trigger on their intentions. At least not on a major scale. In Penn's mind, the occasional bus bomb outside a coffee shop didn't count. It certainly did not warrant a nuclear strike.

But Blanton would not listen. She maintained that the strike was Israel's idea, and that as their primary ally in the world, the United States owed them all the support they needed to protect themselves.

House members' evacuations to the Annex began under the cover of darkness and in absolute secrecy to prevent alarming the nation's enemies that something bad was in play. Once the American government was safely in place, the plan was to alert the Russians and the rest of the world to the imminent strike with as little advance notice as possible. The geniuses surrounding the late president assured everyone that the Russians would understand the necessity of what would follow.

Then the Washington press corps leaked the fact of the congressional migration to Hilltop Manor amid extraordinary security measures and postulated that perhaps the United States was planning a first strike somewhere in the world. Iran connected the dots and launched on Israel without warning, triggering a retaliatory strike that then snowballed into defensive strikes and more retaliatory strikes from every nuclear-capable nation.

The whole war lasted eight hours, and as far as Penn could tell, no one knew the extent of the destruction. He sure as hell didn't.

While the Annex was blessed with the latest communications technology, Penn discovered in the first seconds of the war that communication happens in two parts. It's fine to be able to transmit, but electromagnetic pulses had played hell with the atmosphere, and the electrical grid was apparently down around the world. Penn and his comms were the personification of the tree that falls in the empty woods. While he and the comms staff here in the Annex were quite certain that they were effectively making noise, what difference did it make when no one could hear it?

Once reports of President Blanton's and Veep Jenkins's deaths were confirmed, as Speaker of the House of Representatives, Penn assumed the big chair.

And here again, a crisis of imagination during the planning stages made his presidency vastly more complicated than it needed to be, even under these terrible, extraordinary circumstances. The executive branch of the United States government, or what was left of it, anyway, resided in a different bunker, about one hundred miles away from the Annex. Thus, while Penn Glendale was president of the United States, he had no direct contact with any of his senior staff. Instead, he was ensconced with the legislative branch. That in itself wouldn't be so bad if the two political parties in residence could find a way to be on speaking terms, but that hadn't been in the cards for over a decade.

A knock on the door drew Penn's attention away from his miserable musings. "Come in," he said.

Arlen Strasky pushed the door open and entered. Arlen had been Penn's chief of staff for nearly as long as he'd been a member of Congress. Now that there was precious little staff to manage, Arlen's primary role was to be his friend and confidant.

"Hi, Boss," Strasky said. "How are you holding up?"

"I'm fine. How're the rest of the inmates?"

"Going a bit crazy," Strasky said. "Everybody pretends to be doing something, but at the end of the day, they're as frustrated as we are that there's really not a lot to do."

They'd had this discussion dozens of times, it seemed. Congress was in the business of passing laws and funding government programs. With communications essentially shut down, and without access to the federal treasury, members were left with little to do other than make speeches and yell at each other. Penn was willing to bet that of the remaining population of the world, the few hundred residents of the Annex were among the precious few who had actually gained weight in the weeks since the war. Three squares a day plus snacks, and all of it tasted pretty good.

They ate in shifts, their mealtimes assigned to them by Solara, the consulting firm that ran the joint. The shift was documented on the identification cards they all carried. At first, the mealtimes seemed to have been randomly assigned, with members of the House and Senate eating separately. But given the recent events surrounding Penn's elevation to POTUS over Angela Fortnight, the leader of the opposition party, Solara had been forced to reprogram mealtimes to allow not only for a staggered schedule, but also to take party affiliation into account.

"The problem is," Strasky continued, "that the lack of projects is driving the party divides deeper and deeper. This is America's most desperate moment, and we're all running in circles, like we have one foot nailed to the floor."

"I had a talk with a Colonel Booker, formerly with Fort Hood," Penn said. "At least that's who he said he was. Pete Clostner told me that he was transmitting on an unencrypted short wave channel, so take it for what it's worth." Pete Clostner was in charge of communications at the Annex.

"How did he make contact?"

"From what I can tell, he knew the protocol to get through via radio. Frankly, I didn't ask. I was so thrilled to have news from the outside that I didn't think to ask. We can talk to Scott Johnson after this and find out those details, I suppose." Scott Johnson was the young man in charge of Solara, and by default in charge of the Annex. "Apparently, things are really bad out there."

"What does that mean?"

"According to Booker, the destruction is close to

total. He survived only because he wasn't at work. In fact, he was down in the Big Bend area of the state—"

"Texas, right?"

"Yup. He said Fort Hood is gone. He tried to get back there, but he came to his senses. Every ground zero for a nuke detonation is boiling with radioactivity. The rumor out in the world is that most of what hit us came from the Russians, but there's no confirming that. No one can even confirm who shot what."

Yet more of the stunning miscalculation that defined these attacks and the responses. What the hell were previous administrations thinking when they tied every system to the internet, and every tracking system to a satellite? The government had spent trillions of dollars of taxpayer money building a system that none of them ever thought would be needed.

Or maybe they secretly understood the reality that the greatest protections that money could buy ultimately would fail when confronted by the awesome destruction of an attack.

Another knock on Penn's door.

"Yeah," Penn said. "Come on in. What the hell?"

Strasky reached behind him and turned the knob to expose Burton Sinclair, the eighty-year-old representative from the great state of Oklahoma. Penn had lost track of how many administrations and Congresses Sinclair had served, but the man himself liked to joke about the wonderful conversations he'd had with Abraham Lincoln. He was one of Penn's favorite people on Capitol Hill, just as he was the worst enemy to so many others. There wasn't a committee he hadn't served on or a personal battle he hadn't fought.

"Good afternoon, Mr. President," Sinclair said. "I'd

like to say once again for the record that I think this bunker sucks donkey dicks."

Penn blurted out a laugh and it felt good. Burton Sinclair had a way of boiling observations down to their most basic elements.

"There's a special place in hell for the asshole who designed this shade of blue." Somewhere between baby blue and aqua, the interior portions of the Annex were painted the same color as every munitions facility Penn had ever visited. Even the office of the president of the United States was crappy and ugly. Perhaps the intended alternative Oval at the intended executive branch bunker was nice, but the alternative selected here wasn't even an office. It had existed in the early days of the new bunker as a communications center. As an accommodation to the uniqueness of the circumstances, Scott Johnson had had the space converted to an office for President Glendale.

"Blast protection and fashion are entirely different things, Burt," the president quipped.

"And this shithole doesn't do either one. We can't survive a direct hit, and I'll be goddamned if I'm going to be incinerated in a a reinforced concrete crematory while dressed like Fidel Castro. Jesus, who thought of this crap?"

In a nod to health and efficiency every arriving resident of the Annex was made to strip naked, shower, and dispose of all personal items, including their clothing. On the far side of the shower, everyone was assigned several sets of old-school Army fatigues and government-issued underwear. The ensemble was finished with identical black off-brand high-top tennis shoes.

Penn looked down at his own uniform and pulled at the shirt. "At least gender discrimination is not an issue down here," he said. "Equal ugliness for all. Now, what can I do for you, Congressman Sinclair?"

"I heard about your conversation with the guy from Texas," Sinclair replied. "I wanted to hear what you had to say about it. I called your appointment secretary, but no one answered the phone. What's up?" Sinclair moved with the grace of a man much younger than he was. He grabbed the metal visitor chair next to the one occupied by Arlen Strasky and spun it around to sit with his chest against the back support.

"I was just telling Arlen," Penn said, "it's pretty much what we've heard from everyone we've been able to communicate with. Uncountable numbers of dead, lots of suffering and desperation. No one knows what to do, and no one's out there to help them."

"What about the remaining military units?" Sinclair asked.

"It seems that every military facility on U.S. ground was hit, some by multiple warheads. Some people must have survived, but the vast majority didn't. As for National Command Authority"—he pointed the fingers of both hands at himself—"there are no controls for me to hold. I can't even establish reliable communications with Mount Weather, and they have the same quality comms as us, if not better. The atmosphere is screwed up. We don't know how toxic the atmosphere is, we don't know if there's any fresh water to drink, and we don't know if there are a thousand people left alive or a hundred million."

"I worry about the lawlessness," Sinclair said. "Where there's a lot of fear and a vacuum of leadership, you're going to see a rise in crime. It's almost a physical law. Civilized people will become wild animals pretty quickly."

"That's bad news for the weaker elements of society," Strasky observed.

"Oh, yeah," Sinclair agreed.

Penn pressed his palms over his eyes and inhaled noisily. "And here we are, leading in silence."

"Which is why I'm here," Sinclair said. "We've got to open these doors and get out there."

"You know the rules," Strasky said. "Once the doors closed, they won't open again for sixty days. We're not there yet."

"Rules, my ass. Mr. President, you're the leader of the Free World. Order those pricks from Solara to open the goddamn doors."

"They won't do it," Penn said. "Believe me, I've had this discussion in the context of somehow transferring me up to the other elements of the executive at the other bunker, but they won't do it."

Sinclair screwed up his features. "You can't believe—"

"I have no authority over them," Penn said.

"That's what they said early on, but surely—"

"No, Burt," Penn snapped. "The rules don't relax. That's why they're rules in the first place. These Solara dudes are well trained and highly committed. They specifically don't report to you, and my authority isn't even addressed because no one thought the president would be in the building. Doctors don't let patients dictate their treatment, and patients sure as hell don't get to run the hospital."

"People are dying out there, Mr. President!"

"I understand that, Congressman Sinclair!"

"You've got to show some leadership, sir."

"How, Burt? What would you have me do? Yes, people are dead and more will die, but if we open these doors, they'll still die. All we'll do is add to the body count."

Sinclair reared back in his seat. "Oh, my God, sir. When did you become a coward?"

"Hey!" Strasky snapped.

"No," Penn commanded. "This is a place for honest discussion and that's what we're going to have." His gaze zeroed in on Sinclair. "You're older than Methuselah, Burt. Sorry to say it, but it's true. In the best of worlds, you wouldn't have much of a chance of seeing another ten years. It's easy for you to say, *Just open the doors and roll the dice.* Hell, it's even easy for *me* to say it, because I'm lucky if I have another twenty-five years. But what about everyone else in here? Latasha Washington from New York. Is she even thirty yet? And what about the Solara guys?"

Sinclair rose to his feet. "For God's sake, Penn. Mr. President. Don't kid yourself into thinking anyone in this godforsaken shithole is your first priority. We didn't get special dispensation from the attacks because we've got a right to live longer. We got it because we have a job to do. A job that, I hasten to add, none of us is doing."

Penn slapped his desk. "Okay, Burt. Your way. We open the doors. Now, what?"

"We go out and provide leadership the way it's supposed to be done. Person to person."

"How?" Penn shouted. "How, Burt? You just going to go hunting for these gangs you're worried about and take them on, nose to nose? How do you think that's going to work out for you?"

"It's better than doing nothing, Mr. President."

"Is it?" Penn asked. "I understand the urge to break out of here. I understand the urge to breathe non-recycled air and to be anywhere but here, but that's not our job, either. You ask me, we—us here in this room—need to put some degree of trust in the system. In a few weeks, the blast doors will open again, and then we can take it from there. Who knows? In the intervening time, maybe a satellite will fix itself. With any luck at all, we'll wake up and find out this has all been some CIA experiment in mass hysteria."

Sinclair fell silent, but Penn could tell from the look on his face that he wasn't done yet. He settled himself and resumed his seat, turning it around to face normally. "Mr. President, what about in the meantime? What are people supposed to do while we're waiting for the clock to tick down?"

"I'm telling you that we can't help those people, Burt. Not as individuals. Our only hope of providing any form of cogent help is doing it from here. To do it as the government of the United States."

"There *is* no government, Penn," Sinclair said. "Government is of, by and for the *people*. Remember that? If the people aren't in the loop—if they're not aware of what we're doing—what's the point?"

"The point is to not give up," Penn said. "There's a lot more broken around here than there is fixed, that's to be sure, but we've got to keep tinkering. These are terrible times, and there is no easy resolution. But, Burt, I need you on board. You say whatever you want to me, but when it comes to speaking to others, I need you to project hope."

"I don't *feel* hope."

Penn laughed in spite of himself. "I don't give a shit what you *feel,* Burt. Shit, in all the years we've known each other, *you've* never given a shit about what you feel. This is bigger than that. This is about leadership, and people still look up to you. You're everybody's grandfather. If you show faith, people will see it and feel calmer."

Sinclair allowed himself a chuckle. "You know, Mr. President, that's the second, maybe third, time in the last couple of minutes that you've called me an old man."

"I believe you're right," Penn said. "And I'm far too noble a man to tell a lie."

CHAPTER FIVE

Hell Day + 36 (Sixteen Days Later)

IN THE WEEKS SINCE VICTORIA HAD ARRIVED IN Ortho—in the weeks since Hell Day—empty lots had morphed from green fields to tent cities and now to clusters of two-room houses occupying eight to an acre, more or less. Long-term residents called the area of the main drag Shack City or Shantytown. She couldn't change the label, but she saw it as a community of lifesaving shelters, where immigrating residents could find rest and warmth after what, in many cases, had been weeks of walking.

Eighty percent of the new arrivals brought with them a desire to help build the community. Two more medical doctors helped to take the load off Rory Stevenson—Doc Rory—who had been a one-man show until they arrived. Jayne Young had just started her Pittsburgh family medicine practice with her husband, Leroy Johnson, when the world ended. They'd been camping in the mountains when the bombs dropped, and they'd never bothered to try to make their way back to the city that they knew no longer existed.

Together with Doc Rory, they did their best, with very little medicine or technology, to tend to the sick and injured.

Nancy Hisch was a just-retired dentist living out in the nearby sticks when everything stopped. She'd been waiting out her husband's final deployment to Afghanistan and his subsequent retirement, finalizing plans for their round-the-world cruise. Presuming him to be dead, yet knowing for certain that they would not see each other again for a very long time, Nancy told Victoria that loneliness, combined with a valuable set of skills, inspired her to leave her home and walk into town with her collection of stainless-steel tools wrapped in Baggies in her backpack.

Upon Dr. Nancy's arrival, Victoria had dispatched young Mike Underwood and his ancient El Camino back up the mountain to retrieve the ancient treadle-driven dental drill and chair that had been part of Dr. Nancy's collection of antique dental equipment. They set her up in the back of Doc Rory's office, but she saw precious little business. She had only limited supplies of local anesthetics to limit pain, and there wasn't much interest in retro dentistry. Nancy shared with Victoria that she did far more extracting than she did filling.

Most new arrivals who did not have specific skills that were useful to the greater community were put to work on a construction crew for new homes. Others were sent to work with Ty Rowley, owner of Rowley Lumber, the company that had been in his family for four generations and was blessed with an old steam-fired sawmill that had been little more than a conversation piece back when electricity was a thing. Now the mill worked round the clock by lamplight to keep up with the demand for building materials.

Ty had complained when his priorities shifted from housing construction to deer blinds, but not for long. He'd been able to turn out all they needed within six hours of being asked.

The surrounding forests provided all the timber anyone could ask for. The constant sound of chopping and manual sawing was like something out of a time machine, Victoria thought. She wondered if modern conveniences were forever a thing of the past.

She worried about the approach of winter. The war had already lowered the ambient temperature of the air—at least she assumed that was why the air had seemed chillier—and as the temperatures dropped further, she knew that health issues would increase.

With the help of Grant Zenger, a petroleum hydrologist who'd been visiting his sick grandmother when the war came, at least she was confident with the positioning of the sanitation facilities. Two-hole outhouses had been constructed throughout the town at a rate of about one commode per every ten people, and work was under way to hit the goal of one per five before the ground froze. Near enough to the populations to be useful, but far enough away from fresh water sources not to spread disease, everyone seemed confident that they'd avoid an outbreak of cholera.

Now, they just had to count on people not to take shortcuts as nighttime temperatures plummeted.

Ellie Stewart, a self-proclaimed homemaker in the

before times, had done a remarkable job in organizing the clothing bank. Not only had she proven herself to be a remarkable organizer for storage and distribution, she also turned out to be an excellent salesperson, able to convince residents to contribute clothing and household essentials to the bank. Under the circumstances, she'd told people, it was irresponsible to hang on to outgrown baby clothes or even jeans and business suits that didn't fit anymore.

Victoria had had to dampen Ellie's enthusiasm only once, and that was when she suggested that there was nothing wrong with burying a loved one naked. That was the way we arrived in this world, she'd argued, and that was the way we should depart. Victoria couldn't argue with the logic, but there were limits to how far you could push a point.

Truth be told, Victoria was surprised by the fact that so few people had died in the weeks since Hell Day. There were the expected losses of those whose lives depended on medications that were now unobtainable, but not much in the way of new illnesses. Victoria worried, however, about the high numbers of accidental deaths and suicides. Doc Rory was surprised, too.

A team of five stalwart members of the Foster family—including nineteen-year-old twins Kyle and Caine, with whom Victoria had gotten off to a very rough start—had stepped up to take care of burials. In the days immediately following the attacks, the official strategy for handling bodies had been to put them outside and let the scavengers take care of them au naturel. While efficient, the results were tough on morale, and proper corpse management had taken on special importance.

A team of fifteen volunteers had dug a trench in a

swale near the roadway outside of town. Six feet deep and twenty feet long, this common grave would become the final resting place for departed Ortho residents. Funerals were short. After a linen-wrapped body was laid in the ground, the Fosters would place a plank with the decedent's name burned into it atop the corpse and then cover it with lime and a layer of dirt. Inevitably, the town cemetery became known by locals as Boot Hill.

Marauding animals occasionally visited the community of the dead, but for the most part, they stayed away.

As Victoria strolled down the street toward Lavinia Sloan's welding and blacksmith shop, she allowed herself a moment of contentment. Despite the awfulness that brought everyone to this place, at this time, there seemed to be an overarching sense of community here—such a contrast to the mayhem she'd encountered when she first arrived.

Ortho wasn't exactly what you'd call horse country, but many people owned them and rode them, and before Hell Day, Lavinia Sloan had made much of her living as a farrier, though she'd told Victoria that she did a fair amount of welding as well. These days, now that everything was upside down and difficult, Lavinia had shifted to all manner of construction and repairs. Anticipating the time in the very near future when all manufactured construction materials would have been taken from the lumberyard and other places where such items were sold, Lavinia had shifted much of her manufacturing to casting catches and hinges for doors and shutters.

Because Lavinia had a forge-worthy workspace,

newcomer James Landon had set up an experimental glass-manufacturing operation in hopes of being able to provide windowpanes for the rapidly-rising city center. As it was, the only protection from the elements to be found in the new construction came from old-school hinged shutters. It was going to be a cold and breezy winter for the families who lived in Shanty Town. It would be a boon to morale if residents would be able to bring light inside without inviting the rain and snow with it.

Victoria worried that the close spacing of the houses also posed a fire hazard, made all the more serious by the fact that flame was the source of all heat and light. If one of the cabins went up, the whole community would burn unless the fire was attacked quickly. Working with Joey Abbott and George Simmons as her de facto town council, she'd established a policy whereby every home would have a thirty-gallon barrel of water inside, courtesy of a redirected shipment of empty Nalgene drums that had arrived at Rowley Lumber only the day before Hell Day.

As a condition of residing in one of the houses, residents committed to keeping the drums filled. It had been Joey Abbott's idea to sell the requirement as a convenience, stressing fewer trips down to the river or to the town well to get water. The "law" about water—Victoria hated using the *L*-word for rules that are born outside of a formal vote—carried with it a right for the security committee, led by Joe McCrea, to inspect homes for compliance, but Victoria felt that was a step too far this early in the process of building the community.

Luke's horse, Rover, grazed in the field next to the

blacksmith shop, a leather hobble stretching from her front leg to her rear leg on the right side.

As Victoria crossed the threshold into Sloan's Welding and Rustic Arts, the heat inside made her gasp. It had to be over ninety degrees in here, made to feel even hotter by the chill of the air outside. Lavinia was hunched in front of one of the forges, engrossed in something white-hot at the end of a set of long tongs. Victoria didn't want to disturb her with a greeting, but kept eye contact in case she looked up from her work. As if pulled by the magnetics of Victoria's gaze, Lavinia did look up and she gave a little wave. She had the arms and shoulders of a bodybuilder, but the complexion and smile of a supermodel. As always, she wore her auburn hair in a ponytail that protruded out the back of a sweat-stained John Deere baseball cap.

"I'm here to see my baby boy," Victoria called over the din of the forge.

Lavinia gave a thumbs-up and pointed to the far corner, where Luke was running a large file along the edge of a piece of metal that he'd clamped into a vise. At fourteen, he looked like a child laborer, but he had the heart of a man three times his age. Shirtless, his skin glistened with sweat. His forearms and hands were the kind of black that only comes with hard work and would probably never wash off entirely. A streak of blood shined through the grime on his thumb.

"Baby boy, huh?" he said without looking at Victoria. When he turned, he wiped his forehead with his forearm, deepening the black streak across his brow.

"When you're fifty and I'm old, you'll still be my baby," Victoria said. If he didn't smell so much like a wet goat, she might have gone in for a kiss to seal his embarrassment.

"What brings you into the First Circle?" Luke had always been a big reader and a good student. His references to Dante's Inferno had grown more frequent in recent weeks. For the immediate future, the academic priorities of ninth grade seemed less important to everyone, so his schooling had stopped. Victoria liked to tell herself that the schooling was only on hiatus, but that felt a lot like a lie. Fact was, Luke enjoyed his apprenticeship with Lavinia, and Victoria was happy to see him learn a trade.

"Got a minute?" she asked. "We need to talk."

"Talk to my chief of staff," he said. "He'll tell you if I have a place on my schedule." His smile broadened as he echoed back what he'd heard his mom say to him countless times. He put the file down on the workbench and wiped his hands on a nearby towel. The towel turned black, but his hands did not turn white. "Outside?"

"If you don't mind."

As Luke headed toward the door, Victoria said, "It's chilly. Don't you want a shirt?"

"I figure my core temperature must be about one-thirty," he said with a chuckle. "I think I'll be okay." On the way out the door, he snagged his M4 from its place next to his workbench and slung it over his shoulder.

The colder air felt wonderful. Victoria squinted against the brightness. "Winter's coming," she said. "Look how low the sun is hanging."

"Aye," Luke said, channeling Jon Snow. "Winter's comin' indeed. White Walkers are near the Wall."

Victoria laughed. Luke had always had a light heart and a quick wit, and it was nice to see it returning. They started strolling together.

"You here to talk about yesterday?" he asked. "About killing those guys?"

"How did you know?"

"Paul Copley talked to Caleb and me yesterday," Luke said. "He looked so concerned that I figured he'd say something to you. I'm really fine. Those guys were going to shoot you. Shoot *at* you, anyway. I don't think I had a choice."

"I imagined that would be the case," Victoria said. "I never doubted your decision to shoot."

"First Sergeant Copley did."

"No, that's not true," Victoria said. "He wasn't worried about you. He was worried about me."

Luke screwed up his face and gave her a weird look. "What did *you* do?"

"I'm your mom and you're my son. Plus, I'm sort of the mayor of the town."

"Okaaay . . ."

Victoria stopped, prompting Luke to pull up short, too. He placed his hands on his hips and shifted his weight, exactly how his father would have done it. Could mannerisms be hereditary?

"Actions have consequences," Victoria said. "We have every reason to believe that the people who tried to attack us yesterday will try again."

"I'll keep my watch shift in the deer stands."

"I know you will. But that's also not my point. The fact that we haven't seen them back here indicates to Major McCrea and me that they're organizing something big. Something well *organized*."

"We're organized, too, aren't we?"

Victoria made a growling sound. She wasn't expressing this as directly as she wanted to. "Yes, we're organized, and we've already proven to ourselves and to two other groups that we can hold our own in a fight. But those other fights were sort of pop-up fights, know what I mean?"

"You mean they weren't organized." The way he threw her own phrasing back at her made her chuckle again.

"I guess that was self-explanatory," she confessed. As they started walking again, she put her hand on his shoulder. His skin was still slimy, but there was real muscle under there. "The fact that they're organized means that our side is likely to take more casualties." As the words left her throat, she cringed. They sounded so . . . inside Washington. "More of our neighbors are going to get injured. Maybe even killed."

"Don't even say that, Mom."

"Don't think for a moment that it won't happen, Luke. We hope it won't, but you need to be mentally prepared."

"But what does this have to do—"

"Okay," Victoria said. "When . . . *if* people in Ortho lose loved ones in the battle that we think is coming, they're going to be upset. Of course, they'll be upset. And they may look for scapegoats. You know what a scapegoat is, right?"

"Jesus, Mom."

"Of course, you do. Well, the concern is that people will connect the dots illogically and decide that if we hadn't fired the first shots yesterday, then maybe the attackers wouldn't have felt compelled to come back."

They walked in silence while she let Luke figure out what she was trying to tell him. Arguments always made more sense when people worked the logic out for themselves.

"People are going to think that all this is my fault?"

"Not that it would be—"

"That's *bullshit*, Mom." Luke kicked at the ground. "That's total *bullshit*. You talk about our neighbors dying? See what would have happened if we *hadn't* shot first."

"Luke, you're getting upset."

"Ya *think*?"

"I'm not telling you this to upset you," Victoria assured. "I'm telling you this so that you understand the importance of not telling anyone that you took those first shots."

"But I'm *proud* I took those shots. I saved lives with those shots."

"I know you did."

"Then why don't we go first and just tell everyone that? Don't you always say that if you tell the truth, you never have to worry about being a good liar?"

The kid had an uncanny way of turning valuable life lessons against her. She stopped again and spun him gently by his shoulders, so they were face-to-face. "Think about what you're saying, Luke. Remember how things used to be back before Hell Day. Back when I was in Congress. Remember all the lies people told about the president and members of Congress just to make them look bad. They told the lies knowing that they were lies, simply to hurt the person they didn't like."

"That was bullshit, too," Luke said. "It wasn't right then, and it isn't right now."

"Of course, it wasn't *right*. But it was most certainly *real*." Victoria dialed it back and changed tacks. "What's the worst thing you've heard people call me since we've been here?"

A look of horror flashed over his eyes and he looked at the ground. "I haven't heard anyone say anything bad."

"Who's spewing bullshit now? I'm just trying to make a point. Since we've been in Ortho, what's the worst thing you've heard anyone say about me?"

Luke closed his eyes and kicked at the ground again, more gently this time. He really didn't want to do this. "Bitchy McAss-face."

The guffaw escaped her throat before she could stop it. "Seriously?"

"Hey, you asked—"

"I love it," Victoria said. "That shows real imagination. Someone put thought into that."

"Caleb is the one who said it," Luke said. After a couple of seconds passed, he howled, too, from whatever he saw in Victoria's face. "I'm kidding."

"Who did say that?"

"I'm not telling you!"

And she probably didn't want to know. "When people call me names, why do you think they're doing that?"

"Because they don't like you?"

"I hope that's not right because they probably don't even know me. They see the decisions I have to make. I settle disputes between people, and in every dispute, at least one party walks away unhappy. People coming into town are assigned jobs they don't want, and they have to stay in tents until their homes are ready."

"What do they expect?"

"They don't know what they expect. I think most of the people who've arrived in the past week or so are so tired and scared that they've lost the capacity to think past the here and now. They know that they're so tired of being uncomfortable that they don't care what has to happen to fix that, so long as it happens right away. When it doesn't happen, they need a scapegoat. No matter what people think of this town or of me or of the future, every single person is equally vulnerable to being hit by a bullet after the shooting starts. When something that awful happens—"

"They look for someone to hang blame on, even if there's really no blame to hang."

Victoria replied with an extended shrug that said, *You got it.*

"And if they think I started the war, I'll go the way of Brandon-Lee May." A month earlier, the town had staged a ritual flogging to punish a teenager suspected of killing a truck driver.

"That's the concern, yes."

Luke made a noise that sounded like *piff,* and screwed up his features again. "They wouldn't do that," he said. "They might try, but everybody else would stop them. Brandon-Lee murdered a guy and everybody hated him. I didn't and they don't."

Good Lord, he really was becoming his father. Glenn had always had more faith in people than she had. In many ways, he'd been the antidote to her cynicism, though he rated pretty high on the cynicism scale himself.

"Just don't go boasting about it."

"Who would boast about killing?"

The sound of an approaching horse and wagon drew their attention around to see Mike Underwood heading toward them. The wagon had to be a hundred years old. Much of the wood appeared to be rotted, but the wheels appeared to be in pretty good shape. Victoria hadn't seen the horse before. It looked like it was bred more for work than for recreation.

"Greetings, Emersons," Mike called as he approached. Barely past his teens, if that, his smile was broad and natural, but he listed slightly in the wooden seat. He pulled the horse to a halt.

"Hi, Mike," Victoria said. "How are you feeling?"

"More good days than bad," he said. "Still not shitting right, but it could be worse. Remember, you asked." Mike had taken a bullet in the belly during the shoot-out with the Grubbs gang. For the first few days, it looked pretty dark for him, but overall, he'd pulled through better than most had expected.

Luke went to the horse and patted its snout. "It's Sadie, right?"

"Sadie the Wonder Horse," Mike corrected, "but Sadie to her friends."

"Please tell me you didn't trade your El Camino in for this," Victoria teased. Mike Underwood owned one of the precious few functioning motor vehicles in town. He used it mostly to ferry sick people to and from town and to bring them supplies as they needed them.

"The gas in the tank is getting way low," Mike explained. "I found this piece of shit—excuse me, this valuable investment opportunity—behind a collapsed tobacco barn, up off Poole Road. I'm starting a taxi company. I'll take people pretty much wherever they want to go for ten twenty-twos or two five-five sixes."

Victoria felt a swell of pride that the new currency plan was already taking hold in people's minds. "Just a flat fee? Distance doesn't matter?"

"To start, I guess," Mike said. "Haven't had my first customer yet. Say, Luke, do you think Lavinia might be able to tighten some of the undercarriage?"

"She's in the shop now if you want to talk to her."

"Alrighty, I'll do just that." He started to pull on the rein, but then stopped himself. "Oh, Mrs. Emerson, there's something I've been meaning to tell you."

"It's Vicky. What's up?"

"It's really just a rumor. But people are talking about a Bonnie and Clyde team that's driving around in an old red-and-white SUV—either a Bronco or a Blazer—and killing people."

"Just like that?" Victoria asked. "Just drive into a place and kill?"

"That's the problem with rumors, ma'am," Mike said. "They don't come loaded with a lot of detail. I just thought you should know." He pulled back on the reins and Sadie backed up a few spaces to give him enough room to pivot around to drive back to Sloan's.

"I'm not sure it's right that he's gonna be making more as a cabdriver than I'm gonna make as a sentry. He's gonna get ten twenty-twos, and I'm only making five," said Luke.

Victoria hooked her elbow around his neck and tickled his rib. "Welcome to the world of capitalism, young man."

He giggled like she hoped he would and spun out of her grasp.

"Tell me you're going to clean up before you come home tonight."

"I always do," he said. "I keep soap and a towel down by the river." He squinted up at the sky. "It's getting late. I have stuff I need to finish before I quit for the afternoon."

"What's Lavinia paying you?" As Victoria asked the question, it occurred to her that she had no right to ask it.

"Seven an hour," he said. They pivoted to head back to Sloan's. "Are we ever gonna get our own house?" he asked. "The church is okay, but a house would be better."

"Maybe someday," Victoria said, "but not for a while. In my position, I can't be first in line for anything."

Luke launched a loud, genuine laugh. "When has that ever been true?"

Victoria knew that he was playing the moment for the joke, but she had a serious point she wanted to make. "You probably haven't given this a lot of thought, Luke. But as awful as Hell Day made things, it also presented a lot of opportunity."

"You mean God opened a window as He shut the door?"

This time, the snark pissed her off. But she didn't let on. "Be snide if you want, but listen to my words. We have a chance to build something here from the ground up. I don't know if it was God or Satan Who gave us the opportunity, but this is a chance for a hard reset."

"Of what?"

"Of *everything*." She'd never articulated these thoughts before, and as she spoke, she wondered if it was appropriate to share them with a fourteen-year-old. "We can reset to true fairness and justice. We can pursue what's *right* over what's expedient. We can return governance to the people. We can restore their voices."

A look of concern settled in behind Luke's eyes. "Are you okay, Mom?"

She thought for a few seconds before answering, "Yes, I am. The people of Ortho inspire me. They frustrate me and they piss me off, but at the same time, they've mostly pushed aside their petty jealousies and they've started thinking about others. About the common good."

Luke's scowl deepened.

"Say what's on your mind," Victoria prompted.

"We just talked about Bitchy McAss-face."

She made her own *piffing* sound and swiped the topic out of the air with her hand. "Don't worry about that. People have to let off steam and a cheap laugh is a good way to do it."

Luke rubbed his arms with his hands. "I gotta go back to work. It's getting cold."

Victoria watched as he turned his back and headed back to Sloan's. His was an easy, sauntering stride. "My God," she muttered. "He even walks like his father."

CHAPTER SIX

Hell Day + 41 (Five Days Later)

CAPTAIN COLE PRITCHARD, FORMERLY OF THE MARYland National Guard, assumed command of the company a week ago yesterday, upon the death of that idiot Roy Magill. It was moronic to try to literally wade ashore into a crowd of armed townspeople. What did he think was going to happen? Pritchard got that the guy was upset and unnerved by the events of the war—events that no one understood. It was just a lot of alarms and a lot of fires, and then nothing. Total absence of command and total obliteration of everything.

He supposed the captain had tried his best to show command leadership, but the guy had spent his real career—his day job—running the service department for a Ford dealership in La Plata, and while management skills and leadership skills looked similar during peacetime, they were entirely different animals after the shit hit the fan. To show fear was to show weakness, and the captain had spent every second of the days after the war being afraid-of-the-dark scared.

He'd been able to recover some ground emotionally after the first couple of weeks, but by then, the troops had lost interest in following him.

They were the *Army,* for God's sake. They were an arm of the federal government, and when they needed supplies, they had the moral and legal authority to take whatever they needed. Those are times when you don't bother to ask permission. Those are times when you establish you and your team as the baddest badasses in the room—or the town—and you make people bend to your will.

After they left Ortho behind—for the time being— he and his company of thirty soldiers floated downstream twenty miles to a town called Appleton, still in the belly of West Virginia. This time, they moored the boats out of sight and wandered in like any other band of refugees. By the end of the first day, it became clear to him that unlike Ortho, this place was running out of control. No one seemed to be in charge, though he'd since learned that the place had a mayor who'd chosen to eat a pistol rather than face the stress of a rougher life.

The residents depended on county deputies and state police for law enforcement. Since they were either dead or wandering elsewhere, the good citizens of Appleton were on their own. That made them sheep in a world that only had room for wolves.

Pritchard had ordered his company to break up into groups of twos and threes so as not to draw unwanted attention. Their mission was to wander, watch and take note. Later in the afternoon, at 16:30, they'd meet again down by the boats and decide what the next step would be. They needed provisions, and they would not be leaving without them. It hadn't occurred to him at the time that they might end up staying put.

Within minutes of their arrival, the lawlessness of the place was on full display. A gang of eight, maybe ten, punks were in the throes of ravaging the downtown business district. They'd set a few cars on fire, and now they'd turned their attention to the businesses themselves. The gang was entertaining itself by breaking the windows of the unimpressive low-rise stores and offices and helping themselves to whatever might be left to steal.

They looked like a merged group to Pritchard's eye. Some wore biker leathers and others were draped in the long black coats favored by school shooters.

"It looks like somebody shuffled movie tropes from the eighties and the fifties," said Andy Linx, the lieutenant Pritchard was strolling with. Back in the day, when military discipline still mattered, Andy would have been Pritchard's second in command, but those distinctions had blurred over the weeks since the war.

"What strikes you about what you see?" Pritchard asked.

"That these asshats have their *peaceful protest* vibe going strong." They both chuckled.

"Nobody's fighting back," Pritchard said. "These are people's livelihoods being destroyed, and nobody's fighting to protect anything."

"All respect, sir, there's not a lot to fight for, is there?" Andy said. "If it hasn't already been eaten, it's gone bad. And nobody's going to give much of a shit about the cash in the drawers."

"There's a principle," Pritchard said. It disappointed him that Andy didn't see that for himself. "You'd think that people would fight just to preserve their honor."

Pritchard's real job—his day job when he wasn't doing his guard duty—was as a police officer. If there was one development of the past ten or fifteen years that disturbed him more than the general shithole that the United States had become, it was the fact that the current generations had had all the fight engineered out of them.

It was one thing to tell a kindergartener that he had to tattle on a bully rather than to fight him, but the world was knocked seriously off-balance when those orders followed kids into junior high and beyond. As children, the adults of today learned that principle could be suspended so long as you got what you wanted. Forgiven loans provided free educations that guaranteed A's for every child, lest their precious self-esteem be bruised.

Self-defense, a staple of the America forty years ago when Pritchard was growing up, had come to be seen merely as another form of violence, the defender and offender held in equal disdain.

Pritchard had witnessed the decay in decency and the rise in crime in real time from the front seat of his cruiser. People wanted to be protected by others, yet when the protectors defended themselves, the very community that called for help pilloried them.

The result was a public so angry at the vacuum of leadership at the top that politicians felt compelled to erect razor wire–topped fences around the public buildings that were originally erected as monuments to the principle that governments were subservient to the people they served.

And now, as he watched kids wreak havoc simply because no one would stop them, he felt anger boiling inside his gut.

"I don't like that look you've got on your face, sir," Andy said. "You know there's only two of us, right?"

"Those punks are cowards," Pritchard said.

"You know that for sure, do you?"

"Punks are always cowards," Pritchard said.

"We can't go wandering into that," Andy said. His tone was final and his implication clear: *And if you do, you're on your own.*

"Looks like we won't have to," Pritchard said. He pointed with his forehead to two of the punks who were headed their way.

"Oh, shit," Andy said. "Please don't."

"I'm not going to cause trouble," Pritchard said. "I'm going to prevent it."

Andy groaned and shifted his M4 on its sling. "We're not shooting, are we?"

"I hope not."

The bangers were young—barely out of their teens, if even that old, Pritchard figured—but they showed the kind of swagger that demonstrated more confidence in their badassery than they probably should have.

"Who the hell are you?" one of them said as they approached. "A little late for the Army, don't you think?" The banger doing the talking was a zitty kid, probably not more than 150 pounds, and he hadn't been near a bar of soap in way too long. Greasy black hair hung like dirty laundry over his face, and enormous ears poked through the mane on either side.

Pritchard stood tall and didn't move.

"I asked you a question," Zitface said. He produced a stout revolver from the waistband of his trousers, from under his leather jacket, but he had the good sense not to point it at Pritchard.

"Son, you're on the feather edge of changing your life. The question for you is, are you going to end it today, or do you want to make it better?"

"Listen to you, Mr. G.I. Joe." Zitface tried to be unafraid, but his eyes showed the truth.

Andy slid a few feet off to the side and adjusted his rifle again. No one was aiming at anyone else, but a gunfight now would get very ugly, very quickly.

"What are you guys doing?" Pritchard asked. "Why all the breakage and burning? What's going on?"

"You gonna stop us?" asked Zitface's marauder mascot. This kid was about the same age, but he had some meat on him. If he knew how to throw a punch, it would do some damage.

"Why would I do that?" Pritchard asked. "I got no dog in this fight. Start breaking stuff that belongs to me, then we'll have some words, but for now, I couldn't care less."

"Then why you been eyeballin' us?" Zitface asked.

"It's hard to look away from people doing stupid shit," Pritchard replied.

Zitface puffed up.

"Relax. It just doesn't make sense to me why you would waste your time destroying useless stuff when you could be focusing on getting valuable stuff."

Now he had the kid's attention. "What are you talking about?"

Pritchard offered his hand and the kid jumped back. "Captain Pritchard," he said. "You can call me Cap."

"Davey Priest." He didn't trust the outstretched hand, though.

"This is my colleague, Lieutenant Linx. And who are you?" He addressed that last question to Davey's friend.

The beefy kid stayed where he was and said, "Why is my name important to you? Why do I give a shit what yours is?"

Pritchard suppressed a chuckle. "A hard-ass, I see. That's fine."

"His name is Austin Mills," Davey said. "What do you want here?"

"Same as everybody, I guess," Pritchard said. "Food. Medicine. Shelter."

"Go away, then," Austin said. "We ain't got enough for the people that are already here."

"Are you sure about that?" Pritchard asked. "Have you seen a lot of people starving to death? People gotta be eating something."

Davey's eyes narrowed and he cocked his head. He didn't see where Pritchard was going.

"What have you been eating?" Pritchard asked. "You and your friends?"

"That's none of your damn business," Austin said. "Davey, we don't need none o' their shit."

"Would you lighten up?" Pritchard said. "I'm not a threat to you. Not unless you make me one. I'm trying to present you with an opportunity. My company of soldiers numbers about thirty. I'm here to give you an opportunity to join us."

"And why would we want to do that?" Austin said.

Pritchard looked to Davey. "Is he in charge, or are you? I need to know who to talk to."

"Nobody's in charge of anybody here," Davey said defiantly.

"And that's the problem," Pritchard said. "If you're willing to talk to me a little—willing to put that weapon away for starters—I think there's a real opportunity for all of us."

"What kind of opportunity?"

"Gotta pay to play," Pritchard said, eyeing the revolver. "Are you willing to chat, or aren't you?"

Davey turned to look at Austin, who answered with a noncommittal shrug. Finally, "What do you want to talk about?" As he asked the question, Davey stuffed the revolver back into his waistband. Pritchard would wait till another time to tell him how that's a great way to blow his dick off.

"Is there a place to sit?" Pritchard asked.

"Standing works for us," Austin said.

"Fine." Pritchard took a few seconds to gather his thoughts. "So all this damage I see. Is all that just from you and your gang?"

Davey snorted a laugh. "Do we look like Crips or Bloods to you? We ain't no gang."

"What are you, then?"

"People who want to have a good time."

"By burning the town down?" Andy asked.

"Don't knock it if you ain't tried it," Austin said. "These high-n-mighty assholes with all their money and attitude. Puttin' down people like me, firin' me when they feel like it. Factories open and then close, leaving us to figure out how to eat the next meal. To hell with all of them. Let them burn."

"So you're teaching them a lesson?" Pritchard asked.

Austin puffed up. "You'd best not to mock me."

"I'm not mocking you. I'm trying to understand. You've got all this anger inside, all this rage and strength. You understand that's what armies are made of, right? Take away the uniforms and all the stupid red tape, what you've got in an army is a bunch of folks with a lot of fight in them. I'm just trying to figure out how much fighting you're willing to do."

"More than you want to see," Austin said.

There was a predatory edge to this kid. He was not one to push too far, lest there be consequences.

"I'm glad to hear it," Pritchard said. He wanted to find a way to be on the same side. "Now, what I'm asking you is, how many troops are there in *your* army? How many people were involved in doing all this damage?"

"We've got five other friends we kick with," Davey said. "There's a bunch of *real* assholes that does some, too."

"Who are they?"

Davey looked skyward as he thought. "There's Abe Parrish, Walton Pearce—"

"Not by name," Pritchard interrupted. "I wouldn't know one from the other. Where do they come from? Are they somehow associated with each other?"

"They're younger," Davey explained. "High school, maybe college. They're all the jocks. They think they're tough, but we could take 'em in a fight."

"The trick is to not have a fight," Pritchard said. "The trick is to join forces and work together."

"To do what?" Austin asked.

"To kick ass," Pritchard said. "To *win*."

Davey clearly was not getting his point.

"Come with me," Pritchard said. He turned and walked toward the smoke-stained brick wall of a commercial building of some sort. "What was in here?"

"That was a massage parlor," Austin said.

Pritchard had not turned to address them, so he was pleased to hear the voice so close. That meant that they were following him.

"Why burn down a massage parlor?" Andy asked.

"That wasn't us," Davey said. "That was the jocks. And I don't know why. Probably because it was there."

Pritchard led them to the parlor's façade, where he turned, unslung his rifle, and sat on the sidewalk, his back propped against the brick. "I've been walking a long time," he said. "Have a seat if you want."

Davey and Austin polled each other with a glance and sat. Andy joined them, forming a circle on the sidewalk. Pritchard and Andy sat with their legs crossed, their rifles resting across their knees.

"Do you mind if I ask some questions?" Pritchard said.

"Seems to me that's all you been doin'," Austin said.

Davey shot him an annoyed look. "Go ahead."

"These acts of vandalism," Pritchard said. "What's your goal?"

"This isn't a business," Austin said.

"It ought to be," Pritchard said. "I mean, sure, it's

fun to break things, but if you're not getting something out of it, what's the point?"

"You tell me," Davey said.

"Well, I can't answer for you, but if it was up to me, I'd be collecting stuff. Start with food and go from there. I'll tell you right up front that's why my army and I are here. We're here to forage."

Davey cocked his head.

"It means to find food," Andy explained.

"You mean *steal* food, don't you?" Austin challenged.

Pritchard explained, "In time of war, it's not stealing. An army has a right to feed and equip itself. You've heard of the spoils of war, right?"

"Who are you at war with?" Davey asked. He still wasn't getting it.

"Anyone who gets in my way. Where have you been finding food?"

"Mostly, we've been starving," Austin said. "It was okay for the first few weeks, when we could live on canned shit and squirrels and the occasional deer, but all of that is gone. Have you seen any wildlife around since you got here?"

"Now that you mention it, no. Have you eaten everything?"

Austin looked offended. "Not *me*, no. But I done my part, I suppose."

"The problem is," Davey explained, "everything goes bad so fast. Used to be, you killed a deer and put it in the freezer and it would last a long time. With winter coming, I guess maybe we'll get a break, but the deer are already gone."

"Where have you been finding your canned goods?"

"The whole town raided the grocery store," Austin said. "That place was empty in a couple of hours. All the good stuff was gone in fifteen minutes. Two people got killed in the rush."

"What did you do with the bodies?" Andy asked.

"I don't know. For all I know, they was still in there when the store burned."

"Why don't I see people fighting you back?" Pritchard asked. "I mean, these businesses were people's lives and livelihoods. Why do you have free rein?"

"I dunno," Davey said. "Never thought about it much."

"What about when you go to their homes?"

"We ain't done that," Austin said. "We ain't stupid."

"People 'round here got guns," Davey explained. "You don't want to go chargin' into their houses."

Pritchard and Andy exchanged looks.

"What?" Davey said.

"Spoils of war," Pritchard said with a wink. "How would you guys like to not be hungry anymore?"

CHAPTER SEVEN

Hell Day + 23 (Eighteen Days Earlier)

THE WING OF THE ANNEX OCCUPIED BY SOLARA AND its employees was far more opulent than that which was occupied by congressional personnel. In part, that was because there were only twenty-three Solara employees, as opposed to over two hundred of the bickering children. It was also because Solara employees had been living and working in their quarters for over a decade.

The United States Government Relocation Center had existed in plain sight for its entire life, finding profitable use as the Antebellum Wing of the Hilltop Manor Resort. The chambers designed for the House and Senate had been used hundreds of times over the years as lecture and presentation halls for a variety of conventions and academic forums. The main open space that today was occupied by congressional staffers had been exhibit space.

When CRIMSON PHOENIX—the code phrase for imminent nuclear war—went active, Solara, under the leadership of Scott Johnson, sprang into action to convert the Antebellum Wing into its designed purpose as a bunker retreat for official Washington. It was a metamorphosis that they had practiced countless times over the years, always during off-hours and out of sight of any of the hotel guests or regular staff.

The bowels of the Annex had remained off-limits during ordinary times, blocked by signs that read, DANGER HIGH VOLTAGE. Beyond those doors lay the labyrinth that no one other than Solara employees had ever seen. Two-tiered bunk beds filled long barracks-like rooms as sleeping quarters for members of the House and Senate and their staffs. On the same hallway lay the gang showers and long rows of toilets. Originally some effort had been made to keep those spaces separated by gender, but the effort always failed.

From what Johnson could tell, after the first week, people adjusted to the loss of privacy. Except for Speaker Angela Fortnight, of course, but she was perpetually bent out of shape about *something*.

The secure area of the Annex also featured a state-of-the-art surgical suite and dental office, though in the mad rush of people arriving, none of the medical or dental staff had been able to make it to the bunker before Johnson had to order it to be buttoned up. Everyone on Johnson's staff was former Special Forces of some sort and, as such, had rudimentary combat medic training, but if a resident needed much more than a splint or occlusive dressing, they'd be in trouble.

To the rest of the hotel staff, Solara was the contractor in charge of all things audiovisual. They set up the sound systems for presentations and even made sure that the cable connections in guest rooms were all that they needed to be. In fact, those activities accounted for about 45 percent of their time.

The rest of their time was dedicated to the critical mission of the Annex. They made sure that the stores of rations were rotated out as necessary and that the slate of prescriptions for each member of Congress was current and stocked. The Annex was an entire secret city, known by precious few people even to exist.

Even the members of Congress were kept in the dark because anything a congressman knew at ten in the morning would be on the news by five in the afternoon. Johnson didn't know what they'd been told to cover for the evacuation that brought them here, and he didn't care. They were his concern only insofar as they were the focus of the facilities he ran.

Functioning heat and air-conditioning were his concern. Whether members of Congress were hot or cold was not. They were supposed to be adults, for God's sake. And some were. But most were overprivileged babies who could not wrap their heads around the reality that he and his crew were not their staff.

Johnson's standing order for Solara employees was "Keep the train on the tracks." That meant strict enforcement of rules, irrespective of the personalities involved. To the residents' credit, it had been over a week since anyone had launched the *do you know who you're talking to?* missile. He'd instructed his personnel to respond with, "Of course, I do. It's written right there on your name tag."

Under the long-established protocols under which he operated, everyone in the Annex was an equal. The

Speaker of the House and the majority leader of the Senate were a little more equal in the sense that they shared a room for two rather than be in the barracks with everyone else, but as far as Johnson was concerned, that was the only difference.

The residents had made it abundantly clear that they were not pleased about being forced to wear identical uniforms, but Johnson thought it was good for them. They were sent to Congress by ordinary people to be their mouthpieces for justice. Over the years, with the growth of the professional political class, the access to limitless money from contributors combined with egos the size of Alaska, every one of those assholes had lost track of who they were and what they were sent to Washington to do.

Take away the bling, the status and the television cameras, all that was left was a high-school debate society with no practical skills. Truth be told, that was the one element of the whole CRIMSON PHOENIX bugout that Johnson and his team enjoyed.

The designers of the Annex had been forward thinking enough to include a couple of jail cells for miscreant members or their staffs. Johnson hadn't used them yet, but he'd come close a couple of times. Back before the balloon went up, he'd assumed that the partisan bickering and name calling was just so much posturing for the cameras, but he was shocked to learn that such was not the case. These people truly hated each other.

In addition to being the caretakers and rule enforcers within the Annex, Solara employees doubled as the police force, and were imbued with all the powers normally held by sworn police officers. Under the right circumstances, lethal force was authorized, and the Solara employees were always armed. In addition to the Glock 19s they'd begun to carry on their hips as the tensions mounted among the residents, they also had access to automatic rifles.

Unfortunately, Johnson had had to terminate one of the would-be residents in the early hours of the lockdown. The rules allowed only members of Congress and one staff member each to reside within the Annex. Some bitch member of the House from West Virginia resigned at the blast door when she found out that she couldn't bring her kids with her. Her selected staff member, though, a guy named Oliver Mulroney, had already entered. He was told to leave, but did not. Then, when the war started unexpectedly and Johnson had to button up with virtually no advance notice, Mulroney was still inside. Johnson had no choice but to kill him.

Even his own staff thought that the decision had been too harsh, but as he saw it, killing him was the only option. They couldn't open the doors again to let him out, and every moment Mulroney stuck around was that much more air to be filtered. Every morsel of food was a precious resource that literally was taken from someone else's mouth. Terminating the problem meant terminating the man.

Because someone always had to be with the elected children to provide some semblance of order, Johnson never got to meet with his entire staff at the same time. They worked round the clock on twelve-hour shifts, thus guaranteeing that there were enough people to provide technical support to several residents at once, while at the same time having enough muscle available to break up fights, as necessary.

Currently Johnson was meeting with Bugsy, his second in command, though such ranks didn't really exist. They sat in leather club chairs that years ago had been requisitioned unofficially from the hotel. Because they'd had a long, long time to deck out their spot, they'd turned it into a combination bar, pool hall and break room.

"What's up, Bugs?" Johnson asked as he took a pull on a Budweiser longneck.

Bugsy had been separated from the Army for nearly ten years, but you'd never know from the girth of his neck and biceps. "Have you been keeping up with the transcripts?"

One way to stay on top of security issues among the residents was to listen to their conversations. The congressfolk didn't know it, but they were never alone. Thanks to the genius of Pete Clostner, his chief communications tech, every space was rife with listening devices that were sensitive enough to hear even the slightest whisper. Each mic had its own channel, which was passively monitored 24/7. If necessary, Solara staffers could listen live, but that rarely happened. Each of the channels fed through a computer that listened for concerning words, phrases, or levels of stress. Once detected, it would mark that section of recording for further examination by a staffer. If it was particularly interesting, the press of a button would automatically convert the recording into a written transcript.

"Yes, I have," Johnson said. "The natives are getting more restless, not less."

"Restless doesn't touch it," Bugsy said with a forced

chuckle. "Batshit crazy is more like it. Did you read the convo between Speaker Fortnight and that suck-up from Missouri? Kiser, I think his name is."

"The bit of business about opening the doors and walking away?"

"That exactly," Bugsy said.

"They can try that all they want," Johnson said. "But unless they have the key for the control panel, they're going to be very disappointed."

"I don't worry so much about them actually doing it," Bugsy said. "I think it's a problem that they're even thinking like that. It's like they don't believe that the attacks were real or something."

Johnson nodded. "Yeah, and Glendale is getting to be a problem, too. I haven't ordered it transcribed yet, but when I saw that geezer Sinclair wander into the president's office, I tuned in live. Sinclair was talking about bolting for it, too."

"That guy's got clout with this crowd," Bugsy said. "They listen to everything he says. He's the only one that has more allies than enemies."

"Yeah, well, the president talked him down," Johnson said. "That's enough for now."

Bugsy clearly was not satisfied. He shifted in his seat and recrossed his legs. "Okay, this is going to sound paranoid, but hear me out, okay? I lived through lots of shit in the Sandbox because I trusted my gut and my assessment of people."

Johnson spread his arms in a silent *The floor is yours*.

"The stuff these goobers are talking about is fundamentally stupid, but it's constant and it's spreading. I don't know where the critical mass is, but as time goes on, and they get no rest from each other, this shit is going to boil over."

"They won't be able to open the doors, Bugs. Don't worry—"

"Whether they can or can't is not the issue, Scott. It's the talk itself. As the rhetoric intensifies, the frustration burns hotter. That's a recipe for a riot downrange."

"We've trained for years to control said riot," Johnson said. "One gunshot, and those pussies will scatter like roaches."

"But people will get hurt."

"That's what happens during riots. What are you getting at?"

"I think we need to get out in front of it. Tell them that the shit they're talking about won't work. Tell them what the consequences are if they try."

"We can't do that, Bugs. The only way we can hang their own conversations in front of them is if we tell them that we've been listening to them. You want to see a shit storm start to blow? You tell those pricks that we hear everything they say."

"Come on, Scott, don't dismiss it so fast. There's still a lot of talk about Mulroney among them."

"They don't know anything."

"Oh, yes they do. Every person out there thinks that we shot him."

"Operative word there is *think*. They can think that the world is flat and that pigs can fly, but that doesn't make it true."

"But it *is* true, Scott. You killed—"

"I know what I did, Bugs. You know what I did.

Hell, I imagine that our whole staff knows, but that's different than *them* knowing. Their rods are stuffed so far up their asses that they would never act out on what they *suspect.* Looking the other way and hiding behind plausible deniability is how they drove the world to where it is. They're not going to commit mass suicide by attacking us just because they *think* that somebody was terminated."

"They're all part of the same tribe, Scott. That kind of loyalty drives all kinds of crazy shit."

This time, Johnson's laugh was very real. "They're not part of the same tribe," he scoffed. "Mulroney was regular people. He was a career staffer, never a member of the club. The closest he could ever get to the club room was to man the coat check. Members of Congress are *special,* didn't you know that?" He was tapping into a well of bitterness that spiked his own anger. "They're afraid of real people unless the real people carry cash. Mulroney wasn't even one of theirs. Maybe there'd be a concern if his boss hadn't rabbited on him, but she did. That left him *really* a commoner."

Johnson settled himself before the rant could become a tirade. "Okay, enough of that. I'm telling you, Bugsy. Those roaches out there are way too scared of us to pose any kind of a threat. As long as we keep it that way, we should be good."

Bugsy still didn't look happy, but he did look resigned. "At least it's only for another couple of weeks. What do we know about conditions on the other side of the doors?"

The designers of the Annex had installed surveillance cameras throughout the property, with the intent of keeping hotel guests away from places they shouldn't visit. Since the day of the attacks, none of that equipment had worked.

"Still nothing," Johnson said. "Pete Clostner tells me that those circuits were all fried by the EMP and he doesn't know how to fix it."

"If Pete can't fix it, then it can't be fixed," Bugsy said.

"But I'm pretty sure there are people milling around out there. In fact, I'm certain. The seismographs pick up a lot of what looks like footsteps."

"Sooner or later, they're bound to find one of the blast doors," Bugsy said.

"Good for them. The lightest door is what, thirty tons? They can try to break through, but they'll only die digging."

CHAPTER EIGHT

Hell Day + 48 (Twenty-Five Days Later)

VICTORIA LEANED INTO HER DESK, HER ARMS FOLDED, as she listened to the pleadings of Anthony Sable and his wife, Livvy. He'd been a factory representative for a tractor manufacturer in the before times, and they were having special difficulty adjusting to the new way of doing things. Big Ben Barnett, who used to run the Ortho Grocery and now oversaw the management of community food resources, sat slightly behind her and on her left.

"I'm not a hunter, Mrs. Emerson," Anthony whined. "Never have been. And I don't know anything about construction. It pains me to say this, but I have no skills. I can't just watch my family starve."

Victoria hadn't yet decided if this was the part of her job that she hated the most or loved the most. "Mr. Sable, I don't know how many different ways I can say this. Ben is right. The common stores are not a welfare pantry. They exist as a source of support and sustenance for the people in our community who *cannot* fend for themselves. Your neighbor is able to draw smoked meats and canned vegetables because he's eighty-three and has cancer."

"How is that a good investment?" Livvy asked. "Food is a valuable commodity. Is it wise to waste it on . . ." She looked down as she lost her nerve to finish the sentence.

Victoria felt heat rising in her ears. "Society may have collapsed, Mrs. Sable, but civilization has not. At least not here. Not on my watch." She shifted her eyes to Anthony. "Pardon my French, Mr. Sable, but you are a grown-ass man. I count two arms and two legs, and a head that might not be screwed on straight, but at least it's screwed on. If you need stores, approach your neighbors. They have their private supplies. Buy what you need from them."

"I don't own a gun!" Anthony shouted. "Why would I have bullets to spend if I don't own a gun?"

"Then sell something," Victoria said. "I know for a fact that the construction crews have plenty of unskilled laborers. And you know what? After a week or two on the job, they develop skills that make them even more valuable. We're rebuilding from nothing here. Months from now, some of our residents will be thriving, and, alas, some of our residents will have a very long winter. Perhaps their last, but I certainly hope not."

At the far end of the tavern room, Joe McCrea entered from the sunlight and waited to be recognized. He had with him a young couple whom she did not recognize. The major did not disturb her day on trivial matters.

As Anthony opened his mouth to continue his begging, Victoria stood, a signal that this meeting was over. "Mr. Sable," she said, "I expect this to be the last time we discuss this matter. The food stores are exclusively Mr. Barnett's responsibility. I guarantee you that he has my full support." She extended her hand. "Now, if you'll excuse me."

The Sables looked confused, as if not sure what to do about the proffered hand. After a few seconds, they stood.

"I don't think you understand—" Livvy started.

"Have a fine day," Victoria interrupted. When her gesture of friendliness was not accepted, she shifted her gaze over their shoulders to McCrea and his guests.

Anthony made a point of knocking over his chair and he turned and stormed toward the exit.

"Petulant children," Ben muttered as he stood. "Thanks for the support, Vicky. I'm sorry to bother you with such nonsense."

Victoria smiled at McCrea and beckoned with her fingers for them to come forward. To Ben, she said, "Do you get a lot of that? People wanting handouts?"

"I don't know when a few becomes a lot, but it's more than I'm comfortable with. It's particularly a problem with the newcomers. They have so little, and they're so worn-out."

"We still do the welcome package, don't we?"

"Of course. It's enough rations to get them started for a week, but you'd be surprised how many people can blow through a week's worth of rations in just a few days. I tell them up front very clearly that this is the only handout they can expect, but I'm not sure they believe me."

"My father used to say that hard-learned lessons are often the best learned," Victoria said.

"Far as I know, nobody's starved yet," Ben said.

"Do we need more security assigned to the food?" Victoria asked.

"Not yet," Ben replied. "I promise I'll let you know as soon as I think we do. You know, it's a shame we can't put the new folks straight onto the security teams."

McCrea had approached to within earshot. "Foxes make for terrible security teams at the chicken coops."

"Hey, Major," Ben said. To the newcomers, "If you're planning to stay, I'll be seeing both of you soon."

The couple looked hard ridden and underfed. Victoria guessed their ages to be somewhere in their early twenties, but as drawn as their faces were, they could have passed for fifty. Both wore pistols on their hips.

McCrea said, "Victoria Emerson, meet the Gonzaleses. Greg and Mary. They've got a story I think you need to hear."

Victoria smiled, shook their hands and pointed to the chairs the Sables had just abandoned. "Please have a seat."

They looked relieved to be able to take a load off. "Major McCrea says you're the mayor?"

Victoria blushed. She hated it when McCrea told people that. "Not exactly," she said. "But close enough, I suppose. When the music stopped, I was the one with the chair. So tell me about yourselves."

Mary and Greg polled each other silently to see who

would tell the story. Greg got the nod. "We were on our honeymoon when everything happened."

"Congratulations on the wedding," Victoria said. As they recoiled, she added, "I'm sure it's not what you'd hoped for, but it's better to go through this together than alone, isn't it?"

Clearly, they weren't sure. It had been a long few weeks, after all.

"Tell her where you were staying," McCrea prompted.

"Have you ever heard of the Hilltop Manor Resort?" Greg asked. He looked startled by Victoria's reaction. "What?"

"Oh, I've definitely heard of it," Victoria said. "I'll tell you more when you're done with your story."

"We were sleeping when the explosions happened," Greg continued. "It was terrifying. Was it an earthquake? A war? I mean, literally, no one knew anything—we still don't, really, but we all assumed it was war. Nothing worked. It was dark as a cave in there."

"Was the resort full?" Victoria asked.

"I don't know how many the hotel holds, but there were hundreds of us. Maybe a thousand?"

"It was a *ton* of people," Mary said. Victoria got the sense that she wanted to contribute. "Tell about the staff."

"What staff?" Greg asked.

"That's kind of my point."

"Oh, yeah. So there are all these people, but there was no staff. I don't know where they went, but they weren't anywhere to be found. Well, a few, I suppose, but for the most part, we were on our own."

"Was there any damage done to the resort?" Victoria asked.

"No. Well, not at first. Now it's kind of a wreck."

Victoria cocked her head, waiting for the explanation.

Greg continued, "You know, for the first day or two, everybody was in a panic. No one knew what to do, where to go. We saw those fires on the horizon, and we didn't know if we were going to burn to death or what."

"And there was nothing to eat," Mary said.

"Well, there was for some people, and that's really where the terror started."

Victoria leaned forward. "The *terror*?"

"Wait for it," McCrea said. "This is the part I wanted you to hear."

"There was a guy named Roger there," Greg continued. "I didn't recognize the guy, but others did. He was famous, apparently. A wrestler, I think. I don't do sports. Anyway, he sort of took over as leader of the people who were there, but then he and his followers found the kitchen and the freezers full of food, and they divvied it up however they thought was fit. Some people—his friends and family, apparently—got a lot, but many people got nothing. He took the attitude that if you don't like being there, walk away.

"At the end of that first week, things were already getting desperate. People were hungry and people were dying. I think most of the deaths were medical related. You know, people who didn't get their medications and such. Without power, it was hotter than blazes inside with all those people. No one wanted to stay in their rooms, especially people on the upper floors, so they all gathered in the main salons and ballrooms. Then the plumbing broke, and you can imagine what that was like."

"Were you down there with the others?" Victoria asked. "Down in the ballrooms?"

Mary said, "We started there, but then we decided that it didn't make any sense. Our room was on the third floor, so taking the steps wasn't that big a deal."

"That's when we discovered that the locks are all electric," Greg said. "You get those RFID keys when you check in, right? Well, if the readers aren't plugged in, they can't read anything."

"So, what did you do?" Victoria asked.

"There was a fire ax in a glass cabinet in the stairwell. I only noticed it because you don't see those much in hotels anymore. So I chopped our way into our room."

"Very Jack Nicholson," Mary said. *"Heeere's Johnny!"* They leaned into each other for a loving shoulder bump. Victoria got the reference to *The Shining*.

"But there goes any privacy," Greg said. "One night, we woke up to find somebody rummaging through our minibar, looking for whatever he was looking for. As if we hadn't already cleaned that out. He had some sort of club in his hand—maybe a chair leg?—and when he saw I was awake, he waved it in the air, threatening me with it. It looked so weird in just the moonlight through the window. Kinda terrifying."

"And it all went south from there," Mary said. "People kept arriving. I don't know why. Maybe they thought it was still a functioning hotel. Anyway, as more and more people arrived, conditions got worse and worse."

Greg said, "In the end, we realized that health conditions there were scary. We'd just survived a nuclear war—that's what it was, right?"

"As far as we know," Victoria said. That was more true than false. Well, half and half.

"Anyway, we'd just survived a nuclear war. We didn't want to die from shit-in-the-water disease."

"Talk about the gangs," McCrea prompted.

"They're *terrible*," Mary said. "That Roger guy organized hunts, using the shotguns from the shooting range there on the grounds, but no one really knew what they were doing. I suppose *some* people did, but Roger thought he knew more than anybody else."

"I can't prove it," Greg said, "but I'd swear on a stack of Bibles that he had food stashed somewhere for himself and his cronies. They were the only ones who looked healthy."

"Plus, I think they wanted people to leave," Mary said. "I think part of the plan was to make people so god-awful miserable that they'd pack up their stuff and leave."

"But then the sonsabitches demanded that anyone who left had to leave all their valuable stuff behind."

"Why?" Victoria asked.

"I don't know. I suspect just to be an ass. I mean, what is he going to do with cash and computers now? I think it was a way to be mean."

"Some people just get that way, you know," Mary said.

"I've heard," Victoria said, then instantly regretted her dismissive tone.

"But here's the thing," Greg went on. "As new people came in, most of them were locals. Unlike us, who were all from out of town. *Duh.* Who else stays in a hotel, right? So these new people arrive with guns, and, like, overnight, Roger had an army."

"That's when we knew we had to get out," Mary said. "On our last day, the bullying took a whole new turn once Roger had henchmen."

"How long have you been on the road?" Victoria asked. "And where did you get the pistols?"

In unison, the couple glanced down at their belts, as if startled that they were armed.

"Funny you should ask," Greg said with a playful glare at his wife. "I'm usually always armed. I have a Virginia carry permit—that's where we're from. But *somebody* insisted that I put it in the safe when we got to the Hilltop Manor."

Victoria saw the problem right away. "Electricity."

"Exactly," Greg said, thumping his forefinger on the desk. "The combination is an electronic push button lock, and without electricity, I couldn't open the damn thing. Even the fire ax wouldn't work. I tried to find the emergency key—I figure that staff had to have been able to get into safes when people left stuff behind—but I never could. It would have been nice to ask someone on the housekeeping staff, but, well, we already talked about that."

"How long on the road?" Victoria prompted again.

Greg looked to Mary for input on that. "A long time," she said. "Weeks, certainly. I think we left the Hilltop Manor after only six or seven days of Roger's bullshit. We've been on the road since then, till today."

"What's out there between there and here?" Victoria asked.

"A lot of people who act like wild animals," Greg

said. "I'll go ahead and tell you so you don't find out another way and make it look worse. I had to kill two people out there. They sneaked up on us and tried to steal our *clothes*. I got in a lucky swing to the head with a log I'd been carrying as a club, and I used his gun to shoot the other guy, who was about to shoot me."

"God, it was terrible," Mary confirmed. Her eyes moistened, but she didn't cry. Victoria imagined that was because such scenes were progressively more commonplace.

"But from then on, we were armed," Greg said. "That's better than not being armed. And that's also where the coats came from. A little weird to be wearing dead men's stuff, but you get used to it."

"So you're talking weeks on the road," Victoria said. "How did you survive?"

"We used to do a lot of camping," Mary said. "Both as kids and then together after we met. So we were able to make shelters when we had to. The weather hasn't been that bad, really. We've been eating a lot of fish. Nuts and berries, too."

"The problem with the pistols," Greg said, "is that it's too much bullet for rabbits and squirrels, and not enough bullet for bigger stuff. Not that we haven't eaten a few shredded rabbits and squirrels. It's not much food, but if you don't mind being hungry all the time, you can make either one of them stretch out to two meals apiece."

Victoria couldn't imagine that to be true. At least that explained their gaunt faces.

"Help me understand how you got here," Victoria said. "Many miles separate Ortho from the Hilltop Manor."

"If you decide to stay, you'll discover that we have rules," Victoria explained. "One of them is that everyone who *can* arm themselves *should* arm themselves. We've encountered some of these thugs you've been talking about, and, thus far, our citizens' militia has been able to drive them off."

Greg said, "There's also a rumor of some kind of bunker in the Hilltop Manor, and that you refused to go into it so you could save your family and help people cope."

Victoria was stunned by the efficiency of the rumor mill, even in the absence of party lines and social media. She dismissed the words with a flick of her hand. "That sounds far nobler than the reality of it. The part about my kids was right, but I was just trying to run away like everybody else."

McCrea clapped his hands together lightly, signaling an end to the conversation. "I'm going to take you to the fellow you just saw, Ben Barnett. He'll get you started with some rations and a place to sleep. You look like you need both."

As the door closed on their way out, Victoria closed her eyes, folded her arms on her desk and laid her head on her wrists. She couldn't remember ever feeling this exhausted. When she'd signed on for this leadership gig, she thought she was going to get things stabilized and then move on. That was what she'd promised her boys. She'd sworn to them that they would move on to meet their brother, Adam, at the long-planned postdisaster meeting place called Top Hat Mountain, a couple hundred miles from here.

Now that she'd fallen back into the rhythms of leadership, though, she could no longer see a pathway to a clean exit. People were depending on her, and her efforts were showing fine results.

The events at the Hilltop Manor had not crossed her mind for quite some time. It seemed years ago. Now that she did think about it, she wondered how her former colleagues were faring. Wondered what they were doing. For damn sure, whatever it was had not had much impact on anything she could see.

So many weeks into the post–Hell Day nightmare, she wondered if the federal government had any relevance anymore. Food, shelter and self-protection had always been a personal responsibility, no matter what her political colleagues tried to sell to the media.

Victoria needed rest. On any night, she was lucky to log two hours of undisturbed sleep. Between the inherent discomfort of their digs inside the church and the constant movement of others who occupied the same space, along with the never-ending list of things she needed to do to keep the town running, she worried that she might not be able to keep up the pace much longer.

The flip side of that, of course, was the fact that she was a control freak who doubted that anyone shared her vision for what this community had the potential to become. Here in Ortho, they'd come very close to the point where they'd evolved from merely surviving to truly rebuilding. Under the circumstances, and the short time in which events had transpired, she thought it all to be remarkable.

But Victoria knew better than to get cocky. If the sanitation precautions faltered, or if food in the stores was not properly preserved, they could ignite a fire of disease that could never be put out. From the beginning, she'd put Doc Rory in charge of that slice of the community development, and he'd done a terrific job. Now that he had some extra medical hands to help him out, she was confident that they had a better than average chance of building a real community here.

As she pivoted to review the report on new arrivals, the door opened and Joe McCrea stepped inside again. "Got a minute?" he asked.

"Got a hug for me?" she replied. She pushed her chair back and walked around her desk to greet him, her arms spread wide.

As they embraced, Victoria felt some of the stress drain out of her shoulders. She hadn't felt this close to someone, this vulnerable, in a very long time. She prayed that they might have a long future together, and she knew that McCrea felt the same way toward her.

McCrea had lost everything in the attacks—his wife, his two daughters, his home, his life. They all evaporated in a million-degree fireball while he was doing his duty to escort Victoria to safety. She'd been a bitch to him at the time, but he'd never strayed from his mission. Since then, as the weeks turned to months, he'd become her constant source of strength, her inexhaustible source of counsel and wisdom. While they often disagreed, he'd never let her down after the decisions were made.

But something was off in this embrace. Was he holding her too close? Too long?

She eased away, but kept his hands in hers. "Something's wrong, Joe," she said. "What is it?"

"You need to have a seat," he said.

A block of ice seemed to form in her gut. "What is it?"

"Please," he said, pointing to one of the guest chairs with an open palm.

"I'm not a child."

McCrea helped himself to the other chair and waited. Victoria sat.

McCrea looked to be on the verge of tears. "I've just learned some very, very bad news," he said. He reached out for her hands again. "I heard it once, a while ago, and I chose not to share it because one report is a rumor, but two or more—"

"Oh, for God's sake, Joe. What happened?"

"One of the arrivals today came in from up near Mountain View. If I recall, that was where you originally wanted to go before we diverted—"

"I know what I said, Joe. I know what we did. Is this about Adam?" Her oldest son, Adam, had been attending a boarding school in Mountain View—a military academy—when Hell Day happened.

"I'm afraid it is," McCrea said. "And there's no easy way to say this. They tell me that a fire consumed the Clinton M. Hedrick Military Academy."

Victoria had heard the rumor, too, but she refused to believe it. But this time . . . She brought a hand to her mouth as pressure built behind her eyes.

"Vicky, there were no survivors."

"No," she said. "He survived. I know he did." If she said it forcefully enough, maybe it would be true.

McCrea settled his shoulders, cocked his head. He looked like he wanted to say something, but then he changed his mind. "Okay," he said. "I hope you're right."

"I *am* right," she said. "He's my son. My boy. If something had happened to him, I would know."

McCrea pressed his lips together. His eyes shimmered red.

"Adam Emerson is not . . ." She couldn't bring herself to say the word.

It couldn't be. God would not do that to her. He would not allow her son to burn—

The flood of emotions came from nowhere. This was the horror, the worst nightmare. Without even thinking, she stood from her chair and McCrea was there. As he pulled her close, she could not stop the sobs. They cascaded from her throat, so forceful that they hurt.

Of course, it could be true. God had taken McCrea's family, so why would He hesitate to take hers?

Oh, God, it hurt. It hurt so much.

CHAPTER NINE

Hell Day + 45 (Three Days Earlier)

FRANK ROUSE USED A BUCKET OF WATER TAKEN FROM the bathtub, poured it into the porcelain tank behind the toilet bowl, then pressed the flush lever. Of all the simple elements he missed from the civilized days, the convenience of running water was probably at the top of the list. It was such a pain in the ass to run to the river day after day to keep the tubs full. You never realized how much water a toilet consumed until each press of the handle meant another ten-pound pour to refill the tank.

If it's yellow, let it mellow. If it's brown, flush it down.

Frank's sons seemed to be adjusting better than either Frank or his wife, Paula. In the before times, Paula had taught second grade at John Tyler Elementary, and Frank had taught history at Byrd High School. That made him a specialist and his wife a generalist, which made her by far the most valuable professional asset in the family. When the kids wanted to know about Stonewall Jackson's Shenandoah Valley Campaign, Frank was their man. But if they wanted to know how to work any equation involving mathematics, they knew to turn to their mom.

Now that the weather was changing, Frank worried about how they were going to manage the temperature in their century-old house. They were fortunate that every room had its own fireplace, but most hadn't been used in God knew how long, and it was a crapshoot whether the chimneys were clear, and if they were, if they'd get any meaningful draft to keep the fires burning. Like all fireplaces of the era, these had been built for efficiency rather than beauty, and the fireboxes were very shallow. It was almost like building a fire in the middle of the floor. He understood the physics of it, but he also understood that he had two boys who liked to wrestle on the floor.

All things considered, he knew that they had it better than most. Avid hunters all, they'd had a freezer full of venison and even most of a side of beef when the war happened. Within hours of the attacks, it became clear to Frank that the power outages and the rest of the misery were not transitory—that they would be the rule of life for the foreseeable future—so he, Paula and the boys had spent days salt curing and canning everything they could.

They were able to put up about three hundred pounds of meat before the lack of refrigeration triggered the first bit of spoilage, but that didn't stop them. They spent another hundred hours or so cutting away the questionable parts and continuing on with the rest.

When the music stopped, the Rouse family had well over four hundred pounds of protein to sustain them. That was plenty to get through the winter. After a few months and the return of spring, he'd hoped that they'd be able to turn back to the forest as a source of continuing sustenance, but that was looking less and less likely.

In the earliest days after the war, when the fires were still burning in the distance, his neighbors had panicked and gone on a killing spree in the woods, taking out anything with a heartbeat and fur. He'd never seen anything like it. Now those kills were spoiled, and the woods were hunted out.

More recently, he worried about predators of a different kind. Roving gangs had obliterated downtown Appleton. That they ravaged the grocery stores and the pharmacy made sense at a certain level, especially if you accounted for panic, but he couldn't for the life of him figure out why they would want to burn the buildings down when they were done.

From what he could tell, those perpetrators were mostly young—barely north of teenagers—and he recognized some of them from his classes. Fear and desperation drove people to do unspeakable things, he supposed. That was why he'd instructed Gary and Ronnie to tell no one of the family's food stores. In fact, he'd instructed them to stay on their own property. Not huge by any standard, at a little over five acres, they had ample land to grow enough food in the spring to support their own needs—information that was best left unshared with the neighbors.

Frank was one of the few local residents he knew who did not own a pistol for concealed carry. He had rifles for hunting, and a Colt .44 Magnum revolver he would carry on hunting trips as a backup gun if a boar or a bear startled him, but if confronted for his wallet, Frank's plan had always been to hand over the wallet.

The marauding gangs seemed to be getting ever closer to his little patch of ground. Fires burned every night now, but in his determination to remain isolated and under the radar—what a quaintly-archaic term, now that they'd been delivered back to the Stone Age—he didn't know what the source of the flames was, or who was igniting them.

Sporadic gunfire broke out every night, and the rhythms of it concerned him. These were not the single shots of a hunt, or even the double or triple taps of target shooting. This gunfire came in waves and in different powder loads. In his mind, he was listening to gunfights. And where there were gunfights, there were dead and wounded people.

What could possibly be worth that kind of sacrifice? That kind of brutality?

Outside now, he focused his attention on the business of splitting firewood. He figured that each of the six fireplaces would consume ten logs per day in the dead of winter. He was good enough at math to understand that to be 420 logs per week. And that was before calculating what it would take to cook their meals on campfires outside, or to heat the water for bathing.

It hurt his head to consider that during the twenty-week winter season, he could easily burn through nine thousand logs! Conservatively, then, he needed to chop around ten cords of wood just to get them through the season. He prayed that he'd vastly overestimated the need.

If he could make his daily goal today, he'd be one-fifth of the way to where he needed to be.

And it was only October. At least that's what he figured. Truthfully, he'd lost track, but the leaves looked too far advanced in color for it to still be September, and too many remained on the branches to be November.

He'd just teed up a two-foot-wide hunk of tree trunk and set the maul when he heard Ronnie yell out, "Dad! Look!"

Adolescence had not been easy on his fourteen-year-old. Five feet eight, with a twenty-seven-inch waist, fourteen-inch neck and size-ten feet, he had a comical asymmetry about him that would go away in time, but left him an easy target for derision from his brother and from friends, back when he hung with them. Ronnie stood twenty feet away, his arms filled with another hunk of tree, and he pointed with his forehead toward the end of the long drive that led to the front door.

Down there, at the end of the steep slope, he saw a large group approaching. They were armed, and at least some of them appeared to be military. They had spread out wide in their approach, none of them utilizing the paved driveway, as far as Frank could tell.

"Go inside," Frank said. "You, your mom and your brother stay out of sight. I've got this."

"What's happening?"

"Just do as I say, please," Frank said.

"Gary is out in the woods," Ronnie said.

"Then let him stay. I don't want you out here right now. Remember to tell your mom."

Frank let his sledgehammer fall at the base of the chopping block and tried to remain calm as he strolled thirty feet to the nearest wall of the house and lifted the Beretta over-and-under twelve-gauge that he normally used for doves and sporting clays.

He didn't want to project menace, but he wanted to protect himself.

Frank didn't count the number of people in the approaching party, but he estimated it to be around twenty or twenty-five people. Among them, he recognized Austin Mills and Davey Priest, two boys he'd taught last year, who were bad news in every sense of the word. They walked next to two other boys from the current year, which was still too new when the war came for Frank to know their names. He believed both of them to be stars of the football team.

The center of the approach line seemed dominated by military personnel. They wore uniforms of a bygone era, a camouflage pattern that he hadn't seen in years. The one in the center—the one who seemed to be in charge—wore captain's bars.

Frank walked toward the group with the action of his shotgun closed, but with the breech resting on his shoulder, muzzles facing the sky. He wanted to meet and greet as far away from the front door as he could.

"Howdy!" he called. "How can I help you?"

"Mostly by just staying out of our way," the captain said. He kept his approach steady, neither fast nor slow.

Frank held out a hand, fully aware and embarrassed that it was trembling. "Just a second there, Captain," he said.

"Don't make me arrest you," the captain said. "And for God's sake, don't make me shoot you." He stopped when he was maybe five feet from Frank, but the others continued without stopping. They headed toward the house.

Frank whirled. "Hey!" he shouted. "You can't go there! That's my home!"

"I've declared martial law," the captain said. "Your house now belongs to Uncle Sam's Army."

"That's not what martial law means!" Frank declared, as if arguing the law had any bearing on what was happening. "My family is in there."

"Thanks for letting me know," the captain said. Then he yelled, "Watch out for trouble inside! If anyone poses a threat, shoot to kill."

"Wait! What?" Frank squared off and brought his shotgun off his shoulder.

The captain didn't hesitate. He fired a punch to Frank's throat, the effect of which was to unwire his legs and drop him to the grass.

Frank's throat spasmed. Though his mouth and diaphragm worked to let air pass, breath wouldn't come. He tried to yell, but the effort brought no sound. As he lay on the ground, he saw the throngs of invaders enter through his front door even as they surrounded the house. He thought he was dying.

Commotion erupted from inside the house. Lots of shouting. Paula screamed and there was a gunshot.

Oh, shit. Oh, my God! Frank tried to shout. He tried to stand, but nothing worked. Somehow that punch had paralyzed his whole nervous system.

Another gunshot ripped through the air and Paula screamed again. "Frank! Frank!"

I'm trying, honey. Honest to God, I'm—

Ronnie fell out the front door, holding a spot on his belly as blood seeped through his fingers and down the front of his jeans. He caromed off a pillar at the edge of the front porch, but when he tried to find the step, he ended up tumbling down the three steps into the yard. After he hit, he got to his hands and knees.

"Where's your mom?" Frank asked. At least he could generate a whisper now. And he, too, could get to his hands and knees now. He'd crawled half the distance to Ronnie when he realized that he'd left his shotgun where he'd dropped it. It would have to stay there.

"They shot me, Dad," Ronnie said through a terrified sob. He was sitting upright now, his hands still pressed tightly against his belly. His side, really.

"Your mom?"

As if on cue, Paula exploded out of the doorway. She nearly sailed off of the porch into the grass, too, but she was able to snag the same pillar that Ronnie had bounced off. She appeared unhurt as she scurried over to Frank and Ronnie.

"Ronnie, lie down," she said.

"They shot me."

"I know, sweetie. Lie down." She helped her son lie back onto the grass.

In the distance, off to the right side of the house, Frank detected movement, and he saw Gary running toward them, a .22-caliber rifle in his hand.

"No!" Frank yelled. His voice had returned, and so had his coordination and balance. "Gary, stop! Stop right there!"

The boy slid to a halt, his head on a swivel. "What! What's wrong?"

"Go back to the woods!" Frank yelled. "Don't come any closer."

"You don't have to send him away." The voice startled Frank. The captain had been able to approach without Frank noticing. "How is your boy?" As he spoke, he beckoned Gary to join them.

"No!" Frank yelled. "Don't come any closer!"

"We're not here to hurt you," the captain said. He kneeled on the grass next to Ronnie. "Here, let me take a look at that."

Paula pushed him away. "Don't you touch him!"

"Have a lot of experience with bullet wounds, do you?" the captain mocked.

"Leave my son alone," Frank said, rising to his feet.

"Don't make this worse than it needs to be," the captain said. He stood as well. He extended his hand. "Captain Cole Pritchard."

"I am not shaking the hand of the man who shot my son."

From only a few yards away: "Oh, shit, they shot Ronnie?" Gary rushed in and dropped to a knee. Ronnie and Paula had worked together to unbutton his shirt to expose the wound. At first glance, it didn't look that bad.

"I didn't shoot him, sir," Pritchard said. "But one of my men did. They wouldn't have if the boy hadn't reached for a gun."

"It's our house!" Ronnie grunted.

Pritchard redirected his attention back to the wounded boy. He kneeled, looked at the wound, then stood. "He'll be fine."

"He's been shot!" Frank said.

"And he's been lucky. Embrace the good and move on. Not everyone we've encountered has had the same good fortune."

"I'll see you punished for this," Frank said.

Pritchard's features darkened as he took a menacing step closer. "Don't push me," he said. "You're alive and healthy because I decided to keep it that way. Don't make me worry that I made a mistake."

"I want you out of my house and off my property," Frank said.

Humor returned to the captain's face. "It's not your house anymore," he said. "This now belongs to the United States government. You and your family have fifteen minutes to pack up what you need and get off the property."

"That's crazy!"

"These are crazy times."

"You have no right!"

Pritchard turned and headed back toward the house. "Your clock is ticking."

CHAPTER TEN

Hell Day + 47 (Two Days Later)

ADAM EMERSON TRIED TO IGNORE THE SOUND OF THE retching. He'd seen his share of death and mutilation in the weeks since the war—he'd caused more than his share, for that matter—but active puking was a line he couldn't cross. He felt bad that he couldn't be there to hold Emma's forehead and say those comforting things a good father-to-be should offer up, but it wasn't in him. He didn't see how both of them blowing chunks at the same time would be helpful.

They couldn't know for sure how far along Emma was in her pregnancy, but they figured about six weeks. The last five days had been particularly hard on her. She couldn't keep anything down—not that there was that much to put down in the first place. Emma was losing weight and strength and he worried about her.

Now that the temperatures were dropping near

freezing every night, their tent and sleeping bags were proving inadequate. He'd hoped to be much further along on the construction of their shelter, but no matter how hard he worked, it simply was not progressing fast enough.

Emma emerged from the tree line dabbing her mouth with a towel and forced a smile. "Are we having fun or what?" she joked.

Adam rose from one of the chairs that he'd fashioned out of chopped wood and moss, and met Emma halfway to the fire, where he helped her down into her own chair. The fire never went out these days. They'd found a spot to camp and build the never-completed shelter deep into the forest, probably a half mile from the road where they'd stashed Emma's ancient Ford Bronco. Built in the 1960s, the Bronco was unburdened with the kind of electronics that killed modern vehicles, so it still ran.

He settled in next to her. "I'm worried about you, Em."

"They tell me that having a baby is the most beautiful experience a woman can have."

"Be serious."

"Does that help?" She tucked a strand of impossibly red hair behind her ear. "I'm preggers and I feel like shit. Before long I'm going to be fat and I'm going to waddle when I walk."

"Oh, come on, Em. You're beautiful." Adam cringed when he heard his words. Despite being true, they sounded forced.

"And you are full of crap," she said with a hearty laugh. "I'm just glad that mirrors aren't a thing anymore."

Adam felt guilty that they hadn't taken precautions.

"At first, we were just wandering," Greg said. "We didn't know what we were doing or where we were going. We both worked in DC and lived in Arlington, so we knew that home wasn't an option, and we don't really know this part of the world."

Mary took over. "All over, these camps have popped up. I don't know where they came from, but no one seems to know anyone. They're mostly awful places. Lots of crime, suffering and sickness. I think starvation is the biggest problem, and it's a *really* big one. People say that the woods are hunted out, that there's no more game to support people, but I don't know if that's true. I'm not sure it even *can* be true."

"But we heard about this place several times," Greg said. "People are saying there's food and shelter and that crime is under control. People are calling it Eden."

Victoria scowled and looked at McCrea, who bounced his eyebrows.

"I didn't believe it, to be honest," Mary said. "I mean, it's like the Wild West out there."

"What do you think so far?" McCrea asked.

Mary started to speak, then stopped herself.

"Feel free to speak your mind here," Victoria said.

Greg reached over and gave her knee a squeeze. Victoria couldn't tell whether it was to encourage her to speak or to keep quiet.

"Well, there are a lot of guns," Mary said. "I mean, it's, like, *everybody*. I even saw a little girl, maybe twelve, thirteen, years old, carrying a rifle. I don't think Adam and Eve had an arsenal."

"Don't you think maybe Abel wished he had a concealed club to defend himself with?" McCrea asked. He clearly meant it as a joke, but it face-planted.

He felt terrible that they'd be bringing a baby into a world that had turned to shit.

Emma placed her hand over Adam's and squeezed it. "This is a good thing, Adam," she said. "On the other side of all this, we're going to have a baby. A little human being."

"Who'll be born naked and without an instruction manual." How the hell were they going to care for it?

"As they have for tens of thousands of years. You need to cut yourself a break."

Adam stood abruptly and started to pace. He had something he needed to say, but he didn't want to. It had been festering for a few days now, and he knew it was going to upset Emma.

"What's wrong with you?" she asked.

"We can't do this, Em. Not on our own."

Emma's face darkened. "What are you saying?"

Adam started wandering a long circle around the fire. "We're fooling ourselves when we pretend that we can do everything that has to be done, and do it out here in the wilderness. We need to go into town."

"What town?"

"*Any* town. A place with a doctor. With food and warm clothes. Hell, with *diapers*. What did people do before there were diapers?"

Whatever Emma saw in Adam made her start to giggle.

"What's so funny?"

"Adam Emerson, you're one of the bravest people I've ever met. You've rescued us from fires, from murderers, from nuclear *war,* for God's sake. And your Achilles' heel is a creature that's likely to weigh less than eight pounds."

"I'm serious, Em. It's irresponsible for us to pretend that we know what we're doing."

"I thought you came from a family of preppers," Emma said. Her smile never faded. "You mean child-birth and infant care weren't part of the curriculum?"

"We're a family of three boys. It didn't come up, no."

"And at least one of those boys is quite fertile."

"Dammit, Em, I'm serious. We need to move out of here."

Emma rose to address him, eye to eye. "You know that's not an option. Anybody who sees us is going to hang us for murder. Or worse."

It was odd to hear how nonchalantly she could utter those words. In the early days after the war, they'd been attacked by crazed countryfolk. In the fight that followed, Emma and Adam had been forced to kill both of their attackers. Then, as they left the scene of the attack, the dead couple's family confronted them, triggering another gunfight. Adam didn't know if they'd killed anyone in that exchange, but he feared that they had.

"There won't be any trial," Emma continued, em-phasizing her point. "You said yourself that they're from around here and we're not. That makes us the bad guys no matter where we go."

"There's still gas in the Bronco," Adam said. "We can drive till we get to where no one's heard of us."

"That's even worse. The Bronco is probably the only working vehicle within fifty miles. We were in it that night and being in it now will be like hanging a confession around our necks."

"Well, we have to do something. Look at you. You're going to starve to death."

"I'm fine." The way she said it, though, Adam saw the first glimmer that she was scared, too.

He folded her into a hug. "We've got to get to people. We have to find a doctor for you."

Emma buried her face into Adam's shirt. She allowed herself to be hugged as she hugged him back. "I don't want any more killing," she said.

"I don't want that, either," Adam whispered. "But I can't promise it won't happen. All I can do is promise that I won't start the fight."

"We didn't start the last one."

"Yet here we are."

Emma leaned back to look him in the eye. "Is it ever going to stop?"

He pulled her in tighter. "The rules have changed," he said. "No law matters anymore. I don't imagine anybody gives much of a shit about courts. Every moment of every day is a negotiation. This is why I'm so sorry about the baby."

Emma pushed away from him. "Don't you dare!" she said.

The words startled him.

Emma placed her hands on her belly. "This baby is a new beginning. He won't know it's a shitty world unless we tell him it is. The world's going to be tough, but it's *his* world. It's his only frame of reference. If we make it a good place, then it'll be a good place."

Adam had never heard her go off like this before.

And she wasn't done. "We're not in the driver's seat for any of this, don't you see that? You're trying to engineer a solution, but there's no solution to be engineered. We're having a baby because God decided to give us a baby. That, and because we had a lot of really great sex."

That line caught him off guard and he laughed. On that, she was absolutely right. And, for the record, pregnancy hadn't changed that. Well, not until the puking started.

Emma rubbed her head and shoved her hands into the pockets of her too-thin jacket. "And you're probably right about giving in to winter," she said.

Adam threw his hands in the air and stepped back in feigned shock. "Wait. What? Did you just say I was right?"

"Don't let that go to your head, cowboy. But we can't go shooting our way out of here."

"We can if that's the only way." The thought of more killing sucked the lightness out of the mood. "We won't start any fights, but we can't walk away from them, either."

Emma's hands went to her belly, an unconscious protective move.

"You can't have it both ways, Em. If you believe that God gave him to us, you have to believe that He'll protect him, too."

They embraced again.

"How do we do this?" Emma asked, her voice muffled by Adam's shirt.

"Do what? The move?"

"Getting all the stuff we need back to the Bronco."

"The same way we got it here. We hump it out of the woods."

"Suppose it's not there anymore?" she asked.

"Where would it have gone? I hid it pretty well off the road. A bigger concern is whether or not a bear or some other critter is living in it."

Two hours later, they were done.

The Bronco was, in fact, right where he'd left it, and, yes, a family of squirrels had taken up residence on the floor behind the driver's seat. During the quick battle with the locals a few weeks ago, Adam had to shoot through the windshield, rendering it opaque. First chance they got, he'd pulled over and removed the whole windscreen. That's how the critters had gotten in, along with a lot of water from whatever rain had fallen over the past weeks.

Fortunately for Adam and Emma, yet unfortunately for the mama squirrel, they had a tasty lunch. A little gamy and sinewy, and it needed salt, but these days, everything needed salt.

Emma did her best to keep it down, but she couldn't.

Both of them wore Glock 19s in holsters on their belts, and they each had an AR-15 next to their seats. Adam also wore an old-school KA-BAR knife—a memory of his dad—on his belt on the left side. Their tent and what was left of the contents of Adam's rucksack lay in the cargo section. They'd filled jugs with water they'd boiled from the stream near their campsite and placed them next to the two 5-gallon jerry cans of gasoline that had been part of the Bronco's kit since Emma had first gotten it.

The dry snacks they'd started with were all gone now, but Adam had made about a half pound of venison jerky, which could keep them going in a pinch. So far, of all the hardships they'd faced since the beginning of this adventure, going hungry had not been one of them.

Until the puking started.

With the Bronco loaded, Adam climbed into the driver's seat, inserted the key and turned the ignition. The engine wasn't anxious to start. As it cranked, Adam could hear the oomph draining out of the battery. If this thing didn't turn over, they'd be screwed.

Ultimately the engine coughed to life and they were all set. With the hubs locked and the transmission in four-wheel drive, he was able to back out of the hidey-hole he'd built for it, and in less than a minute, he was back out onto the hard surface of the road.

The mechanical sound of the motor seemed out of place now. These days, silence ruled the air.

As Emma settled into the seat next to him, she said, "I bet people can hear us for miles."

Adam imagined she was right. "It's your truck," he said. "Do you want to drive?"

"Nah. This way, if I need to hurl, I can just lean out the window."

"What a pleasant thought."

He pushed the shifter into gear, engaged the clutch, and they were on their way. If only they knew where they were going.

CHAPTER ELEVEN

Hell Day + 45 (Two Days Earlier)

"**W**HY AREN'T WE FIGHTING THEM?" GARY ROUSE asked as the family rolled their bicycles out of the garage. "Are we just *giving* them our house? Our stuff?"

Frank heard the derision in his son's voice and it tore at him. "Take a look at your brother," he said. "They nearly killed him."

"I'm okay," Ronnie said.

"That's not your doing," Paula snapped. "That was bad aim on their part."

"We should call the police," Gary said.

"There are no police," Frank said. "And if there were, how would you suggest we call them?" He helped the others pull their bikes clear of the garage door and then joined them with his own.

His family stood in a loose arc, looking back at the house, where five of the armed invaders were staring them down, making sure that they got off the property.

"Your time is up in one minute!" Pritchard called from the front porch. "After that, we keep the bikes and the backpacks, too."

"We need guns!" Frank shouted. He heard the crack of emotion in his voice and it angered him. "We need to be able to protect ourselves!"

"Fifty-one seconds!" Pritchard made a show of looking at his wristwatch.

"What an asshole," Gary mumbled.

"Shush," Paula snapped. "This is not a time for heroics."

"If not now, when?" Ronnie asked. The effort from speaking made him wince and touch his side.

"You gonna be okay?" Frank asked.

Ronnie didn't answer. He swung a leg over the seat and headed off down the hill. Gary followed directly behind and Frank and Paula together brought up the rear.

"You had no choice, Frank," Paula said. "There are too many of them. It's only a house. It's only stuff. It's not worth dying over."

"Suppose we offer to join them?" Frank said. As he heard the words, he felt a glimmer of hope. "You know, instead of fighting them."

Paula looked horrified. "We need to get off the land," she said. But she clearly wanted to say more.

She kicked off on her bike. After a quick look back at the home they'd built over fifteen years, he took off after her. The family was waiting for him at the end of the driveway. The boys were straddling their bicycles and Paula was standing next to hers.

"What do we do now?" Gary asked.

Ronnie looked a bit pale, and that concerned Frank.

It didn't look like shock—at least not yet—but it was something to keep track of.

Frank had no idea what to do next. He looked to Paula.

"We ride to Ortho," she said. "It's only a few miles down the road."

"It's *twenty* miles down the road," Ronnie corrected. "Maybe twenty-five."

"I'm open to suggestions," Paula snapped.

"Stop," Frank said. "This is so surreal. So stupid. What the hell are we doing?"

"We're surrendering to the inevitable, Frank," Paula said. "Those people up there are crazy. They're capable of anything. Trying to fight them would be like putting a gun to your own head and pulling the trigger."

"Like Dad said, maybe we could ask to stay," Ronnie said. "You know, maybe we could offer to become one of them."

"We are *not* doing that," Paula said. "We will not stoop to that level of depravity. We are better than that."

"We've got no *home,*" Ronnie said. "We've got no food, we've got no tents. We don't even have sleeping bags. What the hell are we supposed to do?"

"Watch your mouth," she said, earning a look that said, *Are you kidding me?* "Are those people what you want to become? Those *animals*? Do you want to be one of the people raiding other people's homes and stealing their things?"

The thought crossed Frank's mind that in times of crisis, sometimes what you *wanted* needed to take a backseat to what you *had no choice* but to do. It wasn't that long ago that people ignored hateful, violent acts that they knew to be wrong merely out of fear of being shamed on social media by their neighbors. That was accepted behavior. How was it so wrong to hurt those same neighbors when the stakes were your very survival?

But he knew better than to express those thoughts. Certainly not now.

"Is starving and freezing to death any better?" Gary asked.

Paula answered without hesitation: "Yes. There's a time coming for each of us when we'll have to look Jesus in the eye and atone for what we did while we were here on earth. The Rouse family is not going to make victims of other people."

"So we roll over and just let ourselves *be* victims?" Gary asked. "We just say, *Kick me in the balls and take my stuff*? And while you're at it, *Rape my sister, too*?"

"Gary!"

"What! I don't have a sister. The point is—"

"I know what your point is," Paula said.

Frank tried to intervene. "Hey, guys, this isn't accomplishing anything. We need to get going if—"

"Tell him, Frank," Paula insisted. "Tell him that he's wrong."

Frank wanted this talk to stop. It was a stupid time for a stupid argument. But it was also the wrong time to lie. "I don't know that he is, honey," he said. "The moral high ground doesn't provide a lot of physical protection. If you have to do bad things to survive—"

"Don't say it," she said. "If you say the words, I'll never be able to un-hear them." She pushed her bike forward to make room to climb on. "I'm going to Ortho," she announced. "You guys choose whether it's better for me to drive twenty miles alone, or for you to maybe have a place to sleep, but at the cost of your souls."

Frank and the boys mounted their bikes and followed.

CHAPTER TWELVE

Hell Day + 48 (Three Days Later)

ADAM UPENDED THE NOW-EMPTY JERRY CAN AND LET the last few drops of gasoline drip into the funnel that he'd inserted into the filler tube. "That's it," he said, and he tucked the empty can back into its slot. In the weeks since the war, they'd burned through whatever gas had been left in the tank when the bombs dropped, plus two 5-gallon jerry cans.

"How much do you think we have in the tank?" Emma asked.

"Not a clue. All I know is that the extra is all gone. When it runs out, we're walking." There was no way to know. The gas gauge in the old Bronco hadn't worked for the entire time that Emma had owned it, and Adam had been fanatical about never letting it run dry. Thus, he'd refilled partially empty tanks over and over.

The Bronco had been their lifeboat. Without it, they never would have survived the fires that swept through the forests after the bombings. And with it, they'd been able to stock up on weapons and ammo and food from ruined stores. Soon, once the gas was gone, they'd have to make tough decisions about what to take and what to leave behind.

But that was for later. If there was one lesson that had been driven home by recent events, it was that any plan that tried to see more than, say, twenty minutes into the future was just a guess. There was no way to know what lay ahead. That was what survival was all about, he figured: dealing with *now* as best he could, with a jaundiced eye toward what might come next. On balance, he thought they were doing okay.

"Do you recognize where we are?" he asked when he climbed back into the cab.

"Somewhere in West Virginia?" The roads in this part of the world pretty much looked identical. Narrow and winding, with occasional glimpses of breathtaking overlooks.

"The road we'll pass in about a mile is where it happened," Adam said.

For a few seconds, Emma didn't get it. And then she did. "Oh, my God." It was the intersection past the cluster of houses where they'd had the shoot-out that banished them to the woods. "What if they see us?"

"We need to be ready for that," he said. He nodded to the AR-15 that was wedged muzzle down next to her seat. As he did, he lifted his own from next to his leg and propped the barrel shroud on the ledge that used to be their windshield. "If they shoot, we shoot."

"Let's shoot over their heads," Emma said. "I don't want to kill anybody."

"Shoot wherever you like. Just know that they're not going to be as kind."

All Adam knew of the people they'd been forced to shoot was that they called each other Janey and Tommy, and that they had kin who lived a couple hundred yards up the road that the Bronco would soon be passing. All that kin knew was that Janey and Tommy had gone up to steal the Bronco and had never come down. They had no way of knowing that Adam and Emma were not the aggressors.

"What do you think?" he asked. "Should I sneak past and try not to make noise, or just own it and blast through?"

Emma answered without hesitation. "I say blast through. There's only one working motor within God only knows how many miles. I figure they already know we're coming. It's not like they have a lot else to do, you know?"

Adam wasn't sure that last part was true, but he didn't say anything.

He shifted into gear, popped the clutch and took off. As he topped sixty miles per hour, he realized that he would not be doing any shooting. If it came to that, return fire would be Emma's responsibility. He was going to concentrate on driving. The Bronco handled like the *Titanic,* requiring huge movements in the steering to produce any response from the wheels. In normal conditions, that wasn't a big deal, but at higher speeds, on narrow roads, all that slop imparted a zigzag pattern that must have looked like a sine curve from above.

The woods were a blur as they whipped by. He didn't

dare a glance at the speedometer, and he sure as hell didn't sneak a peek to see if the goobers up the road were going to take a shot at him. If they did, he'd know it by other means.

As the intersection approached, he had the terrible thought that they might have put up a roadblock. It would make sense, wouldn't it? As Emma said, precious few cars were functioning after the war, so if they figured the couple that killed their family might drive back by this way, it would only make sense to set up a barrier to stop them.

"We're past it!" Emma shouted over the roar of the engine. "You can slow down."

Not yet, he couldn't. Depending on the gun, bullets could be deadly two miles downrange, and they traveled at three thousand feet per second.

As he navigated a sharp curve to the right, he downshifted and allowed the engine compression to slow him down some, but when the road straightened out, he was back on the gas—with a little lighter foot than before, but still with more speed than he wanted.

After he drifted through another sharp curve, this one to the left, he backed off. He had about a million tons of mountain between him and any shooter from the houses. He figured that was enough.

Adam downshifted again, to back the speed way down. "I didn't hear any shots. Did you?"

Emma had one hand on the Jesus bar on her side of the dash and the other wrapped around the grip of her rifle. "Dying by flipping the truck is pretty much the same as dying from getting shot," she said. Her eyes were two huge circles.

Adam's heart was trying to escape his chest, so he got where she was coming from. But he'd much rather die in a car wreck than be shot, and he had no idea why.

"How are you feeling?" he asked. It was more about changing the subject than actual curiosity, though it had been a long time since the last time she puked.

"Being out and around makes me feel better," she said. "Maybe because I have other things to think about."

"Like dying in a car wreck," he joked.

"Exactly like that." Thirty seconds passed before she asked, "Are we going to be going back through Mountain View?"

"I think we're gonna have to," Adam said. "We won't stop, though."

The once-tiny burg of Mountain View, West Virginia, had been their home before the war started. Emma was a student at the Joan of Arc Academy, which was situated down the road from Adam's alma mater, the Clinton M. Hedrick Military Academy. They'd met at a chaperoned event, dated for a few months and were camping together when the world caught fire. It had taken Adam forever to screw up the courage to ask her out, and he was shocked to learn that she'd been waiting for him to do it. Lust ran strong from their first moments together, but the relationship had grown to so much more since the night of the attacks. They'd barely escaped the forest with their lives. Upon returning to Mountain View, they found that a raging inferno had burned their classmates alive in their dorms.

Of all the awful scenes they had endured together since this nightmare began, the image of his friends' charred remains was the one he most wished he could erase from his brain.

"Is there a way to avoid Mountain View?" Emma asked.

"We don't want to go to the cities," he said. "They'll be hotter than Chernobyl. I know there are some small towns on the other side of Mountain View. Hopefully, we'll find a doctor and supplies there."

"You know they're going to want the Bronco in trade for anything we ask for, right?"

"They're not going to get it."

"That means more fighting."

Adam made a growling sound. "Probably," he said. Violence was the one constant for the future—perhaps for the rest of their lives, even if they pulled off some miracle and lived a long time. "Two choices, remember? We can be victims or victors. That's it. Nothing in between."

"Is that something you learned during your childhood training?"

"I think it probably came up," he said, "but the last weeks have been a master class, don't you think? There's something to be said for us still being alive."

"I just am not sure it had to go down that way."

Emma placed her hand on Adam's, atop the gear shifter, and squeezed it.

Adam smiled.

Mountain View lay at the corner of Routes 44 and 54, in the heart of Coal Country. The fire had ravaged the town, but on the day after the attacks, while the buildings there were still smoldering, Adam had been able to salvage weapons, ammo and food from the hardware store where he'd worked during the summers. He even was able to purloin a few sticks of dynamite and primers, though he had no idea what he might use them for.

That strip of commercial buildings lay directly ahead as they approached the intersection. It appeared that they had collapsed even further since the last time they drove through here. All that remained—where anything remained at all—were the charred brick and stone façades.

"I wonder what became of the Chaney family," Emma said. A local man and his two grown sons had taken an interest in the Bronco while lodging strong objections to them helping themselves to the contents of the hardware store.

"Oh, my God," Adam said, then quickly added, "Don't look."

The burned bodies they'd encountered weeks ago still remained where they'd fallen, but scavengers had gotten to them. What was left was awful to look at.

"Just keep going," Emma said. "Until we're beyond the fire damage, there's going to be a lot of that, I'm sure."

The next twenty miles or so were tough to take. It was like driving into a nightmare. Nothing lived through the fires. Trees were charred black, and even the roadway was scorched. What looked like it might be black ice on the pavement was actually melted and resolidified asphalt. The atmosphere smelled of destruction. The stench of burned hair seemed to have bonded with air molecules.

Adam didn't dare accelerate past fifteen or twenty miles per hour in here for fear of slamming into a deadfall or breaking an axle in the huge divots that the heat had made in the asphalt. As they drove through the moonscape of destruction, a rooster tail of soot and God only knew what else followed them.

"We are literally the only living things here," he said aloud.

He looked over and noted the tears on Emma's cheeks. The awfulness was beyond measurement.

Then, finally, life began to reassert itself. As the charring became less all-inclusive, the first life-forms they saw were turkey buzzards as they circled and soared overhead.

"At least they get enough to eat," Emma said with a humorless chuckle.

Over the next three miles, color returned to the world. Black gave way to brown, which then dissolved into green, but the smell of death remained in Adam's nose. He hoped it was more about some kind of sensory memory than it was a disgusting new reality.

Buildings began to appear on the horizon. Most were empty, some were dilapidated, but a few were sound and displayed signs of life. As they drove on, signs of a community heartbeat continued to grow and multiply. People came to their doors at the sound of the approaching vehicle. Some waved, but all looked startled.

"Ignore them," Adam said. "Don't engage."

"Why not? They're not threatening us."

"*Everybody* is threatening us until they prove that they're not. We keep going until we get to whatever the first town is, and then we take stock."

"We have to trust somebody sometime," Emma said.

"We'll start tomorrow," Adam said. Fewer interactions meant less risk. Hard stop. And it wouldn't be different tomorrow.

Emma jumped in her seat and pointed through the opening where the windshield had once been. "Look out!" she yelled.

Adam saw it at the same instant. A skinny middle-aged man wearing ratty jeans and a tan farm coat was pushing an old Chrysler minivan from his driveway across the road, blocking its entire width. Adam stood on the brakes and the clutch and skidded the Bronco to a halt.

"Get your weapon ready," he said.

He pulled the parking brake and his door handle at the same time and within seconds was standing on the road, his M4 ready at his shoulder. Emma opened her door, but remained inside the Bronco.

The man in the farm coat raised his hands and waved them over his head. "Don't shoot! Please don't shoot!"

Adam thumbed the selector to SAFE, but held his aim. "Get that van out of our way, please." He tried to find the right mix between friendly and authoritarian.

"I heard there was still runnin' cars," the man said. "We heard you comin' from a mile away. What's your name, young man?"

"You first."

"My name is Orrin Hornsby. This is my house, my car."

"You could've killed us, Mr. Hornsby."

"Can I put my hands down, please?"

"I'm not looking for a fight, sir," Adam said. "Please don't start one. You can put your hands down."

As Hornsby lowered his hands, other people wandered from their homes into the street. They seemed far more curious than threatening, but Adam thumbed the switch back to FIRE, just to be sure.

"Y'all please stay back," he said. "We haven't met, and none of us knows what the other's intent is. Please let's just keep our distance."

A kid in coveralls stepped forward. He was about Adam's age, but looked far less healthy. "That the red-and-white Bronco we been hearin' about?"

"Hard to know what you've been hearing," Adam said.

"You killed a bunch of people?"

A woman who might have been the kid's mother bolted from the crowd. "Anse, don't you dare! You don't talk to strangers that way."

Anse shook free from his mother's grasp. "How come your truck still works and mine don't?"

"Because it's old," Adam said. "No computer to get fried."

"D-do you know what happened?" the kid asked. "Why this is happening?"

"I think there was a war," Adam said.

"With who?" That question came from a middle-aged woman dressed in the jeans and flannel of a man.

"I don't know, ma'am," Adam said. "Are y'all all right?"

"We're dyin'," the boy said. "It was the fire, I think. It just kept comin' and comin'. Ain't nothin' alive anymore."

A voice from behind asked, "Where are you goin', son?"

Adam whirled to see a man with a half-black, half-gray beard who'd approached to within ten feet without him noticing. When he saw Adam's reaction, he stepped back and held out his hands. "No need to be jumpy like that. We ain't here to do you no harm."

There were too many of them, and they were situated at too many compass points for Adam to take them all in a fight.

"Where am I now?" Adam asked, changing the subject.

"Appleton County," the man said. "Fifteen miles from Appleton proper. Is that where you're headin'?"

"We're heading to where there are people," Adam said. "Appleton is straight ahead, then?"

"Yes, it is, but you be careful. All these supplies you got, you're gonna get plucked like a chicken."

"I'll be careful," Adam said. He considered asking whether there was a doctor in Appleton, but decided against it. To ask about a doctor would project weakness.

The man with the beard stuck out his hand. "I'm Dirk Harris."

Adam tipped his head, but did not accept the proffered handshake. "Adam. That's my girlfriend, Emma."

"Those folks over there are my wife, Brienne, and my boy, Darrin." He pointed to people at the back of the gathered crowd.

"Pleased to meet you."

"I don't believe you are, son," Dirk said with a laugh. "And I can't say as I blame you. Orrin's hello wasn't the most hospitable I've ever seen, but I imagine he thought he had to stop you."

Here it comes, Adam thought. His finger hovered just outside the trigger guard.

"Orrin's niece is sick," Dirk continued. "I don't

know what it is, exactly, but she needs medications to live."

Adam waited for it. He and Emma were not a delivery service, and the Bronco was not an ambulance. "I'm sorry to hear that."

From behind, a voice called, "Here she is!" It was Orrin Hornsby, and a little girl of about seven or eight stood next to him.

Adam turned toward the sound, then pivoted back to Dirk. "Would you mind stepping back and giving me some space, Mr. Harris? As you might be able to tell, I'm not in a comfortable place."

"Certainly," Dirk said. "I understand completely."

Adam circled to the front of the Bronco so that he could see as many compass points as possible. "Now, then," he said. "Who's the girl?"

"This is my niece, Lisa," Hornsby said. "Lisa Barnes." Blond and freckled, she wore jeans and sneakers and a jacket that clearly belonged to someone else. It looked as if it had consumed her. Adam guessed that someone in the house had tried to cut her hair with scissors that were too dull to do the job.

Her color was wrong. Too red in the cheeks, too gray around her nose and mouth.

Emma got out of the Bronco, leaving her rifle on the seat. "Hi, Lisa," she said. "My name's Emma. The grouchy guy with the rifle is Adam. He's nicer than he looks."

As he watched Emma shake hands with the little girl, Adam's Spidey senses went nuts. Not only were they in the middle of a threatening situation, but Emma had made it exponentially worse by stepping within grabbing distance.

Emma addressed Hornsby. "Your neighbor said she's sick?"

"I have diabetes," Lisa said. Her voice was little more than a whisper, and the effort to speak seemed to tire her.

Hornsby elaborated. "That's exactly right." He put his hand on Lisa's shoulder, and she looked up at him even as she leaned into his side. "This beautiful little girl needs insulin to survive. She was staying here with us on the night of the fires, while her parents went on a date." He grew uncomfortable and cleared his throat. "Well, you know what I mean, right?"

"Yes, sir," Emma said. She stooped to get eye to eye with Lisa. "Parents all need a break from time to time."

"Right. Well, that was weeks ago, you know? We keep an emergency supply of insulin here, and she brought some with her, but it's not enough. Not nearly enough. We've been rationing out what's left, a little at a time to keep her from . . ."

"I get it," Emma said.

Adam saw where this was going, and he moved quickly to intervene. "Um, Emma? Can we talk, please?"

"In a minute," she said. She didn't even make eye contact. To Hornsby: "Does she have more insulin at home?"

"She says yes, but I can't confirm that."

"What about a doctor?"

"Maybe down in Appleton, but I don't know if they have a supply. I imagine everybody's scratching at the same post, if you know what I mean."

"Excuse me," Adam said. "I think I know where this is going, so let me ask you: If the town is only fifteen miles away, why haven't you just walked there and taken her home?"

Hornsby's features screwed into a derisive, patronizing sneer. "Know a lot about diabetes, do you, son?"

Adam felt himself puffing up for a fight, but backed away from it. "No, sir, I don't."

"It's a balancing act in her blood," Hornsby said. "If she eats too much or eats carbohydrates, her sugar levels go up and her need for insulin increases. Exercise requires energy. If she doesn't have enough food, then the body will start turning her own body tissues into sugar and you have the same problem. And before you ask, I don't know why her mama and daddy ain't been up here to fetch her."

"So, what's the . . ."

Emma shot him a look that froze his words in his throat.

As if he could read Adam's mind, Hornsby's eyes reddened. "She needs to be with her family," he said.

Oh, shit, Adam thought. This poor girl was dying.

Emma spoke quickly. "So, Lisa, you want to come with us so we can take you home?"

"I don't know the way," she whispered.

"I can give you directions," Hornsby said. "Come on, Lisa, let's go inside and get your stuff."

As Hornsby walked away, the gathered townspeople went to work pushing the minivan back out of the road.

Adam slung his rifle over his shoulder and walked to Emma.

"Don't you dare say no to this," Emma snapped.

Adam recoiled.

"This is how the world becomes kind again," she said. "We do favors for other people."

"I'm not arguing with you," Adam said. "But what if . . ." This time, he stopped talking on his own without the withering glare.

"*What if* is *what if*," Emma said. "And before you ask, I don't *know* how we're going to feed her when we can barely feed ourselves." She placed her hands on her belly. "But there's a lesson we'll have to learn pretty soon, anyway."

Jesus, what kind of monster did she think he was? He lowered his voice till it was barely audible. "Do you really think I'd let a child die because she's . . . *inconvenient*?"

His question seemed to startle her. She kissed his cheek. "You're gonna be a great dad."

In less than a minute, the minivan had been pushed back into the driveway from which it had been launched. All nine of the surrounding neighbors formed an expectant half circle, waiting for Hornsby and Lisa to re-emerge from the front door.

She had a backpack with her now, and a well-loved stuffed beagle that she held in a way that made Adam wonder if she thought it might float out of her arms.

With wobbly legs, she had difficulty negotiating the front steps, but Hornsby helped her.

Once on the street, Lisa and her uncle walked from one neighbor to the next, accepting hugs and returning them. Every face showed sadness through valiant efforts to smile.

Dirk Harris was last in the line, and when it was his turn, he scooped Lisa off her feet into a giant bear hug. He held her close and kissed her cheek before putting her back down. "You be safe now," he said, but his voice didn't work very well. "Come and visit us again."

Then it was Adam's turn. That tiny creature craned her neck to see him and said, "I'm sorry."

Something in Adam's throat solidified, and he shot a look to Emma, silently begging for help.

Emma picked Lisa up into a hug. "You've got nothing to apologize for," she said. "We're both glad you can join us for our trip."

Hornsby handed a folded sheet of paper to Adam. "You'll get to the driveway before you get to the town," he said. "These are the directions. You're going to see an old mill building on the left side of the road. It's falling in on itself. When you pass that, start paying attention to your right-hand side. There'll be a long split-rail fence that's marked with Posted signs. That's Jacob's property—Lisa's dad. When the fence ends, that's the driveway. It don't look like much from the road, but trust me, it's there. Turn up the drive, and theirs is the only house you'll see. Nearest neighbor is probably two thousand feet away."

Adam glanced at the note and was pleased to see that most of those details were written there.

"I need a car seat," Lisa said.

Emma kissed her forehead. "Not for this trip, you don't. How about I hold you on my lap?"

"Mommy says that's dangerous." Still, she offered no further objection as Emma climbed into the Bronco and hugged her close to her chest.

"I can't thank you enough for this," Hornsby said. He handed over a plastic garbage bag that weighed nearly nothing. "This is all that's left of her insulin. She hasn't gotten a full dose since two or three days after the fires. That's when we realized that this could be a long slog."

"So, how much do we give her?"

Hornsby's shoulders climbed to his ears. "I don't know what to tell you. Our approach has not been scientific. I don't know what the right balance point is. Hopefully, there'll be a doctor in Appleton."

"And if there's not?"

Hornsby looked at the ground. "She needs to be with her family, son."

Words failed. She was so . . . *young*.

"Terrible times, Adam," Hornsby said. "Horrible times."

Adam took the bag and unslung his rifle. As he turned to join the ladies, Hornsby put his hand on his arm. "You be careful, okay?"

"That's always the goal."

Hornsby lowered his voice and pivoted Adam away from the others. "One other thing," he said. "Times like these bring a lot of rumors, you know. And one of 'em is that a boy and a girl, just like you, who was drivin' a Bronco, just like that, killed some boys up on the mountain."

Adam felt color rise in his ears.

"I ain't tellin' you as a threat or nothin' like that," Hornsby said. "Them hill folk can be rough as cobs, and you two don't look like the murderin' sort. Hell, I'm handin' you some damned precious cargo. I just want you to be aware."

How could the news have traveled so far in just a few weeks? Adam didn't reply because he didn't know what to say.

Dirk was waiting for him at the driver's-side door. He offered his hand again, and this time, Adam took it. "I know you're scared, son," Dirk said. "But you're doing the right thing. You're earning a place with the Lord when the time comes."

Adam pressed his lips together to keep the emotion in.

Dirk continued, "It's okay to feel things, Adam. Do yourself a favor and try to remember that." He let go and stepped away. "Good luck."

Adam slid in behind the wheel and handed the folded instructions to Emma. "You're the navigator," he said.

"Thank you for doing this," Emma said.

"I just found out that I'm earning a place with the Lord," he said. "Let's just hope I don't meet Him too soon."

Adam engaged the clutch and eased away from the crowd. By the time he was up to speed, Lisa was already asleep.

CHAPTER THIRTEEN

Hell Day + 46 (Two Days Earlier)

"THIS IS A NICE HOUSE," PRITCHARD SAID AS HE flopped into an overstuffed blue-and-pink plaid sofa and crossed his boots across the top of the coffee table. Unlike most of the other houses in Appleton, this one did not have a monotonous faux-Colonial look. The Rouses' place was old and solid, but it had seen recent renovations. The kitchen, in particular, looked as if it had had a recent makeover. The firebox in the family room fireplace had been refitted with a woodstove, so as the weather cooled, this room would get toasty.

Andy Linx helped himself to the matching recliner, which had been set kitty-corner to the sofa. All around them, the sounds of scavenging made casual conversation difficult.

"Why did you let them live?" Andy asked.

"Who?"

"The people who lived here."

"Why would I kill them?"

"You wounded the boy, you took their property. They're gonna be pissed."

Pritchard laughed. "Do you have any idea how many pissed people there are in this town now? A lot more than *aren't* pissed. But they're also scared."

"I wouldn't get cocky if I were you," Andy said. "Just because we've taken their weapons doesn't mean that they don't have tons of shit that we haven't found. Push them too hard and they'll rise up against you."

"Against *us,* you mean."

Andy blushed. "Yes, of course. Push them too hard and they'll rise up against *us.*"

"I'm not worried," Pritchard said. "Have you seen any sign of an organized response from the fine people of Appleton? Have you met a single person who looks anything like a leader? Individuals don't take on crowds in armed combat. And if they do, or if they try, we'll cut them to pieces."

"Look what's happening already," Andy said. "You've got people roving the streets like packs of dogs. If they find a way to organize—"

"Why on earth would they come against us wolves when they can terrorize all the sheep they want? That makes no sense."

Andy started to answer, but Pritchard silenced him with a raised palm. "Besides, half our numbers started out in those dog packs. Sooner or later, more will join. They'll learn that it's a lot better to fight with us, and that you'll live longer if you don't fight *against* us."

The better part of a minute passed in silence. Andy looked uncomfortable as he crossed and recrossed his legs.

"Are you going to get to what you're here to talk about or not?" Pritchard asked.

"It's the elephant in the room," Andy said.

"That town upstream?"

"Right. Our troops want revenge," Andy said.

"Revenge is a stupid reason to take up arms. Maybe the stupidest. Too much emotion gets people killed. They take chances that they shouldn't."

"So we do nothing about them?"

"I don't think we'll have that luxury," Pritchard said. "Too many people are leaving here and heading to Ortho."

"I've talked to a few who've gone the other way," Andy said. "Come here from there. Apparently, they've really got their shit together. Some former congress-woman is in charge."

"Congresswoman, huh? I guess that was the bitch with the rifle? She's not the one I worry about. It's all those others with rifles and damn good marksmanship that worry me."

"Maybe we should just leave them alone," Andy said. "You know, leave things the way they are."

"We can't do that," Pritchard said. "They're going to hear the stories of your packs of dogs, and the people they inherit from Appleton will demand some kind of action. If we don't go to them, they'll just come to us."

"Then let's dig in," Andy said. "Go defensive and let them come to us."

Pritchard liked the idea in principle, but knew that it wouldn't work in Appleton. "If we organize the dog packs, we can get numbers and we can motivate them to attack. Just spin up enough with the hope of food and they'll walk into a propeller blade for me. But settling in for a defensive posture takes discipline that lasts longer than the moment. There's no way we can make soldiers out of them. Hell, even our own guardsmen have lost their military discipline. We've got to act first, before Ortho does. We need to build up our numbers and take the fight to them. If we do it right, we'll take them out when they're asleep."

"How can that work if you think they're organized and good?"

"Because they won't be expecting it," Pritchard said. "The double reverse."

"When?"

"Sooner than later. Not tomorrow, maybe next week."

Andy shifted uncomfortably. "I don't know, Cole. If they're organized and we just rush them, we're going to have a very, very bad day."

"That's not what I'm suggesting," Pritchard said. The whole truth was that he hadn't given much thought to this at all until right now as he spoke. He knew that it was a thing that needed to be taken care of, but his priority had been—and remained—to bring more organization to Appleton.

Pritchard said, "We need to know what Ortho's capabilities are. We need to know just how armed and organized they are."

"You mean espionage?" Andy asked.

"That's exactly what I mean."

"Ortho is what, twenty miles from here?" Andy griped. "A day's walk, even with a horse. How are we going to send a mole down there with those kinds of distances? It would take too long and be dangerous as shit for whoever we send in to spy."

"I'm not suggesting that we *wait* for people to give us information," Pritchard said. "I'm suggesting that we go down there and take it."

"How?"

"Well, let's talk about that."

CHAPTER FOURTEEN

Hell Day + 48 (Two Days Later)

"WHAT WAS THE QUIET CONVERSATION ALL ABOUT with Mr. Hornsby?" Emma asked. Lisa had not moved.

"Nothing important," Adam replied. "But it's something we need to discuss in private."

"She's sound asleep."

Adam gave her a look. "Trust me on this?"

Emma pointed ahead and to the left, then glanced down at the sheet of directions. "Is that the old mill?"

A brick structure with a near-collapsed roof stood fifty feet off the road, where it was being consumed by what must have been a mile of creepers and kudzu.

"I guess?" Adam said. "Keep an eye out . . . There it is." He pointed out across her nose. "That's the fence."

There was a lot of it, all split rail and chicken wire, leading Adam to conclude that there were dogs or other critters that the owner was trying to keep from wandering off. There was something to admire in that, he supposed.

Hornsby was right to warn about the driveway being at the end of the fence. At speed, it would have looked like a small clearing, but because Adam had been anticipating it, he saw the tire marks in the shoulder of the road, and the gravel drive beyond them. He had to slow nearly to a stop to make the turn, and after that, it was like riding a paint shaker. They bounced all over the interior of the Bronco as they negotiated what became a steep hill after about fifty yards.

"Is she still sleeping through all of this?" Adam asked.

"Even her breathing pattern hasn't changed," Emma said. "Poor little thing."

Adam saw the bonding that was happening, and it brought feelings of sadness and anger. There was no way this was going to end well for Lisa in the long run. He had a friend back at the academy who was constantly checking his sugar levels, and he'd shared with Adam the dire importance of keeping current. Mr. Hornsby was right. It was important for Lisa to be with her family now.

The house sat atop a cleared acre or so of hilltop, with a good view of the valley below. As they approached, the Bronco crossed a charming little brick-and-timber bridge that arched over a stream. The flow wasn't much at the moment, but the width of the streambed spoke of quite a torrent when it rained.

"Should I wake her?" Emma asked.

"Doesn't look like you could if you wanted to," Adam said. "No, let me go up and talk to them first."

"Maybe you should keep the guns down here, so they won't get frightened."

"I'll keep the gun *with* me, so *I* don't get frightened." He said it with enough of a smile not to start an argument.

Adam tried to be quiet as he exited the Bronco and strode up the walk toward the front door. The structure defined his vision of what a farmhouse was supposed to look like. Three steps led up to a porch that wrapped every angle of the house that he could see. The second floor featured three shed dormers. Except for a couple of spots where the paint had begun to dull and peel around the gutters, the place appeared to be in good shape. The wooden steps to the porch didn't even groan when he climbed them.

He cast a look back at Emma, then walked to the front door and knocked. He waited thirty seconds and knocked again. He had a bad feeling.

Just for grins, he walked back down off the porch and over to the detached garage. The doors wouldn't lift—he figured they had an electric opener—so he stood on tiptoes to look through the windows in the door panels. Two late-model pickup trucks sat inside, too young not to be dead.

What to do next? If he entered the house without being asked, he would be inviting another fight. Clearly, the family hadn't driven off anywhere, but he supposed they could have walked into town. Or maybe they were working in the yard somewhere. Or they could be off hunting or fishing. Shit, they could be anywhere.

Adam decided to check the backyard. As he turned the corner from the side of the house to the back of the house, his bad feeling transformed to sheer dread. About fifty yards from the back wall, a bunch of turkey buzzards were chowing down on something. The breeze brought the stench of rotting animal.

"Oh, shit," he moaned. He stopped and looked back, but the house stood between him and Emma. He considered going back and telling her that no one was home and then returning Lisa to her uncle, but he couldn't do that. Plus, as much as he didn't want to see, he still needed to know.

He brought his rifle to low ready, just in case, and approached the birds slowly, dreadfully. They were such god-awful creatures that it was hard not to blast them to hell. But he knew better. They saved countless human lives by consuming the bacteria-ridden remains of other dead animals. Still, it was tempting.

As he closed the distance, Adam told himself that the buzzards could be chowing down on anything. It didn't have to be a human, though from the intensity of the stench and the sheer number of birds, whatever the meal was, it was large.

As he closed to within twenty or thirty feet, the buzzards got spooked and flew away. Once they were gone, Adam at first didn't see anything. Closer still, and he saw the body of a man whose face and much of his head had been blasted away by the shotgun that lay lengthwise down his chest and abdomen. What the buzzards hadn't consumed was bloated and black.

Adam's stomach churned. He took a step back, turned and retched, but everything stayed down.

The man whom he presumed to be Lisa's father had dug his own grave and lain in it to kill himself. The overburden from the four-foot rectangular hole lay mounded at the edge, though much of it had been spread about by scavengers. A D-handled spade lay on the ground.

"Holy shit," Adam muttered.

Taking a few more steps back to gather himself for the task of filling the grave, Adam let his rifle fall against its sling and he planted his hands on his hips, the web between his right thumb and forefinger embracing the grip of his holstered pistol.

He took in the surroundings. A swing sat in the middle of the yard, and three bicycles rested in a stack near a sloped storm cellar door. Two were boys' bikes and the third was a girl's.

Oh, no, no, no . . .

Where were the boys? For that matter, where was their mom? Was that why no one answered the door? Were their bodies scattered somewhere inside? How much of a monster was this guy, whose name, Adam only now realized, he didn't remember?

This—this right here—this kind of bizarre behavior and cruelty—was the reason why you didn't enter people's lives just because someone asked you to. You get sucked into drama that you never wanted and observe things that you can never un-see.

Now he was going to have to search the interior of the house to find child-sized corpses and afterward dispose of them. Or he could just burn the house down with them inside. Wouldn't that accomplish the same goal?

And what of little Lisa? What the hell was going to happen to her now?

"God *damn* it." He kicked the ground.

As he turned to look back at the open grave, he noticed three rectangles of upturned dirt separated from each other by maybe five feet. The mounds had settled some, but not much.

This just got worse. "What the *hell* did you do?"

He caught a flash of white through the corner of his eye and turned to see what appeared to be an envelope enclosed in a plastic lunch bag. It had been nailed to a tree near the open grave with the point of a locking-blade knife.

Adam stared at it, not moving for the better part of a minute. Intuitively, he knew that it was a suicide note, and instinctively, he wanted nothing to do with it. He didn't give half a shit why this guy had offed his family and then killed himself. Knowing wouldn't change anything, but it would draw Adam in deeper to the place where he never wanted to be in the first place.

He found himself hating the dead man. No matter how bad things got—no matter how bad you *think* they've gotten—there was always a way to win. The harder it got, the harder you worked. But you *never* gave up. And you sure as hell don't give up on behalf of others who never had a chance.

If Adam had a brain in his head, he would have ripped the package from the tree and thrown it into the hole, where this entire chapter of the ongoing nightmare that was his life could be buried forever.

But he didn't and he couldn't.

"Adam? Is everything okay?"

He whirled to see Emma emerging from the side of the house, Lisa's hand in hers.

"No," Adam snapped. He moved toward them with his arms spread, as a bouncer would move if he wanted to push revelers off the velvet rope. "You can't be here," he said.

Emma's eyes flashed fear.

"What's wrong?" Lisa asked. "I'm scared."

Adam pleaded silently with his eyes. *She can't be here. She can't see this.*

There was no way to know if Emma had gotten the whole message, or even the right message, but she caught the subtext.

"I'm okay," Adam said. "That's not it."

"Got it," Emma said. She bent and picked up Lisa. "Everything's fine. Let's go back to the car."

"I want to go inside."

Adam shook his head, nearly an imperceptible twitch, but Emma understood. "No, show me around your front yard, sweetie." They disappeared back toward the front.

"Ah, screw it," Adam said aloud. "Time to cowboy up."

Under the circumstances, he decided that the letter could wait. His first task had to be to make sure that Lisa would never see the horror that he'd seen. As bad and broken as the world was, she'd earned the right to remember her father with a face.

Filling the grave took all of five minutes. Because more of the dirt had been scattered than he'd expected, the resulting filled hole left a dimple in the ground rather than a mound. He'd considered plucking the shotgun out of the hole and adding it to his arsenal, but he didn't need that kind of bad juju.

Adam tossed the shovel to the side, into a tangle of weeds along the line where the lawn transitioned to woods. He dislodged the packaged envelope from the tree, folded the knife, then pocketed both before heading up to the house to check the interior. By now, he was convinced that he'd find no bodies, but he wanted to be sure. If he was right, then he could let Emma and Lisa come inside.

The inside of the house was much brighter and more modern than he'd expected, judging from the outside. Where he'd expected lots of tiny squares and rectangles of rooms, he instead found a first floor that was essentially wide open. The sparkling kitchen sat in the middle of the space, with a family room, formal dining area, and breakfast nook arranged in what would have been a circle if the exterior walls had not been at right angles.

The air in here smelled musty, yet clean. It hadn't been closed up for all that long. A flight of eight stairs led to the second floor. At the top, immediately to the right, he found a room with two twin beds and a sporting-goods store's worth of balls and assorted gear. Football helmets and pads, baseballs and bats, seemed to be on display, arranged as if by a model home decorator. The dresser drawers were closed, and the floor was free of laundry and clutter. This clearly was the boys' room, but no real boy had cleaned like this.

To the right of the boys' room, directly across from the top of the stairs, lay another bedroom, this one equally organized and impossibly pink. Here, carefully-arranged dolls and stuffed animals took the place of the sports gear from next door.

Next came a shiny hall bath. Adam noted three toothbrushes in the holder. He pulled open the mirrored medicine cabinet, where a container of stick deodorant and a disposable razor told Adam that at least one of the boys was a teenager.

Mom and Dad's room continued the theme of preternatural neatness. Adam didn't want to poke around in here too deeply, but he did notice the gun rack between the windows and noted that the second set of brackets from the top was missing its gun.

It felt like he'd been wandering this house and its property for hours, but in reality, it had only been thirty-five minutes when he walked back out to the Bronco to give the all clear. Even in that time, though, Lisa had faded further away, and had fallen back to sleep.

"The house is clear," Adam said as he opened Emma's door.

"What's going on?"

"Let's get her down in her bed and we can talk privately."

"Has the family gone away?"

Adam pantomimed a shot to his head with a finger pistol.

Emma's eyes grew huge. "Oh, my God," she whispered.

"There's more. Let's go."

Adam led the way back into the house, and up to Lisa's pink paradise. Emma laid her down on top of the bedspread, then pulled a folded quilt from the end of the bed and covered her with it.

Then they went downstairs and sat in the family room. Adam moaned as he sank into the overstuffed cushion of a leather chair. It had been a long, long time since he'd been truly comfortable.

It took less than five minutes to catch Emma up on what he'd found out back.

"Have you read the letter yet?" she asked.

"No, I figured that could wait till we got Lisa inside."

He pulled the plastic bag and envelope from his pocket and turned it over in his hands.

"Open it," Emma said. Her voice had an anticipatory, Christmas morning lilt to it. "It's not a bomb, right? It's not thick enough."

"Know a lot about bombs, do you?" Adam asked through a grin. "I almost don't want to get my fingerprints on it."

"I imagine those databases are running pretty slowly these days," Emma quipped.

Adam inhaled deeply and unzipped the Baggie. There was nothing special about the envelope inside. Plain white and sealed closed, it was addressed, *To Whom This May Concern.*

Adam tried to be careful not to tear the paper as he opened the seal, but he had trouble getting his finger under the flap. By the time he finally got it open, the top of the envelope was ragged as hell. The content was a letter, written by hand in a careful script on lined notebook paper. To Adam's eye, the blue ink came from an old-fashioned fountain pen.

Emma pressed in close and they read the letter silently together.

> *To whomever finds this note:*
> *If you are reading this, then you know that I am dead. If creatures have not made away with my remains, I lie buried in an open grave near this tree. I suppose it won't matter one way or the other, but please consider it my last wish for my body to be covered with the dirt that I have stacked nearby.*
> *To the right of the tree where you found this letter, you will also find three additional graves. One contains the remains of my wife, Heather,*

*and our children, Michael and Sean, rest in the
others, Sean in the middle grave. Our third
child, Lisa, is staying with her uncle, Orrin
Hornsby, several miles southwest of here. Please
let her remain there, do not seek to find her. She
needn't know how her family came to die.*

*You must think me a monster, but Heather and
I could not endure the future as it is. Michael is
not yet 14 years old, and Sean just turned 10.
How can I inflict a future of misery upon them?
Upon us?*

*Just for the record, the boys never knew what
happened. We drugged them with high levels of
Valium (Heather just recently had her prescrip-
tion refilled before the explosions). We took them
from their beds while they were asleep and shot
each of them once in the head. Then I shot
Heather, and now the plan is that I will shoot
myself.*

God help me. God help us all.

Sincerely,
Jacob Barnes

"Did you finish it?" Adam asked.

"How awful," Emma said. "We need to take her
back to her uncle."

"Not yet," Adam said, and he couldn't believe he
was the one saying it. "We need to tear this place apart
to find her meds. Then we need to go into town and
find the doctor or maybe a pharmacy that can help. We
can't just go back without something to show for the
effort."

Emma put her hand on Adam's thigh. "Do you think she's going to . . ."

"Not on our watch," Adam said. "I made a promise. We'll get Lisa to someplace where she can get help."

Without warning, Emma whipped her arms around his neck and hugged him hard enough to hurt. "You're already a great dad," she said.

"Remember you said that if the baby's a girl and I lock her in her room for her teen years."

Lisa needed to sleep. They decided to make that the first priority for the immediate future. While she was down, they could scour the house for her meds.

"I looked at the package that Orrin Hornsby gave us," Emma said. "The label is pretty specific that it needs to remain refrigerated."

"God grant me the serenity," Adam said, invoking the famous prayer. "We can't create refrigeration."

Emma's face showed excitement. "I just thought of something," she said. "If we can find the bottle for the pills they used to kill their kids, maybe it'll have a doctor's name and address on it. Maybe the doc will be more willing to help out a patient he knows."

That was a good idea, Adam thought.

"Do you mind taking the lead on that?" he asked. "They've got two trucks out there in the garage. They're gonna be dead, but the gas in the tanks should still be good. I'm going to siphon it out and fill as much of the jerry cans as I can. As long as we have gas, we have mobility."

"The garage doors are locked," Emma said. "I checked when we were walking around."

"There's no such thing as a locked door as long as I have my trusty ax."

CHAPTER FIFTEEN

Hell Day + 49 (The Next Day)

*T*HE LURE OF SOFT BEDS PROVED TO BE TOO TEMPT-
ing. Just a few hours, they told themselves, but a few
turned to eight, and then to ten. Somehow the rest and
the deep sleep left Adam feeling oddly more tired than
before.

For good or ill, Lisa slept the night through. The un-
refrigerated mini-dose of insulin Emma administered to
her didn't kill her. It didn't make her much better, either.

It was still early when they were ready to move on.
With both jerry cans filled, plus another he'd found in
the garage, they had fifteen gallons' worth of driving
future ahead of them. Sooner or later, Adam hoped, the
god-awful taste of gasoline would leave his mouth.

Emma had succeeded at finding the family doctor's
name and address. In cross-referencing to an ancient
phone book she'd found in a closet, she discovered
that the address was for a medical office in Appleton.

In a sign that the day might end up being something other than awful, Adam had discovered a trove of road maps, one each for West Virginia, Virginia, Maryland and Pennsylvania. In the garage, Jacob Barnes had mounted a topographical map of the area on the wall behind the workbench. Whereas commercial maps concentrated on roadways and towns, topo maps featured contour lines that showed the slope and elevations of the land. Once they again got to the point where he'd be building another shelter as their home, the topo map would help him find the high ground, which was easier to defend, and the streambeds, where they could find water to sustain themselves.

They searched for food in the pantry, but the shelves were completely stripped of anything useful to eat. Perhaps that explained, in part, why Jacob and Heather Barnes decided to off themselves. Adam and Emma helped themselves to blankets and coats and a block of knives from the kitchen. Adam wasn't sure what he'd use them for, but having them was better than not having them.

"I wish we could stay here awhile longer," Emma said.

"We've got to get to the doctor during the daylight hours. I feel bad that we stayed as long as we did."

"Do you think the doctor is even there anymore?"

"Our luck's got to turn positive at some point," Adam said. "Hey, there's one more thing we need to talk about before we wake up Lisa." He helped himself to a seat at the cherrywood dining-room table and gestured for Emma to join him. She sat directly across from him.

"Remember you asked me what Orrin Hornsby said

to me when he pulled me aside? Well, he warned me that people have been talking about us."

"Nobody even knows us."

"Not by name. Not like that. Word is out that two teenagers in a Ford Bronco—a boy and a girl—killed some people up on the mountain. Mr. Hornsby said he didn't imagine that we did anything wrong, and he acknowledged that some of the folks up there are rough and scary, but he wanted us to be careful."

Emma's expression darkened. "We talked about this happening."

"Yeah, not a surprise, I guess, but it's disturbing how quickly that kind of news spreads. So, when we drive into town, we might be driving into a hornet's nest. People are going to notice."

"What are you saying?"

"I just want to make sure you know what I know. It's a lot of exposure."

Emma thought for a few seconds. "Maybe we just keep going," she said.

Adam didn't get it.

"We don't stop. We drive through the town. We get ahead of the rumors. Literally."

"Then what?" Adam asked. "What do we do with Lisa?"

Emma looked at him with pleading eyes, clearly waiting for him to understand on his own.

"Oh, no," he said. "We can't just keep her, Em. She's not a puppy."

"No, she's a sick little girl." She dropped her voice to a whisper. "Her family's dead. Even if we find her doctor and get her medications, what choice do we have? If we attract a lot of attention, do you want to drive all the way back to Orrin's house just to drive back through the hazard, where they'll be ready for us?"

Adam knew she was right, though he didn't want her to be. He wanted to let it go for now, but Emma wouldn't let him.

"We'll do what we have to do," he said.

"What does that mean?"

"I have no idea. And let's not forget that *you* need to see a doctor, too."

"I don't need a doctor anymore."

"No, that puke-o-rama is really good for you."

"I've been feeling better," she said. "And you're changing the subject." She stood. "I'll go get her. Doctor or no, we've got to do *something*."

"Do you want me to get her?" Adam asked. "To carry her?"

"It's not like she actually weighs anything," Emma said. "I've got her. Is the Bronco ready?"

"As it will ever be."

CHAPTER SIXTEEN

Hell Day + 49 (The Same Day)

P RITCHARD AND ANDY LINX HAD SPENT LAST NIGHT in the living room, finishing off the Rouse family's meager supply of scotch whisky and laying out the details for how they could gather intelligence on the town of Ortho and its defenses. Inserting a spy seemed impractical. The communications lines were too long, and there was no way of knowing whether the spy would come back from the town that was beginning to gain the reputation of a Shangri-La.

"Why don't we just take one of their sentries and pump them for information?" Andy said. "It's high risk, but if we float in under the cover of darkness, maybe we can nab one of them and bring them back."

Pritchard's eyes narrowed as he considered the possibilities. Making a person talk would not be a challenge. "I think you just hit on it, Andy. Well done."

A rapid, urgent knock on the front door turned their

attention to the storm door at the front of the house. One of the high-school recruits stood on the other side. He looked excited and out of breath.

Pritchard motioned for the kid to enter.

He was only partway through the door when he started talking. More linebacker than runner, he looked nearly spent. "I've got news," he said. "You've heard the stories about that red-and-white Bronco? The one with the guy and the girl in it?"

"Rings a bell," Pritchard said. "Bonnie and Clyde, right?"

"I don't know their names. But the Bronco was spotted last night out on Kanawha Road, a few miles outside of town. They were coming this way, but they never got here."

"Where did they go?"

"I don't know. Maybe they stopped for the night. Anyway, I thought you'd want to know that it's nearby."

Pritchard looked to Andy. "It'd be nice to have a running vehicle," he said.

"It'd make a lot of things easier," Andy agreed.

"I want it," Pritchard said. "If they were coming this way yesterday, then they'll come through sometime today. If not today, then sometime. They have to. There's nowhere else for them to go."

Pritchard stood. "Get it."

Andy stood, too. "How?"

"Do whatever you have to do. It's one of one, right? Set up a roadblock if you have to. Spread the word. Take whoever you need. I want that vehicle."

"What about the driver?"

"There's two of them," the kid corrected.

"I don't give a shit about either of them," Pritchard said.

CHAPTER SEVENTEEN

Hell Day + 49 (The Same Day)

*T*HE FIRST COUPLE OF MILES FROM THE BOTTOM OF Lisa's driveway were dominated by hilly and rocky farmland. The crops had all been harvested or died. Adam wondered how the farmers were able to take care of the harvest without the conveniences of modern mechanical equipment. The land seemed excessively disrupted. Overturned. In his mind, he envisioned a mob of people swarming the crops and helping themselves.

Just a little farther down the road, that image was strengthened by the sight of large carcasses that had been slaughtered in the field, their remains left for scavengers.

"Are those what I think they are?" Emma asked.

"Cattle," Adam said. "I guess there's no way to get them to market."

"There must be dozens of them."

"I'm thinking there was a killing frenzy at some point," Adam said. "Hunger can be a hell of a motivator."

"How can they possibly keep that much meat fresh?"

"You can smoke it or dry it," Adam said, "or even can it. The question is, do the people who rustled the beef know how to do any of that? When you're starving—or you think you're about to—maybe you don't think all that straight."

A few more miles down the road, as houses became more frequent, they saw more and more people. They didn't seem to be doing much. Some sat on porches, some sat on steps. Everyone seemed to be armed—most with pistols on their hips, but there were a few AR-15 clones, shotguns and even hunting rifles. And every person seemed utterly shocked to see a moving vehicle. "I feel like an animal in the zoo," Adam said.

"They seem curious," Emma said. "Not threatening."

She was right, he thought, but that could change in an instant. Adam stipulated in his mind that all those people with all that weaponry were merely being careful, but that concerned him, too. Careful people were nervous people, and nervous people were apt to make snap decisions of the kind that would pose a danger to Emma and him. He adjusted the Glock on his hip to make sure he would have easy access if he needed it quickly.

"How far do we have to go?" Emma asked. He heard the nervousness.

"It measured out on the map to be about ten miles from the end of the driveway." Problem was, he didn't know what he was looking for. The address on the bottle talked about the Appleton Medical Arts Building, but without the help of the street view offered by computer mapping services, he didn't know if he was looking for an eight-story office building or a converted ranch house. He did note that the address was an even number, and that even numbers were on the right-hand side. Not that it mattered, he supposed. Without oncoming traffic, what difference would a left turn make over a right turn?

Lisa had barely moved since Emma had plucked her from her bed and carried her out to the Bronco. Before leaving, Adam and Emma had discussed administering another of the insulin doses they'd found to bolster her health a little, but they decided to wait. With medical help this close, why risk a poisonous reaction?

"It's strange," Emma said. "On the first few days after the war and the fires, I really missed seeing people. I worried about how I would exist without having them around me."

"Now they all scare you."

"Exactly. What do you think they do with their days?"

"I think they dedicate every second to just staying alive. By now, I figure their food is all gone or it's all spoiled. Have you noticed that we haven't seen any pets around?"

Emma's expression showed horror. "Do you think they ate them?"

"Meat is meat," Adam said. "It's what I've been telling you from the beginning. When the shit hits the fan, everybody is either hunting or being hunted. Most are doing both at the same time."

"Aren't you cheerful?"

Adam kept the speedometer dancing right around

thirty-five as he approached the denser part of the town. Not fast enough to pose a hazard to unaware pedestrians, but fast enough to discourage people from stepping in front to try to stop them.

As far as he knew, he'd never been through Appleton, so he didn't have a good baseline point of comparison, but it looked like the structures were beginning to show signs of neglect already. Certainly, the roadway did. Many of the homes displayed broken windows. He didn't know what that meant, exactly, but it didn't speak to effective law enforcement.

There seemed to be a hard break between the residential part of the town and the business center. Houses transformed to low-rise industrial buildings—the kind that could just as easily be an automobile body shop or a furniture repair shop. Every food establishment clearly had been looted. Intact panes of glass were a rare commodity. The skeletal remains of a McDonald's looked like it might have burned. The interior had been ransacked.

"I'm getting a bad feeling about this," Adam thought aloud.

Emma said nothing. She pulled Lisa closer.

"Do you need to put her down?" Adam asked. "You know, in case this goes really bad?"

"Nothing is bad yet," she said.

"Yet," Adam said, "is a terrifying word."

Clearly, this part of town had seen rioting. If not rioting, then intense looting. Charred hulks of cars lined the main drag, and every building within sight had been heavily vandalized. Some had been burned, and no windows remained intact.

"There's no way there's going to be an unclaimed pill or vial of any drug in this place," Adam said.

"What's the address number we're looking for?" Emma asked.

"One-eight-two-eight," Adam said.

Emma pointed ahead and to the right. A five-foot sign read, APPLETON MEDICAL ARTS BUILDING, but the two-story structure behind it was charred black. It appeared that the interior floors had collapsed.

"Okay, can you stop for a second?" Emma asked.

"Here? Are you crazy?"

"I want to put Lisa in the back," she said. "I'm beginning to think I might need both hands."

That was as good a reason to stop as any, Adam thought. He pulled to a stop, shifted to neutral and set the parking brake. As Emma struggled to let herself out while holding Lisa, Adam exited and slung his rifle to provide cover if they needed it.

"What are we doing?" Lisa asked.

"I've got to put you down for a while," Emma said.

"I don't want you to."

"I know, sweetie, but I'm going to make a place for you to sleep in the back of the truck."

"I need a car seat."

As Emma bent to put Lisa down, the little girl pulled up her feet and hugged herself tighter. "I don't want to."

Four men ranging in age from late teens to mid-twenties emerged from behind the structure next to the medical-arts building. "Hey!" one of them called. He carried what appeared from seventy yards away to be a sawed-off shotgun. His pals all carried long guns.

"We've got trouble," Adam said quietly. "Get her in the car."

"Come on, Lisa, I need to make a spot for you." Lisa continued to squirm and resist.

"Jesus, Emma. Heave her in if you need to. This is serious shit coming."

Adam positioned himself in front of the left wheel well, putting the engine block between him and the approaching threat.

"Hi, friend!" Shotgun Man called. "Nice wheels." Sixty yards separated them.

"We're not friends!" Adam called back. "But I hope we're not enemies, either." He prayed that he was subtle when he thumbed the lever from SAFE to FIRE. He didn't want a fight, but if it came, he'd be ready. "We're just passing through."

"I can see that," Shotgun Man said. "Nice wheels."

"Emma, get her in. Now. You too." He didn't want to look away from the approaching men. To them, he shouted, "I'd appreciate it if you'd stop where you are. To be honest, you're making me a little nervous."

They slowed, but they didn't stop. "You gonna shoot it out with us? Four against one?"

Adam raised his rifle and pointed it at the sky. He wanted them to know he was armed, but he didn't want to pose an immediate threat.

Lisa was crying when Emma planted her in the back of the Bronco amid all the equipment and supplies. She closed the tailgate and hurried around to the passenger side.

"You're not leaving so soon, are you?" Shotgun Man shouted. "I think that's a bad idea."

Adam didn't respond. Instead, he moved the pistol

grip of his M4 to his left hand and started to slide back into his spot behind the wheel. Keeping the muzzle up, he released the parking brake and shifted into gear.

"Don't do that," Shotgun said. "We're taking the truck. Wrap your head around that. Don't make me shoot—"

That was all the threat Adam needed. He snapped the muzzle down and popped off five rounds in their general direction. In the back, Lisa screamed.

The approaching gang jumped at the sound and instinctively dropped to their knees—exactly the reaction Adam had been hoping for. He popped the clutch, and they were off. "Open fire!" he shouted to Emma. "Keep their heads down!"

Emma shouted over the engine noise, "They're not shooting back!"

He supposed that made sense. It's hard to hit a moving vehicle, and he was zigging and zagging as much as the narrow roadway would allow.

So, why was he troubled by the fact they let him go?

His mom's voice answered in his head in a voice so clear that she might have been sitting next to him. *Trust your instincts,* the voice said. *Trust what you know about the world and trust your sense of danger. Never be embarrassed to react as if you're threatened.*

Up ahead, beyond a trashed streetlight, the road curved to the right, disappearing behind a cliff that had been carved into the mountain to accommodate the road. Beyond that spot, he would literally be driving into the unknown.

What a perfect place to set a trap.

If people didn't wander into it on their own, they would be driven into it by others.

Or he could be totally paranoid and they had nothing to fear.

There's nothing wrong with being paranoid.

"Hang on," he said. Taking his foot off the gas, but without really slowing, he pulled the steering wheel hard to the right and cut down a cross street that took them off the main drag and deeper into the edges of the commercial district.

"What are you doing?"

In the back, Lisa yelled, "You're hurting me!"

"Call it a hunch," Adam said. "Those guys should have shot us. Makes no sense that they didn't." He explained his theory that they were being driven into a trap.

"That's a classic hunting strategy, isn't it?" Emma said. "Flushing the bushes?"

He supposed it was, come to think of it. He'd gotten a lot of quail that way, back before quail got so scarce.

Then he thought he was being stupid. You flush quail from areas where you know quail to be. No one had any way of knowing that he and Emma were going to be there.

Still, it didn't feel right.

He drove a few blocks into a side street and then turned left to run parallel to the main road. Once again, they drew a lot of attention. There was something wrong with the vibe of this whole town. No one—*no one*—appeared to even attempt to project friendliness. Perhaps they'd heard the gunshots and those sounds had put them on edge. Perhaps they were just born mean. Whatever the reason, Adam, Emma and Lisa clearly were not welcome.

"We're collecting a following," Emma said, looking backward.

The rearview mirror was long gone, and the side views might as well have been. Adam shifted in his seat to look behind, and sure enough, people were wandering from the surrounding buildings and falling in behind them. Most were armed, but none were posing an imminent threat.

"Hey!" one of them shouted. "Stop! Where'd you get the wheels?"

"Maybe we should stop and talk," Emma said. "At least find out if there's a doctor nearby."

"Absolutely not," Adam said. "Too many of them. Too few of us." He downshifted, hit the gas, and they lurched forward, leaving the crowd behind.

Emma continued to watch them.

"What are they doing?" Adam asked.

"Most have stopped, a few are following. One is running toward us. Oh, shit. He's aiming his rifle."

Adam jerked the wheel hard to the left and launched the Bronco over the curb and into the front parking lot of what looked like it might have once been a plumbing-supply company. He heard the *tink* of a bullet's impact, followed immediately by the sound of three shots.

The secret to not getting shot was to put distance between you and the shooter, and to do it in as unpredictable a way as possible.

Adam veered back to the right, then back again to the left, as he heard the sounds of more gunshots, but he didn't hear any impacts. He'd take that as a victory.

Up ahead, he saw a hard left that would bring him back to the main road they'd exited. He cut the angle by charging across another parking lot and a lawn.

"As ideas go," he said, "this is not one of my best!" He looked over to Emma.

"What's wrong with these people?"

"We have stuff that they want," Adam said. He had no idea if that was true, but it made sense.

This block looked worse than the others. The buildings here were mostly single-family houses, probably twenty of them, ten on a side, most of which looked as if they dated back to the 1970s. Three had been burned and all of them that Adam could see had been shot up. Bullet holes marred the brick and siding.

"My God," Emma breathed.

Adam backed his speed down as they cruised the street. Ahead and to the right, two human bodies lay sprawled on the front stoop of a house. The blood on the stone steps was still bright red.

"This all happened recently," Adam said.

As he brought his head back around to face front, he damn near jumped out of his skin as a bruised and bloody young man of about twenty staggered away from the curb and fell onto the street in front of the Bronco.

CHAPTER EIGHTEEN

Hell Day + 30 (19 Days Earlier)

ANGELA FORTNIGHT WAS PERHAPS THE LEAST ATTRACtive woman Penn had ever met. He'd stipulate that there'd probably been a time in her youth when there'd been a spark of something that wasn't hideous, but in recent years, she'd had so much work done that her features looked stretched and burned. Throw in a heart as dark as Cruella de Vil's, and her insatiable desire to ruin her political opposition, and there wasn't much to admire.

But she was Speaker of the United States House of Representatives, and as such, Penn needed to find a way to work with her. She'd ascended to that position after President Blanton and Vice President Jenkins had been killed in the attacks on Washington, and Penn moved up to the POTUS slot.

In the weeks that had passed since the war, none of them had had much to do. It was virtually impossible to contact anyone of official status outside of the Annex. The Constitution gave the House of Representatives the power to incur debt and pay the bills, but currency—the very *concept* of currency as was once understood—was a thing of the past. And even if they had a means to pay for the construction of lifesaving or republic-saving materiel, they didn't know what factories had survived the attacks, or what they were capable of manufacturing.

Speaker Fortnight sat in one of the two uncomfortable desk chairs in Penn's presidential office, which was about the same dimensions of the bedroom he shared with his younger brother when they were growing up. The bedroom, however, had been far better decorated.

Arlen Strasky had pulled in a folding chair from the massive workspaces out in the main hall, and set it up in the back corner, away from the fur if it started to fly between the president and the Speaker.

"He's late," Angela said. "This is his power play. This is the way Johnson struts his stuff in front of his minions."

"Alternatively," Penn said, "it's entirely possible that he has critical work to do. As things stand now, his actions have a far more immediate impact on real people than ours do."

"We are the two most powerful individuals on the planet right now, Mr. President. Scott Johnson has no right to ignore—"

"My apologies for being late, sir," Johnson declared as he appeared in the door. "Ma'am. A hotel this size has a lot of moving parts, and between limited resources and high-strung guests, well . . ." He let his

voice trail off. "What can I do for you, Mr. President?"
He helped himself to the other guest chair.

"The topic hasn't changed much, Mr. Johnson. We
need to establish reliable communication with the outside world. What are your people doing?"

"Well, sir, my staff and I have been eating copper
wire with every meal in hopes of shitting out electrons.
So far, we've had only limited success."

"Who do you think you're talking to?" Angela demanded.

Johnson smirked at her. "Due respect, ma'am, we've
had this same conversation for weeks. The comms
aren't working the way they should. Either the government whiz kids who let the contract to the lowest bid-
der didn't know what they were doing, or they didn't
properly understand the nature of the threat."

"Wasn't Solara the selected whiz kid?" Angela
asked. She fired the question as though it were a spear.

"One of many, yes," he said. "And if I were you, I'd
call up Solara's executive management and give them
a severe talking-to. I'm confident that we will do our
very best to make sure that the next war is less inconvenient."

Penn said, "The attitude is unnecessary."

"So is the goddamn question, Mr. President. Do you
think we're not trying everything we can think of? Shit
just does not work. If you'd like, I can bring Pete
Clostner in here to give you the technical problems,
but spoiler alert: Shit's not working."

"Then we need to open the doors," Penn said.

"Chapter two of the same conversation as always,"
Johnson mocked. "And that one ends the same way as
the others. No."

"Goddammit, Johnson," Penn erupted. "I am the president of the United States. I have an obligation to know what the hell is going on outside of these walls. You have an obligation to let me do it."

"No, sir, I don't. Welcome to chapter three. I don't question your obligation to save the world, sir. Certainly not after you did such a great job of breaking it in the first place. But that obligation is yours, sir, not mine. Mine is to make sure that the outside world stays outside. You, sir, run a representative republic. I, on the other hand, run a purebred dictatorship. The Annex was designed with this very discussion in mind. That's why my people have guns and arrest powers, and yours do not."

Johnson stood. "Now, if you don't mind—"

"Sit your ass back in that chair," Penn said. "I'll tell you when it's time for you to go."

Angela looked more startled than Johnson did. Johnson sat.

"Tell me what we know about the environment immediately outside the Annex."

The smirk returned to Johnson's face. "It's been a while since I looked, but I can tell you the daily temperature is dropping, that humidity levels are very comfortable, and that ambient radiation levels are high."

"How high? Put a number on it."

"Two to three roentgens."

"And normal background in Iran is four to five roentgens at some places, correct?" Penn asked.

"That's correct, sir. Well, I imagine it's much higher now." Johnson smiled, but his joke fell flat.

"Now, a *safe* exposure is, I believe, five thousand millirems per year, is that right?"

Johnson seemed genuinely shocked that Penn knew these things. "Yes, sir, that's correct."

"That's five roentgens."

"Yes, sir, but we're kind of talking apples and oranges here. The safety regulations allow that much in a *year*. Here, you're talking—"

"I don't need a physics lecture," Penn said. "And *safe* isn't an absolute term, is it? I mean, isn't there a significant margin for safety built into that number?"

Johnson seemed to search for the answer. "Well, yes, I suppose so. But that's not—"

Penn wasn't in the mood to hear about Johnson's regulations manual. "So, with an elevated background radiation of three roentgens, only slightly higher than what some Iranians have been living with for generations because of Mother Nature's deposits, we cannot say that such a dose is lethal."

Johnson remained silent. Perhaps a good idea.

"And whatever that number is outside, however safe or unsafe it may be, do you agree that it's the same number as is being experienced by all of our fellow countrymen who are not inside this glorified steel drum?"

"But, sir—"

"I'm not done," Penn said. "Every time an astronaut would perform an extra vehicular activity, he would be hit with twenty-five thousand to thirty thousand millirems during the course of his spacewalk. Cancer patients are *deliberately* exposed to six *million* millirems to make them *healthy*." He paused for a few seconds to let it settle in. "Are you following me, Mr. Johnson?"

"Yes, I am, Mr. President. But the point remains—"

"The point remains that I'm still not done. This is wartime, Mr. Johnson. Tens of millions, hundreds of millions—hell, for all we know, *billions* of people have died. Those who are left will be desperate for help."

"I'm not opening the doors."

Penn continued, as if uninterrupted. "Because this is wartime, it's reasonable to expect that we will all shear a few years off our prewar life expectancy. At the end of your prescribed isolation, the ambient radiation levels will be more or less the same as they are now."

"Dammit, Mr. President, I have orders."

"Yes, Mr. Johnson, you do have orders. And here they are: You're going to ignore your standing orders and send a scouting party outside to see what conditions are like out there."

"And here we are back around to full circle. I am *not* exposing my people to that level of risk. If you want to take a shot of gamma rays, you do it yourself, sir."

Strasky stood from his chair and pushed it aside. "Okay," he said. "I'm in. When do I go?"

CHAPTER NINETEEN

Hell Day + 49 (Nineteen Days Later)

*A*DAM SLAMMED THE BRAKES, AND INSTANTLY CURSED himself for doing so. This was another classic ambush tactic. Anything to get your prey to stop.

Except this guy looked genuinely terrible. He was barefoot, wearing sweatpants and a T-shirt soaked with blood.

Adam set the parking brake and opened his door.

"Where are you going?" Emma asked. Her tone sounded borderline panicked.

"I'm not going to run over this guy," Adam replied. "Keep an eye out for threats."

From the back, a weak voice said, "Mommy, I need a shot."

Emma's look of panic deepened. "What do I do?"

"At this point, why not?" Adam said.

The guy on the ground lay on his back, his face partially concealed by the Bronco's front bumper. That's how close Adam had come to crushing his head. He moved to the man's feet and pulled him away from the truck by his ankles.

The man yelped. "Stop. Stop, stop, stop."

"I've got to get you out of the street," Adam said, but he stopped pulling on the guy and moved to his head. "What happened to you?"

"They came last night," he said.

"Who came?"

"I don't know names. It's been bad for weeks, but not like this."

"I don't know what you're talking about," Adam said. "How badly hurt are you?"

"They killed Becky last night."

"Who?"

"Becky. Rebecca Armstrong. The baby too."

"They killed your *baby*?"

"We were gonna call him Trey. Robert Armstrong the Third." A wave of pain washed through him. He winced against it and drew up his knees.

Adam wasn't getting it. Then he did. "Your wife was pregnant?"

The man nodded, knocking tears from the corners of his eyes.

"Are you Robert Armstrong the Second?"

"Junior. People call me Junior."

"So, what happened?"

"It was the Army," Junior said. "A couple dozen of them, loaded for bear. They came to steal shit. When we didn't have anything—thanks to the other gangs that came through here—they set everything on fire. Started shooting anyone who resisted." A cough launched a wad of bloody gunk from his throat.

Adam jumped back to dodge it. "I'll ask you again. How hurt are you? What happened?"

"The guys in uniform—females too, to be honest—crashed into our house." Another wave of pain passed through him. He took ten seconds or so to let it pass. "We were in bed. They didn't say anything. I couldn't have given them anything, but they didn't ask for it, either. They came through the door, shot me, and that's all I know. When I woke up . . . they were . . . It was all over."

"Where are the Army guys now?"

"I don't know. Around. Somewhere. Everywhere. But it's not just them anymore. They're like a disease. They've got regular people joining in with them."

"And they just shoot people and burn things?"

"They recruit. Their thing is to survive by force. It's a goddamn nightmare."

"Let me see your wound," Adam said. Now that he knew what to look for, he could see the hole in his shirt.

Junior slapped Adam's hand away, and the effort seemed to exhaust him. "I'm dying," he said. "I want to die. I want to be with my family." His words carried no emotion. "I'm not doing this anymore. I'm not being without them." He cut his eyes toward Adam. "Would you kill me?"

"No," Adam said. That was a hard stop. No negotiation.

"I figured. You look like a nice guy."

"We're here for a doctor. Where can we find one?"

"They burned the medical building," Junior said. "Stupid shits. They go around looking for drugs, and they burn the medical building and the pharmacy." He laughed, but abandoned the effort when it hurt.

"Do you know where the doctor lives?"

"I don't know any doctors. We go to their offices— used to—but where they live? Not a clue."

"Shit."

"I've heard a rumor there's one about twenty-five miles from here, in a little town called Ortho. Do you know it?"

"No."

"Get back on Kanawha Road and drive. You'll go right through it. Word on the street is that they're pretty organized there, too. Civilized. I don't know if it's true, but that's what I've heard."

Adam's brain felt full. He knew there were a thousand questions he should be asking, but he couldn't think of any of them.

"They're gonna kill you for that truck," Junior said. "I heard about you. Well, about the Bronco."

"Being famous sucks," Adam said. "They already tried to kill us for the truck."

Junior's eyes bulged and his expression cleared. "They know you're here? You've seen people? They've seen you?"

"Yes, but—"

"You need to get out of town. Drive fast. Don't stop for anybody."

"Can I do something for you?" Adam asked.

"Live. Get out. You don't have time. There's nothing valuable left in this whole shitty little town. You're fresh meat. Get out. Please do that for me. Just leave me."

"Adam!" Emma yelled. "They're here!" She fired

three quick shots in the direction they'd just come from.

The crowd fired back.

It was time to go. "Sorry, Junior. Good luck." He was still talking when he whirled, still on his knees, and brought his rifle up to his shoulder. The approaching crowd was maybe seventy-five yards away, and they'd spread out and ducked behind cover.

"Em, you drive!" Adam shouted. He settled the reticle of his four-power scope on the top of a head he saw cowering behind the trunk of a parked car and pressed the trigger. He was rewarded with a pink spray and he shifted to the next target he could find. He had no idea what the target looked like. He saw a hunting rifle and a figure with a center of mass. He drilled it and moved to a third.

Three shots, three kills. That unnerved his attackers. Two took off running back the way they'd come. They were still carrying guns, so he shot them both. One he knew was a kill shot because of the brain spray, but he wasn't as sure about the second one. He knew he'd hit the guy because he face-planted in the street, but the wound might not be fatal.

Behind him on his left, he sensed, more than saw, that Emma had slid into the driver's seat.

With the rifle pressed to his shoulder, both eyes open to scan for additional threats, he circled around the back of the Bronco and moved to the door of the shotgun seat. He was about to slide inside when one of the townspeople peeked around the corner of a house on the left-hand side of the street. He had a rifle and was apparently a right-handed shooter who didn't know how to switch to southpaw. To make his shot, he had to expose his whole body and he paid for it with an exploded heart as Adam drilled him.

Adam's butt had barely hit the seat when Emma popped the clutch and launched them down the street and up a hill.

"Are they following us?" she asked.

"They won't be doing much of anything for a while. I got the sense that they weren't used to people fighting back. Cowards choose their targets carefully. I think I convinced them to look at others."

"Where are we going?"

Adam reached across the center and grabbed the Barneses' old street map, which he'd dropped next to the driver's seat. He opened it to the quadrant that showed their part of the state, and then took a few seconds to orient to where he thought they were. "Here it is. Appleton." But where within the town?

He found the business district, and he found the place where they'd turned off, and then the subsequent turns he'd made. "Read off some street signs," he said. "Give me street names."

"We're in the trees," Emma said. "We just passed Pine, we're coming up on Poplar."

Adam found the spot on the map and put his finger on the page. He looked up. Elm was next, so he knew exactly where they were.

The road dead-ended.

"Shit. Right on Elm."

Emma executed the turn. "Now what?"

Adam looked ahead on the map, trying to find a way back to Kanawha Road that wouldn't take them back into the lion's den.

"We've got more people ahead," Emma said.

"Just go. Don't slow for anything. Two intersections from here, left on Quince."

That would buy them time when he could look away from the map and worry about aiming his weapon. He was tired of being subtle and not the least bit interested in being friendly. The gangs had apparently not gotten to this part of the town yet—or maybe this was the headquarters for the gang—because nothing here had been burned.

As before, the people who gathered seemed to have been caught in the middle of doing nothing with their day. Maybe there was nothing to do. And as before, the Bronco might as well have been a circus train.

"Don't get caught in that truck!" someone yelled. "They'll burn you right along with it!"

"Don't slow," Adam reminded, though her foot remained heavy on the gas. He didn't look, but he guessed their speed to be about thirty-five miles per hour.

Up ahead, a lady stepped off the curb and waved her hands to get their attention, but she backed away when Adam muzzled her with the M4.

"Maybe she was going to warn us about something."

"Not a lot she could warn us about now that we haven't already seen." At least he prayed that was the case.

CHAPTER TWENTY

Hell Day + 45 (Four Days Earlier)

THE TWENTY-PLUS-MILE BIKE RIDE WAS MORE ONEROUS than Frank Rouse had expected. When you have the benefit of motorized transportation, you don't think about how steep the hills are or how long they stretch upward before you get a break to go down. It didn't help that he hadn't ridden a bicycle in over a decade or taken even a quick step in probably three years. Not an old man by any empirical standard, he felt old as dirt, nonetheless, by the time they approached the roadblock on the outskirts of Ortho.

A cluster of four men and two women stood around two ranks of sawhorses that had been stretched across the roadway. They were dressed casually, but each wore a white bandanna somewhere on their clothes. As Frank approached with Paula, he saw that their boys had already been stopped and had dismounted their bikes. People with guns surrounded them.

"What's going on?" Paula asked.

Frank didn't answer because he thought it was a stupid question. All of them would know soon enough.

A nondescript man with a rifle slung across his chest stepped forward and held up his hand, signaling for them to stop.

"Let me handle this," Frank said.

The man with the rifle stopped with five feet separating them. "Good afternoon," he said. "My name is Seth Garner. Welcome to the town of Ortho."

"You don't look too welcoming to me," Paula said.

"What's all this about?" Frank asked.

"Where you coming from?" Garner asked.

"I'm not sure why that's any of your business."

Garner cocked his head. "I'm not here to cause you trouble, sir. But I have a job to do, and if you want to proceed any farther down this road, you're going to have to let me do it. Does any of that seem unreasonable?"

"We're from Appleton," Gary said. "The Army threw us out of our house."

Garner shifted his stance and narrowed his gaze. "Is that true?"

Frank confirmed it.

Garner said, "The older boy—Ronnie, is it? He told us that the people at the house shot him. Is that true?"

"It is," Frank said. It took no more than a minute to fill in the details of his encounter with Pritchard and his gang of soldiers.

"This isn't the first we've heard of trouble up that way," Garner said, "but this is the worst we've heard about. How widespread is it?"

"Hey, Seth?" It was one of the female guards. Maybe

twenty-five, with a ponytail hanging from the back of a Smith & Wesson ball cap, she had a pleasant, if malnourished, look about her. "Maybe we should just take his info and tell 'em where to find Doc Rory." She looked at Frank and extended her hand. "I'm Jeannie Garner. His wife."

Frank tipped his head toward her, left the proffered handshake hanging. "You have a doctor here?"

"A few of them, actually," Garner said. "I don't have your names yet."

Frank introduced himself and the rest of the family. "Paula and I were teachers before the war. I don't suppose you've got school happening again?"

"Not yet, but we have an education committee planning for the future. Right now, we're just trying to figure out the logistics of day to day."

"Committee?" Paula asked.

"Yes, ma'am," Garner said. "We've got committees on committees. It's not as bad as it sounds, but there's a lot of work to do on housing and shit—sorry—before we get to the soft stuff like schools."

Frank felt stunned. "You mean, you've got infrastructure?"

Garner coughed out a laugh. "Mr. Rouse, I'm a construction worker when I'm not pulling my shift out here on security. I don't know if what you're thinkin' of when you say *infrastructure* is anything like what I'm thinkin', but if it is, we got a long way to go. We've got food and water, and we got places for everybody to sleep. It ain't all comfortable, but the harder you work on your cabin, the sooner you'll get outta the tents."

Frank still didn't get it. Didn't know what to say.

Garner went on, "Listen, it'll make sense when you see it and after you've been here a little while. Is it your plan to stay here, or are you just passin' through?"

Frank looked back to Paula. "We don't know yet," she said. "But we'd like to get Ronnie to a doctor."

"Course," Garner said. He looked back to the other guards. "Hey, Levi, it's your turn."

A young man stepped forward. A boy, really, seventeen at the oldest. He carried his rifle slung on his shoulder, muzzle up, and he wore flannel and denim with well-worn Western-style boots. He looked familiar.

"Hi, Mr. Rouse," he said. "Levi Willis. You kicked me out of your sixth-period U.S. history class last year." He said it with no sign of hard feelings.

Frank remembered. The kid had a smart mouth and a way with spitballs. "Oh, yeah," he said. "Sorry about that."

"Don't be," Levi said. "I was shocked you let me stay in as long as you did." He stepped all the way up to Frank and offered his hand. "Welcome to the shitty new normal."

Frank shook his hand and waited till Levi made personal contact with the rest of the family. "You got no weapons?" he asked when he was done.

"They wouldn't let us take any," Gary said.

"Well, we've got some extras," Levi said. He cocked his head as he looked more closely at Ronnie. "You're lookin' kinda pale. Do you want to wait here and I can send a wagon back to get you?"

Ronnie shook his head. "No, I'll be all right. I figure if I was gonna die, I'da done it already."

Frank felt a surge of pride at his son's toughness.

Levi chuckled. "That attitude's gonna get you a long way with Major McCrea and Mrs. Emerson. C'mon, let's get going. Gonna ask you to walk the bikes 'cause I don't have one, and the new rules are that newcomers need to be escorted into town."

The guards lifted the sawhorses out of the way to allow them to pass, and then closed them up again after they were on their way, walking five abreast, spanning the road from shoulder to shoulder. The woods out here looked just like the woods they'd been passing since they left home. Hardwoods on both sides vibrated with autumn colors.

"You mentioned Major Somebody and Mrs. Somebody back there," Paula said.

"Right," Levi said. "Major McCrea and Mrs. Emerson. Victoria Emerson, Vicky."

"The House member?" Frank asked.

"Yep, that one. Kind of a long story how she got here, but when she found out that the rest of the government was going into a bunker to protect themselves and they wouldn't let her bring her family, she told them to pound sand. Said she'd take her chances with the people she loves. Kinda cool, right?"

The admiration invaded Levi's entire demeanor—a kind of respect that he'd have been incapable of showing to school faculty or staff. Frank was embarrassed by the pang of jealousy he felt.

"So Major McCrea was, like, her bodyguard, and when Hell Day happened, they lost their ride—"

"Hell Day?" This from Gary.

"That's what we call it here. Fits pretty good, if you ask me."

"I think it's a cool name," Ronnie said.

"Anyway, him and Mrs. Emerson and her kids wandered into town, along with this buff boy named First Sergeant Copley, and sort of took control of stuff."

"What does that mean?" Frank asked. *"Took control?"*

"I'm not even sure how she did it," Levi said. "She started telling people what to do, and people started doing it. You know, right after the explosions and the smoke and the fire and shit, we was fightin' each other. Nobody knew what to do, and she just seemed to. She put people in charge of stuff, assigning work details, that sort of thing, and people said okay."

"What about fighting and killing?" Paula asked. "What about gangs?"

"There's been some of that, to be honest with you. I mean people are naturally assholes, right? Had a thing blow up down here a couple of weeks ago. Well, maybe not that long. Days all run together, you know? Anyway, some Army asshats tried to storm the beaches in boats, but it didn't go good for them."

"What happened?"

"We killed some of them and they ran off. Kinda sounds like the same people who've been messin' with you guys. A bunch of bad dudes."

"You said that the major and this Vicky chick are going to like us," Gary said. "Why?"

"Word of advice," Levi said. His tone was at once light and deadly serious. "You call her *that Vicky chick* to her face, or around some of the other folks in town, and it's gonna hurt. I didn't much like hearin' that myself."

Gary blushed, but said nothing.

"It's part of the new rules," Levi went on. "The major

and Mrs. Emerson take the security of the town really seriously. You don't want to break laws around here. We got a lot of new folks comin' in, and everybody expects everybody else to behave civil and keep a civil tongue in their head." He made a point of craning his neck to look right at Gary. "I'm not tryin' to make you feel uncomfortable or nothin', but I thought you should know."

"So, is there a police force?" Frank asked.

"You're lookin' at it," Levi replied. "Pretty much everybody's expected to be part of the militia. That's what we're calling it. Don't got no cops that we know of—not real ones, anyway—so all the policing falls on us. That's what these white scarves is all about. They identify us as us—as opposed to *them*—if fighting starts."

Levi hurried ahead a few steps, then turned and walked backward while he continued to talk. "Don't got no jail, either, so lawbreakin' is handled the old-fashioned way. In the town square. Well, we don't really got one of those, but there've been a few public floggin's. Tough to watch, but everybody gets a turn with the whip. One lash per person until the right number is delivered."

"That's barbaric," Paula said.

"It works," Levi said. "And if you see anybody with a *T* carved into their foreheads, be careful around them. They're thieves who got caught."

"Oh, my God," Paula said.

Levi smiled. "Mrs. Rouse, your husband can tell you what an asshole I was when I was in his class, but I tell you what. I ain't that kinda asshole no more. And that's because of the public floggin's. I ain't keen about bein' trussed up naked and havin' people I've known my whole life takin' turns strippin' skin from my back with a knotted wet rope."

"I can't say that I approve," Frank said.

"And I'm pretty sure that I never asked you," Levi replied. He turned back around and they walked in silence.

Levi fell back into line between Paula and Gary. As they continued down the road, the woods became a town. Frank had driven through here dozens of times over the years—maybe hundreds—but he'd never paid it much attention. The homes were modest, as were the business establishments. Everything he saw appeared to have been frozen in time. None of the vehicles moved, of course, and electricity was a thing of the past, but he found it remarkable that the abandoned vehicles sat unmolested. From what he could see, all of the glass in the buildings was intact.

In the distance, he thought he could hear the sound of hammering.

On their left, the wooded lots gave way to views of the river, where people in boats had fishing lines in the water. On the right, a man in his fifties was sweeping the porch of his house. He stopped his work and waved. "Hey, Levi!" he called. "Your shift at the roadblock over?"

"No, sir, Mr. John. Just walkin' some newcomers in to meet Mrs. Emerson."

"Welcome," Mr. John said. "Now be sure to do your part. Pull hard on whatever oars they give you."

Something about the words bothered Frank. "Pull an oar?"

Levi laughed. "Ain't got no slave ships here, Mr. Rouse. He just means, *Don't be a load.*"

As if that clarified things. Frank decided to let it go. He assumed that everything would make sense soon.

The sounds of construction crescendoed as they moved closer into the center of the town. Levi explained, "Whatever other work assignments you get from Mrs. Emerson and her people, your very first and most important job is going to be helping to put up the new houses. We got a flood of new people and now we gotta have a place to put 'em. You, among 'em."

"What kind of place is this?" Paula whispered. "Work details?"

Levi pointed ahead and to the left. "See that reddish building up there near the water? That there's Maggie's Place. Used to be a diner before Hell Day, and since then, it's kinda become the town hall. In there's where Mrs. Emerson set up her office. That's got to be your first stop to get settled."

"What about seeing a doctor?" Paula asked.

"I'm okay," Ronnie said.

"You been shot, bubba," Levi said. "If I was you, seein' a doc would be, like, the very first thing on my list." Then, to Paula: "I can take him there. If one of you wants to come along, that'd be fine, but you really need to sit down in Maggie's with Mrs. Emerson or one of her people. Especially with it getting dark soon. You're gonna need a place to sleep and somethin' warm to sleep in."

"You take Ronnie to the doctor," Frank said. "I'll take care of this meeting."

"Y'all can put your bikes right over there," Levi said, pointing to what looked like a corral filled with bicycles.

"That's okay," Frank said. "We'll keep them."

Levi shrugged with one shoulder. "Suit yourself. I don't want to steal Mrs. Emerson's thunder or nothin', but just know that if you stay, you gotta give your bikes to the town. You can use them if they're available, but so can everybody else."

"Is that one of the new town rules?" Paula asked. She clearly was not pleased.

"Yes, ma'am, I suppose it is." Something changed in Levi in that second. "You know, this is a nice place. A lot of shit has changed since Hell Day, but me and the other people here in Ortho wouldn't mind bein' your friends. We help people out here. We ain't tryin' to steal your stuff."

Paula looked at her feet, cleared her throat.

"Now let's get Ronnie here over to Doc Rory."

Frank watched after them for a few seconds, and then set off for Maggie's Place.

CHAPTER TWENTY-ONE

Hell Day + 30 (15 Days Earlier)

"YOU'LL DO WHAT?" THE PRESIDENT ASKED. ARLEN Strasky was amused that the president, the Speaker, and Scott Johnson all stared at him with the same expression, a combination of horror and confusion.

"I'll go outside on a scouting mission," Strasky said. "Somebody has to do it sooner or later, and the president is correct when he says that a few extra days or weeks won't make a difference in terms of the level of hazards we face. We need to know what's going on out there."

"You could die," Speaker Fortnight said. "For all you know, the radiation levels are unsustainable."

"For all you know, they're not," Strasky countered. It was a stupid rebuttal, but he felt compelled to say *something*.

"All due respect, Mr. Strasky," Johnson said, "you just said a stupid thing. We do, in fact, know that radiation readings are elevated. After all, sir, there was this bit of a war that happened. Perhaps you might have heard about it."

"Watch your attitude, Mr. Johnson," the president said. "That man is my chief of staff."

"I know who he is, sir. I made his sleeping arrangements, remember?"

"You can't have it all ways, Johnson," Strasky said. "Am I scared to go there? You bet your ass I am. I have no idea what I'll find. But we have to see. You don't want to send your troops because they're too important to you, and you don't want to send out any of the elected members in residence because your job is to protect them. I get that. But I don't fit into any of those categories."

"You are *all* my responsibility," Johnson answered.

"As was Oliver Mulroney," Strasky said.

Hearing the name caused Johnson to physically recoil.

"You think there are secrets in this cave?" Strasky said with a laugh. "I know you killed him. Everybody does. You were just doing your job, as I understand it, and that's fine, I guess. I only bring it up to demonstrate that there are exceptions to your protection mandate."

Johnson's ears turned red. "The incident with Oliver Mulroney—"

"Nobody cares," Angela said. "What's done is done. I think what Mr. Strasky is saying makes a lot of sense."

Of course you do, Strasky thought. *I'm one of the peasants, after all.*

"If we open the doors, we'll break the seal," Johnson objected. "We'll contaminate the Annex."

"We'll be doing that, anyway, in a couple of weeks," the president said. "If radiation is the concern, we're talking half-lives measured in millions of years. Weeks won't make a difference to our survival. But we cannot do our jobs in a vacuum. We literally don't know what is happening out there. A recon mission is essential. And if Arlen is willing to take the chance, I think we should let him."

Johnson clearly did not like the idea. Strasky could see it in the way that he straightened his posture. The scowl told him that Johnson was trying to construct a counterargument.

"So here's what you're going to do," the president said. "You're going to outfit Mr. Strasky with a firearm and whatever survey instruments you can muster, and you're going to open up the door long enough for him to sneak out, and then, at a prearranged time, you are going to open the door again to let him back in. Do you have any questions, sir?"

"Mr. President," Johnson said as his ears grew even darker, "I don't think you understand the chain of command here in the Annex. You run the country. I run—"

"The goddamn bunker," the president said. "If you say it one more time, I'm going to puke. What you're hearing from me is not a request, Mr. Johnson. It is an order."

"One that I cannot obey," Johnson said.

Bugsy stepped forward out of the corner he'd been occupying. "I'll open the door for him," he said.

"Bugs!" Johnson shouted.

"Come on, Scott, get your head out of your ass. This

is not a time for posturing and dick knocking. This is not a debate society. The whole goddamn world is suffering, and while every single resident here acts like a petulant child—"

Angela Fortnight puffed up. "I beg your pardon—"

"And you're one of the worst of the lot, Madam Speaker. All the infighting, all the bullshit. You people eat like locusts and you go about accomplishing tasks as if you've got one foot tied to the floor."

"Look, Bugsy—" the president said.

"No, sir, I won't *look*. I started this exercise with little faith in politics and politicians, and now that I see up close just how ineffective you are, how you value yourselves over just about everything else—other than food—my patience is gone. So, if I offend you, get over it. Sir."

Johnson looked pleased with his second in command.

Bugsy wasn't finished. "But no matter how much I loathe the process, it *is* the process. Y'all have responsibilities to do *something* to help the public, and you sure as hell are not getting anything done now."

Bugsy turned to face his boss. "It's up to you, Scott. There are only a few choices. You do as the president asks and let people out, or I will mutiny and let them out myself. Then it's your choice whether to kill me in the process, and/or assassinate the president of the United States. Call the ball."

Strasky was impressed. That took guts. He moved to seal the deal quickly. "Let's go now," he said. "I'll take whatever you want me to carry, except I won't carry a gun."

Bugsy recoiled at the words. "Are you sure, sir? I

mean, you don't know what you're going to find out there."

"Be reasonable, Arlen," the president said. "Better to have one and not need it than the other way around."

"No firearms," Johnson said. "I do draw the line there. I don't know what his training is, if he's had any at all. That's a deal breaker."

It was as if Johnson needed to win on a point. At least *deal breaker* meant that there was a deal.

It was the president's turn to puff up. "Mr. Johnson, there comes a point—"

Strasky held up his hand. "Mr. President, please stop. You can order Mr. Johnson all you want, but even if he gives me a gun, I'm not going to use it. I'm not going to carry it. That's just not my thing, sir."

Now the president looked as if he needed to prevail in the argument. Lots of red faces to go around inside the room.

"Unless you want to choose one of the other volunteers," Strasky said, driving the final nail into the coffin.

CHAPTER TWENTY-TWO

Hell Day + 49 (Nineteen Days Later)

"WE NEED TO PULL OFF FOR A WHILE AND GET our shit together," Adam said. "Whatever's happening in this town, we need to get it behind us and return to sane people. What did he call that town down the road? Ortho?"

"That sounds right," Emma confirmed. She pointed ahead and to the left. "There's a spot up there to stop."

Emma pulled the Bronco off the road, onto what looked like it might have started as a fire road back in the day, but had narrowed to little more than a deer trail. Tree limbs scraped the sides of the vehicle as she nosed into the point where the back bumper was off of the road and out of sight, but the doors could still open enough to let them get out.

Adam had the map open in his lap, trying to orient himself to the strange surroundings. He found their street, and then he found the nearest intersection with Kanawha Road that would get them back on track.

"It's not that far back to the main road," Adam said. He moved the map so Emma could see. Behind them, Lisa moaned from the bed, drawing their heads around.

"Do you think she's in pain?" Emma asked.

"Were you able to give her the shot?"

"Yes, but I didn't give her much."

"It's probably just a bad dream," Adam said. He wanted that to be the case, because if it was something else, there was nothing they could do for her. "We've got to be careful," he thought aloud. "Word is out about us now. They keep attacking and we keep defending ourselves. They're going to want revenge. It's not just about stealing the Bronco and our stuff anymore. For them, this is about winning a war."

"Then why are we still sitting here?"

"Because they outnumber us by a lot. Sooner or later, they're going to realize that our plan is to get outta Dodge, and according to this map, there are only a couple of routes to do that."

"All the more reason for us to be driving fast and taking chances," Emma said.

He liked her choice of words. "Oh, I think we'll be doing that in spades," he said. "But I want to be smart about it."

"You have a plan, then?"

"Absolutely not."

"Sometime soon?"

Adam switched the road map out for the USGS topographical map. It took another minute to orient himself to the landscape. He turned the map like a big steering wheel to get to the point where the direction they were facing matched the same compass point on the map.

For as long as he could remember, Adam had been fascinated by maps. Even as GPS guidance took over all route planning when going from point A to point B, he liked to see the route on a real map. His mind worked in a way that allowed him to translate contour lines into accurate imaginary images. As the lines became closer, the hills and cliffs appeared to him, as did the rivers and streams and buildings.

During orienteering races at the academy, he was the person team members depended on to bring them consistently in among the top three finishers. Often as not, in first place.

As Adam studied the map, Emma leaned over the seat to check on Lisa. "She's still breathing," she said. "But otherwise, she looks awful."

Adam stayed focused on his research.

"Okay, I think I see what we need to do," he said at last.

Emma settled back into her seat behind the wheel.

Adam pointed straight ahead through the windshield into the woods. "It's all forest that way for about a hundred twenty yards before the ground drops off to the road. Just down from there is the intersection between this road and Kanawha Road. If I were them, that's where I'd put up roadblocks, or whatever, to stop us."

"Should we just go back the way we came, then?"

"No. Well, I don't think so. That's where all those wounded and dead people are. I imagine they're still there. Within an hour or two, they're going to find some kind of organization, and if they do, they're going to drive us in the direction of the roadblock."

"The roadblock that you're not sure is even there," Emma said.

"Yeah, that one. What I want to do is walk to where the road was cut through the woods and see what they've got set up, if they have anything set up at all."

"And then what?"

"And then we'll know what we need to do to get out of here."

"Driving fast and taking chances won't accomplish what you're looking to do?"

"What I'm looking to do is get out of here alive and then get down the road to the doctor. Are you coming with me?"

Emma looked into the back of the Bronco. "What about Lisa?"

"That's your call. I've got to go, and we can't bring her along."

"Wouldn't it be wrong to leave her here all alone? What if she had a . . . I don't know, a medical crisis? Don't I need to be here for that?"

"If that's what you think is right," Adam said. "I can do this alone. Won't take more than a few minutes."

"But I should be there with you, too," Emma said. "If things go bad, you'll want an extra set of hands and another head."

Adam didn't know what to say that hadn't already been said.

"You're not helping!" Emma accused.

"I'm trying to," Adam said. "You go, or you stay. If I could think of another option, I'd give it to you. You're not going to hurt my feelings either way."

Emma clearly was torn, and Adam got it. Sometimes Karma trumped logic. If she came along and

something bad happened to Lisa, she'd feel terrible.
On the other hand, staying behind while he got whacked
by a band of crazies wouldn't make her feel very good,
either.

"It won't take long," Adam said. It was a test balloon to see which way she was leaning. *Won't take
long* cut both ways, to either decision.

"I think we should be together."

This wasn't going as smoothly as he'd hoped.
"Which *we*?"

"You and me."

"Good," he said. "That's what I was hoping you'd
decide." He opened his door and grabbed his rifle, plus
two spare thirty-round magazines.

Emma grabbed the same load-out. As they started to
head off, she said, "Aren't you going to take the map?"

He felt like an idiot. "You already earned your keep.
Thanks."

The woods were classic West Virginia forest. Hardwoods, pines, wicked sticker bushes, and rocks. Lots
and lots of rocks. The leaves were well into their au-
tumnal art show, and with the low sun streaming
through the leaves, the scenery gave the false hope of
peace.

Adam let his compass lead him forward, but he
needed to hedge his bets for the return trip. When
walking through the woods—particularly if you're in a
hurry—shooting reverse azimuths could get confusing.
Planning for that possibility, he paused every twenty
yards or so to scrape a vertical stripe out of the bark of
a tree, with the stripe facing forward—the direction
from which it would be most visible for the walk back
to the Bronco.

It took less than ten minutes to hike to the edge of the cliff that dropped down to the roadway below.

As they watched, armed locals streamed to the intersection through which they needed to drive fast and take chances. It appeared to be just as Adam had anticipated. They were setting a trap.

"That looks bad," Emma whispered.

Yes, it did. The crowd of ambushers was too far away to hear what they were saying, and they were mingling too much to get an accurate count, but they numbered at least a dozen. Adam saw many AR platform rifles and a smattering of bolt-action hunting rifles.

"We can't win a fight with them," Emma said.

"And yet we have to." The common theme of all the training he'd received from his dad and later from his mom was that in a life-and-death encounter, surrender was death. If you quit running from a fire, you die. If you don't try to fight the current, you drown. If you don't fight the bad guys, you get torn apart.

"We *can't*," Emma said again.

By any reasonable assessment, she was stating not just fact, but plainly obvious fact. The townspeople were dug into defensive positions. Adam watched as they established fields of fire. Whoever was in charge here knew what he was doing. Moreover, he looked as if he'd done it before—for real.

Adam, on the other hand, had read books and participated in war games at Hedrick, but that wasn't the same. In fact, his instructors had told him that very thing—many, many times. "Real warfare is gritty and loud and bloody," Sergeant Major Sturgen had told the class. "It smells bad and it's terrifying. Anyone who thinks that studying these things in the classroom can prepare you for real conflict is lying to himself."

These were not helpful thoughts, Adam realized, but they kept him from getting cocky.

Sergeant Major Sturgen also stressed that there was more to winning a battle than mere numbers. Stonewall Jackson had kicked Yankee ass up and down the Shenandoah Valley for the better part of two years with far fewer Johnny Rebs than the other side had Billy Yanks. The trick was to be smart, to find a way to reduce the advantage projected by the other side.

"Be nimble and be smart," Sturgen had said. "And be relentless. Never give the enemy a second to breathe or shift strategy to adapt."

"We have dynamite," Adam thought aloud.

Emma's eyes turned round and frightened. "You can't be serious," she said.

"That's our advantage," Adam said. "That, and the fact that we know where they are and what they're preparing to do."

"That's not a plan," Emma objected.

"Not yet, it's not. But it's the beginning of one."

They talked through their options, risks, and opportunities, and five minutes later, the whole plan had taken form. All they had to do now was live through its execution.

The first step was to return to the Bronco and figure out how to insert blasting caps into sticks of dynamite.

CHAPTER TWENTY-THREE

Hell Day + 30 (Nineteen Days Earlier)

FEARING MASS PROTESTS AMONG MEMBERS OF CONgress if they witnessed a blast door being opened—or, alternatively, a rush of members to get the hell out— Johnson, Bugsy, Speaker Fortnight and President Glendale made the decision to release Strasky through a supply tunnel that the residents knew nothing about. The twenty-five-ton hatch was in the part of the Annex where residents were prohibited from entering.

A steel door at the end of the hallway that housed dormitories for members led to a second door, beyond which the facility blossomed into brighter light and more vivid colors. Gone were the military-industrial khakis and aquas, and in their places, the walls featured whites and yellows. The lighting in here was much brighter, and the artwork on the walls was mostly inappropriate for any other workplace in America.

"What is this place?" Speaker Fortnight asked. Her tone dripped with disapproval.

"These are my staff quarters," Johnson said without apology.

"And this?" the president asked, stopping in front of a comfortable and well-appointed tavern room.

"Exactly what it looks like, sir," Johnson said. "Follow me, please."

Strasky admired how Johnson made no effort to explain the opulent cheeriness of their spaces. Frankly, he got it. These guys were 24/7/365 staff and had been for many years in anticipation of a catastrophe that no one really expected and everyone prayed would never happen. Strasky couldn't imagine the shit Johnson was going to take from the Speaker, in particular, when the chance came around.

The brightly-lit spaces led to what could have been the engine room of a warship. Dominated by catwalks and huge storage tanks, it vibrated with a constant hum that made shouting necessary if one was to be heard.

"This is the heart and lungs of the Annex," Bugsy shouted over the noise. He pointed. "That's the potable water there. The diesel fuel for the generators over there. The facility and cooling water—the nonpotable stuff—over there."

"I wasn't aware of nonpotable water," Speaker Fortnight said.

"We didn't anticipate a lot of water being consumed out of the toilets, ma'am," Johnson said. "And I understand that radiator water tastes pretty awful."

Strasky laughed at the absurdity of it all.

"I don't appreciate your attitude," the Speaker said.

"Duly noted about a thousand times, ma'am," Johnson said.

The twenty-five-ton door looked like a hatch from a submarine. Perfectly round and hinged on the right side, the hatch was held fast by a locking mechanism that might have been a stout ship's wheel.

When they arrived at the door, Johnson pointed to the watch on Strasky's wrist. "Is that digital or windup?"

"As old technology as you can get," Strasky replied. "It was my father's. I have to wind it twice a day."

"Good for you," Johnson said. "How long do you figure you need out there?"

As the reality sank in that he truly was going to do this crazy thing, it began to feel like a bad idea. But he was in too deep now. "An hour?"

"That's a long time," the president said. "That's a lot of exposure."

"We're all going to have to do it sooner or later," Strasky said. The calmness in his voice surprised him.

"It's important that you choose wisely," Johnson said. "As soon as you clear the opening, we're locking it down again. If it's an hour, it's an hour. If it's fifteen minutes, it's fifteen minutes. Whatever you choose, at exactly that time, we're going to open up again. You'll be there or you won't. If you're not, then this is it. Are we clear on that?"

"Why do you insist on being such a hard-ass?" the president asked.

"Because we all know how stupid an idea it is to break the seal on a fallout shelter," Johnson said. "We all know that we're going to be introducing toxins into our atmosphere, and that is what this facility is designed specifically to protect against."

Bugsy said, "But seriously, Scott—"

"You shut up," Johnson snapped. "It is with great objection that I'm violating established procedure, and I will mitigate the damage caused in any way that I can. In this case, it means opening the door long enough for you to get out, and then long enough again to get you back in."

Sensing that there was nothing left for him to do, Strasky accepted the old-school thirty-five-millimeter single-lens reflex camera that Bugsy handed him.

"I know it's got film in it," Bugsy said. "To my knowledge, it's never been used, but beyond that, I have no idea if it works."

"I thought you checked and rechecked everything in here," Speaker Fortnight said.

"The camera is not official gear," Johnson said. "It's always been here. For all I know, a guest left it behind in their room, and somebody from a previous era snagged it."

Strasky turned the camera over in his hands, familiarizing himself with the moving parts. He'd always been more a point-and-shoot snapshot kind of guy. With his phone. He'd long ago forgotten how to adjust apertures and f-stops.

"Anything, in particular, you want me to get pictures of?"

"This is your mission, not mine," Johnson said. "There's only a moderate likelihood that the thing will even function."

The president asked, "Do we even have the capability to develop film?"

"Not to my knowledge," Johnson said. "That's not to say we don't have the trays and chemicals stashed somewhere, but they're nowhere on any of our checklists."

"Why bother to take the camera, then?" Speaker Fortnight asked.

Strasky answered without hesitation. "Posterity, Madam Speaker. This is a little like walking on the moon again, you know? That's what it feels like to me, anyway. Documenting what I find will at least provide a historical record."

Again, he surprised himself. He hadn't really thought it through until he articulated his rationale.

The president said, "You make a good point, Arlen." He extended his hand. "Good luck with this."

Strasky forced a smile as he accepted the president's handshake. "I'm just going for a stroll, Mr. President. Don't look so glum."

"Come back whole and healthy," the president said.

That sounded like a good plan. "Yes, sir," Strasky said. He looked to Johnson. "All right, young man," he said. "Let's do this thing."

Johnson nodded to Bugsy, who went to work on spinning the codes that would unlock the blast door.

"Remember the rules," Johnson said. "In one hour on the dot, I will open this door. It will stay open for one minute, and then it will close for the remaining weeks we have scheduled. Am I clear?"

Strasky decided not to give him the satisfaction of an answer.

Over at the hatch, Bugsy spun the wheel. When it was hard over, he gave it a yank, and the hatch pulled free of its housing with a substantial *clunk*. It seemed to take little effort to pull it open.

"This is it, sir," Bugsy said. "From the outside, this entrance is pretty obscured. When you get to the end of the tunnel, I recommend giving a hard look to the surrounding landmarks. You'll remember from when you arrived how that blast door was pretty obvious. This one is the opposite of that, so leave yourself enough time to get oriented and not get lost on the way back in. We'd hate to lose you that way."

Angela Fortnight's face remained impassive as Strasky climbed the two expanded metal steps that brought him up to the hatch, where he changed places with Bugsy. The other man handed him a two-foot-long Maglite.

"Be careful, Arlen," the president said. His voice was thick with emotion.

"See you in an hour, sir," Strasky said. He squared against the door as it opened, and then he stepped outside.

CHAPTER TWENTY-FOUR

Hell Day + 49 (Nineteen Days Later)

ADAM'S ENTIRE PLAN HINGED ON A NINETY-DEGREE dogleg in the street that would dead-end at Kanawha Road. The curve rested sixty yards up the hill from the intersection. If they approached it carefully and quietly, with minimum engine noise, and if they didn't run into any townspeople, and if the commander of the town militia had not placed guards that far up the hill, Adam figured they had a solid 40 percent chance of pulling this off.

Hey, it was better than zero. He took solace in the fact that they never should have survived the explosions and the aftermath in the first place.

Emma coasted to the spot they'd determined along the side of the road. She kept the engine running, but at low idle.

"Having second thoughts?" Emma whispered.

"Hell yes," Adam whispered back. "Tenth, eleventh

and twelfth thoughts, too. I think this is the best bet, though. But as they continue to organize, our chance of success shrinks."

He climbed out of the Bronco again, and after adjusting his gear, he reached back into the cab and folded two sticks of dynamite into his fist. It didn't occur to him till right then that the orange sticks were such a cliché. About the same size as a standard road flare, they actually bore the inscription DYNAMITE along the side. If it were made by the Acme Dynamite Corporation, it would have been the same product that Wile E. Coyote used.

Only with better results, he hoped.

Lisa opened her eyes and moaned before closing them again. He wasn't sure that she'd even awakened.

"Her color's getting worse," Emma said.

Adam didn't understand how the blasting caps worked, per se—not at the mechanical, chemical level—but it was pretty clear that the thin metal tube needed to be inserted into the pinched circle at the end of each stick. He assumed that the markings along the length of the fuse indicated burn time, but that was just a guess. He used his knife to cut what he believed to be thirty seconds' worth for each and inserted the detonators.

"I hope I know what I'm doing," he said.

"You do have an idea, don't you?" Emma's stress came through in her voice. "I mean, didn't your mother train you in explosives?"

"In theory, yes," Adam said. "But not so much on the practical. Even serious preppers have difficulty finding range time for explosives."

"Do I want to know what Santa Claus brought you boys for Christmas?"

Adam set the second and final cap. "Okay, let's go through it one more time. We won't get a second chance."

Emma clearly did not like reciting back like this, but she did it, anyway. "I wait for gunshots. That means things are about to begin. When I hear an explosion, that's my cue to drive like crazy."

"Right," Adam confirmed. "Just do me the favor of waiting for me to hop in before you drive off for real."

"Maybe I will, and maybe I won't," she quipped.

"Right. See you in a few." He took off toward the woods again.

"Adam!"

He stopped, turned.

Emma said, "I'll wait no matter what." Her voice cracked as she spoke.

Adam puckered an air kiss at her and went to work.

The flow of people to the roadblock had slowed to a trickle, but the crowd had grown by a few. Adam didn't count, but he guessed it was as many as twenty. As before, the tall guy in the uniform was directing people to different stations, each of which provided clear lanes of fire to the intersection.

His heart told him that negotiation was the proper move here, to find a peaceful solution to the conflict, but his head told him that these folks were not in the mood to talk. Too much blood had already been shed.

He wasn't going to take the chance.

Adam moved slowly as he approached the cliff above the road, trying his best to stay away from sticks that could break and dry leaves that could rustle. The folks down there clearly weren't concerned about making noise, shouting to one another as they were. Adam couldn't make out the words and didn't care to.

He slid in behind a stout gray limestone rock that provided as much cover as he could want, while not impeding his ability to run like a bunny rabbit when the excitement started in a few minutes.

With a fresh mag in the well, Adam performed a quick press check to make sure the chamber was loaded and then he worked the forward assist to make sure the breech was thoroughly closed. He rested the forestock on a V formed in the edge of his cover and practiced pivoting left and right to acquire targets and simulate shooting them. The commander would have been on that target list if he hadn't inadvertently put a tree between himself and Adam's muzzle.

No more excuses. No more equipment checks. It was time to do this thing.

With his heart bruising itself behind his breastbone, Adam struggled to keep his hands steady enough to get a flame out of his Zippo lighter, and then again to touch the tip of the flame to the fuses. First one, then he counted to ten and lit the other one.

Ticktock.

Now there was no turning back.

As the fuses burned at his knees, Adam thumbed the safety on his rifle to FIRE, acquired his first predetermined target and fired five quick rounds.

The gunfire had exactly the response he'd been hoping for. The assembled enemy scrambled for cover, firing randomly and wildly at the wind, just the way untrained shooters were inclined to do. He felt good to see the people who wanted to kill him spraying the air with bullets that would have no effect but to drain their precious resources.

Ticktock.

They were still scrambling when Adam heaved the first stick of dynamite in their direction. The smoke trail from the burning fuse looked like a rescue flare as it arced high past his rock and down toward the road.

He didn't bother to watch where it landed because the location didn't matter. What mattered was the explosion. It was awesome, a heavy bright burst of pressure that seemed to make the world shake.

It was time to go.

Adam shifted his rifle to his left hand as he darted out from behind his cover, randomly firing in the direction of the bad guys. If there was return fire, it was lost in the booming of his heart and the blasting of his own rifle.

After three or four steps, he heaved the second stick of dynamite.

The explosion came way sooner than he'd expected, detonating in the air, just past the apex of its airborne arc.

The pulse of pressure hurt Adam's ears and made him stumble to his right. He kept his balance, but barely.

Now it was all about the running. If the timing was perfect—an achievement that never occurred in the real world—Emma and the Bronco would be gliding through the intersection at the exact instant Adam arrived. He'd hop into the passenger door and they'd be off to whatever the name of the next town was.

He tore through the woods, his rifle in a death grip in front of him to keep it from slapping. He ignored the scrapes and tears at his flesh from the branches and thorns. He didn't think he was visible to the people he'd just shot at and maybe blew up, but that didn't matter. If he was, he was. He'd find that out soon enough, the hard way. At least he was making himself a difficult target to hit.

Without warning, he found himself airborne as he encountered his own corner of the roadway cliff and the ground went away under his feet.

He didn't fall so much as he slid, first on his ass, then on his side as he finished with a somersault that wouldn't have hurt nearly as much if it hadn't been for the slung rifle, which gouged him hard under his armpit.

Somehow the somersault ended with him on his feet. He'd stuck the landing, as they used to say when people cared about Olympic competitions. Once he'd restored his balance, he headed again for the roadway.

The timing wasn't perfect, but it was damned close. Emma approached fast from his right and hit the brakes hard, skidding to a halt five feet in front of him. He dashed forward and around the Bronco's passenger side just as someone in the crowd noticed them and snapped off a few quick shots.

Tink. Tink.

He had one foot inside the door and his hand barely gripped the A-pillar when Emma engaged the clutch and they were off. In his head, he'd planned to return fire to provide them cover, but it was all he could do not to tumble out onto the street.

The air filled with more gunshots, but he didn't think any more hit their targets.

Seventy-five yards later, they'd made a sweeping

turn to the right and they had a mountain between them and the people who were trying to kill them.

"Slow it down, Em," Adam said. "Let me get in all the way."

It wasn't a matter of speed as much as it was a matter of centrifugal force. Once their path straightened, he could pull himself in safely.

"Are you okay?" Emma asked.

"A little bruised, but I think I'm fine. You?"

"I'm goddamned tired of being shot at," she said. "But otherwise, I'm okay. Check on Lisa."

Adam shifted his rifle around to the side, and turned in his seat, pressing the backrest against his chest as he reached down and around to check on her.

She was anything but okay.

CHAPTER TWENTY-FIVE

Hell Day + 30 (Nineteen Days Earlier)

WHEN THE SOLARA GUYS USED THE WORD TUNNEL, Strasky had envisioned something confining and frightening, a la The Great Escape or maybe an air shaft. In reality, the exit tunnel was built more in the scale of what a narrow-track railroad might use.

Thank God for the Maglite. The generators that kept things running inside the Annex spared no power for the lights in this space—assuming there were lights in this space, to begin with. The Maglite beam was more than enough illumination for him to see the entire length of the tunnel, which appeared to run about fifty, maybe sixty, feet. The walls and ceiling (where does one become the other in a circular space?) were lined with the same military-style piping and conduits that ran down the length of the space inside the front entrance, where they'd all arrived on the night of the war.

The temperature out here was chilly, but not cold.

All the surfaces looked impossibly clean. Scott Johnson and his Solara team might be asshats, through and through, but they clearly did their jobs in the years leading up to the deployment of CRIMSON PHOENIX.

Other than the pipes and conduit, though—and the thick, dormant, explosion-proof overhead lighting that tracked along the top—the space contained nothing. Just concrete and an occasional puddle of water. He had the sense that the tunnel was once used for storage, but whatever had once been here was now gone.

The tunnel terminated at a steel door, which was not unlike the other steel doors throughout the Annex, though this one had a heavy crossbar on the interior, which was as effective a locking system as Strasky had ever seen.

When he could progress no farther, he steadied himself with a deep breath—perhaps the last lungful of clean air for the next hour—and slid the crossbar out of its hooks on either side of the door and lifted it out of the way. It was heavier than he'd expected—every bit of thirty-five pounds—and he had some difficulty balancing it as he placed it off to the side.

As he grasped the knob, he closed his eyes and said a quick prayer. If it was to end now, let him go quickly and with as little pain as possible.

A quick glance at his watch showed that he'd already burned two of his sixty minutes. It was time to go.

Strasky turned the knob and pushed on the door panel. It resisted his efforts at first, but after he put his shoulder into it, the door moved. It swung free from the environmental stripping along the ground with a chilling metallic shriek, and then he got his first blast of unfiltered air. He detected the slight aroma of char, but it was not unpleasant. In fact, it was quite the opposite.

When the opening was wide enough for him to clear it, he found himself in the woods. It felt like a physical non sequitur, and for a brief instant, he recalled reading *The Chronicles of Narnia* to his kids many years ago. Step into a wardrobe and step out into another world.

The exterior of the door had either been deliberately camouflaged to look like mossy overgrowth on the side of a hill, or Mother Nature had taken care of that by herself. Either way, he now understood the warning to note the entrance's location to be able to find it on the return trip. To make it even more exciting, the knob and the locking mechanism did not exist out here. He pulled the door wide open and then opened the other side, blocking them both open with rocks so they wouldn't blow shut and leave him stranded out here.

As bad an idea as this clearly was, he'd raised his hand for the duty, and he'd by God see it through.

As he stepped farther away and got a broader perspective, he could make out the remains of what might once have been an access roadway to the doors. It veered off a larger paved road.

Twenty paces later, Strasky could see the imposing edifice of the Hilltop Manor Resort.

He snapped a picture, mainly to show that the physical structure and the surrounding property and woods remained untouched by bombs. Call that a bullet dodged.

As he walked up the road toward the resort itself, the smell of char grew stronger, and as it did, he began to hear the sounds of people moving about and talking. It was very faint, and he couldn't yet see anyone, but it sounded like more than a few. The char aroma was becoming less pleasant. In fact, it was damned *un*pleasant.

It was the stink of burning meat, but more . . . unsettling.

The service road swung wide to the right and steeply uphill. Within only a minute or two, his body was reminding him of its age, and of the fact that far too much time had passed since it had seen any exercise.

As he crested the hill, and the magnificent architecture of the grand old hotel became visible, he stopped cold and drew in a quick breath. The grand expanse of the sloping front lawn teemed with people, hundreds of them. Some stood in lines—for what, he had no idea—but most seemed to be lounging about in the grass.

The source of the smoke and the stench revealed itself as a large bonfire that had been constructed in a rocky swale that would have been mostly out of the view of the others on the lawn. A dozen or more corpses lay in a heap at the edge of the fire pit—men, women, children of all ages. A group of five men, all naked, were tending to them, stripping them of their clothes and shoes, and presumably their jewelry, too, judging from the way the men manipulated the people's arms and hands. Once the corpses were, likewise, naked, the men grabbed them by their wrists and ankles, swung them for momentum, and then heaved them in a high arc onto the flames. Upon impact, each of them launched an eruption of embers into the column of smoke.

Strasky felt his stomach churn.

As he continued up the paved driveway toward the hotel, he made a deliberate effort to look away from the desecration. What the hell happened here? Why had all these people gathered?

And why the hell was he still walking closer?

Every step made it clearer to Strasky that these people were ill. He could smell it on them, a combination of shit, dirt, piss, and sweat, all of which became more vivid as he left the stench of cremation behind him.

Strasky knew that the right thing to do here would be to engage these poor wretches in conversation, find out what was going on, but the thought repulsed him. To a person, they were difficult to look at. Such was their suffering. Bottom line: Whatever they had, he didn't want.

A voice called from behind, startling him. "You there!"

Strasky whirled to see a young man in his twenties approaching him, a rifle slung across his body, his hand resting on the grip.

"You're new," the young man said.

Strasky remained silent. He didn't understand what was happening, but he sensed that silence was his friend.

"I'm talking to you," the young man said.

Strasky held out his arms and shrugged. *I'm listening*.

"Where are you from?" the guy asked.

Strasky said, "Around. Who are you?"

"You can call me Mr. DeWilde."

Strasky detected attitude in this kid. The *mister* honorific added a note of danger, but he couldn't say why.

"I haven't seen you here before," DeWilde said. "Are you in the Army or something?"

Strasky had forgotten about the uniform. "These people all look sick," he said. "What happened here?"

"A war," DeWilde said.

Strasky rolled his eyes. He supposed he opened the door for that. "You don't look sick," he said. "What did you do that they didn't?"

DeWilde's expression changed to something darker. "Are you armed?"

"No, sir, I am not."

"Why are you here?"

"Just looking around."

"What's with the camera?"

Strasky had forgotten about it. "Posterity? A century from now, everything that happens here is going to be important to history."

"I don't think Roger's going to be happy about you taking pictures."

"Who's Roger?"

"Roger Parsons?" DeWilde seemed incredulous that anyone wouldn't know the man.

Strasky waited for it. This felt like very dangerous ground all of a sudden.

"I think you need to come with me," DeWilde said.

"I'm fine where I am," Strasky said. "I'm just getting the lay of the land. Maybe talk to a few of these people."

"You're coming with me," DeWilde said. The point clearly was nonnegotiable.

DeWilde stayed behind Strasky as they walked through the crowd up the hill toward the massive stone-columned main hotel building. The suffering wretches on the lawn paid little notice and made no effort to move out of the way as the two-man parade wound around them. The stench of illness and sweat burrowed into Strasky's sinuses and churned his stomach.

It was time to test DeWilde's commitment to his task. Strasky stopped near a man who could as easily have been forty as sixty. He shivered in the chilly air despite a heavy hooded sweatshirt that displayed the logo for Virginia Tech. The sweatshirt was at least three sizes too large for him, making Strasky wonder if it had fit well before the war. The man's eyes showed the thousand-mile stare that was so common among trauma survivors.

He stooped to get down to eye level.

"Keep moving," DeWilde said.

"Shoot me," Strasky replied. *Hey, if you're going to play a bluff, play it big, right?* "Excuse me, sir," he said to the man in the sweatshirt. "My name is Arlen Strasky. Are you ill?"

The man didn't respond. He just kept staring.

The last thing Strasky wanted was to make physical contact with this shell of a human being, but he forced himself to put a hand on the man's shoulder.

The guy twitched, and the contact brought his eyes around, but they still seemed incapable of seeing anything.

Strasky craned his neck to look at DeWilde, who, in turn, looked bored. And angry. "What is wrong with these people?"

"What do you *think*? They're dying. They're starving to death."

"Well, feed them," Strasky said.

"With what?"

"With whatever you've been eating. You look healthy enough."

DeWilde laughed heartily, but without humor. "What's ours is ours," he said. "Now stand your ass up and get going. Up to the hotel."

Strasky returned his attention to the pitiful creature in the sweatshirt. "What's your name, sir?"

A shove from DeWilde's foot placed between the shoulders sent Strasky sprawling into the man. They both hit the grass, Strasky straddling the man with his arms. Their heads nearly knocked. Strasky rebounded instantly—recoiled, really—but the man stayed down, his forehead touching the grass.

"He'll be dead within the hour," DeWilde said. "We see it here all the time. Now get on your feet."

Five minutes later, they were inside the grand foyer of the hotel. In here, things looked entirely different than they did outside. To begin with, these people looked healthy. Well fed. A line of armed sentries stood five feet inside the main entrance, each armed with a rifle, and each with deep scowls carved into their faces. Intentional intimidation.

"Who's this?" one of them asked. The man wore jeans and flannel and looked like he was used to hard work in the outdoors.

"I just found him wandering the grounds. He had this on him." DeWilde displayed Strasky's camera.

The interior guard took the camera and turned it over in his hands as a curiosity. "You spyin' on us?" he asked.

"Yeah, I'm a Russian agent," Strasky said.

The new guard gave him a long, hard look. "Under the circumstances, how can you think that's a funny joke?"

"Under the circumstances, how can you give a shit

about spying?" Strasky countered. "Am I under arrest or something?"

"Not yet," the guy said.

"What's going on here?" Strasky asked. "This looks like an armed camp."

"It *is* an armed camp," boomed a voice from behind.

Strasky turned to see a tall, very fit man in his forties approaching. He looked vaguely familiar, but Strasky had no idea where they might have met.

The man offered his hand. "Roger Parsons," he said. "I run the place."

Strasky hesitated, but ultimately shook the man's hand. "Arlen Strasky. What happened to Victor Vanden? Last time I was here, he was the general manager."

Parsons didn't like the question and it showed in his eyes. "We had a difference of opinion on how things should run." He nodded to DeWilde and the other guard. "I've got this. Follow me, Mr. Strasky."

"Where are we going?"

"To a comfortable seat. How's that?"

Strasky checked his watch.

"You've got somewhere else to be?"

"Actually, I do. But that's none of your concern."

Parsons led the way across the reception lobby to a cluster of opulent overstuffed sofas and precious antique padded wooden chairs. Strasky took one of the chairs, while Parsons helped himself to a spot on the sofa.

"Do I look familiar to you, Mr. Strasky?"

"In fact, you do."

"You a wrestling fan?"

That was all he needed. "You're The Mauler."

Parsons beamed. "Undefeated in thirty-seven matches. I came here with my training staff to do a little gambling and to blow off steam. Who knew the world would come apart while we were here?"

"Such a tragedy," Strasky said. "Listen, can you tell me—"

"You know, we've met, right?" Parsons said. "It was a fund-raiser in DC. About five years ago. We were at opposite poles of a ten-top."

Strasky had been to so many of those events over the years, met so many celebrities, that he couldn't pull up that particular dinner.

"I was in my penguin suit, of course," Parsons said. "Hair pulled back in a man bun that made me look respectable."

"Oh, sure, I remember," Strasky lied. It seemed like the best way to move the discussion forward. Ticktock and all that.

"You're big-time in the political sphere," Parsons went on. "Somebody's chief of staff?"

The vibe here was all wrong. The chitchat was supposed to be casual, but it was filled with menace. "Feels like a long time ago. Like the Stone Age feels like a long time ago."

Parsons pretended to laugh. "The Stone Age *was* a long time ago. Yet, now it seems to have returned. Why do I suspect you had something to do with that?"

Strasky's stomach knotted. "I don't know what you're talking about." Even as he spoke, he could feel his poker face failing him.

"Your boss is Penn Glendale, right? Speaker of the House?"

"He was, yes."

Parsons leaned forward. *"Was."* He leaned on the word. "Past tense. Now, that's interesting. You could mean that he used to be your boss, or he used to be the Speaker of the House. Which is it?"

"Mr. Parsons, with all due respect, I'm not here to discuss me. I'm here to ask what is going on with the people—"

"I imagine Mr. DeWilde already told you," Parsons said. "They're starving to death."

"But why? Clearly, there's food. Clearly, *you're* not starving to death."

"I think there's a good chance that we will, sooner or later." Parsons leaned way forward. "Where did you come from, Mr. Strasky?" It was the posture of someone who already knew the answer and was setting a trap. "I mean, look at yourself. Tell you what. Let's start with something easier. You appear to me to be a bit old to have recently enlisted in the military, yet here you are in military dress. Not only that, but the military dress looks freshly laundered. You want to tell me how that is possible?"

Strasky said nothing. He couldn't think of any words that would not pose a threat. In a wash of realization, he suddenly knew that Scott Johnson had been correct, that he never should have ventured out of the Annex.

Parsons stood. "Come on," he said. "Let's take a walk. I know I promised comfortable seats, but I realize what I really want to do is give you a tour of the grounds."

Strasky considered declining the offer, but as armed men took a step closer, he realized that there was nothing optional in the invitation.

"Mr. DeWilde!" Parsons called.

The young man didn't snap to attention in the classical sense, but he certainly became attentive.

"I'd like you to come along on this," Parsons said.

DeWilde waited as Parsons and Strasky approached, and then he fell in line. They walked back outside.

"It's really a terrible, terrible thing when you think about it," Parsons said as they reentered the sunshine. "You think you've got all kinds of time left on the planet, and then *boom!* It all goes away. Look at these people out here. Every one of them is of means. If they didn't have piles of money sitting in their accounts somewhere, they couldn't afford to vacation in a place like this. You following me?"

"I hear your words," Strasky said. "But I'm not sure I'm following." Rather than tracking through the lawn as he had when DeWilde was in charge, Parsons took them along the paved driveway, back down the hill toward the crematory fire.

"Fair enough," Parsons said. "The point I'm trying to make is a little convoluted, but it makes sense to me. These people thought they were being successful, and that their government would make decisions that would keep them safe. They had homes, they had money, they had educations, and now all of those things don't mean anything because the leaders they trusted let them down."

"Are you getting to why these people are starving?"

"Charles Darwin," Parsons said. "Survival of the fittest. When resources are scarce, the herd has to be culled."

The horror of it hit hard. "You're deliberately starving them?"

"Nothing is stopping them from leaving," Parsons said. "Nothing is stopping them from hunting or fishing on their own."

"Except we took all their weapons and gear," DeWilde said with a giggle.

"Yes, there's that," Parsons agreed, though he looked perturbed to have been interrupted. To Strasky, he said, "No guns allowed. We don't need a bunch of panicky, clueless people wandering around armed. They'd just do something stupid and I'd end up having to kill them."

Strasky had difficulty wrapping his head around it. "You're starving them because they're weak?"

"Not at all. They are choosing to let themselves starve. There's a difference. New people wander in every day. They come from all over, and most of them are tired of being out in the elements. Especially with winter approaching, they want to have a chance at being warm. If they can demonstrate to me that they can be useful, they might be allowed to stay. That's how Mr. DeWilde here came to join us. He's a fine trapper and guard."

The stench of burning flesh was beginning to crescendo again.

"That's a god-awful smell, isn't it?" Parsons said. "Nothing reminds you of how fragile society is quite like the stink of shit and dead people. Once the pumps go out, the toilets back up fast. Sanitation is a real concern."

Strasky understood the fires now. What appeared at first glance to be desecration was, in fact, survival. Better to burn the bodies than let them contaminate everything.

"I saw the pyre as I was coming in," Strasky said.

"Those workers I saw. The ones handling the bodies. Are they volunteers?"

"They decided that getting fed is better than not getting fed. Again, they made themselves useful."

"And their clothes?"

Parsons laughed again and rolled his eyes. "They don't get to all the corpses in what you'd call record time. Since it's easier to wash death rot off of skin than off of fabric, they choose to work naked. I'm betting that will change as soon as the temps drop."

"This is about where I found him looking around," DeWilde said.

"Care to tell me now where you were coming from, Mr. Strasky?"

Strasky drew up short. Hard stop. "What are we doing here?"

"Let me add this up in my head and see if I get it right," Parsons said. He shifted his rifle on its sling, and for a second, Strasky thought he might shoot. Was that a deliberate move to make him uncomfortable?

To DeWilde: "But first, go and gather as much of the guard team as you can find. Bring them down here and make sure they've got all their gear."

DeWilde looked like he wanted to salute, but he didn't. He turned and headed back up the hill at a run.

"Keep walking with me," Parsons said, and he continued their stroll down the hill. "You confirmed my suspicions when you looked at your watch. I mean, the uniform was a pretty big clue, too, and the fact that you actually look *well fed* is another, but those things alone could be explained in many ways. Really, it was the look at your watch."

"I'm sorry, Mr. Parsons, but I'm still lost."

"Now you're lying," Parsons said. "I understand. It's pretty much your only play at this point. So I won't ask you to confirm or deny anything."

"Why did you send that young man back to get more people?" Strasky asked. He was stalling for time, trying to find some leverage in this encounter.

Parsons continued, as if uninterrupted. "This place— the Hilltop Manor—is an oddly designed place. Me and my people have wandered the grounds a lot during the past weeks. Lots of quirky details to take in." He stopped and pointed to a spot in the distance behind Strasky. "Like over there. There's a concrete block building that's marked *Danger, High Voltage*. Not exactly a hazard anymore, now that electricity doesn't exist anymore. So I went in. Do you know what I found?"

"I have no idea."

"Well, neither do I, to be completely honest. But what it *wasn't* was high-voltage equipment. Looked more like a smokestack, only there wasn't any smoke coming out. My guess is that it's an air intake. Anyway, the point is, it wasn't what it said it was. Now, I asked myself, why would a hotel do that? Why would they deliberately camouflage a pipe in a concrete room with a label that was a lie?"

This was the first Strasky had heard about any of this. He found it interesting. "To prevent vandalism, maybe?"

"Maybe," Parsons said. They started walking again. "But a heavy-ass lock would do that, wouldn't it? Why would the managers of this place want people to think that a building was something it wasn't? Then you've got to take it in context with everything else."

Strasky recognized the pause to be his opportunity to urge him on, but he remained silent.

"Did I tell you I was staying here when the war happened? With all the flashes and explosions, everybody gathered down in the main lobby—well, a lot of us, anyway—and there was a buzz from a sizable group of guests that they had been forcibly moved out of their rooms just a few hours before the explosions. All of them came from the Antebellum Wing. Some were upgraded and were happy about it, others were pissed that they got moved to smaller rooms."

"What's your point?" Strasky was playing the bluff to the end.

"I'm just talking context here. Paying customers being evacuated from their rooms in the middle of the night. Camouflaged buildings. Heavy-ass blast doors."

That last one startled Strasky, and his step faltered.

Parsons caught it. "Yeah, blast doors. At least that's what I assume they are. Like the biggest, baddest bank vault doors you've ever seen. You can't even get into the Antebellum Wing now because of one of those doors. Isn't that wild?"

Strasky could tell that the other man was studying his expression.

Parsons laughed. "Yeah, keep that blank face going. It's working for you. Since we're in this deep, I'll tell you that there's more than one of them doors. There's five that we know about, but there again, they're hidden and camouflaged. There's a set of heavy doors down this hill and around to the left that have been camouflaged as greenery. Tell you the truth, if we hadn't seen the blast doors and were out looking for more, I don't think we ever would have noticed the doors down here."

At the bottom of the hill, they made the turn to the left, stopping at the intersection of the roadway and the path that led to the steel doors, which were now propped open.

"Which brings us to your wristwatch," Parsons said. "I believe you were sent out here on a mission to look around and then sneak back at a given time. That you looked at your watch tells me that that time is soon." Parsons offered an ostentatious smirk. "How am I doing? Pretty close?"

Strasky felt dumbstruck. He wasn't sure that he could form words, and if he could, he had no idea what he would say.

"So let's recap," Parsons said through his smirk. "The chief of staff for the Speaker of the United States House of Representatives appears out of nowhere, well fed and recently washed. The bunker he came out of goes to extravagant lengths to hide its true identity. It's time for you to come clean."

Strasky looked to the ground, ran his options. Did he even have any?

No, he didn't. So he changed his thoughts over to what needed to happen next. What were the upsides and downsides? That the blast door would open was inevitable. In about thirteen minutes, if he calculated properly (he didn't dare look at his watch again), the blast door would open to grant him access back into the Annex. Parsons and his team would be there, whether Strasky was with them or not.

So, what was the smart play? If Strasky stonewalled

and said nothing, the door would open and Parsons would storm the place. If they didn't know the truth, they would expect the worst, and that would cause people to get hurt.

On the other hand, if Strasky could broker a peaceful opening, maybe everything would go without anger and violence.

No, that was not possible. Scott Johnson would not sit passively while strangers wandered into his clean safe spaces. One way or another, there was going to be violence.

But did it have to go that way? Strasky's only option for brokering peace was out here with Parsons. No matter how this went down, the people inside the Annex were going to go berserk. But if he could talk Parsons into taking things easy, maybe there'd be a chance for everyone to come out a winner.

"All right," Strasky said. "Kudos to your powers of deduction." As he spoke, he could hear Parsons's reinforcements arriving down the hill. "The official name for this facility is the United States Government Relocation Center, otherwise known as the Annex." He took the better part of five minutes to describe the nature of the operations inside.

"But there's a more important piece to this that you need to know and pay close attention to," Strasky said. "President Blanton and Vice President Jenkins both perished in the initial attacks. That means that Penn Glendale is no longer Speaker of the House. He's president of the United States."

Parsons's jaw dropped as a murmur rippled through the assembled crowd.

"So, you see, Mr. Parsons, the Annex is now doubling as the White House. This is the center of the Free World."

Parsons looked genuinely impressed. "Well, holy shit," he said. "I had not expected that. So y'all have this unlimited supply of food and water?"

Something terrifying changed behind Parsons's eyes. *"Unlimited?"* Strasky said. "Not hardly."

"But it's dry in there, am I right? And you have electricity because of generators and such? I'll bet you even have medical facilities."

What started out as an expression of admiration had morphed into anger.

"When do they reopen the door to let you back in?" Parsons pressed.

"Look, I'm sure we'll be willing to share what we have," Strasky said.

Parsons laughed. "Oh, I know that. In fact, if there's anything I'm sure of, it's that y'all will be willing to share. The better question is, will I be willing to share with you?"

Parsons gave that a long, few seconds to sink in.

"What time do they open the door?" he asked again.

Strasky gaped. He didn't know what to say.

"Oh, to hell with it," Parsons said. "We'll figure it out." He turned to the others who had gathered around. "Mr. DeWilde," he said, "do me a favor and kill this sonofabitch for me."

Strasky started to object, but he never got the chance.

CHAPTER TWENTY-SIX

Hell Day + 49 (Nineteen Days Later)

"THEY SHOT HER," ADAM SAID, HIS VOICE A RASPY croak. "Oh, my God!" Emma swerved the Bronco.

"She's dead. Oh, God." A one-in-a-million shot, a bullet had pierced the Bronco's tailgate and hit her high in her chest, just at the tip of the unicorn's horn on her T-shirt. "Those assholes killed her."

Emma stopped the truck. "Sweet Jesus, Adam. What are we going to do?"

"Don't stop," Adam said. "We've got to put distance between us and them." He eased Lisa's body over to her side and covered her as best he could with the corner of the plastic tarp they'd taken so long ago from the hardware store in Mountain View.

Emma set the brake and kneeled on her seat, looking back. "Oh, God, Adam." She covered her mouth with her hands. "What are we going to do?"

Adam turned around and settled himself back into his seat. "Come on," he said. "We have to keep going."

"I want to go back and kill them," Emma said. "Oh, my God, she's so . . . tiny."

"We can't win that fight," Adam said. His emotions were slipping beyond his control. "We have to move on."

"But Lisa—"

"Is dead. We can't change it."

"Adam, we can't—"

"Drive, Em," he snapped. "Please. Just drive. We'll bury her later. We'll make this un-suck somehow. But *later.*"

"We can't just drive around with her body," Emma protested.

"We don't have time to bury her," Adam said. "And I'm sure as hell not leaving her on the side of the road." Adam stared straight. He couldn't bring himself to make eye contact. For the first time since any of this started, he felt that hope had evaporated. He saw no future. "Please, Em," he whispered. "Just . . . please."

Tears pressed behind his eyes and he squinted them tight.

Emma gripped his wrist gently. "Adam . . ."

He shook his head. This was not a time to speak.

His eyes were still closed when Emma engaged the clutch and they were moving again.

This really was the way of the future, wasn't it? For all those years, through all those drills and exercises, they'd talked about the challenges of survival and the risks of death, but now he realized that death was all they had to look forward to.

Maybe Jacob Barnes wasn't a monster, after all. Maybe Lisa was blessed to die so quickly.

No. You can't do this.

"This isn't your fault, Adam."

He opened his eyes as Emma squeezed his arm again.

"We did everything we could," she said. "You could not have saved her."

"I know," he said.

"Do you?" She'd slowed to about thirty-five miles per hour, an easy speed for the road conditions.

"Do we have to talk about this?" Adam asked. "Just give me some time. I'm fine."

That was a lie. But if they could drive in silence for a while, he could make it the truth.

CHAPTER TWENTY-SEVEN

Hell Day + 30 (Nineteen Days Earlier)

SCOTT JOHNSON CHECKED THE WALL CLOCK YET AGAIN as he paced his third mile around the utility room. "This is the slowest goddamn hour in the history of time."

"We need a set of eyes out there," Bugsy said. They were sitting on barely-padded government-issued metal chairs at the foot of the steps that led to the blast door.

Johnson glared at him. "This would be the perfect time for you to keep your mouth shut," he snapped. "You're the reason we're going through this." Johnson would never admit that he agreed, that operating in a vacuum as they'd been doing was counter-productive for everyone.

"I know this is a huge violation of the rules," Bugsy said, "but you have to admit that pretty much nothing has gone the way it was supposed to."

Understatement of the decade. Given the thousands

of daily checks that had been performed on all the communications equipment, you'd think that it would have occurred to someone that one-way communication was no communication at all. You'd think that someone would have thought that congressional authority to let contracts to help America rebuild would require a functioning currency and factories that would be capable of producing things.

He couldn't imagine how frustrating it must be for the president—elevated by accident, in the first place, and currently unable to actually *control* anything.

Johnson wondered what was left standing on the other side of the walls. Was there any point in attempting to reconstruct life as it once was? In the first weeks after the war, he'd been consumed with the day-to-day activities of keeping the Annex running—and that was a task that never slowed. As they passed the halfway point of statutory isolation, he couldn't help but think of what lay beyond.

He realized now, as the time ticked down to the moment the doors would open to let Strasky back inside, that if he, Johnson, had been given the opportunity to trade places with the president's chief of staff, he'd have done it in a heartbeat. Beyond the blast door lay the newest, greatest frontier. Who *wouldn't* want to be one of the first to set eyes on the new world?

It was far too great a risk for him to inflict on any of his staff—and, given his responsibilities, it was, likewise, too great a risk for himself—but it would have been magnificent to try.

"Three minutes," Bugsy said.

"Where's the president?" Johnson asked. "I expected him to be here at the door."

"Last I saw him, he was headed back to his office. He had meetings scheduled with the House and Senate leadership."

Johnson chuckled. "Gotta keep the pot stirring, I guess. Gotta pretend that they're getting something done."

"What do we do if the door opens and Mr. Strasky is not there?" Bugsy asked. "Are we really going to maroon him outside?"

"That's what I believe *he* believes," Johnson said. "That should be enough for him to make sure he's out there."

"But if he's not?"

"We'll figure it out on the fly."

Bugsy shifted in his seat, crossing his legs and adjusting his M4 so it would rest more comfortably across his lap. "So, what's your bet, Scott? What do you think he found? Is the world still intact?"

"Oh, I don't doubt that it's intact," Johnson said. "The fact that we're still here talking about this means that no warheads landed within a few miles. The real question is about critters. Human and otherwise. Are they alive or dead?"

"The president was right about the radiation levels," Bugsy said. "They're way higher than anybody would want them, but we don't know that they're not survivable."

"So, what does *your* crystal ball say?" Johnson asked, throwing the question back at Bugsy. "Zombies and three-eyed rabbits?"

Bugsy laughed. "I'm going with Godzilla."

Johnson glanced up at the clock on the wall. "It's time," he said. He stood.

"No, let me open the hatch," Bugsy said. "You stay put. Let me suck up a little for not sticking up for you during the meeting."

"All right, then," Johnson said. "You've earned penance."

They were still a minute early when Bugsy went to work on the lock. He punched in the numbers, spun the big wheel, and pushed the heavy circle of steel outward, away from its seat and seal.

It had only moved about five inches when it lurched open so fast that it overbalanced Bugsy and made him fall forward into the opening. He yelled something that might have been "Hey!" or might only have been a grunt.

Johnson put it together right away. When he saw the face of the first stranger, he realized that the nightmare of nightmares was coming true. When he saw the number of gun barrels, he knew that he was too far outnumbered to make a difference from here.

He dropped to the floor and scrabbled on hands and knees to the steel door that led to the hallway. His rifle clattered across the floor tiles as he brought his microphone to his lips. "Code red, code red. We've been breached. Utility Corridor Bravo. This is not a drill."

What happened to Bugsy would happen to Bugsy. They'd kill him, or leave him alone, or do something in between, but he was no longer Johnson's concern. When he got to the steel door to the corridor, he opened it, tumbled through the opening and slammed it behind him.

In yet another failure of imagination on the part of the Annex's designers, the locks all worked the wrong way. The locks had been designed to keep people out of the utility room, not the other way around. Once the hatch was breached, essentially nothing stood in the way of an invading force.

Then again, who in his right mind would have considered that there'd be an invading force to contend with? No one ever truly expected that the Annex would be used in the first place. And if it ever was, the assumption was that everyone else would be dead.

A Klaxon blared over loudspeakers throughout the Annex. A mechanical voice droned, "This is an emergency. This is an emergency. All residents are to return to their dormitories immediately. This is an emergency. This is an emergency . . ."

Once in the corridor, Johnson sprinted down the hallway to the next door, the one to the staff dormitories. Into his radio, he shouted, "No! Not to the dormitories! The breach is in Utility Corridor Bravo!"

The design protocols assumed that any emergency they would deal with would have to do with radiation or physical damage to the Annex itself. By having all members report to their dormitories, they would be able to conduct a headcount and deliver instructions to a small, captive audience.

Now that emergency protocol was summoning all members of Congress to the very spot where a violent conflict was nearly inevitable.

When he reached the end of the corridor, with the door to the dormitories to his back, he turned and leveled his rifle at the door at the far end, the one he'd just scampered through. That door posed a choke point, just as the corridor itself did, and choke points leveled the playing field. It didn't matter how big your army was if it couldn't get past the portal in enough strength to exploit their tactical advantage.

He keyed his mic again. "Tactical team, report to Door Seven-Two Bravo. Full gear."

Down on the far end of the corridor, the steel door opened.

Johnson did not hesitate to send five rounds downrange. He never saw whom he was shooting at, but he knew that they were human and that they didn't belong here. Bugsy, he was sure, had already made the supreme sacrifice.

The door slammed the instant Johnson fired his first shot. It didn't matter. Johnson's 5.56-millimeter bullets would punch through the light steel door panels as if they weren't even there. Into his mic, he said, "Shots fired. Shots fired. Tactical team, expedite."

The door at the end of the hallway seemed to disintegrate as the attackers fired through it, sending God only knew how many rounds through the panels and toward Johnson. An invisible fist punched Johnson hard in the chest, and then again in the stomach. As his legs went numb, he collapsed straight down, forming a heap of bone and flesh right there on the floor at the foot of the door to the dormitories.

The door crashed open then and the flood of people started. He didn't know how many, but many more than a few. They streamed at him. He thought they might have been shooting, but maybe not. He intended to announce that the breach was complete, but nothing worked.

As they passed, they kicked him aside, rolling him against the wall, facedown.

CHAPTER TWENTY-EIGHT

Hell Day + 45 (Fifteen Days Later)

"*T*HEY EXPECT US TO LIVE *HERE*?" GARY ROUSE asked. It clearly was not a question. It was a statement of horror. "We left our house for *this* shithole?"

"Watch your mouth," Paula snapped.

"If it's a shithole I should be able to call it a shithole," Gary said. This place wasn't a house. It wasn't even a tent, not really. Somebody had sewn plastic tarps together and staked them into the ground. The floor wasn't really a floor at all, but rather a series of old pallets—the kind they use to transport bricks—pressed together, with a plywood sheet on top. "What are we supposed to sleep on?"

His mom looked as horrified as he felt, but she was trying to put a good spin on it. "I'll ask around," she said. "It looks like others were able to find padding to put down on the pallets."

"I hope so," Ronnie said. "Lying down at all will be tough. Doing it on a wood floor would be impossible."

The doctor—his name was Rory—had diagnosed his bullet wound as little more than a scrape, which was good news because the doctor's office looked more like an old house with medical tools in it than a real office.

"When your father gets back, we'll go exploring for supplies. There's got to be a way to get things."

"I want to go home," Gary said. This was the stupidest thing they'd ever done. He couldn't believe that Dad just gave away their house. He didn't even try to negotiate. Hell, he'd have joined their gang or whatever they called themselves. Why not? If you have the choice of being part of the strong team or the weak team, you'd be stupid not to choose the strong team. Yeah, they brought violence, but for crying out loud! They'd been through a goddamn war. Of course, there was going to be violence.

The thought of someone else sleeping comfortably in his bed—the one with the magazines under the mattress and the other stuff in the nightstand—pissed him off beyond belief.

From what Gary could tell, Ortho was divided between people with and people without, and somehow, the Rouses were people without. He didn't understand how those asshats on the other street had houses, while they had a shitty tent with a wooden floor.

"I'm going to go look around," Gary said.

"No, you're not," his mom said. "You're going to stay right here."

He pretended he didn't hear. Mom had been knocked off her parenting game since the night of the explosions. It was like she never quite knew what to do, while in the before days, she always had a plan and a string of orders to go with it. In the before times, she would have shit a brick if he'd walked away from her like that.

The tent city looked a lot like the refugee camps he'd seen along the Texas border in the news. If he used his imagination, he could see roadways of a sort—more like aisles, really—separating the various tents by three or four feet. There must have been a hundred of them. Maybe two hundred. Gary was only about five-five, so from his vantage point, the tent tops printed as a kind of patchwork quilt that stretched out everywhere. And what was with all the open-top drums filled with water?

Most of the tents were empty. There were a handful of moms with little kids and quite a few old people, but most people were somewhere else.

Three tents away from his own, a twenty-something lady in a dress that looked too big, and blond hair that hadn't been washed in a very long time, was tending to a baby's diaper. Gary walked that way and waited till she was done before he cleared his throat.

"I got nothing for you," the lady said.

"Um . . . okay."

She seemed startled by his voice, and she pivoted around to look up at him. "Oh, I'm sorry," she said. "You're not who I thought you were. Hi."

"Hi. I'm Gary Rouse. We just got here."

"Meg Sullivan," she said. "And this is Toby. We've been here about two days. No, three. We walked in from Linden. Took us about a week."

"Where is everybody?" Gary asked.

"Doing their committee work, I suppose," she said.

"I'm supposed to be on the clothing committee starting in a half hour."

Gary didn't get it.

"Yeah, that's how things work here," Meg explained. "You've got to earn your keep. Ain't nobody here gonna help you with nothin' if you ain't on a committee doing something for the town."

"What kind of things?"

Meg told him about the security committee, the clothing committee, the sanitation committee, and a half-dozen others, most of which sounded like a lot of physical work.

"Kids too?" Gary asked.

"How old are you?"

"Twelve."

"Absolutely," Meg said. "Your first thing will be to build your cabin. Do you have parents with you?"

He pointed at their tent, where Mom was talking to Ronnie about something. "And my dad's checking in at the office or whatever."

"Yeah, that's important. They'll give you some basics to get you started, and they'll give you an orientation of the camp, but after that, you'll be on your own. You and your family. Do you have guns?"

"No, ma'am," Gary said. "What about food? What do we eat?"

Meg pointed to a stack of green plastic pouches and some canned goods. "They'll give you a starter pack of food to get you going, but that'll only last so long. What you see there is all I've got left."

"What happens when it's gone?"

"Get a job," Meg said. "That's the solution. Get a

job, you get money—bullets, really, but that's our currency. Get money, you can buy stuff. You're free to forage out in the woods on your own, but with winter coming, I don't think that's a great strategy. Some of the folks like to hunt, but because we're getting so big, you have to get a permit to do that."

"A permit?"

"Up at the office, where your dad's at. The worry is that the game will get hunted out."

Gary listened and tried to sort out what it all meant to him. "So we need to build our own house? Is that what you're telling me?"

"Yes," Meg said. "I mean, not by yourselves. There's a building committee to help you. That's what they do. But you've got to be on your own crew, if that makes sense."

"Is that where your husband is?" As soon as the question was out of his mouth, and he saw the reaction on her face, he wished he could take it back.

"My husband was traveling that night," she said. Her voice thickened. "I waited for as long as I could, but it all got too dangerous. We had to sneak out at night. Like I said, we walked for a long time to get here."

"Why here?"

"We heard that Ortho is a safe place. Well, a safer place."

Gary realized it was time for him to shut up and be quiet. This was a town of losers, right? A town filled with people like his father, who ran away from everything they'd built over a lifetime to hunker down in tents and shacks. How could that be safer?

"It's nice here," Meg said, as if reading his thoughts. "I know it's all startling, but it's nice to have neighbors again. And organization."

"Organization?"

"The lady in charge here really knows what she's doing. Used to be in Congress. She's tough as nails, but fair. I don't know how she keeps it all straight."

"Are you building a house, too?" Gary asked.

"With Toby here, that's a little tough for me. Vicky—Victoria Emerson, the lady in charge—makes exceptions for people who can't take care of everything themselves. Sick people, old people . . . people with little kids."

"Gary!" His mom's voice cut through his thoughts and stopped their conversation.

He looked up to see her pointing in the distance, where his father was returning from wherever he'd been.

CHAPTER TWENTY-NINE

Hell Day + 30 (Fifteen Days Earlier)

*P*ENN GLENDALE, PRESIDENT OF THE UNITED STATES, was in one of the small lounging spaces adjacent to the House Chamber, deep into a discussion of funding options with Speaker Fortnight and the Senate minority leader, Dennis Laraja, and the rest of the leadership teams, when the alarm went off.

This is an emergency. This is an emergency . . .

"What the hell is that?" Laraja said.

Penn stood. He feared that he knew exactly what it was. Arlen Strasky was due back from his recon mission, and now the Annex was rocked with an emergency.

Then they heard the first gunshots.

Speaker Fortnight let out a little *yip* and jumped to her feet, too. "Who's shooting?"

As if to answer her question, the building reverberated with a long fusillade of additional shots. From the deep percussive nature of them, Penn knew that it was rifle fire.

"Oh, my God, are the Solara people following through with their threats?" asked Randy Banks, House minority leader. "Are they shooting our people?"

"What do we do?" Angela shouted.

"The first thing we do is stop shouting," Penn said.

The door to the lounge crashed open, revealing a Solara employee who was dressed for war. "Mr. President, we're under assault. I need you to take cover."

"Where?" Penn asked. "Where the hell do you go to hide in a concrete bunker?"

"Standard procedure, sir."

"To hell with your standard procedure. Tell me what is going on."

"I don't know, sir. Something about a breach of the facility."

"Oh, my God," the Speaker said. "What does that mean?"

Penn said, "It means that you need to go to work, young man. Don't worry about me. Don't worry about us. Go do your job."

"But, sir—"

"Do it."

As the Solara soldier left them, Penn followed.

"Where are you going!" Angela demanded.

Penn didn't bother to answer. If there was one person on the planet to whom he owed nothing, it was Angela Fortnight. What he knew for certain was that Arlen Strasky was no doubt in peril. He knew that this place—their home, their sanctuary, the seat of power for whatever was left of the Free World—was under attack.

He was commander in chief, goddammit. He was going to find the battle and be in charge. He was tired of hiding, tired of being told what to do. He was sick to death of not actually being in charge of *anything*.

If a war was coming to this space, he was, by God, going to run it. As he made his decision, he wondered if he'd be alive tomorrow—in twenty minutes, for that matter—to reflect on the wisdom of his choice.

Penn had no idea that Solara had this many employees, far more than he'd ever seen. There must have been a robust behind-the-scenes staff. All of them were streaming toward the dormitory wing—the very location where the droning alarm voice told the members of Congress to assemble.

The Solara troops carried long guns and pistols and were in various stages of kitting up for war. While some were fully dressed and armored, others clearly had been sleeping just moments before the alarm went out.

Penn joined the stream of responders, though with greater effort and significantly less speed. House and Senate members, plus their staffers, were caught in transit from their respective chambers to the assumed shelter in the dorms.

"Everybody get down!" Penn yelled. "On the floor! Everyone get on—"

He'd made it nearly halfway to the door to the dormitory hallway when someone grabbed his shoulders from behind and pulled him down onto the floor. It was a Solara employee he knew to be Billy St. James.

"This isn't for you, Mr. President," St. James said. "You need to stay down, too, sir."

"You need to not worry about me," Penn said, and he pushed the man away.

The world erupted in gunfire, and St. James lost his focus on the president. In the enclosed space of the bunker, gun smoke hung like fog. The concussive pounding of the gunfire left his head feeling as if it were stuffed with cotton.

The attackers looked like everyday citizens. Dressed in worn civilian clothes, the heavily armed men and women flooded into the common work area from the dormitory wing, weapons up and hammering away at everyone they saw.

Solara formed a skirmish line of sorts, using thick reinforced concrete roof supports for cover as they mowed down the first wave of attackers.

Panicked members and staff reacted blindly and awkwardly. Some squirmed along the floor, others stood and started to run. A few were hit and fell. Many screamed.

The gunfire was relentless.

Penn found a pillar for his own cover and hunkered behind it. He was watching Billy St. James when a bullet slammed into the pillar he'd chosen, spraying spalled concrete into his face. St. James yelled and brought his hands to his eyes, exposing himself just enough to get shot through the forehead.

The attackers seemed fearless in Penn's eyes, and the Solara defenders powerless to stop the flow through the door. As the attackers flooded in, they spread out, forming a rough circle that effectively eliminated any reliable cover for the Solara shooters. They were being hit from all sides.

The attackers killed indiscriminately, so far as Penn could tell.

Two minutes into the fight, it had devolved into a bloodbath.

Penn needed to do something.

And he knew exactly what the something was.

Saying a silent prayer not to get blown in half, he stood and stepped out from behind his cover, waving his hands over his head like a football ref declaring a dead ball.

"Stop!" he shouted. "Cease-fire! Everybody stop shooting! Everybody stop shooting!"

Maybe the attackers recognized him. Maybe they were startled by the stupidity of an old guy wading into the middle of a battle. Whatever the reason, no one shot him.

"Solara employees, cease-fire!" he yelled. "You other people! Whoever you are, stop shooting. You're in! You won. There's no reason for the slaughter to continue."

"Who the hell is that?" someone from the attacking force said.

A tall man with blond hair, and more muscles than any one person should have, said, "That is Pennington Glendale, I believe. President of the United States of America."

CHAPTER THIRTY

Hell Day + 49 (Nineteen Days Later)

*E*STABLISHING A COMMON CURRENCY TURNED OUT to be a key to returning a trace of normalcy to Ortho. In the early days, hunters and preppers were inherently "wealthier" than others, but a certain equality emerged within a few days as shop owners reopened and were able to start selling their wares again.

Within the first few days, households with extra clothes or dishes or tools opened up retail outlets from their homes. People with smarts, but few manual skills, started charging to educate children. Depending on the weather and the flow of the breeze, the air would sometimes be heavy with the aroma of smoking meats. Farmers were beginning to find a market for their animals and autumn vegetables. People with the means and knowledge to can such products, likewise, opened retail establishments.

And then there were the Sables. Anthony and Livvy

had only days before been whining to Victoria about their lack of skills to find a means to make money, but now it turned out that the Sable family were wine affi- cionados, with a collection of truly fine vintages. Mostly full-bodied reds, but with a smattering of most every varietal. Their solution to their financial woes was to open up a sidewalk bar and offer libations to passersby who felt the need.

Victoria first became aware of the Roadside Vint- ner—that was what their handwrought sign read— from a huffy octogenarian Baptist who took umbrage at the boldness of selling "Satan's nectar" out in the open. If only to get the woman out of her office, Victo- ria had agreed to speak with the Sables.

She and McCrea rode up together on bicycles, their rifles slung across their backs—and thank God for Paul Kinkaid, who first thought of the idea of a bicycle bank (now the "bike bank"). The more she realized how well citizens understood their own needs in their own communities, the more she wished that she had pushed harder for less government when she was in Congress.

Livvy and Anthony Sable had opened their shop— their stand, really—on the sidewalk outside their home on Jubal Early Street, one of the older residential sec- tions of the town. To Victoria's eye, they'd carried a portable bar, which might have been in their den, out to the sidewalk, and then placed two bar stools and two club chairs in the street, immediately in front of the bar.

"Afternoon, Vicky," Anthony said as they ap- proached. "Major."

Victoria made a point to look pleasant and wave as she braked to a stop just short of the club chairs.

"You're not here to complain that we're blocking traffic, are you?" Livvy quipped.

"Selling liquor without a license?" Anthony added.

Victoria dismounted the bike and propped it against its kickstand. "Why do I get the feeling that you opened this establishment with one thumb in my eye?" She sold it with a flash of a smile.

"Why, whatever do you mean?" Anthony asked with a feigned Georgia accent. "I presume that Anita Steele walked her crazy ass down to you?"

"Casting no aspersions toward Ms. Steele's hind-quarters, I will confirm that, yes, she came to see me."

"You told me to find a way to make money, Vicky."

"Yes, I did," she confirmed.

"So now you're going to shut me down?"

McCrea had dismounted as well and had joined Victoria at the bar.

"I'm not sure I have the power to do that," Victoria said.

"To the degree that I get a vote," McCrea said, "I hope she doesn't. I'm surprised you're the first person with this idea."

Anthony looked surprised. "Really?"

"What's your plan for the wintertime?" Victoria asked. "Or for bad weather in general?"

The Sables exchanged confused looks. This clearly was not the way they'd thought this confrontation was going to go. "I–I guess we move it into the house," Anthony said.

"And you're welcome to do that," Victoria said. "But let us offer you an alternative."

McCrea took it from there. "As you know, there's a number of unoccupied storefronts downtown. I think probably some of them closed before Hell Day, but others have closed more recently. Would you consider moving this into one of those?"

"We've got to get a sense of community back," Victoria expounded. "If we're going to survive the winter at our strongest, we need to bring businesses downtown. Centralize them so people don't have to wander all over creation to load up on essentials."

"We'll get a wagon, or maybe Mike Underwood's El Camino, down here to help you move your supplies," McCrea said.

Livvy and Anthony looked at each other again.

"Tell you what," McCrea said. "While you think about it, what do you have in a bold cabernet?"

Anthony's face brightened. "Now you're talking. I have a really nice Stags' Leap—"

Victoria raised her hand, asking for silence. "Do you hear it?" she asked.

McCrea scowled and closed his eyes.

"It sounds like whistles to me," Livvy said.

The screech of the whistles was still far away, but it traveled on the breeze, nonetheless. She concentrated on the pattern of the blasts. They were staggered.

"Oh, shit," McCrea said.

Victoria came to the same conclusion at the same instant. "Blue fire," she said, and she darted back to her bicycle.

CHAPTER THIRTY-ONE

Hell Day + 30 (Nineteen Days Earlier)

ROGER PARSONS WASN'T SURE WHAT HE'D EXPECTED the outcome of this raid to be, but he expected the fight to be more vigorous than what they encountered. He also expected the interior of the seat of government for the Free World to be a little less spartan. Before signing on with the world of professional wrestling, he'd served for twelve years in the United States Navy, most of that afloat off the coasts of America's many enemies. He had to say that the Annex, as the locals called it, was shittier than his shittiest ship. He couldn't imagine what a transition it must have been for these political elites to shift into the life of a wartime grunt.

His first order of business was to gather up all the weapons and ammo. Then he separated the politicos from their protectors. Even though everyone wore uniforms, there was no mistaking the physique and bear-

ing of the mercenaries from those of the people they
failed to protect. He rounded up what was left of the
Solara crew and locked them into the jail cells that
came with the Annex.

Why the hell would war planners include jail cells
in a facility designed to shelter lawmakers?

Then he thought back to the decades-long dysfunc-
tion that defined Washington politics, and it made sense.
Shit, if they'd put those bastards in jail for malfeasance
and treason a long time ago, maybe the world would
still be intact.

Out there—in the world beyond this bunker—people had been left to fend for themselves, while these
privileged few had all the comforts and luxuries of
home. They had electricity, which meant that they had
running water and heat and air-conditioning. They had
laundry. These were all consumables with limited shelf
life, but at this stage, as the world outside ran low on
everything, this was a gold mine for Roger's people.

The members of Congress were docile to the point
of compliance. Roger's people ordered them into their
respective chambers and assigned sentries both within
and without the doors. Most were so terrified they might
get hurt that they didn't even offer up a complaint.

Kenny DeWilde waved at Parsons from across the
massive room that looked like it had once been display
space for conventions. Parsons waved back and waited
for him to walk the distance.

When he arrived, his face was a massive grin. "We
found the food stores," DeWilde said. "You won't believe how much they've got. Everything from canned
goods to frozen meat. What they've got may get us

through the winter, if we don't become pigs. They even have cookies and cake. Ice cream. You wouldn't believe it."

Parsons liked what he was hearing. This could very well be the stroke of good fortune they needed to live another six months. He figured that planning out further than that was an exercise in futility.

"Kenny, I need you to get together with one of these Solara guys and learn everything you can about how this place works. I mean, I want to know about the fuel tanks and the electrical system, the whole nine yards."

"What if they refuse?"

"Shoot the sonofabitch. You'll only have to do that two or three times before people will be aching to give you all the help they can."

DeWilde laughed. "I like your management style." He started to walk away, but then stopped and turned. "Oh, I almost forgot. The president would like to speak to you."

"Where is he?"

"He has his own office," DeWilde said, pointing. "That one over there. I assigned Thibodeau as guard to make sure he didn't go anywhere."

Parsons shrugged. "Sure, why not?" He started walking that way.

"He's not alone in there," DeWilde said. "He's got the congressional leadership team with him. They demanded to be treated differently than the others."

Parsons shook his head in disbelief. The level of cluelessness among politicians never ceased to amaze him.

Thirty seconds later, he pushed open the president's door without knocking. Glendale sat behind a meager

metal desk, and three others—a woman and two men—
sat gathered around. They looked startled, triggering
concerns about what they might be discussing.

"Good afternoon, Mr. Glendale," Parsons said, deliberately avoiding the honorific for the office.

No one rose from their seats.

"You have the advantage," the president said. "We
don't know your name."

"I'm Roger Parsons. I'm in charge now."

A stocky guy, sixty-something, snorted a laugh. "Not
hardly," he said. "This is the president of the United
States, and that lady there is Angela Fortnight, Speaker
of the United States House of Representatives."

"Pleased to meet you all," Parsons said. "And who
are you?" That last question was directed at the man
who just spoke.

"Dennis Laraja, Senate minority leader. And this is
Nick Barker, Senate majority leader."

Barker looked short and skinny, though he did look
familiar.

"Your man Strasky told me that there'd been a shake-
up in leadership," Parsons said.

"Where is Mr. Strasky?" the president asked.

"Dead. I had him shot."

While the others gasped, the president's gaze hardened.

"I'm sorry it had to go down that way," Parsons explained, "but I didn't see that we had any choice. We
couldn't risk him sounding an alarm. He said he was
your staff manager or something."

"Chief of staff," the Speaker corrected.

The president continued to glare.

"Right. Like I said, sorry about that." Parsons returned to the door and opened it. "Do me a favor," he said to Thibodeau. "Bring me a chair."

He turned to the president and his team. "Y'all have made a hell of a mess out of the world. What do you have to say for yourselves?"

Speaker Fortnight leapt from her chair. "Listen here—"

Parsons put one hand on the Glock at his hip and the other on the Speaker's shoulder. He pushed her down. "Ma'am, I don't make a habit of shooting women, but don't think I would hesitate to blow you to hell. Are we understanding each other?"

The president cleared his throat. "Okay, Mr. Parsons, dial it down a bit. I concede that you've got the upper hand, at least for the time being."

It was Laraja's turn to stand. "Mr. President, what are you saying?"

"The obvious, Dennis," the president replied.

This wasn't going as Parsons had expected, and the difference made him uneasy. He'd essentially just commandeered the White House, yet the president seemed damn near complacent.

A knock on the door announced the arrival of the new chair. Parsons set it up behind the president, forcing the other man to pivot to face him. "I believe you were about to explain how you screwed up the entire world, and killed a billion people."

The president looked mildly amused—again, not what Parsons had been expecting. "I'm not sure what game you're playing, Mr. Parsons, but I'm going to do my best to disappoint you. That said, a lot went wrong on the night when the war started."

"And ended," Parsons said. "Right? From outside, it sounded like it didn't last more than a few hours."

"You are correct," the president said. "And while it is my long-standing policy never to apologize for the actions of my colleagues, I will tell you that the people in this building had nothing to do with the events of that night. That's all on the president."

"But that's you," Parsons said. He was being deliberately obtuse, to see how the others would react.

"Not then, it wasn't. I ascended to the presidency only after the rest of the executive chain was killed."

"Ah," Parsons said. "So you're only responsible for the country's *response* to the attacks. You're responsible for taking care of the injured, burying the dead and putting out the fires?"

The president started to answer, then chose not to. Perhaps he'd seen the rhetorical trap that Parsons had set for him.

"In case you were wondering, you sucked at your job."

"Tell me," the president said. "What *is* it like out there?"

"Exactly how you'd think," Parsons said. "The people who haven't yet died are trying to. Nothing works. There's no infrastructure left. Water has to be pumped by hand. But I'm glad y'all were able to stay comfortable and well fed."

"The communications challenges were much worse than any of us had anticipated," the president said. "We've been working day and night to fix it."

"And then what?" Parsons asked, genuinely baffled. "You get it fixed. Say you find a way to go on television and tell us all what to do. Who the hell is going to see or hear you?"

Speaker Fortnight said, "You need to realize, Mr.

Parsons, that the purpose of government is to find a way to provide—"

"Stop!" Parsons shouted it because he couldn't deal with his anger any other way. "Stop talking! Do you even hear yourselves? Do you have any idea what the world is trying to do while you sit in here and play government parlor games? They're fighting to stay alive. In some cases, they're fighting each other, and even when they're not, they're fighting to feed themselves and their families."

"What about you?" asked Nick Barker, his first words since Parsons had arrived. "What have you been doing to stay alive?"

"I've been providing for my people. I'm not always great at it, and I've failed maybe more than I've won. But at least I was out there."

"We all have our roles to perform in emergencies," the Speaker stated.

"Oh, good Lord. Shut. Up." Parsons realized in a flash that he did not have the intellectual or emotional bandwidth for talking with these people anymore. "Mr. Thibodeau!" he yelled.

The guard appeared in the doorway. A physician by trade, Thibodeau was the first face Parsons saw when everyone gathered in the lobby on the night of the attacks. His wife had passed just last week, having run out of her heart medicine.

Parsons said, "Mr. Thibodeau, these people are under arrest."

That got the president out of his seat. "Wait one minute, Mr. Parsons—"

"I've waited forty minutes too long, as it is," Parsons said.

"On whose authority?" Laraja objected.

"Whatever is your authority of choice, *Dennis,*" Parsons said, leaning on the name that he'd heard the president utter.

"Mr. Thibodeau, if they attempt to leave this room without permission, and without escort, you are to shoot them to death. No hesitation, no questions."

"You do realize that I am president of the United States, right?"

Parsons turned on him. "I don't give a shit what you think you used to be, or what you want to call yourself. Any of you. President, pope, king, queen, I don't care. What you specifically are not is in charge of anything here anymore."

"I presume you're placing *yourself* in charge?" Laraja asked.

"That's exactly what I'm doing," Parsons said. "The good news is, I couldn't possibly do a worse job than you have."

CHAPTER THIRTY-TWO

Hell Day + 49 (Nineteen Days Later)

ADAM AND EMMA DIDN'T SPEAK MUCH FOR THE rest of the trip away from Appleton. Adam thought he'd hardened to the notion of death and destruction, but the burden of having Lisa's body bouncing in the back of the Bronco unnerved him. Maybe Emma was right. Maybe it was disrespectful to drive with her like this. Maybe it was bad juju, as his mother liked to say.

But what was the alternative?

He was going to have a baby of his own soon. What if this upset the karmic balance for his son or daughter? He knew it was ridiculous at its face—such things did not exist. He had a hard enough time accepting that God Himself was actually a thing. To accept that random events could affect a person's life in perpetuity was even sillier.

But suppose . . .

"Stop this," he muttered.

"What?"

He didn't realize that he'd spoken aloud. Now that he had, he didn't want to pull Emma into his troubling thoughts. "Nothing," he said. "I'm just going a little crazy." He took a settling breath. "I'm really sorry about this, Em."

She gave him that little smirk that renewed his faith in humanity. "I am too. It's all so—"

Adam heard it, too.

"Whistles?" he asked.

"That's what it sounds like to me. But it's not natural."

"They sound like lifeguards," Adam said. "Stop the truck."

Emma pulled to a stop, but kept the engine running. Sure enough, it sounded like lifeguard whistles blaring out of the woods. But the pattern was irregular. One long, two shorts and a long.

"What the hell?" Adam said.

"Signals, maybe?" Emma asked.

"I guess. I mean, why not? The day is already off-the-charts weird."

"What should we do?"

"Well, we're sure as hell not going back to Appleton," Adam said. "That means going forward. But carefully."

"What does *carefully* mean?"

"I have no idea. Let's just try not to get shot."

Emma engaged the clutch, and they started driving again. "We must be getting close to the town," she said.

Adam knew she was right. What he didn't know was whether that was a good thing or a bad thing. Ju-

nior in Appleton had said that Ortho was more organized. Maybe they'd established some kind of an alert
system. If so, then they were *really* organized.

The whistle blasts seemed to be following them as
they navigated the winding mountain road.

No, that wasn't right. The whistles seemed to be
leading them. And as they progressed, the code patterns changed. One long, two shorts and a long became
one long, one short, one long, one short.

Adam harbored no doubt that they were driving into
a trap. But that didn't have to mean violence. Maybe it
was just a checkpoint.

But what would they be looking for?

A dead little girl in the back wasn't going to play to
their benefit, but the truth was the truth, and they had
the battle damage on the Bronco to prove it.

"Talk to me, Adam," Emma said. "You've got your
plotting face on. I don't know what I'm to think of
that."

"They have all the advantage here," he said. "They're
expecting us. Well, not *us,* but someone. They know
we're coming. Since they have a signaling system set
up, that probably means they have defenses set up."

"Wherever we're going is getting closer every second," Emma said. "Can you put all of that in the form
of a plan? A direction?"

Adam saw only one way. "We keep weapons ready,
but at neutral. If their intent is to kill us, they're going
to be able to do it without us even knowing it."

"How do we explain about Lisa?" Emma asked.

"We just have to be honest," Adam said. "In fact,
honesty about everything is going to be our best plan.
The whistle signals tell me that they're not happy about

getting new people into town, but if they wanted to take us out, they could have sniped at us instead of blowing whistles about us. Let's see what happens."

A half mile later, they found out.

The sound of whistles in the air reminded Victoria of cicada season from the before days. The shrill screech seemed to shimmer in the air, a sound that was as disturbing as it was unignorable.

She and McCrea raced toward the center of town far faster than her biking skills could justify. The handlebars vibrated in her grasp as they flew down the long hill without touching the brakes. As the cross street loomed at the bottom, though, she couldn't take it anymore. She tightened her hand around the brake lever for the rear tire—a little too tightly at first, causing her to fishtail. She recovered, but it was close.

Amazing how quickly childhood skills become forgotten when they go unused.

By the time she turned left onto Kanawha Road, the militia lines were already forming. The defensive shooting positions had already been predetermined and assigned by McCrea and First Sergeant Copley. George Simmons and Joey Abbott were in the thick of it all, making sure that positions were manned appropriately. From the whistle signals, everyone knew that whatever the threat was, it was coming from the south. The town militia was forming accordingly, taking up V-shaped skirmish lines on both sides of the road, facing the same direction, but staggered so as not to pose a friendly-fire threat by encroaching on each other's lines of fire.

"The training seems to be paying off," Victoria said

as she slid to a stop five seconds behind McCrea. He'd taken a position near the boat launch, in plain sight, but probably out of harm's way, at least for the initial confrontation.

"Right now, it's all a parade," he said. "Everything can go to shit after the first shot is fired. I want to know what the hell the threat is."

Instinctively, Victoria cast a look up and behind to see her boys in the windows of the hardware store, right where they belonged. Caleb saw her looking and waved. A second later, Luke waved, too.

"Good God, how life has changed," she thought aloud.

McCrea followed her eyeline and chuckled. "If President Blanton knew about this, she'd be shitting pickles," he said. "Abolish the Second Amendment, my ass."

Victoria's mind flashed to the place she chose not to go—in a bunker with a bunch of suits who were trying to run the world from a basement. There wasn't a single attractive thing about cowardice. She was unspeakably glad that she'd raised her kids to be different than their peers.

The sound of galloping hooves drew Victoria's attention toward the south. Young Levi Willis was squeezing everything he could out of the mare as he screamed into the center of town. "It's the Bronco!" he yelled. "It's the Bronco!"

At first, Victoria wondered what she was hearing, her mind going to a rodeo horse. Then she remembered the buzz about a red-and-white old-model Ford Bronco that had a reputation as a killing machine. Wherever it went, the rumors went, people died in its wake.

She stepped forward and raised her hand to be recognized. Levi saw her and waved back. Regaining control of his horse, he got it stopped, then walked it in. Behind him, George Simmons jogged to keep up.

"Okay, Levi, settle down," Victoria said. "First of all, were you up at the roadblock to see with your own eyes, or are you repeating rumors?" It was a problem in these days without instantaneous communication for stories to become embellished by the time they reached ground.

"I saw it," Levi said. "I was there on the line."

McCrea took control of the horse's reins at the bit and held him steady. "Why don't you climb down?" he said. "Take a breath."

Levi seemed to eject out of the saddle in a dismount that only young people can pull off. "You can believe me," he said after the dismount. "I really did see with my own eyes."

"I'm not doubting you," Victoria said. "I just need to know the details."

George Simmons finally caught up. "What did I miss?"

"Nothing yet," Victoria assured. "Just that a Ford Bronco has been sighted."

"Not *a* Ford Bronco," Levi corrected. "*The* Ford Bronco. Red and white, blistered paint. And listen to this." He could barely control his excitement. "They've got a dead child in the back."

McCrea recoiled. "You're shitting me."

"I shit you not, Major," Levi said. If there'd ever been a note of revulsion, it had been replaced with pure adrenaline. "Just dead in the middle of a bunch of guns and ammo. They even had *dynamite*."

"Can that be possible?" George asked.

"Of *course,* it's possible," Levi said. "I told you, I *saw* it."

"Where are they now?" Victoria asked.

"They were at the first roadblock when I left. So about a mile out. Eric Lofland zip-tied them. A man and a woman, and he's walking them into town now."

"What about the Bronco?" McCrea asked.

"I don't know," Levi said. "Once we saw who they were, and I knew that the alarms were sounding, Eric told me to bust ass into town and let people know what we have."

"All right," McCrea said. "I don't know if this is a big deal or not, but I need you to bust ass back that way and make sure that the roadblock stays manned. We don't need everybody and his brother walking these people into town. For all we know, this could be a ruse, a bluff to get us distracted."

Victoria admired the way that McCrea was perpetually on a war footing in his head. Every town needed someone like that. But she had other concerns. "And, Levi," she said, "when you go back up there, take the pulse of the crowd. The air is filled with rumors of them being Bonnie and Clyde, but not one person has actually seen them do anything. I don't want to hear stories of this man and woman being lynched and hanged from a tree."

"I don't think anyone would do that, ma'am," Levi said.

"Tell Eric Lofland what I told you," she said. "Tell him if justice needs to be done, it's going to be done in a civilized way."

"I don't know—"

"Just tell him exactly what I told you," Victoria said. "He'll understand."

"Yes, ma'am," Levi said. He remounted the horse in a single hop, barely touching the stirrup. McCrea only just got his hand out of the way before Levi turned the horse and launched back the way he'd come.

"Ever get the feeling that someone is having the time of his life?" McCrea asked with a chuckle.

Victoria ignored him. "Gentlemen," she said, "I need you to make sure that no one is trigger-happy on this thing."

"You act like we've let you down in the past, Vicky," George said.

"The militia is trained," McCrea said. "They know what to do and what not to do. Get into their heads now, and you can cause an avalanche of unintended consequences."

George touched the brim of his John Deere baseball cap. "I'm gonna get back with the troops." He walked away.

"Where do I need to be?" Victoria asked, barely above a whisper.

McCrea gave her a curious look. "What do you mean?"

"Being in charge," she said. "What's the best place for me to be?"

McCrea placed his hands on his hips and side-stepped away so he could see her better. "You run the town, Vicky," he said. "Troops and tactics are mine."

She took no issue with that, but the question remained. "Should I be on the front line with the others?"

McCrea's look of confusion deepened. "What are you *really* asking me?"

Victoria wasn't sure she knew how to put it. In fact, she was sorry that she'd opened the door. "You've said a thousand times that leadership is fragile. That optics matter. I want the people to see that, well, that—"

"Stop," McCrea said. "There's not a soul in this town who follows you because you can wield a rifle. They follow you because of who you are. They walk through fire for you because they respect the fact that you respect them."

"They're all putting their lives on the line. I can't just hang back in the rear."

McCrea shrugged. "Then don't hang back in the rear. Do what you want, Vicky. Do what you think is the right thing to do. This isn't a fashion show, and it's not an audition. Whatever you do, do it *because* it's what you think is the proper action. The whole concept of optics died weeks ago in a million-degree fireball."

Victoria didn't understand her own climb to power. It never was what she wanted—though McCrea and her boys would argue otherwise—but it was hers, nonetheless. And at every step, with every decision, she felt like an imposter.

The buzz from the assembled militia told her that their prisoners were approaching.

"Okay," McCrea said, "I do have a suggestion for where you should be."

Victoria waited for it.

"Go back to Maggie's. Be at your desk. Look official when you greet these people you'll have to pass judgment on. Go be the judge."

Victoria saw the rationale. That was the sensible thing to do. Project justice to be the key to everything. As she turned to head to Maggie's, she heard shouting from the direction of the hardware store. She thought she heard a *holy shit,* which was entirely in character for either of her boys, now that they'd pushed societal niceties off to the side.

When she looked to the windows, she saw them darting away from their posts, and she got a bad feeling. What could that mean? What had they seen?

Ten seconds later, they both crashed out of the hardware's front door, their rifles slung and slapping across their backs.

"What the hell?" McCrea muttered.

"Luke!" Victoria yelled. "Caleb!"

They were both running full tilt down the road, toward the approaching killers.

"Boys!" Victoria called again. "Stop!"

If they heard her, they made no indication.

"Oh, this can't be good," she said. She started after them.

Adam hated the perp walk. With his arms pinioned behind him, he had no choice but to endure the steady flow of blood from his nose, just as he had to endure the repeated shoves from behind that seemed designed to make him fall on his face. He hadn't gone down yet, but he was sure it was only a matter of time.

The sentries at the roadblock had taken them down hard, dragging him and Emma both out of their seats and onto the street. He sensed that these people had been expecting them. He assumed it was the Bronco that gave them away. The stories preceded them yet again.

Roughness transitioned to brutality after they discovered Lisa's body in the cargo bed. He was pretty sure they'd broken a rib or two with the massive kicks after his arms had been taken out of service. If something in his gut hadn't been ruptured, too, it was a matter of Providence more than of planning or restraint.

Because the Bronco sat between them as they were manhandled at the roadblock, Adam had no idea what they'd done to Emma, but her swollen eye and bloody lip spoke of violence.

Throughout the ordeal on the street, everyone seemed to talk *about* them, but no one spoke *to* them. There was talk about shooting them on the spot, but that was quashed right away.

"That's not the way we do things," someone said. "They'll get a trial."

"And then we'll shoot them," someone else said, earning a guffaw from the crowd.

"Holy shit, they've got a whole arsenal in here," a voice said.

"What're you gonna do with the dynamite?" somebody else asked. The question immediately preceded the big kick to his ribs.

"All right, stop that!" said the same voice that had assured a trial before their execution. "We're not doing this. We're taking them into town."

"Ow!" Emma yelled. "You're hurting me!"

"She's pregnant, goddammit!" Adam yelled. "Whatever you're doing, stop it! We're not fighting you!"

That earned him the gut kick.

Hands grabbed his biceps on both sides and he was lifted/assisted to his feet.

He got a first look at Emma's swelling face. "Are you okay?" he asked.

Before she could answer, someone pushed him forward. "Get going, kid killer."

And the long walk started.

The level of organization here impressed him, despite the pain. This group had its share of assholes, but they also had the benefit of leadership.

"We're going to be okay, Em," he said.

"Be quiet," a guard replied.

And so it went for the better part of a mile, Adam figured. At one point, a teenager galloped up on horseback and spoke to a guy named Eric, whom Adam figured to be the man in charge, but he couldn't hear what was said. Whatever it was, the guy named Eric seemed insulted.

After about five minutes of walking, the forest started to give way to businesses and then to homes. The number of armed people surprised Adam and confirmed his suspicion that the shrillness and tempo of the whistles were some form of signal.

He wanted to ask what the plan was—what the citizens' army planned to do with them—but decided not to. He might not want to hear the answer.

As in Appleton, a number of businesses displayed broken glass and signs of vandalism, but unlike Appleton, the broken windows had been boarded up and the glass disposed of. The townspeople seemed curious, but they did not swarm in. Nor did they run away. This place was as close to being civilized as any he'd seen since the night of the war.

With each additional step, and each additional observation, he gained hope that whatever lay ahead, they weren't on the edge of being lynched.

Far in the distance, he thought he heard his name

being called. He strained to look ahead, but the way the little parade was organized, he couldn't see past the escorts immediately in front of him.

"Adam! Adam!"

There was no mistaking it now. Someone definitely was calling his name. When he looked over to Emma, she was scowling. Clearly, she'd heard it, too.

Ahead, Eric looked back at him. "Is your name Adam?"

"Yessir."

"Huh."

Eric stepped aside, and Adam saw two familiar-looking, skinny young men with rifles running straight at him. His first instinct was to brace for conflict. He stopped, spread his stance, bent his legs a bit. But then it clicked in his head.

He straightened and his whole face lit up. "Holy shit!" he yelled.

He should have stayed braced because when his brothers hit him at a run, they all tumbled to the pavement.

CHAPTER THIRTY-THREE

Hell Day + 49 (The Same Day)

*B*Y THE TIME VICTORIA CAUGHT UP TO THE ACTION IN the street, a scrum had started. There was wrestling, there was shouting, but there also seemed to be laughing. Eric Lofland was trying to break it up, but only halfheartedly. Everyone in the crowd looked confused. Among them stood a beautiful young lady with the kind of red hair that rarely happens outside of Ireland. She was yelling at the clutch of people on the ground and more upset than anyone else. Her hands were tied behind her.

"Hey!" Victoria yelled. "What is this? What's going on?"

Eric Lofland turned at the sound of her voice and said, "I have no idea. Ask your sons."

Victoria took two steps forward and froze. "Oh, my God," she breathed, and she brought her hands to her mouth. "Adam?" Could this possibly be true?

"What is it, Vicky?" McCrea asked.

She couldn't make her voice work. She walked forward carefully, as if being drawn by a supernatural force. Yes, she knew that was stupid and impossible, but that's what it felt like. All three of her boys were wrestling on the street, it seemed, the oldest with his hands rendered useless.

Luke was the first to see her approaching. "Mom!" he shouted. "It's Adam!"

Caleb added, "Look, Mom, Adam's here!"

Eric arrived at her side. "What's happening, ma'am?"

She looked at Eric through blurred vision. "That's my son," she managed to say. "Please help him stand up."

"Ma'am, he and that girl over there were driving the red-and-white Bronco we've been hearing about."

"Please," Victoria said. "Help him to his feet."

"Get away from him!" Caleb snapped as Eric stepped up to do as he'd been asked.

Eric jumped back as Caleb and Luke brought Adam upright, and then to his feet. He looked stunned. Disoriented. "Mom?"

Victoria glided to her eldest son, her arms spread wide. She still couldn't bring her voice to work, so she folded him into a hug and pulled his face down into the crook of her neck just like she used to do when he was little. He smelled terrible. Wonderful.

She felt his shoulders shake as the emotions caught up with him as well.

"What are you doing here?" he rasped.

"Free his hands," McCrea said from behind.

"But—"

"Now," McCrea said.

Victoria sensed movement, and then a few seconds later, Adam's arms were around her, too. Then the other boys joined in for a family embrace.

"I thought you were dead," Victoria whispered.

"Almost was. A couple of times."

"Vicky." It was McCrea's voice in her ear, from very close by. "There's a better place for this."

Victoria wanted to tell him to go to hell, to bother someone else, but she knew he was right. She put her hands on Adam's shoulders and eased him away. Then she placed her hands on either side of his face. She'd never seen him in a beard before. Even though he'd just turned eighteen—on the night of the attacks, in fact—a few flecks of gray were already visible. His eyes were those of an old man.

"How are you?" she asked, emphasizing each word with a gentle shake of his face.

Then came that grin that he'd learned to weaponize even as a little boy. "All things considered, I've been better." He pulled away, hooking his brothers into another quick embrace around their necks, and then turned toward the redhead.

"Mom, this is Emma Carson." He led Victoria closer, his brothers still hooked in his elbows. "She and I are going to make you a grandmother."

Victoria halted—hard stop. Someone had pulled all the air out of the atmosphere.

Adam laughed—it was a good laugh, a sound of real happiness. "These things happen, you know."

McCrea snapped his fingers for attention. "See to the young lady's hands."

Eric said, "Major, they killed a little girl. Her body is in their Bronco."

Victoria looked at Adam, aghast.

"We didn't kill her," he said. "It's a long story. We were trying to save her life. We got jumped and a bullet came through the tailgate."

"It was terrible," Emma said, her first words in Victoria's presence. Her tone carried a pleasing Southern twang, but not from this part of the South. Atlanta, maybe.

"Ma'am, they have dynamite in their truck," Eric said.

"It's a hard thing to walk away from when you find it," Adam said.

Caleb said, "This is bullshit," and he flicked open the locking-blade knife from his pocket. He circled around Emma and cut her zip ties.

"Mrs. Emerson!" Eric shouted.

"What do you want from me, Eric?" Victoria said. "This boy—this *man*—is my son. I promise you, he is not a danger to anyone here. And if he's a flight risk . . ." She turned to Adam. "You're not a flight risk, are you?"

"No."

"Do you plan to blow up any part of this town?"

The grin happened again. "No, ma'am."

"There you have it, Eric. They are risks neither to people nor property, and they promise that they'll stick around. If it helps, I will vouch for them."

"There has to be due process, Vicky." This from George Simmons.

"It'll come," McCrea said. "I promise you, it will come. But for now, how about we get out of the way of this family reunion?"

Adam spun away from his mom. "No," he said. "I'm sorry, what's your name?"

"McCrea. Major Joseph McCrea."

Adam offered his hand. "Nice to meet you, Major McCrea. But the reunion has to wait till we bury Lisa."

Victoria said, "Lisa is—"

"Lisa Barnes. The little girl in the car. She had a terrible last couple of days. And then . . . I owe her a dignified funeral."

"Trying to bury the evidence?" Eric asked.

Adam took a menacing step forward, drawing aggressive movement from the crowd. Weapons clattered. If Adam heard it, he made no indication. "We don't know each other yet, *Eric*." He leaned on the word as if to mock the name. "And I'm not sure I want to get a lot closer. But whatever you *think* you know about me, you're wrong. When that Bronco gets up here, you're gonna have to make a choice. You can shoot me, or you can let me do a kind thing for that little girl."

Eric started to answer.

"No, don't tell me," Adam said. "I want to be surprised in the moment."

Victoria saw the fear in Eric's eyes and in his body language. Her little boy Adam, now in the costume of an adult, projected real menace that she'd never seen before.

Now that Emma's hands were free, Adam took one of them and led her over to Victoria. "I think you're going to like each other," he said.

"I've heard a lot about you, Mrs. Emerson," Emma said. "You should be very proud of Adam. I know I am."

The way they stood together, the way they bumped shoulders while Emma spoke, told Victoria that there was hope that the world might one day return to normal. She was happy that this couple was right for each other.

"Look what a nice lady he chose," Victoria said. "How could I not be proud?"

Emma laughed, the same kind of guffaw she'd heard from Adam a moment ago. "There's the politician he told me about."

The sound of an approaching vehicle drew Victoria's attention back toward the direction Adam had come from. Kyle Foster was at the wheel of the fabled Bronco, his brother, Caine, in the shotgun seat. They pulled to a stop behind the gathering crowd.

Adam shot Victoria a look that was pure angst. "Mom, who's in charge here? I need to see to Lisa."

"Your mother's in charge," McCrea said. "Why is this so important to you?"

Adam started to answer, but stopped as his eyes turned red and glossy. "Say yes, Mom," he said. "Please, just say yes."

"Hey!" Kyle yelled from the open window. "I got all kinds of shit in here. We can arm an army. Plus, we've got a dead little girl Caine and me ought to take care of. Don't want her to get gamy, you know."

Victoria saw Adam puff up. "Mom. Please."

"Major McCrea," Victoria said. "Please clean out the contents of the Bronco. All weapons, ammunition and tools need to be off-loaded and inventoried. Then I'd like you to escort Adam and Emma up to Boot . . . to the burial grounds with the Foster boys and make sure that little Lisa gets all the dignity that the circumstances allow."

"Not a problem," McCrea said.

Victoria kept her eyes on Adam as she finished with, "And when that's done, I want to convene a hearing in Maggie's Place. The public will be invited. We're going to find out the truth of the rumors."

CHAPTER THIRTY-FOUR

Hell Day + 49 (The Same Day)

AS THE BRONCO DROVE OFF WITH THEIR BROTHER, Luke and Caleb turned on Victoria. "What are you doing, Mom?" Caleb said. "A hearing? Adam didn't do anything!"

"Not here," Victoria said. She turned and headed back toward her office.

"Mom!" Luke called. "We need to talk!"

She ignored them. If they wanted to talk, they'd follow.

As Victoria entered the door to Maggie's Place, she saw that Lavinia Sloan was waiting for her. They'd been scheduled for a supply chain meeting before the excitement with the alarm broke out. "Oh, hi, Lavinia," she said. "I'm sorry about—"

Her boys stormed in right behind her. "How can you walk away like that?" Caleb demanded. He saw Lavinia and retreated.

Lavinia stood. "Looks like we should reschedule," she said, and she gathered her notes.

"I'll come to you next time," Victoria said as they crossed paths.

The transition from daylight to lamplight was always a difficult one. She consoled herself with the knowledge that these were conditions in which the Founding Fathers built an entire nation out of nothing. If they could do that, then managing the problems of Ortho shouldn't be overwhelming.

"Say what you have to say, boys," she said as she approached her desk.

"You're treating Adam like a criminal!" Caleb said.

"You're going to have a *trial* for him?" Luke asked. He looked as if he couldn't believe he was speaking the words he heard coming from his mouth.

"I mean, Jesus, Mom, aren't you even happy to see that he's alive?"

"I'm not even going to honor that question with an answer," Victoria said. She walked around the desk and sat in her chair. "Have a seat."

"I want to stand," Caleb said.

"Sit."

They both sat.

"You've heard the stories of the red-and-white Bronco," she said. "We've all heard them. The serial killers with a river of blood in their wake. The stories have painted a picture of the new boogeyman."

"You can't believe that," Luke said.

"I've never believed it," Victoria said. "Even before I knew that it was Adam and his new friend."

"Emma," Caleb prompted.

"Right. Emma. Even before that, I didn't believe

that the stories were true, simply because they were so over-the-top."

"Then why—"

"Still, in my experience, every frightening tall tale is rooted in some bit of reality. What do you think the rest of the town thinks of Adam and Emma?"

The boys stared back at her.

"It's a real question," she said. "When the town saw the red-and-white Bronco, what do you think their first thoughts were?"

"Scared?" Caleb guessed.

"Both scared and relieved that they no longer had reason to be," Victoria said. "The good news—the really *encouraging* news—is that no one opened fire on them."

"God, Mom," Caleb said.

Victoria pointed her finger at him. "What would your first reaction be if you opened a closet and there was a clown inside?"

Caleb deflated a little. He'd always been terrified of clowns.

"He'd shit his pants is what he'd do," Luke said through a laugh, earning himself a punch in the shoulder.

"That Bronco is this town's scary clown. The boogeyman. Jack the Ripper. Pick the one you want."

"But he wouldn't *do* those things!" Caleb had a hard time moving past that one point.

"He did *something*," Victoria said. "Those kinds of rumors don't grow from the ether. He's got a dead little girl in his truck, Caleb."

"He explained that."

"Yes, he did. And I believe him. But this isn't about

me. Really, it's not even about Adam. It's about the rest of the town."

"So, are you going to have him whipped like you did Brandon-Lee?" Luke asked.

The phrasing of the question, and the tone with which it was asked, tripped something in Victoria. Brandon-Lee May had been part of a gang of marauders who killed an innocent man on the night of the explosions, merely to steal his cargo. Unable to prove the charges against him, yet knowing that the town would tear him apart if he got off entirely without punishment, Victoria had ordered him to be flogged. It was an ugly sight, and an ugly day.

"The faster we get the real stories out in the public, the better off it's going to be for Adam. The better it's going to be for all of us."

"Because you don't want people to think that you'd give a break even to your own kids," Caleb said. "We're not even supposed to be here. We were supposed to just pass through, and then you started getting high on power again."

He was baiting her. She knew better than to rise to it. With just the three of them in the room, she'd give him that much leeway.

"Luke," she said. "Remind me *why* we were just going to pass through Ortho. Better yet, remind Caleb. He seems to have forgotten."

Luke cleared his throat and looked at the floor. This was not a role he wished to play. "We were going to find Adam."

"You remember that, don't you, Caleb? You remember that we wanted to find Adam? Shall we still leave

here and head off to Top Hat Mountain? That seems
oddly imprudent under the circumstances."

"You can't whip Adam!" Caleb shouted. "He's your
son! He's our brother!"

As they got louder, she got softer. It was a tactical
move she'd learned decades ago, and it always worked
in an argument like this. De-escalating the tone also
de-escalated the words. "Caleb, listen to me," she said.
"The very last thing in the world I want to do is anything that will bring harm to Adam. I know you know
that, but I also know that you are angry. And that part
of your anger comes from the fact that you've been
dreaming about this reunion for so long—wondering
for so long if it would ever be possible—and this is
nothing like what you wanted it to be."

Caleb's jaw muscles worked like he was grinding
his teeth to powder, even as his eyes reddened, and his
lips trembled.

"You saw how they brought him in here," she continued. "You saw the fear and the anger. You saw that
everyone in this town is wanting revenge. But they
also untied their hands, didn't they? They also let them
go up to Boot Hill and bury that little girl. Why do you
think the town did that?"

Caleb mumbled what he clearly thought to be the answer she wanted to hear. "Because you told them to."

"No," Victoria said. "My words carry no more
weight than anyone else's. If people follow me, it's because they *choose* to. They can just as easily choose
not to. At any given second, of any given day, my
words can be shut out like *that*." She snapped her fingers.

"The reason they're willing to give Adam some benefit of the doubt has everything to do with you two."

That startled the boys. Got their attention.

"Yes, you," Victoria said. "Everyone sees how you comport yourselves every day. They see how you work hard at your jobs, how you help people who need it and how you show courage when it is called for. Because you are who you are, they are willing to cast the dice on the possibility that Adam is just like you."

"Because we're brothers?" Luke asked.

"Exactly that," Victoria said. "That is the same benefit of the doubt that will grant him a fair hearing. Do I think that he had to kill people in the days since Hell Day? Yes. Who among us has not? Of all the rumors that have been spread about him, not one person purported to be an eyewitness. That means that the only eyewitness accounts we will hear will come from Adam and his friend . . ."

"Emma," Caleb reminded again. "But what happens if people *don't* believe he's justified in whatever he did?"

Victoria took her time answering that. If the results of today's hearing showed probable cause that he and *Emma* had committed murder, or had killed unjustly, then there would have to be a trial. At the conclusion of the trial, a verdict would have to be rendered. If the verdict was guilty, then . . . Well, that would be bad.

"Let's just see what happens," she said. "And then we can go from there."

* * *

"Let me help," said one of the twins as Adam reached into the back of the Bronco to lift Lisa's body.

"I've got her," Adam said. He knew that his tone sounded snappish, but that's not how he meant it. Major McCrea stood nearby, but out of the way, and he kept the others, who had come to observe, out of the way, too.

He could see the fatal wound now, a hole no larger than the diameter of a #2 pencil, through-and-through the top of her breastbone and out the back. It wasn't until then he realized how close he had come to being shot by the same bullet.

Lisa weighed nothing, but rigor had set in, making handling her an awkward challenge in balancing.

When he nearly dropped her coming through the door, a twin whispered in his ear, "My name is Kyle Foster, Adam. That's my brother, Caine, and this is what we do."

Adam twisted his head to look at the man. He was too close to really focus, but Adam could see kindness in him.

"I know this is important to you," Kyle said. "I don't know what happened, but I can see this is important. You don't want to drop her. Not in front of all these people. She needs more dignity than that."

This wasn't what Adam had been expecting. In fact, kindness had been nowhere on his radar. His throat thickened.

Kyle beckoned for his brother, who joined them at the open door.

"Go be with your lady," Kyle said. "What's the little girl's name?"

"Lisa Barnes." It came out as a rasp.

"We'll wrap Lisa in a blanket. Wrap her tight, okay?"

"There's Mr. Beagle, too," Adam said. He pointed his forehead to her stuffed dog, now spattered with her blood.

Caine reached around to grab Mr. Beagle, which he held close, presumably so that others could not see the blood.

"Where are you taking her?" Adam asked.

"The other side of that rock over there," Kyle said. "It's a, you know, preparation area. Not the kind of thing you want to see. I promise she'll see nothing but respect, Adam."

"How long?"

"Not very."

"I want to stay for the burial."

"Sure."

Adam didn't know what to do. He'd never failed at anything so utterly and completely. He felt that it was his duty to stay with Lisa, but he knew that the *preparation* was not an image he needed to have bouncing around in his memory for all time.

"Adam?" It was Emma's voice.

He turned.

"Come hug me," she said. "I need you."

He felt Emma's hand on his shoulder, and the quick squeeze she gave it. The slight tug to urge him away from the Bronco. "Come on, Adam. We've done our best. Let these men do their jobs."

Kyle and Caine moved together to take Lisa's weight away from Adam. "We've got her now," one of them said. He couldn't tell one from the other.

Adam felt like he was weightless, drifting as Emma pulled him back and folded him into her arms.

Something broke inside, a torrent of emotion that overwhelmed him as he allowed himself to be embraced. "I tried," he said, and the word broke as a sob. "I didn't—"

But he couldn't finish the sentence. He clenched his jaws hard and tightened his gut, trying to force the anger and the hate and the loathing to stay down in his belly.

It was his job to make sure that everything turned out well. To make sure that no one got hurt on his watch, and that if anyone did, it would be him. He had *one job*. Lisa's father had entrusted him to bring his daughter to a doctor. Instead, he dragged her into a running gunfight. He got her killed.

Emma was wrong when she said this wasn't his fault. Mr. Hornsby's little niece was killed on Adam's watch. That laid the responsibility at Adam's feet. He had done this terrible thing.

Big boys don't cry. *Leaders* don't cry. They don't have the luxury. They can't afford the self-indulgence, yet here he was, sobbing like a baby, being mothered like a baby. And he couldn't bring it under control. He was fighting a whale with a two-pound test line, and he had no chance of reeling in this awful thing.

In time—he didn't know how long—he became aware of Emma's touch, the gentle strokes along his back. Her efforts to soothe him.

"We'll be okay," she whispered.

He felt her hand in his hair at the back of his head, just like his mom used to do when he was little.

"You didn't do this. You did everything you could."

Adam let the words settle in. He didn't fight them, didn't argue. But he didn't believe them.

He took a deep breath and held it. Then he let it out slowly, over a ten count.

What was done was over now. He couldn't turn the clock back, couldn't undo anything that had been done. All those decisions, good or bad, were in the past now. It was time to concentrate on the future, however much of that was left for him.

He eased away from Emma and swiped at his eyes. "I'm okay," he said. "Sorry for that."

As he cast a glance around to the others, they all looked uncomfortable, looked away. All except for Major McCrea. He looked sympathetic. Pleased, perhaps, if that was possible under the circumstances.

Twenty minutes later, it was finished. The Foster brothers had done a fine job of wrapping Lisa's body in a blanket, and as they laid her into what clearly was a mass grave, they'd been able to make it look less like one, with a plank divider separating her from the others.

One of the brothers asked Adam and Emma if they'd like to say a few words, but both declined. One of the brothers said a meaningful Our Father, and then it was time to go back down the hill to whatever lay ahead for them.

CHAPTER THIRTY-FIVE

Hell Day + 49 (The Same Day)

"**D**ON'T YOU WANT SOME TIME ALONE WITH ADAM before this hearing starts?" McCrea asked as the makeshift courtroom filled with observers. "Maybe do it tomorrow, instead?"

He and Victoria stood together at the table that served as her desk in Maggie's. Night had fallen and the flickering light cast by candles and hurricane lamps made shadows on the wall appear as if they were alive. The look would have been spooky on Halloween, and romantic if it were a five-star restaurant. Tonight it just reminded Victoria how long a day it had been.

There hadn't been many trials in this space—and this would be the first hearing, per se—but they'd developed a pattern. A lectern that Victoria understood used to support a dictionary in Maggie's house had been placed atop the desk to give it the feel of a judicial bench, and a bar stool would serve as Victoria's chair so that she could see over the lectern.

"I don't think that would be a good idea," she said. "We can't be seen together until this is done. It wouldn't be right."

"He's your son."

"Exactly," she said. "Trust me on this. Every movement I make, and every word I speak, is going to be scrutinized. We've got dozens of people in here who've never attended one of these. They're all newcomers, and they're the ones who brought the word of the marauding Bronco in the first place. They need to trust the proceedings. More than anything else, they need to trust that the process is fair."

McCrea arched his eyebrows. "I gotta tell you that seems kind of harsh. You've been waiting for this reunion for a long time."

"We had that reunion outside," Victoria said. "And when this is over, we'll have time to catch up."

"I'm just saying—"

"This conversation is over, Major. See to the security concerns, will you?"

"Okeydokey," he said.

Victoria settled into her official station and gaveled for order by rapping her knuckles on the lectern. "Please have a seat, people. Wherever you can find a spot."

Word had traveled quickly and at quite a distance. She saw the usual players from way back to Hell Day, but to her eye, the preponderance of people in the space were newcomers. In the dim light, they all sort of melded together in her vision as a single organism, a moving black shadow.

Adam and Emma had been given seats directly in front of Victoria's bench. They both looked exhausted. And filthy. Emma looked terrified, while Adam, through his thick beard, looked angry. In the dim flickering light, their eyes showed as black hollows. Luke and Caleb had wanted to sit with their brother, but Victoria didn't allow it. This was not yet a family event, after all. Instead, they commandeered a patch of floor immediately to the subjects' left, Victoria's right.

"Ladies and gentlemen, boys and girls, thank you for attending this hearing this evening. The sheer number of you present in the room—and the overflow into the street—indicate to me that you are already aware of the topic at hand." She shifted her gaze. "Major Mc-Crea, can you assure me that we still have our defenses manned, just in case?"

"Yes, ma'am, I am confident that they are. But just to be sure, I have asked First Sergeant Copley and Joey Abbott to make sure. If we're shorthanded, I'm equally confident they'll fix whatever needs to be fixed."

"Thank you." It occurred to Victoria that her question might have been a delaying tactic to give herself a chance to gather her thoughts.

"Just to be up front and transparent," she continued, "the young man we're about to hear from is named Adam Emerson, and he is my eldest child. The young lady next to him is Emma Carson, and if the rumors are true, she's got my first grandchild in her tummy."

"You can't be judge under those circumstances," someone called from the crowd.

Victoria rapped on the lectern again. "That's enough of that," she said. "To the noisy gentleman, I'll state that this is not a trial of fact. This is an opportunity to hear the truth, or lack thereof, of the rumors we've been hearing about the dreaded red-and-white Bronco. To the rest of you, especially those of you who are new to town, everyone will have a chance to ask whatever questions they wish, but that will not be until I am done. Those questions will not be shouted out. Rather, you will raise your hands and I will call on you."

Victoria squinted out into the crowd. "George Simmons, where are you?"

He raised his hand from the back of the room.

"George, I will task you and Major McCrea to escort interrupters and shouters out of the building."

"Happy to do it, ma'am," George said.

Victoria turned her attention to Adam and Emma. "Let's get a couple of things on the record." Since no one actually kept records of these things, that was merely a rhetorical flourish. "Did I identify you properly?"

They nodded.

"The people in the back of the room can't hear you nod," Victoria said.

"Yes," Adam said, and Emma echoed him.

"Tell us how you came into possession of the red Bronco."

Emma explained that it had been a dream of hers to own an old-school Bronco, clarifying that she'd owned it long before Hell Day.

Victoria said, "Over the course of the past weeks, we've heard a growing body of rumors that a young man and young woman in a red-and-white Bronco have been terrorizing the countryside. So let me ask you this, and please answer honestly. Have either one of you killed anyone over the time since Hell Day?"

"Mom!" This from Caleb.

"Don't think I won't have you thrown out, too," she said. "Adam? Emma?"

The two of them exchanged glances, but neither of them spoke. As a murmur grew among the assembled crowd, Victoria encouraged Adam with a nod. *It's okay.* With an upward pump of her hands, she encouraged him to rise.

Adam stood from his chair, cleared his throat and said in a loud voice, "Yes, I have. We both have. Would you like to hear the details?"

"The floor is yours."

"On the night of the bombings—what do you call it? Hell Day? That's, like, perfect." He told the story of him and Emma on a camping trip when they heard the bombs exploding. Then he told of their panicked drive out of the forest, barely ahead of a fire that consumed everything—including the schools where he and Emma were boarders. "If you look closely at the Bronco, you'll see blistered paint. That's where that happened."

He then told of an encounter on the first day after Hell Day, where a family of three guys wanted to take the Bronco away from them. "We were loading up supplies from a hardware store, where I used to work, and when we came out, these guys—the Chaney family, I think their names were—were all over the car."

"Is that where you got the dynamite?" Victoria asked.

"That's where we got pretty much everything," Adam said. "Looking back, that Bronco was the best thing and the worst thing. Everywhere we went, people wanted it. Or they wanted our stuff."

Emma stood. "The first time we had to kill was on the night when a man and his woman wanted *me.* He was going to rape me and then he was going to kill us both. He actually said that."

"I got the best of the guy," Adam said. "I killed him with his own gun."

"And I killed the woman when she was trying to kill me."

"After that, we knew we couldn't stick around, but as we were driving away, the family of the people we'd just, well, you know . . . Their family blocked the road and that got ugly. That was another fight. Some of the holes in the car tell that story."

As Victoria listened to the stories, she watched the crowd. Every one of them seemed focused on their words.

"We even made it to Top Hat Mountain," Adam said with a smile.

Victoria beamed and fired off a laugh. "Did you really?" To the others, she explained that Top Hat Mountain was the meeting place that they as a family had established in case of a major emergency—like Hell Day.

It took every bit of twenty minutes, but when he was done, Adam had explained everything that Victoria wanted to hear. She thought he kept it together well, until he got to the events of that morning, and little Lisa's death. At that point, he choked, and Emma had to take over for him.

When she finished, the room was silent.

"Okay," Victoria said. She cleared her throat. "I had no idea. Thank you for your bluntness and honesty." She looked to the crowd. "Does anyone else have questions?"

Mr. Jake stood from the same seat he occupied every time he came into this space. He brushed his beard as if to ensure that no crumbs were in residence. "Yeah, I've got a question. Tell me more about this gang over in Appleton."

Another man stood. Victoria recognized him as a recent arrival, but she couldn't place his name. "If I may," he said. "Not to interrupt, but my name is Frank Rouse, and everything that young man described about Appleton is absolutely true." He told a story about being forced out of his own home by a band of thugs.

McCrea stepped forward as the man was talking and placed a hand on Adam's shoulder. He whispered something and Adam sat back down.

"These thugs you're talking about," McCrea said. "Were they military? Or at least pretending to be?"

"Come to think of it, yes," Frank Rouse said.

A boy, the older of the two who sat with Rouse, stood. "They said they were Maryland National Guard."

McCrea looked back at Victoria. This was not a good development.

"They're like locusts," Rouse said. "They'll take anything that's not nailed down, and they don't hesitate to shoot."

"They shot me," the boy said. "My name's Ronnie. Ronnie Rouse."

"Why did they shoot you?" Victoria asked.

"I guess because I wouldn't move fast enough."

A woman stood, clearly the mom, because the boy looked exactly like her. "Because they were taking over our home and we objected."

"How many of them are there?" George Simmons asked.

"I don't know."

Adam stood again. "A lot. Dozens, for sure."

Frank Rouse said, "They seemed to be recruiting. A lot of boys from the high school where I taught are among them."

Victoria asked, "Who else has had experience with this group from Appleton?"

At least ten hands went up.

"And we told you about the gangs between here and the Hilltop Manor," said Greg Gonzales. "People are like wild animals."

Mr. Jake stood again. "Ma'am, if I may?"

"The floor is yours," Victoria said.

"First things first," Mr. Jake said. "To clear the deck of this hearing crap, I think we can all agree that the horror stories we've been hearing about Freddy Krueger in a Bronco are all bullshit, right? Anybody want to argue otherwise?"

Mr. Jake made a point of scouring the room, turning his whole body 360 degrees over fifteen or twenty seconds, waiting for someone to object. No one did.

"All right, then. Mr. Adam Emerson, and Ms. Emma Carson, welcome home. This place is Eden compared to the rest of what's out there." He clapped his hands once and pivoted to a new topic. "You know, I hear these stories about what's going on beyond our town, and I think back to that attempted invasion escapade a while ago, and there are two things that come to my mind. First of all, the assholes that shot that young man over there, and the ones who ultimately killed young Lisa Barnes, are the same ones who tried to start trouble at the boat launch."

Victoria watched the crowd as Mr. Jake spoke. He'd lived here for dozens of years, doubled as Santa for the young ones at Christmas, and he had them drilled to their seats with his words.

"We've come a long way here since Hell Day, and while we have a long way to go, it sounds to me like we're a lot further along than pretty much everybody else. I know we've got bars opening up—about god-damn time for that, too—and some folks are starting to sell wares and make things. That's all great. But I think there's a message that some of you been missin'."

He continued to rotate his body as he spoke, addressing as many of the people in the room as he could, simulating eye contact as best as possible in the dark.

"Our first priority—first over everything else—is our defense. Those sonsabitches are gonna come back. They're locusts. Cockroaches. All we got is ourselves. We got this immediate threat that I predict is gonna come to a head, one way or the other, in the next couple of days. I'll leave it to Vicky and the leadership team to figure out what to do about it, but I'm talkin' to each and every one of you in this room. I'm also talkin' to everybody in this town that *isn't* in the room when I say we can't never let our guard down."

Half-a-dozen hands went up.

"In a second," Mr. Jake said. "I've still got the floor. I'll give it back shortly. A lot of you are thinkin' that we need to stop letting new folks come in here, but think again. What we got here is an alternative to hell out there. We might not have no government to think of no more, but we sure as hell got our conscience, and most of us walk with God in our hearts. We owe folks kindness. We owe them a chance."

More hands went up.

"I'm not done yet, goddammit. You new folks listen up, too. Ain't none of us your servants. We'll give you a leg up and a head start when you arrive, but after that, you take advantage of that kindness to figure out a way to make it on your own. If you ain't willin' to do that, then get the hell out. If you ain't willin' to pick up a weapon to defend this Eden of ours, then you better be good at loadin' magazines or doin' somethin' for the common good. We ain't got room for people who hide from protectin' this thing we're tryin' to build. Everybody's a coward in their heart, but don't let me see it showin' if you don't want an ass whuppin'." He took a breath. "Okay, I'm done." He sat back down.

No other hands went up.

CHAPTER THIRTY-SIX

Hell Day + 50 (Hours Later)

BEST AS LUKE COULD REMEMBER, IT HAD BEEN NINE months since he'd last seen Adam. It was Christmastime. He looked so much older. The beard was a big enough surprise, but the gray was a real shock.

"He looks like an old man," Caleb said, speaking Luke's thoughts. "He looks sad."

"Sounds like he's been through a lot," Luke said.

The family reunion had only lasted a few minutes before Caleb and Luke had to head out to relieve Anton Cole and Maris Garcia on roadblock duty. As their mom had said, Adam would still be there in the morning, and the previous shift deserved a break.

Luke and Caleb rode bikes together through the black night, the sky exhibiting a near-perfect starfield. Tonight would be a new moon, so the world was creepy-dark. An old-fashioned kerosene lantern dangled from Caleb's handlebars—the kind they used to see in cowboy movies—but he hadn't lit it. As long as you stayed on the road, which was a different shade of black than all the surroundings, it was just as easy to navigate in the dark and you didn't ruin your night vision.

"You know, if it had been anybody else under the same circumstances, Mom would have let us trade shifts with somebody so we could be with Adam," Caleb said.

"He's gonna be shit company," Luke said. "You saw him. He's ready to sleep standing up."

"I can't believe he knocked up his girlfriend," Caleb said.

"She's gorgeous!" Luke said. "I'd do her in a heartbeat."

Caleb laughed. "Your only girlfriend is your hand."

"Like you've done any better."

"You have no idea what I've done," Caleb said. "Or should I say *who* I've done."

"That's such bullshit."

"I know you want it to be," Caleb teased. "Nobody likes to be the last virgin in the family."

"I've seen your dick, you know. Tiny little thing that it is."

"Of course, you'd be peeking," Caleb said. "You perv."

Luke wasn't going to say anything, but Caleb was wrong. Well, mostly. It wasn't only his own hand that had—well, you know. Sara Jenner was about his age and had wandered in from somewhere up north. They'd had a couple of adventures down at the river, but so far, they'd never gone all the way. From the way she handled him, he guessed that he was not her first. As for him returning the favor, he had no frigging clue what he was doing, but she didn't yell and she didn't make fun of him.

But Sara Jenner was no Emma Carson, not by a long shot.

There was a lot to hate about the world after Hell Day, but there were also a few things that he appreciated. One was the peaceful darkness. With the skies so impossibly dark, and no drone of machinery to interrupt the silence, the nighttime had taken on a soothing quality for Luke. He found it easier to think than he used to.

The thoughts weren't always happy ones, but at least they were there, without interruption. When he was bedded down in the church, surrounded by the sounds of other people sleeping, he'd think up stories in his head. Not all of them involved Sara Jenner, but a good number of them did. Other stories would be about fictional adventures with fictional characters. None of the stories had endings in his head, but they had whole story lines. He wondered if one day he might grow up to be a writer.

He could write about all the crap they'd endured since Hell Day. But who'd want to read something so depressing?

About ten minutes into their ride, they encountered the sentries at the inner checkpoint. They were a husband-and-wife team that Luke recognized, but he didn't remember their names. As if to deliberately piss off Caleb, they raised their lantern up to eye level to see who was approaching.

"It's the young princes," the guy said.

"Get that thing out of my eyes," Caleb commanded. "Dammit, you'll never see anything past the light."

The whole *prince* thing had grown old a long time ago, but Luke had stopped rising to the bait. If anyone thought that he and Caleb got special treatment from anybody because of who their mother was, that person needed to take a much harder look.

The guy lowered the light and apologized. "Are you guys our relief?"

"Nope," Luke said. "We're outer perimeter tonight."

"Well, shit," the lady said. "Who's supposed to relieve us?"

"Shoulda read the list more carefully," Caleb said, and they pedaled past.

"No need to be shitty," the lady mumbled. Neither Luke nor Caleb bothered to respond. But the truth that Luke knew better than most was that if Caleb really *wanted* to be shitty to someone, he was well-trained for the task.

Major McCrea and his team had dreamed up this tiered security plan. The outer perimeter was arguably the most dangerous because those would be the first sentries that invaders would encounter if they attacked. That outer roadblock was about a mile out of town, with the inner checkpoint they'd just passed sitting at about a half mile.

All along the way, the trees were manned by watchers with whistles.

In theory, everyone cycled through every position on a rotation. But in practice, while they'd only been doing this for a little while, the weakness of the everyone-cycles-through plan had become obvious. Some people of a certain age were less . . . *efficient* in their tree-climbing skills.

Luke had pulled tree frog duty twice, and he hated it. The shifts ran longer, and there were only so many times you could shift to a different butt cheek. When the penalty for a slip was to plummet fifteen feet to the ground, it was impossible to relax up there.

The outer roadblock itself wasn't much, just two ranks of sawhorses manned by four sentries during the day and two at night. Fact was, without streetlights or flashlights, people just didn't travel much after dark. In the three times that Luke had worked the perimeter, not a single person had wandered up.

As they approached the sawhorses, the first thing Luke noticed was that no one was there. The second was that one of the sawhorses had been knocked over. They stopped in unison.

"Where are they?" Caleb asked.

"Do you remember who we're looking for?" Luke asked.

"Anton Cole was one of them," Caleb said. "Pretty good carpenter. And Maris Garcia, I think. She's one of the original townspeople."

"Anton Cole!" Luke shouted. "Are you here?"

"Shh," Caleb hissed. Then he whispered, "What if there are people out there?"

Luke feigned a shiver. "Maybe it's a clown."

"Eat shit, dickhead."

The brothers dismounted their bikes and laid them on the ground. Luke slid his M4 around from behind his back, slipped the safety to FIRE and tucked the buttstock into the soft spot in his shoulder.

"Mr. Cole!" Caleb shouted it as a whisper. "Mrs. Garcia!"

"What do you think?" Luke asked.

"I don't know any more than you do," Caleb snapped.

"Maybe we should light the lantern," Luke suggested.

"No way," Caleb said. "If someone's out there, we don't want to give them any better a target than we already are."

Luke dropped to a knee at the thought of being an easy target. "We have to do *something*," he said. "They wouldn't both have just wandered off."

"They didn't wander," Caleb said. "Not with the barricade knocked over like that. I think they were attacked."

Luke started to fish his whistle out of his shirt.

"No, don't," Caleb said. "Not yet."

"Why?"

"Because I might be wrong, and we don't need that kind of shit flooding down on us. Let's make sure."

"That's stupid," Luke said. "The whole reason we're out here is to warn people."

"Speaking of stupid, Stupid, what are we going to warn them about? We're going to alert the whole militia because Anton Cole went into the woods to take a dump?"

"You just said they were attacked."

"I said, I *thought* they were attacked. Before we send up flares, I think we need to know for sure."

"Shit." Luke knew that Caleb was right. Their mom had as much as told them that they were under greater scrutiny for mistakes than anyone else in the town. First Sergeant Copley did the same after Luke had fired the first shot, back then at the boat launch.

"Be careful," Caleb said.

"Ya *think*?"

"You go along the right side of the road. I'll take the left," Caleb said.

Luke settled himself. He took a huge breath and forced his shoulders to relax. They'd trained for this kind of thing. Operations in the night were about all of the senses that we don't pay much attention to during the day. With low-to-zero visibility, sight took fourth or fifth place behind hearing, smell and touch.

He set off walking. Very slowly, very carefully. He didn't plant his footsteps along the pavement so much as he rolled them on.

The trick was to listen, sniff and feel for anything that was unusual. Like when tracking game (or people, for that matter), you didn't look for footprints so much as you looked for things that didn't belong. Why would a branch be broken at a particular spot? Why would hair or fur be on this particular tree? Why would—

He smelled shit. Literally, shit. But there was more than that, too. He smelled . . . unpleasantness. He smelled the stench of a recent kill.

He pulled his rifle in closer, checked again that the safety was off, and he bent low at the waist. His nose would bring him to what he was looking for, while at the same time presenting a smaller target for whatever was out there.

In his head, the threat was human, but now that the world had changed in every conceivable way, the threat could be some hungry animal. Except a cougar attack wouldn't explain both sentries going missing.

He wanted to shout out to Caleb, but that was a bad idea. He'd sell his left nut for a flashlight.

The stink kept getting stronger. After fewer than a dozen steps, he saw a shape on the road near the shoulder.

"Pssst." He didn't want to verbalize anything, but maybe a hissing sound might make it move.

Two steps later, it became clear that the form was a person, and that the person was an adult. It was the source of the foul odor.

When he was still a few feet away, he paused again and crouched lower. He held his breath, hoping to hear movement—and dreading hearing movement—but the hammering of his heart drummed out any hope for that.

With his right hand still wrapped around the pistol grip of his M4, Luke put his left knee on the pavement and reached out with his left hand to shake the man. He thought he could make out the white patch that was his face, and below that, he thought he could see the shimmer of fresh blood.

In fact, he was kneeling in it.

He was opening his mouth to call out to Caleb when he heard the *clack* of metal on metal from the woods on his right. It was the sound of a firearm being handled by someone. Certainly, it was a sound that was beyond the capability of a bear or a mountain lion.

When milliseconds matter, be sure to be the one who shoots first. God, how many times had he heard that from his mother?

He reacted instantly, spinning on the ball of his left foot, and firing randomly into the foliage. He thought he was aimed at the source of the noise, but there was no way to know. This was all spray-and-pray. Otherwise known as spray-and-slay.

At one round per trigger pull, a thirty-round magazine goes fast. Ten seconds, max.

When he received no return fire, he scrambled back
to his feet and darted back to where they'd laid down
their bicycles and lanterns.

"Jesus, Luke!" Caleb shouted. "What the hell?"

Luke wasn't sure he had enough breath to form words.
"One of the sentries." He managed. "Dead. People in
the woods."

"Who? What people?"

"They had a gun. They were getting ready to shoot."

"Did you get him?"

"How the hell should I know? I shot and I ran."

In the distance, the shrill blast of whistles bloomed
like a cloud all around them.

Twenty minutes later, a dozen people were mingling
around the outer perimeter roadblock, along with lamps
and flashlights. The night was alive with light and activity. Townspeople arrived on foot, on bicycles and on
horseback.

Victoria and Adam were among the first to arrive,
along with Major McCrea and First Sergeant Copley.

It took Luke all of two minutes to describe what had
happened, along with some narrative assistance from
Caleb, who clearly didn't want to be left out of the
loop.

The body that Luke had stumbled upon turned out
to be Anton Cole. His throat had been cut, so the fact
that he'd been murdered was not in dispute. Now that
they had light, and the blood pattern was visible, it was

clear that Mr. Cole's body lay at the spot where he'd been killed—that he hadn't been moved there.

"Who was Anton on duty with?" Victoria asked.

"Maris Garcia," McCrea replied. "One of the original residents."

"Just the two of them?"

"It's a two-man shift this time of night."

"Have we spoken with the tree frogs?" Victoria asked. Luke was pleased to hear her using his vernacular for the tree stand stations. "I figure they've got to be in this crowd somewhere."

"Maybe not," Caleb said. "When you're on tree frog duty, you're supposed to stay at your station—no matter what."

"Unless you're being fired upon," McCrea said. He sounded a little defensive. Luke figured that was so Mom wouldn't worry about her baby boys being trapped in the trees during a gunfight. To be perfectly honest, Luke thought that might be the safest place, but he'd had limited experience with *real* gunfights.

Up ahead, beyond the body, George Simmons and Joey Abbott were poking through the woods.

"Hey, Luke, is this the direction you were shooting?" Joey called.

Before answering, Luke stepped into the bushes and tree branches to see what they were looking at. The bodies of two adults—a man and a woman, each in their mid-twenties, Luke guessed—lay sprawled on their backs, their bodies torn by bullets. The wounds all looked recent, which meant that Luke had inflicted them.

"Do you recognize them?" Joey asked, though it wasn't clear to whom he was addressing the question.

"I don't," Luke said. Neither did George Simmons.

Both of the bodies had dropped rifles when they died.

"You okay, Luke?" George asked just as Victoria pushed her way through the foliage. "Your kid has good ears and good instincts," George said.

Victoria placed a hand on his shoulder. Adam appeared on his other side.

Is it okay to be okay? Luke wondered. He'd just killed two people and he didn't feel anything.

"Interesting first night," Adam said. "No idea who these folks are?"

Joey kneeled to the side of the lady's head and brought the light close. When he did, a sparkly hair clasp glinted in the light.

"Wait a second," Adam said. "I might know her, after all. She was on the roadblock I ran up against at Appleton. It's the weirdness of the hair thing. That's why I remember her."

"What about her?" Victoria asked.

"That's it, really. Just that she was there. All of that went down really fast, but the image I have of her is diving for cover."

"Karma," McCrea said. "Sooner or later, cover runs out."

"Why are they here?" Victoria asked.

"Hey, look here, Major," Copley said from fifteen feet away. He'd wandered down to the river's edge. "Somebody parked a boat here."

They all walked down to see what First Sergeant Copley was looking at. The mud along the bank clearly showed the imprint of a flat keelboat. A bass boat maybe.

"That print looks fresh," Copley said.

"A boat," Victoria thought aloud. "Why a boat?"

"It's our weak spot," McCrea said.

"Okay, but why did they come here to kill Anton?" Victoria asked. "And where do you suppose they went?"

"I've got a better question," George asked. "Where is Maris Garcia? I'll bet you a hundred that if you find her, you'll find the boat. And vice versa."

It all came together for Victoria with a snap that she was nearly certain others could hear. "They took her," she said. "They're going to attack, and they want to know everything they can about us before they do."

CHAPTER THIRTY-SEVEN

Hell Day + 50 (The Same Day)

*P*RITCHARD HEARD THE SOUND OF OARS IN THE WATER long before he saw the boat. He'd taken a position along the riverbank, on the opposite shore from Ortho and a mile and a half downstream. When he thought the boat was close enough to hear, he whistled his best whip-poor-will impression—the only birdcall he could pull off. He hoped the sound wouldn't travel back to the extraction point, yet would be audible to his crew.

The explosion of gunfire had startled the shit out of him even as it heralded the loss of surprise. Whoever shot whom, the residents of Ortho would now be very much on edge.

With surprise lost, the smart move would perhaps be to postpose the attack till another day, but he didn't know how long his army of frightened recruits would hold out. They'd walked nearly twenty miles through the darkness to the encampment they'd established another mile downstream, bitching and complaining with every step. He'd already suffered losses through desertion in the darkness, but that was to be expected.

His Guard troops did their best to keep order in the ranks, but he was disappointed by their lack of discipline as well. Just as an untended lawn grows weeds and sprouts unwanted saplings in just a few weeks' time, military discipline and chain of command disintegrated without the hope of a larger mission.

Pritchard hoped that if he could conquer Ortho without doing too much damage to the only true infrastructure that seemed still to exist in this corner of the world, he'd be able to stabilize the decline in discipline and morale.

Surely, the residents of Ortho would fight back, or at least attempt to, but the lady in charge of the town was rumored to be a career bureaucrat—an elected one at that!—so he didn't imagine that her followers would stick around to fight past the first volley of shots. Pritchard fully expected that to be the case with his own citizen conscripts, but at least he had a core of professional soldiers under his command. They would understand tactics and were unlikely to run away at the first sound of gunfire.

The one thing that was certain was that this daily existence of foraging and scrounging had to end. It was no way to live. In fact, it felt a lot like a good way to die.

Once he got a feel for how Ortho's defenses were designed, he was confident that the battle would be short and decisive. He longed for the days when night vision goggles, combined with infrared illumination and sighting, allowed him to overwhelm enemies in darkness, when they were unable to defend themselves.

These days, night attacks were out of the question. Instead, nighttime hours were dedicated to maneuvering troops into position so they could attack at dawn, when the enemy was least prepared.

Perhaps one advantage of the unexpected gunfire on the opposite shore was the fact that the defenders of Ortho would be exhausted when Pritchard's militia attacked, having been awake and on point all night long, waiting to learn what the next phase of the attack was going to be.

Yes, Pritchard's troops would, likewise, be tired after marching all night, but they would have been bolstered by foreknowledge of what lay ahead. They'd be focused on the jobs they had to do. As opposed to the enemy, who would have been debilitated by hours of worry.

Pritchard heard the return whistle of a whip-poor-will as the boat coasted to the shore.

"Can you hear my voice?" Pritchard whispered.

"They shot us to pieces," a voice said from the night. Pritchard thought it belonged to Dell Cheatham, an E5 from the Guard, but he couldn't be sure.

"Save it for later," Pritchard said. "Did you complete your mission? Did you grab someone?"

"Yeah, but—"

"That's all I need to know. Bring him up into the woods. Away from the water so the sound won't travel."

Pritchard let Andy Linx and Sergeant Teddy Rehm manage the business of bringing the boat to the shore and tying it off. As he watched the ballet of silhouettes against the movement of the water, he saw only two forms in addition to Andy. One of those forms most definitely was Dell Cheatham, and the other moved awkwardly, hesitantly. The plan was to put a bag over the captured sentry's head, so that explained the awkwardness, at least in part.

But there was more than that. The prisoner's legs wobbled. Had he been hit?

Pritchard's head swam with questions, but he pushed them aside until they had retreated into the woods.

"Teddy," Pritchard whispered.

"Sir?"

"Stay with the boat so we'll be able to find it again."

"Sir."

The absolute blackness of the night surprised Pritchard every new moon. You never knew how much illumination invaded the night sky from man-made sources until all of those sources were snuffed. He didn't wander far, just deeply enough into the tree line to break up sound waves and make it more difficult to be heard by the enemy.

After he stopped, he whistled again, to make his location known.

Within a minute, they were ready to begin the debrief. Pritchard struck a match and touched it to the wick of a hurricane lantern, whose wick was barely exposed, and placed it on the ground next to the spot where they planted their prisoner, whose shirt shined black in the dim light. Pritchard felt confident that it was blood.

"What the hell happened down there?" Pritchard asked.

"I told you," Cheatham said. "They opened fire on

us. Killed Manford and Rosilla. And they hit their own sentry here. She says her name is Maria."

"I didn't say *Maria,*" the prisoner said, her tone muffled by the burlap bag over her head. "I said *Maris,* and, yes, I've been shot. Hurts like shit, too."

"Where were you hit?" Pritchard asked. He yanked the bag from her head.

"Belly. It's bad." A few years either side of fifty, Maris had a hard look about her. Maybe she'd been a laborer or a farmer in the before days.

"You don't know that. Your hands are bound."

"They weren't when I felt my guts hanging out."

The matter-of-fact delivery counterbalanced the stress of her pain and fear.

"I have some questions for you," Pritchard said. "Then we'll get you some medical attention."

"There ain't no medical attention to be got," Maris grunted through a wave of pain that brought her knees to her chest. "And I'd rather choke to death on my own blood than answer any question you got to ask."

Pritchard felt his gut tighten at her words, but he had to admire the grit. "Does your militia have a name?" He thought easy questions might grease the skids for tougher ones.

Maris ignored him.

"I don't want to have to hurt you, Maris," he said. "But don't think that I won't."

She raised her voice and tried to yell: "I'm Maris Garcia! The enemy is on the opposite shore!" Yelling required flexing the gut muscles, however, and her attempt came out as something barely north of a mumble.

She was fading.

"This woman is of no use to us," Andy Linx said.

Maris collapsed in on herself, heaved one rattling breath and then was gone.

"I don't think that's true," Pritchard said. "Look at that armband."

"What about it?"

"I remember seeing that before, at the boat launch. That must be how they identify themselves from whoever they're fighting."

And if that was the case, Pritchard had just the plan.

CHAPTER THIRTY-EIGHT

Hell Day + 50 (The Same Day)

*A*DAM HAD BEEN AWAY FROM PEOPLE FOR TOO LONG. When life is one continuous battle, you lose sight of the fact that people can be good to each other and help each other out—even when the common goal was to fight others. The people of Ortho—Or was it Eden? He'd heard it called both, and in equal measures—mostly seemed to like each other. Certainly, they seemed able to pull on the same oar, in the same direction, when needed.

His mom had dug up space for him and Emma in St. Thomas Church, where the rest of the family lived, along with another family and the two military guys. The place felt more like a barracks than a church, given all the firearms and ammunition strewn about. This would do for a while, but he needed to find another place pretty fast. Within a week or so, he and Emma needed to be someplace else, even if it was in one of the tents. Even better, he'd like to take another stab at building a shelter for them in the woods.

From the very first moments when Emma met Mom and Major McCrea, she said there was a romantic thing between them. Adam didn't see it, but Emma said it had something to do with the way they looked at each other. From Adam's viewpoint, McCrea just followed the orders Mom issued, like everyone else in history who had interfaced with his mom.

Leave it to her to assume command of a town in the aftermath of a war.

Emma was appalled by the lack of motherly coddling during the family reunion, but he got it. First of all, *coddling* had never fit into Mom's parenting model. She believed in responsibility and accountability, as if she'd somehow foreseen the madness of the world as it now was and raised him and his brothers accordingly. He saw the love in her eyes, felt it in that long, emotional first embrace.

The big surprise for Adam was the degree to which his brothers had changed. It hadn't yet been a year since they'd seen each other, but both of them seemed to have aged a decade. Caleb, in particular, had bulked up and had grown a good couple of inches. In Luke's case, the changes weren't so much physical as they were in the cast of his eyes and the seriousness of his demeanor. Of the three Emerson brothers, while Adam had been the most rebellious—thus the military boarding school—Luke had been the most compliant. He knew he was the baby of the family and he used it to his advantage, sucking up to Mom and obeying all the rules—at least when she was watching.

Now Luke showed no lingering signs of boyhood.

Emma told him those were a lot of conclusions based on an hours-long reunion, but Adam knew what he saw.

Write it off to the fact that at fourteen, Luke had been through more gun battles than most military veterans three times his age.

Adam had just fallen asleep when everyone inside the church leapt into action, grabbing weapons, and pulling on clothes. As he'd suspected when he heard the coach whistles, that was their general alarm signal. The general scrum of motion confused him at first, and then he got protective of his gear, for fear that someone might take it in the darkness.

That turned out not to be a concern, however, because everyone in here had accumulated a wide variety of weaponry. In those first moments of the general alarm, he learned of the responsibility of every resident to be prepared to defend against invaders. That begged the question of training, but that was for later.

With the alarm sounding, he followed suit and gathered his stuff. As Emma was arming herself and preparing to join with everyone, he tried to talk her out of it.

"Kiss my ass," she said. "I'm not *that* pregnant."

His mom had overheard and said, "Well, she'll fit right in with the family."

"You really should think of the baby," Adam said.

"Fighting and dying are different things," she replied. "Isn't that what you've told me a thousand times? I'm no more important than anyone else."

"Are your rifle skills as wicked as your brothers'?" McCrea asked as he pulled on a ballistic vest.

"I taught them everything they know," Adam said. It

was as true as it was false. Fact was, if it hadn't been for his mom and dad's training since forever, none of them would have the fighting skills they had.

In the minutes that followed, Adam learned that bicycles were community property, available to whoever got there first.

When he arrived at the scene of the shooting, he was concerned, but not surprised, to see that Caleb and Luke were involved. He was impressed, however, with their telling of the story.

Now, as they stood over the bodies of the two dead strangers, Adam realized just as his mother had that this had been an espionage mission on the part of the nutjobs he'd encountered up in Appleton. The lady they'd taken—whoever that was—would be grilled for information about Ortho, its people and its defenses.

"When do you think they'll attack?" his mom asked.

Even in the dim, flickering light of the lantern, Adam could see the major's face crinkle into a scowl. "Hard to say," he confessed. "I didn't see this coming."

"This lady they took," Adam said. "How much did she know?"

"*Does* she know," Victoria corrected. "We have no reason to believe that she's not alive."

Adam thought the dead body on the street was an omen of murder, but he didn't press it.

"Everybody knows everything," McCrea said. "Otherwise, none of this would work."

"Maris knows everything," George said.

"It doesn't matter all that much," McCrea said. "There are only two roads into this town."

"Plus the river," Victoria reminded. "You said yourself that's the weakest spot."

"It's also the least practical," McCrea said. "We're not talking men-o'-war here. We're talking fishing boats and pleasure boats."

"Like the ones that attacked a couple of weeks ago," said a guy Adam didn't recognize.

"Exactly that. They can sneak in stealthily that way, but then what?"

"We've seen these guys in action," Emma said. Adam didn't know she'd sidled up next to him. "They like marauding. They're like roving street gangs."

"I didn't see anything that looked like organization," Adam agreed. "Think zombie movies, okay? They sort of swarm and attack the weak."

"You don't have to be weak for them to attack you," said a kid Adam recognized from the hearing earlier. He'd been with the guy who talked about being kicked out of his house.

"I'm Ronnie Rouse. My dad spoke up earlier."

"I'm right here," said the dad. "And not to disagree, I think it's a mistake to assume that the Appleton gang is incompetent."

"It's always a mistake to underestimate your enemy," McCrea said. Adam heard it as an effort just to say something to stay in the conversation.

Frank Rouse went on, "When those military guys first arrived, they were hungry and desperate and violent, and everybody was their enemy. Then they started turning the locals to their side. I thought of it as building an army. When I saw some of my students in the crowd that stormed my place, I knew we were in trouble."

"Yeah," Adam said. "I don't know when you guys

left town to come here. But I was there, what, twelve hours ago? What I saw was confusion, but it was organized confusion. With a little training and attention to detail, I think they could be a real threat."

"Meaning no disrespect," George Simmons said. "I know you're the oldest Emerson and all that, but who are you to speak to strategy and tactics?"

Caleb and Luke laughed in unison, drawing angry glares from pretty much everyone.

"Sorry," Caleb said. "But you obviously didn't grow up with Mom as your mother. Believe me. If there's one thing every Emerson understands, it's strategy and tactics."

Adam gave Caleb's hair a tousle and earned an angry glare again. "Your name is George, right?"

He got a nod.

"I don't claim to be an expert in anything," Adam said. "But I know chaos when I see it. There's a shit ton of chaos to be seen out there. But by contrast, I also know organization when I see it. And that's what I saw forming up in Appleton."

"The fact that they're gathering intelligence speaks to that," Victoria said.

"We're going to assume they're organized," Mc-Crea said. "And now that they've shown their hand—now that they know that we know that they're planning an attack—I figure it has to come soon."

"Why is that?" Joey Abbott asked.

"Because if they don't, they know that we'll attack them," Victoria answered.

"Why would we do that?" Joey pressed. "*Would* we do that? I mean, why not let sleeping dogs lie?"

"Because the dog's not sleeping," McCrea said. "It's

wandering and it's growling. And we need to be ready for it when it attacks."

McCrea gathered all present into the roadway, surrounding the sawhorse roadblocks, to discuss strategy.

Only two roads passed through Ortho. Kanawha Road, the one where they stood, paralleled the river. Aptly named, Mountain Road came down from the mountain and intersected with Kanawha Road in the vicinity of Maggie's Place and what used to be Simmons Gas and Goodies Exxon Station.

"Anything they'd want to have as spoils of this battle are there at the intersection, at the center of town," McCrea explained. "We don't want them to get that far. Once they have access to buildings and the cover they provide, this thing becomes urban warfare, and we haven't trained any of you for that."

"I bet the other guys haven't been trained in that, either," Victoria said.

"Probably not," McCrea conceded, "but room-to-room fighting is a thousand times more difficult and deadly. You just don't have the maneuverability that you have outdoors."

Joey Abbott asked, "So you think they're going to play Redcoat and march in straight lines down the street?"

"I don't know about the straight lines," McCrea said, "but you've seen the terrain around here. Coming in through the woods would be awkward as hell. And very slow."

"Okay, Major," one of the new arrivals said. "What would you do if you were them?"

"My first choice would be to stand my ground and fortify Appleton against attack."

"That's what I said," Joey objected.

"But I think they've shown their hand that they have different intent. So, what would I do then? I'd cheat. I'd set up diversions. I'd try to figure out a way to create panic in the ranks and break people's resolve to fight before the fighting began."

"And how would you do that?" Victoria asked.

"I don't know." He sold it with a shrug. "Not a great answer, but it's the best I've got."

"So, what's the plan?" Victoria asked.

The basic plan remained the same as what they'd trained for. Militia members would take up positions along the sides of the road in chevron formations, creating a punishing gauntlet for anyone attempting to travel toward them.

"We're going to set up two more-or-less-identical patterns," he explained. "We'll set up here, of course, but then we'll also set up along Mountain Road."

"That's a lot of open country up there," said First Sergeant Copley. "We've got trees and stuff here. Up there, it's mostly fields and structures. Houses."

"I'm aware of that," McCrea said. "Place your troops carefully. That's your segment of the battlefield."

Copley looked pleased by his assignment.

"Getting access to Mountain Road from up by Appleton is a long detour," George Simmons said.

"How long?"

"Thirty miles, easy."

"That's a six, seven-hour walk if they really push it hard," McCrea said.

Caleb raised his hand and waited to be called on. "Do you think they'll do both? Come both ways?"

"Yes, I do," McCrea answered. "Which brings us

back to diversions. We're going to split the militia between the two entryways. Whichever one gets hit first, it's going to make a lot of noise. Don't let yourself get drawn away from your posts. Stand your ground. Your bit of turf is every bit as important as the bit of turf that's getting pounded."

"What if we need help?" Frank Rouse asked. "I'm a high-school teacher. My family and I haven't trained for this kind of thing."

"Thanks for asking that," McCrea said. "We're going to set up a messenger chain. I don't know why I didn't think of this a long time ago." He looked to George Simmons. "George, you're in charge of this front on Kanawha Road, okay? You assign your people as you see fit, but I need you to keep me informed of major developments, particularly if things go south."

McCrea explained that people who couldn't or wouldn't fight would be messengers, carrying notes from the front to the command post, and then bringing back the answers.

"So you're going to be running things from Maggie's?" George asked.

"No," McCrea said. "That's no doubt one of the questions they'll ask Maris Garcia when they interrogate her. I'm going to set up command in your old station."

"Roger that."

McCrea looked like he was done. "Is that everything you had?" Victoria asked.

"Just the obvious. Commanders, make sure your people have all the ammo and supplies they need. This could be a long slog. Have everyone bring food and water."

"To that point," Victoria said, raising her tone from conversational to oratorical. "This is our town, people, and a decisive moment is upon us. This is likely to be a big fight. I don't care how you divide up your manpower for this, but I want to make it abundantly clear that this fight is for *everyone*. No one will hide. I want every door knocked on, and every person standing at a battle station or a support station. When we prevail in this, the victory will be shared by everyone."

"Suppose we lose?" someone asked from the crowd.

Victoria ignored the question. "Let's get to it."

CHAPTER THIRTY-NINE

Hell Day + 50 (The Same Day)

PRITCHARD WISHED THAT HE COULD SEE THE FACES OF the men and women assembled in front of him. With dawn still an hour or more away, his thirty troops printed as a moving mass of silhouettes against a darker darkness. Their white armbands, however, glowed despite the gloom.

After the abortive attempt to interrogate the sentry, he'd reboarded their skiff and paddled a half mile back downstream to rejoin his team of conscripts. More than a few of the men and teenagers in the crowd wore white undershirts, so he ordered them to be cut into strips and tied around their arms.

Now they were waiting for the time to set out.

Hours ago, he'd sent Andy Linx with a group of twenty to march with haste through the woods to intersect with Mountain Road and engage their enemy from the rear.

Pritchard understood the nature of warriors, just as he understood the nature of nonwarriors. Whoever was in charge of Ortho's militia would have no choice but to assume an attack down Kanawha Road, and if not via the road itself, then via the river. That was where they would have to deploy their assets. While they may suspect a rear-guard action, they would have neither the will nor the logistics to command two fronts at one time.

Andy's orders were to be in position by 7 a.m. to begin the mayhem from the least protected angle.

"Squad leaders, step forward," Pritchard said to the cluster of silhouettes. He spoke at increased volume, but nowhere near a shout. Even with a half mile separating him from the enemy, he worried about being overheard.

The squad leaders were professional soldiers and their responsibilities had as much to do with keeping the conscripts from running away as it did engaging the enemy.

As the squad leaders advanced from the crowd, Pritchard led them into the tree line, where they could speak in private.

Teddy Rehm spoke before Pritchard had a chance. "I still think this is a bad idea, Captain. These people are scared. They're not happy to be here."

"Nobody's happy to be here, Sergeant," Pritchard said. "And it's too late. Lieutenant Linx is already in play. It's not like we can make a radio call." As soon as he spoke, he regretted his words. They sounded defeatist. "And it's entirely unnecessary. We need to hit them while they're still upset about losing their guard."

"They're going to be *pissed* about losing their guard,"

said Alma Boatright, a noncom from Pennsylvania who numbered among the survivors of the bombings. "That makes them motivated."

"Refresh my memory," Pritchard said. "When did I ask for your opinion?"

"All due respect, sir," Rehm continued, "we're all in this together."

"All due respect, I am in charge, and this is still the United States Army."

"Is it, sir?" someone asked. Pritchard couldn't identify the voice, and there was no follow-up.

"Sergeant Rehm, repeat to me the plan of action," Pritchard said.

"We're going to advance a few hundred yards and then we're going to wait until we hear Lieutenant Linx's element engage the Ortho militia in the town. That will be our signal to advance."

"Specialist Boatright," Pritchard said. "As we advance, what are the most important considerations?" He'd gone through all of this, and now he wanted to make certain the strategy had been absorbed.

"Speed and brutality," she said.

"Specialist Anson," Pritchard said.

"Sir."

"Which elements of our group advance down the center of the road?"

"No one, sir."

"What do we do, instead?"

"We advance down the sides of the road and we engage every person we see."

"Specialist Boatright, back to you," Pritchard said. "What is our key element of surprise?"

"The armbands, sir." Her tone sounded bored.

"Sergeant Rehm, when do we stop shooting?"

"When the enemy is dead, or they've dropped their weapons."

"Very well," Pritchard said. "Make sure your people understand the goals and the concerns. Our key advantage in this fight will be the confusion caused by the double whammy of the diversions, combined with the infiltration of their ranks. Both of those have short shelf lives, but bullets travel at two thousand feet per second. If we do our jobs right, we won't need a lot of time to succeed."

"Captain," Rehm said, "I don't mean to be a broken record on this thing, but these are not reliable troops. We can't possibly know how they're going to perform under fire. Most of them are only here because we didn't take all their stuff."

Pritchard lowered his voice and leaned in closer. "Those troops are cannon fodder, as far as I am concerned. They are numbers. The more of us there are, the more the enemy will be startled and rocked back on their heels."

"Can I ask where you're going to be, sir?" Specialist Boatright asked. "You know, during the battle?"

Pritchard bristled at the implication of cowardice, but he didn't rise to the bait.

"Gather your people and start your advance. At the second dogleg to the right, stop and hunker down for daylight. In a couple of hours, this will all be over."

CHAPTER FORTY

Hell Day + 50 (The Same Day)

A S DAWN APPROACHED, THE CENTER OF ORTHO WAS a hive of activity. Like any complicated plan with lots of moving parts, the first real test exposed unexpected weaknesses.

First, they'd never given a lot of thought to handling emergencies that would arrive in the darkness of the night. Fact was, some people slept more soundly than others. That was particularly true of those who continued to live in the homes they'd occupied before Hell Day. And why not? They were warm, dry and in comfy beds with covers on them. Real walls separated them from the hubbub outside. She'd dispatched a dozen or more citizens to pound doors and rouse the occupants.

Doc Rory was ready with medical supplies, but he was short on paper towels, linens and blankets. With the assistance of medical newcomers Jayne Young, Leroy Johnson and Nancy Hisch—who was really a dentist, but this was wartime—he'd set up as good a field hospital as he'd been able. He had ample ether and chloroform—the last of the nitrous oxide had been used up a week ago—but without electricity and adequate lighting, the best they'd be able to pull off was what Rory liked to call *cowboy surgery*. A lot closer to biting the bullet than it was to modern medicine.

Victoria had ordered the weapons supply room to be opened for all who needed ammo, mags and other supplies, but her efforts to keep track of who got what broke down almost instantly, and she reverted to the honor system—where people would return what they didn't use when the battle was over. She told herself that she had high hopes that people would do the right thing.

While she remained armed and ready to fight as necessary, McCrea had asked her to be the traffic cop when the shooting started. He wanted her to make sure that supplies got where they needed to go and to the people who needed them. Essentially, Victoria was in charge of everything that didn't directly involve shooting or the supervision of people who were pulling triggers.

On balance, people were anxious and ready to either fight or help with the effort. That warmed her heart.

At McCrea's new headquarters in the old Exxon Station, a steady stream of messengers on bicycles buzzed in and out. Most of the messengers were kids under, say, twelve years old, and that made sense to Victoria. First, they were involved in a vital function, and second, they were used to riding bikes. Hell, they probably had grabbed the bikes that originally belonged to them.

She was surprised when one of the kids, a little girl with a ponytail and teeth she hadn't yet grown into, jogged from McCrea's HQ directly over to her and handed her a folded note. She opened it to reveal hurried script that she thought she recognized as McCrea's handwriting.

> *Copley reports sounds of large force moving ~ 1 mile up Mtn Rd. Tell docs to get ready.*
> *JM*

"It's time," she mumbled. She considered asking the messenger girl to ride the note down to Doc Rory's place, but the child was already off, back to the HQ. And why not? She probably was following orders that told her to do exactly that.

Victoria took off at a run.

She'd made it about halfway when movement in the sky caught her attention. A black dot arced high through the air and seemed to be heading toward Shanty Town.

She never did figure out what it was before it exploded.

First Sergeant Copley had assigned Luke and Caleb to find good sniper perches as far up Mountain Road as they could get.

"You guys are going to be the point of the spear here," Copley had said. "You're going to be the first to hear anything and the first to see anything."

"How far out ahead are we going to be?" Caleb asked. "First to see and hear is also first to get shot at."

"I'll leave the specific location to you," Copley said. "You've both got good skills and good instincts. You understand the mission. If you're not willing to take the chance, I can assign someone else."

"No, we'll do it." Luke spoke quickly to get the word out there before Caleb might say something different. Other people in town understood stalking and hunting, but their mom had trained them to be *snipers*. The skills were similar, yet very different.

To start with, deer and rabbits didn't shoot back.

"I'll make sure you have at least two messengers at your disposal," Copley had said. "Whatever you see, if it's out of the ordinary, I want to know about it."

"Where will you be?" Luke had asked.

"I'll be at the Carter house, about a quarter mile up the road."

"So you want us up farther than that, right?" Caleb asked.

"Don't go crazy, but yes. Remember, you don't want to be so far out that the runners can't get back to me."

"Or so far out that reinforcements are too far away," Caleb said.

"You know the drill," Copley said. "Your job is less to engage than it is to give the rest of us advance warning. That's why you'll have the runners. If you can harass them without overexposing yourself to return fire, knock yourself out. But that's not your primary goal." He looked at each of them. "Are we clear on this?"

Luke was clear, and Caleb stated it aloud for both of them, but it wasn't the job he really wanted. He was used to providing overwatch, reaching out to people at a distance when they posed a big risk. But, hey, the job was the job.

Both of the Emerson boys chose to stick with their M4s as their weapon of choice, if only because of its rapid rate of fire and the fact that their scopes were already zeroed to one hundred yards. Luke couldn't imagine a circumstance when that wouldn't be enough distance, but with his 4x scope, he could reach out to three hundred yards and hit some part of the target if he could see it. Past that, he just wouldn't take the shot.

Ronnie and Gary Rouse had been assigned to them as their runners. Luke didn't particularly like either of them because they whined too much and didn't do a lot of work. Ronnie had been shot a week or so ago, but it was a nothing wound. The way he complained, you'd think the bullet had taken off his leg. Just a couple of weeks before that, Caleb had been shot in the ass—a real bullet wound—and while he still limped some, he didn't complain.

Ronnie and Gary had been issued the Ruger 10/22s that had been part of Luke's and Caleb's bug-out packs, back before Hell Day. It was a great choice for people who needed to be armed, but didn't know much about shooting. It made little noise, had zero recoil and launched .22 long-rifle ammo that was every bit as deadly as a cannonball, if it hit the right spot.

They rode bikes to get to their preferred sniper's nest. They chose the Nowakowskis' farm because it was one of the first real structures that an approaching army would encounter on the way into town. The main house sat about fifty yards off the road, but Luke and Caleb were more interested in the barn that sat fifty yards behind that. Built back in the heyday of barns—whenever that was—it looked like the cliché, complete with the angled roof and the hayloft window.

It was that window that made the barn their first choice.

Mr. Nowakowski was a cranky old bastard under the best of circumstances. When he was awakened at zero-dark-early by four kids with guns, he got downright unpleasant.

"I ain't lettin' you use my barn for no target practice," the old man said when he heard the plan.

"I wasn't asking," Caleb said. "I'm just telling you that we're going to be back there."

"You two're that queen bitch's kids, ain't you?"

Luke felt his ears go hot, and he felt Caleb puffing up next to him.

"Have a good morning," Caleb said through a tight jaw. "You might want to put on a bandanna if you step outside. You're gonna want the good guys to know you're a good guy."

The old man bitched like a wet hornet as the boys headed into the barn, but he didn't do much to stop them. Best of all, he didn't shoot them in the back.

It was damp in the loft. And dusty. Every move they made launched a whirlwind of motes that irritated the back of Luke's throat and made him sneeze.

"Way to be stealthy," Caleb said.

"So, what do we do now?" asked Ronnie.

"We wait and watch," Caleb said. "Then, if we see anything, I write it down and one of you two busts ass to get it to First Sergeant Copley."

"Why does everybody call him that?" Gary asked.

"Because that's his name?" Luke said.

"The whole *First Sergeant* thing."

"Because that's his rank," Caleb said. "It's how we came to know him. Him and Major McCrea both."

"Just seems weird to me," Gary said. "Like the Army even matters anymore."

Caleb and Luke exchanged glances. Neither of them chose to engage.

"What are we looking for?" Ronnie asked.

"Anything," Caleb snapped. "Now hush. Open up all your senses."

They hadn't been in place for a half hour when Luke heard the first sounds of movement. There were some voices, but there was also the clatter of equipment. The clatter of stuff. Whatever it was, was still on the other side of a rise, out of sight.

Caleb pulled the spiral-bound reporter's notebook from his back pocket and used a well-chewed Bic pen to write a note. He folded it and gave it to the closest Rouse. Gary. "Get this to First Sergeant Copley."

"What does it say?"

"That we hear stuff. Get it to him."

"Shouldn't we wait—"

"Now!" It was a whispered shout, but the nonnegotiable nature of it was clear to all.

"You don't have to be rude," the boy grumped, but he headed down the stairs.

"And stay off the road as much as you can," Caleb ordered. "You're going to be a target if shooting starts."

"What do you think the noise is?" Luke asked.

"Only one reason we're up here," Caleb said. "We assume this is the beginning of an attack."

Dawn had bloomed full when Luke wasn't paying attention—as the others, whoever they were, continued moving forward, into view. He brought his binoculars up to his eyes. He counted ten people, but there might have been more. They looked like regular folks—

not military types, or even particularly nasty types—and they moved loosely in a group, keeping to the sides of the road. All of them carried weapons—who didn't these days?—and two of the weapons, in particular, caught his attention.

"Caleb," he whispered. "Do you see the grenade launchers?"

"These are the same guys from the boat launch," Caleb said.

"They're wearing white bandannas, too. Are they on our side?"

"I don't think so," Caleb said. "This could be bad news." He jotted another note and tore it off. "Ronnie. Your turn. The note says we think we see grenade launchers and that they're dressed like us. Come back with instructions on what we're supposed to do. Hustle."

Unlike his brother, Ronnie went right to it, without any lip.

The crowd, such as it was, had stopped their advance, and instead seemed to be settling into the woods, preparing to do something.

"Should we take them out?" Luke whispered.

"You heard the orders. We are to observe and report. That's it."

"What do you think they're waiting for?" Luke asked.

"I don't know. Orders, maybe?"

When Luke saw one of the guys look at his watch, and then when a lady looked at hers, too, he understood. "I think they're waiting for a specific time. Two of them looked at their watches."

"Now, there's a plan that wouldn't work for us,"

Caleb joked. Before Hell Day, everything they knew about the time of day was determined by their cell phones. "Where the hell is Gary? We need to know what to do."

"I don't see any more grenade launchers," Luke said. "But I've got a guy with a good long-range rifle. Tall kid with the WVU baseball cap." Judging from the size of the scope, Luke decided he must be good at long ranges.

"Got him," Caleb said. "Do you see the dude climbing the oak tree on our side of the road?"

It took Luke a few seconds, but then he got him. Another bolt-action rifle.

"They're deploying snipers," Luke whispered. "You take the kid in the cap, and I'll take the guy on our side."

"No," Caleb said. "They haven't done anything yet. We don't know what First Sergeant Copley wants to do. If we shoot too soon, we can screw everything up."

This made no sense to Luke. None at all. The strangers already killed one citizen of Ortho, and they apparently kidnapped another one. Why wait until they killed more to eliminate the threat?

While they watched, more people arrived to join the group of presumed invaders. The one guy who appeared to be in charge wore a uniform like the ones worn by the marauders at the boat launch. Luke couldn't hear the orders, but, clearly, they were being given. The troops—if that's what you'd call them—responded by taking positions in the road, but stayed behind the established first line.

"What are they doing?" Luke whispered. "They're just standing there."

"Waiting for their signal, I guess," Caleb said.

The people down there with watches were checking them more frequently now, making Luke think that the time was getting close when they planned to do something.

"Grenade Launcher Guy is moving," Caleb said, his tone urgent and his voice tight.

The soldier with the launcher stepped out of the trees, tucked the shoulder stock of his M4 into the crook of his elbow and fired a round. It was more a *thunk* than a *boom*. That round was still airborne when the shooter slid the launch tube forward and inserted another round.

Down to the left, about three hundred yards away, in the center of town, a flash of light pulsed at the spot where the round landed, followed immediately by a fireball and a dull explosion. A second later, another one.

The shooter prepared to launch a third time.

CHAPTER FORTY-ONE

Hell Day + 50 (The Same Day)

P RITCHARD HAD GIVEN HIS WATCH TO ANDY LINX, figuring that since Andy's element would be the first to engage, he, Pritchard, had little use for it. In the stillness of the early-morning hours, the sound of the explosions would be plenty of warning.

Still, the sound of the distant booms surprised him.

"Okay, squad leaders," he said, "this is it. We'll move on my order. For those of you who count this as your first battle, just do your job. Follow your leaders and everything will be fine."

As he scanned the faces, he saw a mixed bag of determination and abject terror. One young man in Sergeant Rehm's squad openly cried. The sight and the sound disgusted Pritchard. He turned away.

"Good luck to you all," he said. "Now take your positions. When you hear the third grenade, it's time to go."

The plan called for Pritchard's troops to advance

through the forest in lines of three and four, parallel to the roadway. The instant they saw a target, they were to shoot it and continue the advance. Advance, advance, advance. That was the secret to success on this day. If a friend or fellow combatant fell, they were to make a mental note of the location so the injured could be tended to later. But the advance was never to stop.

He watched as the different elements split, more-or-less-evenly, to the two sides of the road, climbing the steep banks to do so.

He was the last to climb the bank, choosing the left side of the road as his own. He worked his way to the front of the line with the intent of demonstrating the leadership of a professional soldier. Perhaps the sight might inspire greater things from the troops.

He'd kept the last M203 grenade launcher for himself, along with the final three grenades. They were high-explosive dual-purpose rounds—HEDPs—designed to rattle the cages of the enemy and knock them off their game. While they were still trying to stuff their thoughts back into their heads, Pritchard and his troops would be on them.

It was important not to attack too quickly. He wanted to give his opposing force time to think about turning their backs on Kanawha Road and returning back to town to assist their friends.

In the distance, as additional explosions shook the air and the sound of gunfire blossomed, he counted silently to thirty.

Then he placed the first grenade into the launch tube under the barrel shroud of his M4, slid it shut and launched the round.

CHAPTER FORTY-TWO

Hell Day + 50 (The Same Day)

VICTORIA FELT THE PULSE OF HEAT AND PRESSURE AT the same instant she heard the explosion. Instinctively, she dropped to her knee and brought her rifle to her shoulder. There were no targets to shoot, but as debris was still falling, a roiling fireball erupted from the center of Shantytown.

Three seconds later, a second explosion erupted close enough to the first one to be called the same spot. Screaming started instantly and people started to run. Panic arrived, fully formed and without delay.

The third explosion transformed panic into chaos.

People of all ages and in all stages of dress flooded from their homes into the street to get away from the fires, which, left unattended, would expand geometrically and threaten to destroy the whole town.

"No!" Victoria yelled. "Put the fires out!" Perhaps it was counterintuitive, but there was no place to run to. It

wasn't as if there was a shelter to hide in—and even if
there was, hiding in a shelter did nothing to protect Ortho.

As one of the newcomers darted past her on his way
to somewhere, she grabbed his arm. "Hey!" she said.
"Greg Gonzales, right? From Hilltop?"

"Right."

"Where's your wife?"

A look of panic crossed his eyes as he shot a look
back toward the fires.

"You left her in there?" Victoria was horrified.

Then, as if to answer her question, his head exploded in gore and his body dropped to the street.

"Shit." Victoria dropped to the ground as well. *Snipers.*

"This is bullshit," Caleb said, speaking Luke's thoughts
aloud. "Snipers first. I'll take the far one."

Either one was an easy shot, but it was best when
everyone knew what to do. "If we're shooting together, I don't have a shot yet," Luke said. The sniper
had positioned himself in the tree in such a way that a
big limb blocked the sweet spot for a shot.

"Nope, one at a time," Caleb said. "My guy is prep-
ping for his next shot." Caleb's rifle barked and the
civilian soldier on the far side of the road tumbled out
of his tree.

The shot caught everyone's attention on the ground.

It also captured the heart and mind of Luke's target,
who turned toward the sound of the shot. Luke drilled
him through the chin.

As soon as his bullet was away and he'd confirmed
the kill with a glance, Luke shifted his aim to find the
guy with the grenade launcher, but he never got a chance

to take his shot. The whole world opened fire on the hayloft.

The building vibrated with bullet impacts, each of which registered louder in Luke's ears than any of the gunshots that were propelling them. Shards of wood flew and the air filled with the residue of a century's worth of wood rot and hay dust.

"Out!" Caleb yelled. "We've got to get out!"

Luke was perfectly happy pressing himself as deeply through the hay and bird shit as he could go, thank you very much. The smaller the target, the less likely to get hit.

His jacket went tight around his chest and shoulders as Caleb grabbed his collar and dragged him over to the stairs that led down.

"We can't stay here!" Caleb yelled over the cacophony. "Are you going to climb down or am I going to throw you?"

A lot of times, when Caleb made threats, he was just talking tough. This was not one of those times. Luke could see it in his eyes. It was a fifteen-foot drop to the barn floor, much better walked than flown.

"I'm going!" Luke said.

"Hurry. They know where we are. We're trapped if they come in."

"Shit." Luke hadn't thought of that. He slung his rifle behind his back, turned and faced the ladder and let himself down. He might as well have fallen, for all the contact he had with the rungs, but he made it to the floor unhurt. Good thing he moved fast because Caleb hit the ground at the same instant.

"Okay," Caleb said. "We've got to—"

Contained as it was inside the old wooden structure, the force of the exploding grenade was beyond belief.

The pain from the fireball was even worse.

"It's starting," Emma said, straightening her posture to get a glimpse of what was happening back in town.

Adam heard it, too, of course, and he pulled Emma down closer to the roots of the tree that formed the spot of forest it was their duty to defend. "We stay where we are."

"But if they're attacking down there—"

"Remember what the major said about diversions. I don't know what we're going to be up against, but Warfare one-oh-one teaches the advantages of dividing your enemy."

"We don't know that anyone's on their way here."

"They'd be foolish not to be," Adam said. "If the town needs reinforcements, they'll send for them."

The way George Simmons had distributed his fighters was different than anything that Adam had read about or experienced before. He placed everyone in staggered lines along both sides of the roadway, forming a kind of chevron. They had strict instructions to stay high enough on the embankment not to get caught in a friendly cross fire. As the incoming troops traveled via the roadway, they'd walk through a punishing gauntlet of fire.

On the other hand, if they decided to bypass the roadway and come in through the trees, the woods were already occupied with armed people who could engage them there as well.

Adam didn't like the arrangement at all. Not only were the good guys facing each other, they couldn't see each other's positions. Maybe this was a strategy for people who had trained extensively, but he didn't imagine that to be the case here among all these civilians.

Emma got mad sometimes when he referred to others as *civilians,* when he was one himself—military high school didn't count, and he admitted that—but his entire childhood had been about planning for the war that his mom thought was inevitable. Granted, she didn't think it would start with global nuclear war, but rather as the direct result of the death of political compromise, but she knew it was coming. Hell Day just sped up the inevitable.

Whether he liked it or not, this was the strategy du jour and he intended to do his part.

He and Emma were situated in what he figured to be the middle of their line, two of probably fifty volunteer warriors. George Simmons said there was a similar number of militiamen back in the town, plus all of the noncombatants who were slotted to stop an attack down Mountain Road.

Now it was a matter of numbers and marksmanship. If the attacking force threw two hundred people at this spot where they had only fifty, Adam and his team were screwed.

Emma showed that fierceness in her eyes and in her demeanor that he admired so much. When this whole nasty business started weeks ago, she seemed constantly afraid and had a hard time adjusting her classy, well-bred ways to the new world of feral humans. Now she was ready for a fight and knew how to handle herself when they got into one. "I do love you, you know," he said.

Emma looked startled. Then she laughed. "You sure know how to charm a girl." She leaned in and kissed him. "I love you, too." She touched her belly. "Now let's get past this thing so little Ignatz can love both of us."

"Ignatz?"

A distant thump caught his attention. *What was—*

Behind them, on their left, on the other side of the road, a blast detonated in the tree line, shearing off at least one tree and sending splinters and shrapnel in all directions. The leaves and tree bark just above Adam's head sheared away as shrapnel shredded the air.

Acting from reflex, Adam cupped his hand around the nape of Emma's neck and pushed her down into the mulchy forest floor.

Another explosion ripped the woods somewhere near them, closer than before, because he felt the vibration through the ground like a heavy punch to his chest.

A third explosion seemed farther away than the first one, but back toward town.

Someone yelled, "I'm hit! I'm hit!"

Even if Adam could have recognized the face, he hadn't been in town long enough to know whom it belonged to. And it didn't matter, anyway.

"Are you okay, Em?" He realized that he was shouting, but he also realized that was the only way he'd be able to hear anything.

"I think so. I feel a little crushed by my boyfriend, but other than that . . ."

This wasn't a time to talk. Emma looked fine. He saw no blood, and she was able to communicate clearly. Under the circumstances, that would do as a complete physical.

The explosions had stopped, at least for the current few seconds. In Adam's mind, that meant that the real fight was about to begin.

CHAPTER FORTY-THREE

Hell Day + 50 (The Same Day)

*P*ANIC IS A DISEASE. A VIRUS. IT STARTS WITH PATIENT zero and progresses with breathtaking speed unless somebody intervenes.

As the fires in Shantytown grew, Victoria felt like a rock in a stream as people swarmed past her, seemingly without any idea of where they were going or what they wanted to do. Lots of screaming and crying, and little action.

Shantytown was on the brink of igniting past the point of being stoppable, people were trapped, yelling for help, and no one was helping them. She had to do something.

And it would be the first time in her life to do it: She screamed.

It was a classic horror-movie shriek that split the air more surely than any whistle or gunshot could have done. People stopped. They stared.

She knew their attention span was fragile at best, so she wasted no time.

"Everybody stop, goddammit! Just stop! Get in there and help people. Put those fires out!"

"People are shooting at us!" someone yelled.

"Then die with dignity! Stop this panicky shit and act like grown-ups!"

That was all the speech she had time for. She turned and shed herself of her rifle and ammo chest rig, dropping them both to the ground as she strode into Shantytown, resisting the urge to run. In her experience, people in the midst of an emergency could run or they could think, but they couldn't do both at the same time. She grabbed the nearest two pressurized water cans, praying that people would be following, but not daring to look, for fear that they weren't and that she would lose her own nerve.

Victoria didn't know what started these fires—obviously some kind of incendiary artillery, though she couldn't imagine the source. Their points of impact were aflame beyond the point of stopping them.

If she could wet down the surrounding structures, maybe she could keep the fires contained, at least long enough for the intensity of the burning structures to settle down.

The heat was nearly unbearable. As she pulled the pin on her first water can and squeezed the lever to release the water, she started by wetting her own skin.

"Help me!" a voice called. "Please help me. I think I'm bleeding to death."

Victoria turned and saw a young woman on the ground, a shard of wood protruding from her abdomen.

There wasn't much blood on the ground, but that didn't mean she wasn't bleeding to death internally.

And then there was the fire.

"Mrs. Emerson!" She turned to see Joey Abbott approaching. He carried an ax and a water can. A train of other townspeople trailed behind him. "Let me take care of the fires."

"You've got to wet down the structures," Victoria said.

"I know exactly what I need to do," Joey said. "Out of the way. Please, ma'am. I've got this."

Victoria turned her attention to the wounded woman. "Okay, you poor thing," she said. "I'll help you out of here."

"Help Baz first," she said. "I can wait."

Victoria had no idea who Baz was, but then she saw the little boy's body. He was beyond hope. "He's already on the street, ma'am," Victoria lied. "We've got to take care of you."

"He's out already? Where?"

"He's waiting for you. He sent me in to get you." Victoria hated the lie, but she dreaded the fight more. This woman and her son were only two of God knew how many dead and wounded. Neither one of them had time to negotiate.

The woman howled with pain as Victoria tried to move her.

Behind her, Victoria heard chopping sounds, a symphony of destruction as a team of citizens hacked away at fragile cabins. Joey Abbott caught her looking at him. "Gotta reduce the fire load, ma'am. That sonofabitch can't spread if it don't have fuel." He went back to chopping away at the walls of a perfectly good wooden shack.

"What's your name?" Victoria asked the lady in her arms.

"Tina. You're sure Baz is all right?"

"Listen to me, Tina. I can't lift you by myself. You're going to have to help me. On *three,* okay?"

Victoria voiced the count, and on a grunted *three,* Tina got her feet under her, and Victoria got the victim's arm over her shoulder and around her neck.

They'd only taken a few steps before they came face-to-face with Maggie, of Maggie's Place. She was carrying two 5-gallon pails of water. Eighty-five pounds. God bless her.

"Put those down," Victoria said. "Take Tina to Doc Rory's."

"But the fires—"

"I got these," Victoria said. She winced as she lifted the pails. It wasn't the absolute value of the weight so much as it was the skin on her left arm. She was pretty sure there were going to be blisters there tomorrow.

As she walked back to the inferno, she heard more explosions, distant this time. And then a fusillade of gunfire from much closer up Mountain Road.

All her boys were at war now, and she couldn't do a damn thing to help any of them.

The attackers must have used the same kind of firebomb on the barn as they'd used on the town. In a single tick of the second hand they didn't have, the interior went from no fire at all to completely engulfed. If the boys had stayed in the loft three seconds longer, they'd have been barbecued.

And that remained a very real risk even now, as a fireball rolled across the high ceiling and banked back down as it reached the front wall.

"We've got about thirty seconds to get out of here alive," Caleb said.

Luke thought he was being overly generous. He gave them fifteen, max.

"Back door!" Luke said. "They'll be looking for us coming out the front."

Now they just had to find the back door.

Turned out they didn't need it. More than a few of the wall boards down here were loose, leaving gaps big enough for Luke to stick his hands through and yank. The boards were tougher than he'd expected, but they gave a bit more with each tug.

"Pull!" Caleb shouted, and he went to work on the plank next to the one Luke was trying to remove.

It took Caleb two yanks, and Luke two more. Both planks broke simultaneously, and the boys fell back on their asses in unison.

"Ow, shit!" Caleb yelled.

Luke couldn't contain his chuckle as his brother landed on his bullet boo-boo.

He didn't realize how hot he'd been in there until he got outside into the cool air. The first breath of fresh oxygen made him cough.

As they ran away from the barn, Luke dared a look back and saw that the fire had already chewed through the roof and was blowing like a torch out of the upper windows.

The barn was between them and the road now, so it felt safe to take a quick inventory.

"Are you okay?" Caleb asked. "Burned or anything?"

"No, you?"

Caleb shook his head.

The whole world shook with gunfire now, but Luke didn't understand from where or by whom. In their struggle to get out of the barn, he'd lost all perspective on the battle.

"Sounds like First Sergeant Copley's attacking," Caleb said. "Let's get back in it."

"Wait," Luke said. "Let's catch our breath for a second."

Caleb didn't bother to respond. He just started running at a crouch, back toward the roadway and the troops they'd seen there.

"God, I hate him," Luke grumbled, not meaning a word of it.

He was still running to catch up when he saw his brother go down.

CHAPTER FORTY-FOUR

Hell Day + 50 (The Same Day)

"Now!" Pritchard yelled. He started off at a jog, his rifle at his shoulder, safety off as he watched the roadway pass below and on his right. When he saw a target, he would shoot it. He trusted that Sergeant Rehm, on the other side of the road, would do the same thing.

It unsettled him to plow forward like this, essentially blind to the plans of the enemy. It was like traveling in time back to the tactics of the Roman centurions, but with different weaponry. Two groups of combatants rushing headlong at each other.

But where was his enemy?

He'd expected them to be amassed in defensive lines along and across the roads, but thirty seconds into the attack, with not a shot yet fired, the roadway remained bare.

"Hey!" someone shouted. "What are you doing out here? You're supposed to be hunkered down."

The voice belonged to a man in his thirties who was practicing exactly what he'd preached. He'd dug himself in behind a tree in a well-constructed defensive position.

The defender had assumed that Pritchard had made a mistake and had moved out of position. The ruse of the armband was working.

Pritchard shot the defender through the forehead, drawing the attention of another defender he hadn't seen, hunkered behind a different tree. That guy got a shot off before Pritchard killed him, but the shot went wild.

The fight was on, and the score was two-zero.

"Faster!" he yelled to his troops, and he broke into a run.

From the other side of the roadway, the sound of pounding gunfire seemed to make the foliage vibrate.

"What the hell are you doing?" another defender asked from the shadows. "Are they coming?" His face turned confused. "Oh, shit."

He didn't have time to raise his weapon, either.

Adam realized right away that the invaders' plan of attack was not a nuanced one. It was built around the model of a human wave. Or maybe like the old Confederate charges made so famous by the Army of Northern Virginia back during the Civil War. Well, the first Civil War, anyway.

The attackers did not come down the road, as everyone had expected. Instead, they were coming through the woods at a run, presumably to intimidate and over-whelm the Ortho troops.

The war came to Adam and Emma like a wave at a football game, starting out distant and then growing in size and volume.

As the gunfire increased, so did the yelling. He heard shouts of anger and adrenaline, shrieks of pain. The noise of the approaching attackers reminded Adam of what he imagined a line of fleeing dinosaurs would sound like. Only with firearms.

Emma saw the actual soldiers first as they sprinted right at them through the woods. "There they are," she said, pointing.

Both of them raised their rifles. Adam thumbed the safety off and settled his scope on the first form he could make out.

"No, don't," Emma said, and she grabbed his arm. "They're ours."

"What?"

"Look at the bandannas. The white bandannas."

"What the hell? Why are they running away?"

The guy he was about to shoot caught a glimpse of Adam and snapshot a round in his direction. It missed, but not by much.

"God *damn* it!" Adam shouted, and he took the guy out with two rounds to his center of mass.

"Adam!"

"They know about the bandannas, Em! That's their trick."

"No retreat!" Adam shouted. "Stand fast! The enemy is wearing—"

He didn't finish the sentence because he saw a clutch of three soldiers close together, plunging through the woods and firing as they ran. Emma took two of them out, and Adam nailed the third.

Immediately behind them, another cluster of attackers skidded to a halt and turned to go the other way.

"Hell no!" someone yelled. "They just killed your friends. Go get them!"

If they'd kept running, if they hadn't turned back, Adam would have let them live.

The resistance was tighter than Pritchard had anticipated, and the marksmanship more accurate. Behind him, he heard the cries of his troops who had been shot, and he'd seen at least two of his soldiers take hits and fall.

Behind him, he heard his noncoms yelling at troops to run, run, run. "Keep shooting! Keep the pressure on. Forward, forward!"

Pritchard no longer knew what the score was. While it was not the rout that he was hoping for, he sensed that he still had the upper hand. One of the first sights he took in when he started his charge were the shredded remains of two fighters who had taken shelter behind a tree that took the brunt of one of the grenade explosions. The HEDP rounds had shaken the Ortho defenders, killed a few and injured a few more, but as he'd feared, the foliage had dampened the effect of the shrapnel. He could only assume that Sergeant Rehm was encountering the same results on his side of the road.

The sight of the shredded bodies unnerved his conscripts, made them pull up short. "Ignore them," Pritchard commanded. "Look away. Keep going. Keep shooting.

We've got them beat." He planted his hand between the shoulder blades of the man in front of him and pushed.

If they kept pressing forward, he felt they could still carry the day, but they had to keep pressing. They couldn't cower and they couldn't retreat. Either action would lead to disaster.

"Go, go, go," he yelled as he ushered troops to move ahead of him. Better to be able to see that they were fighting than to learn that they'd run off when he wasn't looking.

There was no strategic victory to be had in a battle like this. Success or failure lay in the final body count, strictly a numbers game. Numbers and willpower. The first team to lose the will to fight would lose the war, and there was no more direct route to a loss of will than to see your friends and neighbors dying by the dozens.

Ahead, he saw a cluster of high-school kids running and shooting blindly, but then they hesitated, clearly startled. They'd allowed themselves to group together. They exchanged gunfire with someone on their right and they all fell. Just from the way their bodies collapsed, Pritchard could tell that they were dead before their knees buckled.

Another cluster of locals—these immediately in front of Pritchard—stopped in their tracks. They started to turn to run.

"No!" he yelled. "Hell no. They just killed your friends. Go get them!"

He physically pushed them forward and they raised their weapons, but it was too late.

As they fell, Pritchard felt an invisible fist hammer

him in the right side of his rib cage and he stumbled to the left. He tried to shoot back, but his feet tangled, and he went down hard. The force of the impact forced him to bark a cough, which, in turn, triggered a wave of agony.

Jesus, he thought. *Could this be it?*

"This is dog shit," Adam said. The attackers were playing them. He didn't know what the endgame was going to be, but he'd be damned if he was just going to let the enemy flood past their positions. He decided to take the fight to them.

He stepped away from the cover of his hardwood barrier and took a knee in front of it. Another plug of people was sprinting toward him—or sprinting as best they could through branches and briars—and he started picking them off, one at a time, starting as soon as he got eyes on them. At this range, even if a tree branch deflected the shot, there was a high likelihood of a hit.

He took another three out before the others stopped and reassessed what they were doing.

Stopping in the middle of a charge is a bad idea. Adam dropped one of them, and then the other two whirled and took off running the other way.

The next wave of attackers slid to a stop, turned and ran back through the gauntlet of Ortho militia that they'd already engaged. The explosion of gunfire was stunning.

Behind him and on the left, the war raged on for another minute, maybe two, but then the shooting stopped.

* * *

Caleb had fallen face-first into the grass, but as Luke got three steps closer, he saw that his brother had assumed a prone shooting position. That was a sure sign of an imminent hazard, so Luke slid to a stop and fell to his belly, too.

Caleb fired twice and held his aim. Then he stood cautiously, staying at a low crouch.

Luke did the same and approached slowly, his weapon up to his shoulder, his finger just outside the trigger guard, ready to fire if needed.

As he closed the distance, he saw the lady Caleb had shot. Her dead eyes stared up at the dawn.

"Don't shoot!" someone yelled.

Luke and Caleb both whirled on three high school–aged boys who were emerging from the tree line with their hands held comically high over their heads. None appeared to be armed.

"Please don't shoot!" one of them yelled. "We give up!"

"I didn't want to fight in the first place!" another yelled.

"What do we do now?" Luke asked.

"Wait," Caleb said. "The shooting stopped."

"Yeah, okay, Captain Obvious. What about these guys?"

"Shit, I don't know. Take them to Mom, I guess."

Beyond Adam's line of sight, the forest still vibrated with noise, but it now was mostly yelling and moaning. He heard orders for people to drop their weapons. To get on the ground.

Some people yelled for help. Some called for a doctor. One shouted twice that he was dying, but then he fell silent.

"Is it over?" Emma asked, joining him on his side of the tree.

"I hope so."

"Now what do we do?"

Movement to the right caught Adam's attention. He brought his rifle to his shoulder. "Show yourself!" he yelled.

"I can't," a man's voice answered. "I've been shot."

"Who are you?"

Silence.

"Answer me, or I'll open fire," Adam said. As he spoke, he inched forward. Emma edged away a few feet, but stayed with him, step for step. "Who are you?"

"Pritchard," the man said. "Cole Pritchard. Captain. United States Army National Guard."

Adam and Emma exchanged glances. The bad guys were supposedly led by Army reservists. "You're the enemy," Adam said.

"I'm surrendering."

It wasn't what Adam had expected. Sotto voce, he asked Emma, "Are we taking prisoners?"

She didn't know, either.

"Throw your weapon away!" Adam commanded.

"I can't. I landed on it. Please help me."

Adam sensed a trap. He brought his finger to his lips.

Emma scowled. *What are you going to do?*

Adam pointed at Emma's chest, and made a circling motion, indicating that she should circle around to the right, and then he pointed at himself to indicate that he would circle around to the left.

He moved as silently as the dry leaves would allow, his rifle at the ready, his finger resting on the trigger.

"Are you coming or not?" Pritchard yelled. "Jesus, this hurts."

As Adam scissor-stepped around to the left, the captain became visible to him a little at a time. He saw the baseball cap first, then the profile of his face. It was bloody. He lay at the bottom of a swale. The rocks around him were smeared with fresh blood.

Three steps later, the captain sensed Adam's presence and he rolled his head to look at him. As he breathed, blood bubbles appeared at the corners of his mouth.

"Are you the one who shot me?" Pritchard asked.

"Probably."

"Good shot."

Apparently not, if you're still alive. Adam thought the words were too harsh to be spoken aloud.

"I need a doctor," Pritchard said.

"No, you don't." That came from Emma, who'd materialized from the far side of a towering hardwood. "Not in a few minutes, anyway."

Pritchard had, indeed, landed on his rifle. It was twisted around behind him with the barrel shroud protruding from behind his knee. There was no way he could shoot it, and judging from the pallor of his skin, he didn't have the strength to try.

"Don't you have a warm heart?" Pritchard faked a laugh, but it hurt. The blood around his mouth had begun to foam.

"I used to," Emma said.

"Why this way?" Adam asked. "Why not just ask? Why did you have to attack?"

Pritchard was drifting away. "You've got to choose," he said. "You're either a sheep or a wolf." His chin sagged.

Adam watched as Emma raised her rifle to shoot the man.

"Hey, Em," he said.

Her eyes shifted to him.

"Not worth the bullet." The guy was on his way out, anyway.

He gestured with his head that they should rejoin their team. Leaving Pritchard to die on his own terms, he walked back the way he'd come and waited for Emma. He could see a few bodies among the foliage nearby, and cringed at the sounds of the wounded. Judging from the way other Ortho troops emerged from their cover and scanned the woods around them, the day had not gone well for Captain Pritchard's team.

Emma joined him and they hugged. "Are you okay?" They asked it together, triggering a chuckle and a tighter embrace.

CHAPTER FORTY-FIVE

Hell Day + 52 (Two Days Later)

DAVEY PRIEST, FORMERLY WIDE RECEIVER FOR THE Appleton Wildcats, sat in a hardback wooden chair, his hands on his lap, looking up at Victoria Emerson through wet red eyes. Major McCrea and First Sergeant Copley towered over him, one on either side. Most of the people packed into the gallery no doubt thought that the men were there to keep young Mr. Priest from bolting and running away. The reality of it was that they were making it difficult for anyone in the ersatz courtroom to get a decent shot at the prisoner.

Priest was one of nine people in the room who had participated in the invasion of Ortho and had chosen to surrender. The others' hands remained bound behind their backs, with their eyes blindfolded. They, too, were surrounded by a security detail.

"Ma'am, I'm really sorry," he said, and his words launched an angry murmur through the crowd. "I didn't mean for what happened to happen. I really didn't. I didn't even want to join that damn army. Nobody's happier than me that that Pritchard asshole is dead."

"Watch your mouth, Mr. Priest," Victoria cautioned.

"I'm sorry."

Victoria's eyes narrowed as she leaned into the lectern that doubled as her judicial bench. "That word comes to you pretty easily, doesn't it?" she asked.

"Excuse me?"

"You apologize a lot. You know, when you deploy the same word, as you just used, in response to your participation in the killing of twelve Ortho citizens and the wounding of twenty-three more—"

"I didn't kill anybody."

She rapped her gavel to silence him. "When you use the same word not only for that, but for your participation in the killing of thirty-two of your own—"

"At least ten of them was only wounded," Priest interrupted.

"And they are now dead."

"Because you let them die."

This was a sore point not only to the young defendant, but it also weighed heavily on Victoria's conscience. With medical supplies as scarce as they were, and the numbers of her own townspeople needing attention, she had made the decision to let wounded invaders go without medical intervention. She was confident that some must have survived and wandered off from the spot where they fell, but most did not.

She did not honor Priest's comment with a reply.

"When you use the word *sorry* for such momentous events, and then you use it just seconds later to apologize for using a bad word in my courtroom, I think that perhaps you're not really sorry at all."

"Ma'am, I'm only seventeen."

"And Basil Witworth was only four. Lisa Barnes was only nine. Anton Cole was only thirty-seven. You argue to me that you were forced into joining Pritchard's army, but from where I sit, you had far more opportunity to make a choice than the people I just mentioned. Or the others that I haven't mentioned."

"But it's true, ma'am. I didn't want to fight. I didn't kill anyone. I don't know what else I can say."

Victoria leaned back in her chair and rubbed her eyes vigorously with both hands. "And you know what, Mr. Priest? I believe you. In fact, I don't believe there is anything that you can possibly say that would have any relevance to this court."

She cleared her throat and leaned forward again. "Are you other defendants listening? Nod your heads if you are."

All of the heads nodded, and George Simmons gave a thumbs-up to confirm.

"We have a lot to do in this town, not just to grieve the lives you took, but also to rebuild what you destroyed. I am confident that if I brought you up here to the bench and interviewed you one at a time—tried you one at a time—each of you would have some version of the story Mr. Priest here tells me. That you really didn't *want* to do that which you did, anyway. That is why I am treating Mr. Priest as your exemplar before this court."

She steeled herself with a breath. "Like you, I don't *want* to do that which I am going to do, anyway. I find each of you guilty of premeditated murder, and order that you be taken to a place in the forest where you will be shot to death, and your bodies left exposed to the elements so that you might at least benefit the turkey buzzards."

Davey Priest's shoulders sagged at the sound of her words, and his head dipped. He might have passed out, and Victoria didn't care. In the back, some of the blindfolded defendants cried, but most sat unmoving.

Everyone else in the courtroom applauded.

Acknowledgments

They tell me that nothing ever disappears from the internet. If that's the case, there's a picture of me back in the day when I was a U.S. representative to the International Atomic Energy Agency on issues related to radioactive scrap metal. The picture shows me in the company of Ray Turner, the mentor who taught me more about radioactivity than any college professor ever could. He continues to be my friend to this day, and he did much to keep me on course for some of the technical details in *Blue Fire*. Thanks, Ray.

Thanks also to the whole team at Kensington Publishing who I'm blessed to have gathered in my corner. The fine editing of Michaela Hamilton, combined with the creative business savvy of Steve Zacharius (the guy in charge of it all) and the rest of the production cast, all come together to make my writing so much better than I could ever make it on my own. Words cannot address my gratitude. Thanks also to Anne Hawkins, my longtime agent and friend, whose constant guidance keeps me out of trouble.

Closer to home—and deep in my heart—there's Joy, the unwavering love of my life. Without her, none of the rest would matter. Thirty-seven years and going.

Don't miss the next gripping thriller in John Gilstrap's

Victoria Emerson series

WHITE SMOKE

Coming soon from Kensington Publishing Corp.

Keep reading to enjoy a sample excerpt . . .

CHAPTER ONE

Hell Day + 67

VICTORIA EMERSON HOPED THAT HER SURPRISE DIDN'T show as Althea Mountbank entered Maggie's Place and approached. "This a good time?" Althea asked.

Victoria rose from her chair and the square table that served as her desk in what used to be the dining room of Maggie's Place, a tavern that had been converted to an ersatz town hall in the aftermath of the eight-hour nuclear war that changed everything.

"Now is fine," Victoria said. From the name alone, she had not been expecting someone quite so young and attractive. "Please, have a seat."

Althea chose to sit at Victoria's nine o'clock, rather than taking the seat that would have placed her back to the door. Victoria noted it, but from the young lady's demeanor, she was not concerned.

"Mr. Barnett told me to come in and talk to you."

"I know," Victoria said. "Ben told me to expect you."

"Are you, like, the mayor or something?" Althea asked.

"Not the mayor, no. Nobody elected me to anything, but somehow, every time the music stops, I'm the only one willing to take the chair." Victoria shifted in her seat and crossed her legs. "Tell me something about yourself."

Althea started to lean back into her chair but abandoned the effort halfway. She looked nervous, and Victoria wanted to know why. "What would you like to know?"

"Anything," Victoria said. "As we try to rebuild something that will look something like a real society, and more people flood into Ortho, I think it's important that we all get to know each other. We don't have to become besties, but there's a lot of fear and loneliness out there. Start with where you're from and what you did before the war."

Althea cleared her throat and shifted again. "I'm from up near Appleton," she said. "I was a music teacher. Which is why I'm here."

"Did you come to Ortho alone? Do you have family?"

Althea cast her eyes down. "No children. My husband was killed in the days after the war."

"May I ask what happened to him?"

"It was the gangs," Althea said. "In the weeks right after the war, during the panic, it seemed that everybody was shooting everybody else."

Victoria waited for more.

Althea grew uncomfortable. "That's it."

"Tell me the circumstances surrounding your husband's death."

"Circumstances?"

Victoria hiked her shoulders and held out her hands. "How did it happen? Was he trying to defend you? The house?"

Althea's gaze shifted to the floor.

Victoria pressed harder. "Or was he maybe threatening someone else who defended *themselves*?"

"We were hungry," Althea said.

"Everybody was hungry," Victoria said. "Did he kill?"

Althea's head snapped up and her eyes were hot. "What difference does that make? He's dead himself now."

"Where were you when he was killed? Were you with him?"

Althea lost some of her attitude. "I tried to stop him."

"What was your husband's name?" Victoria asked.

"Jamie. He was a good man, I swear he was."

"How many people did Jamie kill?"

Althea shook her head aggressively. "No one. I swear."

"Okay, then how many people did he threaten?"

The eye contact disconnected again. "He was just trying to provide for his family."

"By stealing from other families." Victoria took a deep noisy breath. "Look at me, Althea."

The young teacher rocked her gaze up to meet Victoria's.

"We can't allow that." Victoria kept her tone even. "You need to understand that here in Ortho, we expect people to earn what they have."

"That's what I want to do."

"Here in Ortho," Victoria continued, as if she hadn't been interrupted, "we punish thieves severely. You can tell a thief from the rest of the community by the T that's been carved in their foreheads. Men, women, children, it doesn't matter. You need to understand that."

"But I didn't steal anything," Althea said.

"I don't care about the past, Althea. But I do care about the future. I'm sure you noticed the burned structures down the street in Shanty Town?"

Althea nodded.

"Do you know who set those fires?" Victoria asked.

"No."

"They came from up your way. From Appleton. They attacked Ortho." Victoria leaned into her side of the table and made sure she had Althea's full attention when she said, "Every one of those attackers are dead. Those who survived were tried and executed."

"But I've heard people call this place Eden," Althea said. She seemed genuinely confused.

"Perhaps it's because we still believe in justice here," Victoria explained. "Ben Barnett gave you your first week's rations and supplies, right?"

Althea bobbed her head. She seemed grateful to be talking about something else. "And he explained about the currency system here." In Ortho, ammunition doubled as money. It had inherent value—unlike the green pieces of paper that had meant so much before Hell Day. "Thing is, I don't have a gun."

"Nor will you before you prove yourself to be trustworthy. What committee did you choose to participate in?"

"Education," Althea said. "That's why we're talking, as I understand it."

"That's one of the reasons," Victoria confirmed. "You want to teach music lessons as a means to support yourself."

"Exactly. Is that a problem?"

"Not as far as I'm concerned," Victoria said. "But I think you might want to think it through. Winter is marching straight at us. You'll have a tent for shelter until your cabin is built—and it will only be built with you as one of the construction workers. You've got provisions for a week. Maybe two if you don't mind being hungry, but after that, you're on your own."

"What are you suggesting?"

"I'm suggesting that in the short term, you might want to focus on the committees that the town will pay you to be a part of. Those include the construction committee and the security committee, but without a firearm, the security slot doesn't do much for you. Or for Ortho."

"I don't know anything about construction," Althea said.

"Most newcomers don't," Victoria said with a smile.

Althea seemed more confused than ever.

"You're going to have to get your hands dirty, Althea. You're going to have to perform physical labor before you can fulfill your entrepreneurial urges."

The young teacher wanted to say something, but it seemed that the words wouldn't come.

Victoria stood, ending the meeting. "Of course, you can always choose to move on down the road, leaving those provisions here, of course."

The front door opened, revealing the familiar silhouette of Joe McCrea, the Army major who had endured every second of Victoria's Hell Day nightmare. "Excuse me, Vicky," he said. "There's something you've got to attend to here." An M4 rifle hung from its sling across his chest. Pretty much everyone who was old enough to carry a weapon did so as a form of citizen militia—which had proven its worth more than once.

"We're finished here," Victoria said. She offered a handshake. "Welcome to Ortho."

Althea hesitated, then accepted the gesture.

"Remember everything we talked about," Victoria said. "On reflection in the coming hours and days, if there's any element of what you discussed with me that you wish to backtrack on or change, I invite you to do so." She tightened her grip just enough to make sure the young teacher was listening. "Just do it before I hear from others that you lied to me."

A bit of color drained from Althea's cheeks. "I-I didn't lie."

"Then you have nothing to worry about." Victoria let go of her hand and watched as she pressed past McCrea to walk back outside.

"The hell was that?" McCrea asked.

"I'm seventy percent sure that she was part of the gangs in Appleton," Victoria said.

"And?"

"And I told her that the past was the past. That last part was a not-so-subtle warning that witnesses to her past are likely here." Victoria walked toward the door. "What's so urgent outside?"

"Stay where you are," McCrea said. "I'll bring him in."

Victoria didn't like these kinds of buildups to a surprise.

Thirty seconds later, McCrea returned with an emaciated young man in a tattered uniform that looked like a product from a war long in the past. "Vicky," McCrea said, "allow me to introduce you to Jerry Cameron."

Victoria wondered if this guy was going to live till morning. He looked awful. She offered her hand. "Pleased to meet you. And please sit down." She looked to McCrea. "Get him something to eat, please."

"On it already," McCrea said. "I asked Joey Abbott to get him some food and drink."

"I don't have time for a meal, ma'am," Cameron said. "You're Mrs. Emerson, right?"

"Victoria. Yes. Now sit. We're not talking until your butt is in a chair."

Cameron seemed annoyed, but he sat in the chair that Althea Mountbank had just vacated. "*Congresswoman* Victoria Emerson?"

"Not anymore. It's just Victoria now." She and McCrea both took chairs at the same table. "Vicky, if you prefer."

"Yes, ma'am, but you *were*—"

"Yes, what is this about?" Victoria had a bad feeling. A glance at McCrea's body language didn't make her feel any better.

"Okay, ma'am," the young man said. "Well, here's the thing. . ." Then he seemed to get lost inside his head.

"Sometimes it's easier if you just spit out the words," Victoria said with a soft smile.

"Yes, ma'am. As your friend said, my name is Jerry Cameron. I used to work at the Annex. A bunker that was used to house—"

Victoria's gut tumbled. "I'm familiar with the Annex, Jerry. The Government Relocation Center." Located about one hundred miles east of Ortho, the Annex was an elaborate bunker complex built into the bedrock, beneath the lavish vacation resort that called itself Hilltop Manor. It was to that very facility that Army Major Joseph McCrea and First Sergeant Paul Copley had been escorting Victoria on the night before Hell Day. She had refused to enter, however, when the managers of the place—Cameron's coworkers, apparently—wouldn't allow her children to accompany her.

"Why do you look like you're going to have a heart attack?" Victoria asked. Even as the words left her throat, she knew she didn't want to hear the answer.

"Well, ma'am, here's the thing. The president of the United States and the leadership of the House and Senate have all been arrested and charged with treason. The president has ordered me to find you and ask if you would preside over the trial."

His words seemed to suck the oxygen out of the air. She understood what he was saying, but the meaning seemed impossible.

"Wait," she said. "What?"

"There was an uprising around the Annex. Around the whole hotel complex. A lot of people were killed."

Victoria asked, "So, were you with the security firm that oversaw the Annex?"

"Yes, ma'am. Solara. Most of us didn't make it. The

civilians up there are furious that the government took care of itself but ignored the people. They're looking for blood."

Victoria tried to make the pieces fit in her head. "You said that the president was in custody?"

"Yes, ma'am."

"You're lying," she said. "The president is at a different facility. She would not be at the Annex."

Cameron looked hurt. "I'm not lying, ma'am." Then his face showed an *aha* moment. "Oh, I get it. I see the confusion. President Blanton and Vice President Jenkins were both killed in the attacks. The office slipped to the Speaker of the House."

"Penn Glendale?"

"Yes, ma'am." Cameron shrugged out of his backpack and reached into a side pocket. He extracted an envelope and handed it to Victoria. "The president asked me to give this to you. He asked for you personally."

McCrea spoke up. "Are you telling us that the government of the United States has been overthrown?"

The question seemed to startle the young man. "I guess so, yes. Roger Parsons has charged Mr. Glendale with treason. Like I said, they've charged everybody with treason."

"And Parsons is the leader of the uprising?" Victoria asked.

"Right."

"I'm confused," McCrea said. "You said that the president sent you, yet this Parsons guy is in charge?"

"Yes, sir. The president himself asked me. I don't think Parsons knows that he did it, though."

"How long have you been on the road?" Victoria asked.

"Eight days, ma'am. It was a long ride. A tough ride, too. It's brutal out there."

"Brutal how?" McCrea asked.

"Gangs. Warlords, really. Lots of suffering. Lots of awfulness."

"How close to here?" Victoria asked. "To Ortho?"

"Quite a ways," Cameron said. "Five, maybe seven miles."

"What are they doing?" Victoria asked. "Are they organized? Are they on the march?"

Cameron laughed. "I didn't see much about them that was organized. They just kind of wander around. I don't know what they're thinking. I tried to get through them as fast as I could."

"Did you *walk* all the way from Hilltop?" McCrea asked.

"No sir, I have a horse. He's grazing in the field across the street."

The door to Maggie's Place opened and Joey Abbott stepped in from the cold, balancing a plate of food in his right hand. The ever-present AR-15 was slung behind his back. "Here's some scrambled eggs and venison sausage," he said as he walked in. He handed the plate to Cameron. "You look like you could use this." The proprietor of Joey's Pawn Shop in the years before Hell Day, Joey had stepped up to be one of the town's leaders.

As Cameron dug into the food, McCrea asked, "Do you have any reason to believe that there'll actually be a trial, or are they just going to hang the president from a tree?"

"Holy shit!" Joey exclaimed. "What president? *Our* president?"

Victoria took thirty seconds to catch Joey up.

"I don't know one way or the other," Cameron said. "All I know is that everybody was arrested, and the president asked me to come and get you."

"How does he even know I'm here?"

"I don't have an answer for that, ma'am," Cameron said. "It's probably because everyone knows you're here."

Victoria looked to McCrea for clarity but got a shrug instead.

"A lot of the people I passed on the way here from Hilltop said they were on their way to Eden," Cameron said.

"That's here?" Victoria asked.

"Yes, ma'am. Turns out you can kill electronics and email, but the rumor mill survives Armageddon."

It was too much. Victoria stood and prepared to leave. "Thank you, Mr. Cameron," Victoria said. "I'll have an answer for you in the next day or two."

Cameron stood, too. "Um, ma'am? We don't have a day or two. Roger Parsons is a scary dude. He's champing at the bit to hang the lot of them."

"I'll give you my decision in a day or two," Victoria repeated. "Take your time eating in here. Do you need a place to shelter for the night?"

"No, ma'am. With you or without you, I need to get back to Hilltop."

"Why?" McCrea asked.

Cameron sat back down and addressed his plate. "You were an Army officer, right?"

"Major," McCrea said.

"If you'd left a bunch of your comrades in danger, wouldn't you want to get back to them?"

McCrea knitted his brow, looked at Victoria, and then put his hand on the young man's shoulder. "Yes, I would," he said. "But do you and me both the favor of resting for the rest of the day and we'll find shelter for you. Start fresh tomorrow. If we end up going, we'll want you along. Any extra hands we can get."

"Not to mention the extra gun," Joey said.

Cameron finished the remaining eggs and sausage with a single scoop of his fork. "I guess I gave you a lot to think about," he mumbled around the mouthful. "I can stay for a night, but then I've got to get back." He stood.

Victoria said, "If you go around the corner to the next building, you'll find Ben Barnett. He's a big man, can't miss him. He'll find a place for you to stay tonight."

"I'm serious about leaving first thing," Cameron said.

"I understand," she said, and they shook hands.

As he exited, Victoria sat back down and opened the letter. "Joey, could you find George Simmons and ask him to join us?"

"What about your boys?" McCrea asked.

"Yeah, them, too."

Within fifteen minutes, Victoria's family had all gathered in the main room of Maggie's Place. Adam was the oldest at eighteen, and his girlfriend, Emma, was pregnant, though not yet showing. At sixteen, Caleb had grown two inches in the past two months.

He spent his days helping Doc Rory Stevenson work on patients and learning cowboy medicine as a trade. Luke would turn fifteen soon, and his work in Lavinia Sloan's blacksmith shop had broadened his shoulders and blackened his hands without darkening his outlook. Just like his father had been, Luke was an unapologetic optimist in all things. Thanks to a lifetime of training, all her boys were expert marksmen.

First Sergeant Paul Copley was there, too, along with George Simmons and Joey Simmons. George, like Joey, was a lifelong resident of Ortho and its environs, and through them, Victoria avoided some of the social landmines that were so common in small towns. They knew the personalities, and friendships. More importantly, they knew the lifelong enmities that existed between some.

The letter was real. There was no forging the elaborate scrawl that was Penn Glendale's handwriting. Written on the reverse side of the stationery for the House of Representatives, on which the logo on the front had been marked out with heavy black ink, the letter explained much of what young Mr. Cameron had told her. Penn's was a personal plea for assistance.

As she read the letter aloud, her voice choked at the concluding paragraphs.

> *"Vicky, I ask you to do this thing—to preside over our trial—not to avoid punishment or to evade responsibility for the mess that the war has wrought. I ask so that some semblance of sanity might reign over this last gasp of government as we once knew it.*
>
> *"If my colleagues and I are to be executed, let*

*it be done mercifully and in a lawful manner.
Decades from now, long after the government
has fallen, the United States of America will remain as a population of citizens who are striving
to thrive in the wilderness, much as our ances-
tors did. What succeeds the present must be built
upon principles of freedom and the rule of law.*

*"I believe that you are uniquely suited to the
task of leading the way. No matter what you
choose to do, know that I am grateful for your
consideration, and stand in admiration of what
you have achieved while so many have
foundered.*

*"Your obedient servant, Pennington
Glendale, President of the United States of
America."*

Victoria folded the letter and wiped her eyes with
her palms.

"So, it's all gone," Joey Abbott said, his voice barely
a whisper. "The government is gone."

"How the hell did everything go so wrong?" George
Simmons wondered aloud.

"The government is *not* gone," Victoria said. Under
the circumstances, the strength of her voice surprised
her. "*We* are the government. The *people* are the government. All that's gone are the trappings of power."

"And electricity," Luke said, drawing a laugh.

George stood, but it took some effort. He'd said
something about pulling a muscle during last week's
fight with the Appleton gang. "You gotta go," he said.

Victoria waited for the rest.